DEAR EDWARD

This Large Print Book carries the
Seal of Approval of N.A.V.H.

DEAR EDWARD

ANN NAPOLITANO

THORNDIKE PRESS
A part of Gale, a Cengage Company

Copyright © 2020 by Ann Napolitano.
All scripture quotations are from the King James Version of the Bible.
Thorndike Press, a part of Gale, a Cengage Company.

LIBRARY OF CONGRESS CIP DATA ON FILE.
CATALOGUING IN PUBLICATION FOR THIS BOOK
IS AVAILABLE FROM THE LIBRARY OF CONGRESS

ISBN-13: 978-1-4328-7340-0 (hardcover alk. paper)

Published in 2020 by arrangement with The Dial Press, an imprint of Random House, a division of Penguin Random House LLC

Printed in Mexico
Print Number: 04   Print Year: 2020

For Dan Wilde, for everything

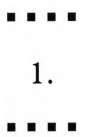

1.

"Since death is certain, but the time of death is uncertain, what is the most important thing?"

— PEMA CHÖDRÖN

JUNE 12, 2013
7:45 A.M.

Newark Airport is shiny from a recent renovation. There are potted plants at each joint of the security line, to keep passengers from realizing how long they'll have to wait. People prop themselves against walls or sit on suitcases. They all woke up before dawn; they exhale loudly, sputtering with exhaustion.

When the Adler family reaches the front of the line, they load their computers and shoes into trays. Bruce Adler removes his belt, rolls it up, and slots it neatly beside his brown loafers in a gray plastic bin. His sons are messier, throwing sneakers on top of laptops and wallets. Laces hang over the side of their shared tray, and Bruce can't stop himself from tucking the loose strands inside.

The large rectangular sign beside them reads: *All wallets, keys, phones, jewelry, electronic devices, computers, tablets, metal objects, shoes, belts, and food must go into the security bins. All drink and contraband must be thrown away.*

Bruce and Jane Adler flank their twelve-year-old son, Eddie, as they approach the screening machine. Their fifteen-year-old son, Jordan, hangs back until his family has gone through.

Jordan says to the officer manning the machine: "I want to opt out."

The officer gives him a look. "What'd you say?"

The boy shoves his hands in his pockets and says, "I want to opt out of going through the machine."

The officer yells, apparently to the room at large: "We've got a male O-P-T!"

"Jordan," his father says, from the far side of the tunnel. "What are you doing?"

The boy shrugs. "This is a full-body back-scatter, Dad. It's the most dangerous and least effective screening machine on the market. I've read about it and I'm not going through it."

Bruce, who is ten yards away and knows he won't be allowed to go back through the scanner to join his son, shuts his mouth. He doesn't want Jordan to say another word.

"Step to the side, kid," the officer says. "You're holding up traffic."

10

After the boy has complied, the officer says, "Let me tell you, it's a whole lot easier and more pleasant to go through this machine than to have that guy over there pat you down. Those patdowns are *thorough,* if you know what I mean."

The boy pushes hair off his forehead. He's grown six inches in the last year and is whippet thin. Like his mother and brother, he has curly hair that grows so quickly he can't keep it in check. His father's hair is short and white. The white arrived when Bruce was twenty-seven, the same year Jordan was born. Bruce likes to point at his head and say to his son, *Look what you did to me.* The boy is aware that his father is staring intently at him now, as if trying to deliver good sense through the air.

Jordan says, "There are four reasons I'm not going through this machine. Would you like to hear them?"

The security officer looks amused. He's not the only one paying attention to the boy now; the passengers around him are all listening.

"Oh God," Bruce says, under his breath.

Eddie Adler slips his hand into his mother's, for the first time in at least a year. Watching his parents pack for this move from New York to Los Angeles — *the Grand*

11

Upheaval, his father called it — gave him an upset stomach. He feels his insides grumble now and wonders if there's a bathroom nearby. He says, "We should have stayed with him."

"He'll be okay," Jane says, as much to herself as to her son. Her husband's gaze is fixed on Jordan, but she can't bear to look. Instead, she focuses on the tactile pleasure of her child's hand in hers. She has missed this. *So much could be solved,* she thinks, *if we simply held hands with each other more often.*

The officer puffs out his chest. "Hit me, kid."

Jordan raises his fingers, ready to count. "One, I prefer to limit my exposure to radiation. Two, I don't believe this technology prevents terrorism. Three, I'm grossed out that the government wants to take pictures of my balls. And four" — he takes a breath — "I think the pose the person is forced to take inside the machine — hands up, like they're being mugged — is designed to make them feel powerless and degraded."

The TSA agent is no longer smiling. He glances around. He's not sure if this boy is making a fool of him.

Crispin Cox is in a wheelchair parked nearby, waiting for security to swab his chair for explosives. The old man has been stewing about this. Swab his wheelchair for explosives! If he had any spare breath in his lungs at all, he would refuse. Who do these idiots think they are? Who do they think he is? Isn't it bad enough that he has to sit in this chair and travel with a nurse? He growls, "Give the boy his goddamn pat-down."

The old man has been issuing demands for decades and is almost never disobeyed. The tenor of his voice breaks the agent's indecision like a black belt's hand through a board. He points Jordan toward another officer, who tells him to spread his legs and stick out his arms. His family watches in dismay as the man moves his hand roughly between the boy's legs.

"How old are you?" the officer asks, when he pauses to readjust his rubber gloves.

"Fifteen."

He makes a sour face. "Hardly ever get kids doing this."

"Who do you get?"

"Hippies, mostly." He thinks for a moment. "Or people who used to be hippies."

Jordan has to force his body to be still. The agent is feeling along the waistline of his jeans, and it tickles. "Maybe I'll be a hippie when I grow up."

"I'm finished, fifteen," the man says. "Get out of here."

Jordan is smiling when he rejoins his family. He takes his sneakers from his brother. "Let's get going," Jordan says. "We don't want to miss our flight."

"We'll talk about that later," Bruce says.

The two boys lead the way down the hall. There are windows in this corridor, and the skyscrapers of New York City are visible in the distance — man-made mountains of steel and glass piercing a blue sky. Jane and Bruce can't help but locate the spot where the Twin Towers used to be, the same way the tongue finds the hole where a tooth was pulled. Their sons, who were both toddlers when the towers fell, accept the skyline as it is.

"Eddie," Jordan says, and the two boys exchange a look.

The brothers are able to read each other effortlessly; their parents are often mystified to find that Jordan and Eddie have conducted an entire conversation and come to a decision without words. They've always operated as a unit and done everything together. In the last year, though, Jordan has been pulling away. The way he says his brother's name now means: *I'm still here. I'll always come back.*

Eddie punches his brother in the arm and runs ahead.

Jane walks gingerly. The hand dropped by her younger son tingles at her side.

At the gate, there is more waiting to do. Linda Stollen, a young woman dressed all in white, hurries into a pharmacy. Her palms are sweaty, and her heart thumps like it's hoping to find a way out. Her flight from Chicago arrived at midnight, and she'd spent the intervening hours on a bench, trying to doze upright, her purse cradled to her chest. She'd booked the cheapest flight possible — hence the detour to Newark — and informed her father on the way to the airport that she would never ask him for money again. He had guffawed, even slapped his knee, like she'd just told the funniest joke he'd ever heard. She was serious, though. At this moment, she knows two things: One, she will never return to Indiana, and two, she will never ask her father and his third wife for anything, ever again.

This is Linda's second pharmacy visit in twenty-four hours. She reaches into her purse and touches the wrapper of the pregnancy test she bought in South Bend. This time, she chooses a celebrity magazine, a bag of chocolate candies, and a diet soda and carries them to the cashier.

Crispin Cox snores in his wheelchair, his body a gaunt origami of skin and bones. Occasionally, his fingers flutter, like small birds struggling to take flight. His nurse, a middle-aged woman with bushy eyebrows, files her fingernails in a seat nearby.

Jane and Bruce sit side by side in blue airport chairs and argue, although no one around them would suspect it. Their faces are unflustered, their voices low. Their sons call this style of parental fight "DEFCON 4," and it doesn't worry them. Their parents are sparring, but it's more about communication than combat. They are reaching out, not striking.

Bruce says, "That was a dangerous situation."

Jane shakes her head slightly. "Jordan is a kid. They wouldn't have done anything to him. He was within his rights."

"You're being naïve. He was mouthing off, and this country doesn't take kindly to that, regardless of what the Constitution claims."

"You taught him to speak up."

Bruce tightens his lips. He wants to argue, but he can't. He homeschools the boys and has always emphasized critical thinking in their curriculum. He recalls a recent rant about the importance of not taking rules at

16

face value. *Question everything,* he'd said. *Everything.* He'd spent weeks obsessing over the idiocy of the blowhards at Columbia for denying him tenure because he didn't go to their cocktail parties. He'd asked the head of the department: *What the hell does boozy repartee have to do with mathematics?* He wants his sons to question blowhards too, but not yet. He should have amended the declaration to: *Question everything, once you're grown up and in full command of your powers and no longer living at home, so I don't have to watch and worry.*

"Look at that woman over there," Jane says. "There are bells sewn into the hem of her skirt. Can you imagine wearing something that makes a jingly sound every time you move?" She shakes her head with what she expects to be mockery, but turns out to be admiration. She imagines walking amid the tinkle of tiny bells. Making music, and drawing attention, with each step. The idea makes her blush. She's wearing jeans and what she thinks of as her "writing sweater." She dressed this morning for comfort. What did that woman dress for?

The fear and embarrassment that crackled through Bruce's body next to the screening machine begins to dissipate. He rubs his temples and offers up a Jewish-atheist

17

prayer of gratitude for the fact that he didn't develop one of his headaches that make all twenty-two bones in his skull throb. When his doctor asked if he knew what triggered his migraines, Bruce had snorted. The answer was so clear and obvious: his sons. Fatherhood is, for him, one jolt of terror after another. When the boys were babies, Jane used to say that he carried them like live grenades. As far as he's concerned they were, and still are. The main reason he agreed to move to L.A. is because the movie studio is renting them a house with a yard. Bruce plans to place his grenades within that enclosure, and if they want to go anywhere, they'll need him to drive them. In New York, they could simply get in the elevator and be gone.

He checks on them now. They're reading on the far side of the room, as an act of mild independence. His youngest checks on him at the same time. Eddie is a worrier too. They exchange a glance, two different versions of the same face. Bruce forces a wide smile, to try to elicit the same from his son. He feels a sudden longing to see the boy happy.

The woman with the noisy skirt walks between the father and son, cutting off the connection. Her bells chime with each step.

18

She is tall, Filipino, and solidly built. Tiny beads decorate her dark hair. She's singing to herself. The words are faint, but she drops them around the waiting room like flower petals: *Glory, Grace, Hallelujah, Love.*

A black soldier in uniform is standing by the window, with his back to the room. He's six foot five and as wide as a chest of drawers. Benjamin Stillman takes up space even in a room with plenty to spare. He's listening to the singer; the woman's voice reminds him of his grandmother. He knows that, like the screening machine, his grandmother will see through him the minute she lays eyes on him at LAX. She'll see what happened during the fight with Gavin; she'll see the bullet that punctured his side two weeks later, and the colostomy bag that blocks that hole now. In front of her — even though Benjamin is trained at subterfuge and has spent his entire life hiding truths from everyone, including himself — the game will be up. Right now, though, he finds peace in the fragments of a song.

An airline employee sashays to the mouth of the waiting room with a microphone. She stands with her hips pushed to one side. The uniform looks either baggy or too tight on the other gate agents, but hers fits as if it were custom made. Her hair is smoothed

19

back into a neat bun, and her lipstick is shiny and red.

Mark Lassio, who has been texting instructions to his associate, looks up. He is thirty-two and has had two profiles written on him in *Forbes* magazine during the last three years. He has a hard chin, blue eyes that have mastered the art of the glare, and short gelled hair. His suit is matte gray, a color that looks understated yet expensive. Mark sizes up the woman and feels his brain begin to turn like a paddle wheel, spinning off last night's whiskey sours. He straightens in his chair and gives her his full attention.

"Ladies and gentlemen," she says, "welcome to Flight 2977 to Los Angeles. We are ready to board."

The plane is an Airbus A321, a white whale with a blue stripe down the side. It seats 187 passengers and is arranged around a center aisle. In first class, there are two spacious seats on either side of the aisle; in economy, there are three seats per side. Every seat on this flight has been sold.

Passengers file on slowly; small bags filled with items too precious or essential to check with their luggage thump against their knees. The first thing they notice upon entering the plane is the temperature. The space has the chill of a meat locker, and the air-conditioning vents issue a continuous, judgmental *shhhh!* Arms that arrived bare now have goosebumps and are soon covered with sweaters.

Crispin's nurse fusses over him as he moves from the wheelchair into a first-class seat. He's awake now, and his irritation is at full throttle. One of the worst things about being sick is that it gives people — *goddamn strangers* — full clearance to touch him. The nurse reaches out to wrap her hands around his thigh, to adjust his position. *His thigh!* His legs once strode across boardrooms, covered the squash court at the club, and carved down black diamonds at Jackson Hole. Now a woman he considers at best mediocre thinks she can gird them with her palms. He waves her off. "I don't require assistance," he says, "to sit down in a lousy seat."

Benjamin boards the plane with his head down. He flew to New York on a military aircraft, so this is his first commercial flight in over a year. He knows what to expect, though, and is uncomfortable. In 2002, he would have been automatically upgraded from economy to first class, and the entire plane would have applauded at the sight of him. Now one passenger starts to clap, then another joins in, then a few more. The clapping skips like a stone across a lake, touching down here and there, before sinking below the inky surface into quiet. The noise, while it lasts, is skittish, with undertones of embarrassment. "Thank you for your service," a young woman whispers. The soldier lifts his hand in a soft salute and drops into his economy seat.

The Adler family unknots near the door. Jane waves to her sons and husband, who are right in front of her, and then, shoulders bunched, hurries into first class. Bruce looks after his wife for a moment, then directs the gangly limbs of Jordan and Eddie into the back of the plane. He peers at the seat numbers they pass and calculates that they will be twenty-nine rows from Jane, who had previously promised to downgrade her ticket to sit with them. Bruce has come to realize that her promises, when related to work, mean very little. Still, he chooses to believe her every time, and thus chooses to be disappointed.

"Which row, Dad?" Eddie says.

"Thirty-one."

Passengers unpack snacks and books and tuck them into the seat pockets in front of them. The back section of the plane smells of Indian food. The home cooks, including

22

Bruce, sniff the air and think: *cumin.* Jordan and Eddie argue over who gets the window seat — their father claims the aisle for legroom — until the older boy realizes they're keeping other passengers from getting to their seats and abruptly gives in. He regrets this act of maturity the moment he sits down; he now feels trapped between his father and brother. The elation — *the power* — he felt after the pat-down has been squashed. He had, for a few minutes, felt like a fully realized adult. Now he feels like a dumb kid buckled into a high chair. Jordan resolves not to speak to Eddie for at least an hour, to punish him.

"Dad," Eddie says, "will all our stuff be in the new house when we get there?"

Bruce wonders what Eddie is specifically worried about: his beanbag chair, his piano music, the stuffed elephant that he still sleeps with on occasion? His sons have lived in the New York apartment for their entire lives. That apartment has now been rented; if Jane is successful and they decide to stay on the West Coast, it will be sold. "Our boxes arrive next week," Bruce says. "The house is furnished, though, so we'll be fine until then."

The boy, who looks younger than his twelve years, nods at the oval window beside him. His fingertips press white against the clear plastic.

Linda Stollen shivers in her white jeans and thin shirt. The woman seated to her right seems, impossibly, to already be asleep. She has draped a blue scarf across her face and is leaning against the window. Linda is fishing in the seat-back pocket, hoping to find a complimentary blanket, when the woman with the musical skirt steps into her row. The woman is so large that when she settles into the aisle seat, she spills over the armrest into Linda's personal space.

"Good morning, sweetheart," the woman says. "I'm Florida."

Linda pulls her elbows in close to her sides, to avoid contact. "Like the state?"

"Not like the state. I *am* the state. I'm Florida."

Oh my God, Linda thinks. *This flight is six hours long. I'm going to have to pretend to be asleep the whole way.*

"What's your name, darling?"

Linda hesitates. This is an unanticipated opportunity to kickstart her new self. She plans to introduce herself to strangers in California as *Belinda.* It's part of her fresh beginning: an improved version of herself, with an improved name. Belinda, she has

24

decided, is an alluring woman who radiates confidence. Linda is an insecure housewife with fat ankles. Linda curls her tongue inside her mouth in preparation. *Be-lin-da.* But her mouth won't utter the syllables. She coughs and hears herself say, "I'm getting married. I'm going to California so my boyfriend can propose. He's going to propose."

"Well," Florida says, in a mild tone, "isn't that something."

"Yes," Linda says. "Yes. I suppose it is." This is when she realizes how tired she is and how little she slept last night. The word *suppose* sounds ridiculous coming out of her mouth. She wonders if this is the first time she's ever used it in a sentence.

Florida bends down to rearrange items in her gargantuan canvas bag. "I've been married a handful of times myself," she says. "Maybe more than a handful."

Linda's father has been married three times, her mother twice. Handfuls of marriages make sense to her, though she intends to marry only once. She intends to be different from everyone else in the Stollen line. To be better.

"If you get hungry, darling, I have plenty of snacks. I refuse to touch that foul airplane food. If you can even call it food."

Linda's stomach grumbles. When did she last eat a proper meal? Yesterday? She stares at her bag of chocolate candies, peeking forlornly out of the seat-back pocket. With an urgency that surprises her, she grabs the bag, rips it open, and tips it into her mouth.

"You didn't tell me your name," Florida says.

She pauses between chews. "Linda."

The flight attendant — the same woman who welcomed them at the gate — saunters down the center aisle, checking overhead compartments and seatbelts. She seems to move to an internal soundtrack; she slows down, smiles, then changes tempo. Both men and women watch her; the swishy walk is magnetic. The flight attendant is clearly accustomed to the attention. She sticks her tongue out at a baby seated on her mother's lap, and the infant gurgles. She pauses by Benjamin Stillman's aisle seat, crouches down, and whispers in his ear: "I've been alerted to your medical issue, because I'm the chief attendant on this flight. If you need any assistance at any point, please don't hesitate to ask."

The soldier is startled; he'd been staring out the window at the mix of grays on the horizon. Planes, runways, the distant jagged city, a highway, whizzing cars. He meets her eyes — realizing, as he does so, that he has avoided all eye contact for days, maybe even weeks. Her eyes are honey-colored; they go deep, and are nice to look into. Benjamin nods, shaken, and forces himself to turn away. "Thank you."

In first class, Mark Lassio has arranged his seat area with precision. His laptop, a mystery novel, and a bottle of water are in the seat-back pocket. His phone is in his hand; his shoes are off and tucked beneath the seat. His briefcase, laid flat in the overhead compartment, contains office paperwork, his three best pens, caffeine pills, and a bag of almonds. He's on his way to California to close a major deal, one he's been working on for months. He glances over his shoulder, trying to appear casual. He's never been good at casual, though. He's a man who looks best in a three-thousand-dollar suit. He peers at the curtain that separates first class and economy with the same intensity he brings to his workouts, his romantic dinners, and his business presentations. His nickname at the office is the Hammer.

The flight attendant draws his attention for obvious reasons, but there's more to it than sheer beauty. She's that magic, shimmery age — he guesses twenty-seven —

27

when a woman has one foot in youth and one in adulthood. She is somehow both a smooth-skinned sixteen-year-old girl and a knowing forty-year-old woman in the same infinite, blooming moment. And this particular woman is alive like a house on fire. Mark hasn't seen anyone this packed with cells and genes and *biology* in a long time, perhaps ever. She's full of the same stuff as the rest of them, but she's turned everything *on*.

When the flight attendant finally steps into first class, Mark has the urge to unbuckle his seatbelt, grab her left hand with his right, wrap his other arm around her waist, and start to salsa. He doesn't know how to salsa, but he's pretty sure that physical contact with her would resolve the issue. She is a Broadway musical made flesh, whereas he, he realizes suddenly, is running on nothing but alcohol fumes and pretzels. He looks down at his hands, abruptly deflated. The idea of clasping her waist and starting to dance is not impossible to him. He's done that kind of thing before; his therapist calls them "flare-ups." He hasn't had a flare-up in months, though. He's sworn them off.

When he looks back up, the flight attendant is at the front of the plane, poised to announce the safety instructions. Just to keep her in their eyeline, many passengers lean into the aisle, surprised to find themselves paying attention for the first time in years.

"Ladies and gentlemen," her voice curves through the air, "my name is Veronica, and I am the chief flight attendant. You can find me in first class, and my colleagues Ellen and Luis" — she gestures at a dimmer version of herself (lighter-brown hair, paler skin) and a bald, short man — "will be in economy. On behalf of the captain and the entire crew, welcome aboard. At this time, I ask that you please make sure your seat backs and tray tables are in their full upright position. Also, as of this moment, any electronic equipment must be turned off. We *appreciate* your cooperation."

Mark obediently powers off his phone. Usually he just tucks it in his pocket. He feels the sonorous welling in his chest that accompanies doing something for someone else.

Jane Adler, sitting beside him, watches the enraptured passengers with amusement. She was, she figures, actively cute for a few years in her twenties, which was when she met Bruce, but she's never come close to wielding Veronica's brand of sex appeal. The flight attendant is now showing the passengers how to buckle a seatbelt, and the Wall Street guy is acting like he's never heard of a seatbelt before, much less how to operate one.

"There are several emergency exits on this aircraft," Veronica tells them. "Please take a few moments now to locate the one nearest to you. If we need to evacuate the aircraft, floor-level lighting will illuminate and guide you toward the exits. Doors can be opened by moving the handle in the direction of the arrow. Each door is equipped with an inflatable slide, which may also be detached and used as a life raft."

Jane knows that her husband, somewhere behind her, has already mapped out the exits and chosen which one to push the boys toward in case of an emergency. She can also sense his dismissive eye roll during the comment about inflatable slides. Bruce processes the world — and decides what's true — based on numbers, and statistically no one has ever survived a plane crash by using an inflatable slide. They are simply a fairy tale intended to give passengers a false sense of control. Bruce has no use for fairy tales, but most people seem to like them.

Crispin wonders why he never married a woman with a body like this flight attendant's. None of his wives had an ass to speak of. *Maybe skinny girls are a young man's game,* he thinks, *and it takes years to appreciate the value of a cushion in your bed.* He's not attracted to this woman; she's the age of a couple of his grandchildren, and he has no more fire in his loins. The very idea of two people writhing around in a bed seems like a distasteful joke. It's a joke he spent a lot of time cracking himself, of course, when he was a younger man. He realizes — gripping the arms of his chair as hot pain blinks on and off in his midsection — that all the major chapters in his personal life started and ended on wrinkled bedsheets. All the wives, the would-be wives, the ex-wives, negotiated their terms in the bedroom.

I get the kids.

We'll be married in June at the country club.

I'll keep the summer house.

Pay my bills, or I'll tell your wife.

He peers at Veronica, who is now explaining how a life vest can be inflated by blowing through a straw. *Maybe if the women I chose had a little more heft,* he thinks, *they would have stuck around longer.*

"We remind you," the flight attendant says, with a slow smile, "that this is a nonsmoking flight. If you have any questions, please don't hesitate to ask one of our crew members. On behalf of Trinity Airlines, I" — she lingers on the word, sending it out like a soap bubble into the air — "wish you an enjoyable flight."

Veronica steps out of view then, and, without a focal point, the passengers pick up books or magazines. Some close their eyes. The vents hiss louder. Partly because the sound comes from above, and partly because it is combined with blasts of icy air, the hiss makes people uncomfortable.

Jane Adler pulls her sweater tighter to fight off the cold and nestles into her guilt for not finishing the script before this flight. She hates to fly, and now she has to fly apart from her family. *It's punishment,* she thinks. *For my laziness, for my avoidance, for my taking on this crazy assignment in the first place.* She had written for a television series in New York for so long, partly because it involved no travel. But here she is, taking another chance, another job, and another plane ride.

She follows her thoughts down a familiar path; when she's anxious, she replays moments from her life, perhaps to convince herself that she has a history. She has created memories, which means she will create more. She and her sister run on a flat Canadian beach; she silently, amicably, splits the newspaper with her father at the kitchen table; she pees in a public park after drinking too much champagne at a college formal; she watches Bruce, his face wrinkled in thought on a street corner in the West Village; she gives birth to her youngest son without drugs, in a hot tub, amazed at the bovine noises rising from her lungs. There's the stack of her seven favorite novels that she's been curating since childhood, and her best friend, Tilly, and the dress she wears to all important meetings because it makes her feel both pulled together and thin. The way her grandmother puckered her lips, and blew air kisses, and sang greetings: *Hello, hello!*

Jane tills through the inane and the meaningful, trying to distract herself from both where she is and where she's going. Her fingers automatically find the spot below her collarbone where her comet-shaped birthmark lives, and she presses down. This has been a habit since childhood. She presses as if to make a connection with her real, true self. She presses until it hurts.

Crispin Cox looks out the window. The doctors in New York — the best doctors in New York, and doesn't that mean the world?

— assured him that it was worth undergoing treatment at a specialized hospital in L.A. *They know this cancer inside out,* the New York doctors told him. *We'll get you on the drug trial.* There was a light in the doctors' eyes that Crispin recognized. They didn't want him to die, to be beaten, because that would mean that they, one day, would be beaten too. *When you're great, you fight. You don't go down. You burn like a motherfucking fire.* Crispin had nodded, because of course he was going to beat this ridiculous disease. Of course this wasn't going to take him down. But a month ago, he'd caught a virus that both sapped his energy and soaked him with worry. A new voice entered his head, one that forecast doom and made him question his prior confidence. The virus passed, but the anxiety didn't. He'd barely left his apartment since then. When his doctor called to make a final preflight appointment to do more blood work, Crispin said he was too busy. The truth was that he was scared the blood work would reflect the way he now felt. His only concession to this new, unwelcome unease was hiring a nurse for the flight. He didn't like the idea of being alone in the sky.

Bruce Adler looks at his boys; their faces

are unreadable. He has the familiar thought that he is too old and out of touch to decipher them. A few days earlier, while waiting for a table at their favorite Chinese restaurant, Bruce watched Jordan notice a girl his age walk in with her family. The two teens regarded each other for a moment, heads tipped to the side, and then Jordan's face opened — it might as well have split in half — with a grin. He offered this stranger what looked like everything: his joy, his love, his brain, his complete attention. He gave that girl a face that Bruce, who has studied his son every single day of his life, had never seen. Never even knew existed.

Benjamin shifts in his cramped seat. He wishes he were in the cockpit, behind the sealed door. Pilots speak like military men, in a scripted code, with brisk precision. A few minutes of listening to them prepare for takeoff would allow his chest to unclench. He doesn't like the combination of chitchat and snores going on around him. There's a messiness to how civilians behave that bothers him. The white lady next to him smells of eggs, and she's asked him twice whether he was in Iraq or "that other place."

Linda finds herself engaged in a strange and exhausting abdominal exercise as she tries to steer away from the wide mass of

Florida without touching the sleeping passenger on her other side. She feels like the Leaning Tower of Pisa. She wishes — her obliques engaged — that she had bought more chocolate. She thinks, *In California, with Gary, I will eat more,* and she's cheered by the thought. She's dieted since the age of twelve; she never considered lifting that yoke until this moment. Thinness has always seemed essential to her, but what if it's not? She tries to imagine herself as voluptuous, sexy.

Florida is singing again but from so deep within her chest, and at such a low volume, that the noise comes out like a hum. Around her, as if cued by the sound, the plane's engine thrums to life. The entry door is vacuum-sealed shut. The aircraft shudders and lurches, while Florida murmurs. She is a fountain of melodies, dousing everyone in her vicinity. Linda grips her hands in her lap. Jordan and Eddie, despite their silent feud, touch shoulders for comfort as the plane builds speed. The passengers holding books or magazines aren't actually reading anymore. Those with their eyes closed aren't sleeping. Everyone is conscious, as the plane lifts off the ground.

JUNE 12, 2013
EVENING

The National Transportation Safety Board's "Go-Team" is at the site seven hours after the accident — the length of time it takes them to fly from D.C. to Denver and then drive rental cars to the small town in the flatlands of northern Colorado. Because of the long summer daylight, it's not yet dark when they arrive. Their real work will take place at sunrise the following day. They are here now to get a sense of the scene, to simply begin.

The town's mayor is there, to greet the NTSB lead investigator. They pose for a photograph for the media. Except for the handshake, the mayor — who is also a book-keeper, because this town can't afford full-time employees — tucks his hands in his pockets to hide the fact that they're trembling.

The police have cordoned off the area; the NTSB team, wearing protective orange suits and face masks, climbs over and around the wreckage. The land is level in every direction, the surface burned, charred, a piece of toast blackened under a broiler. The fire is out, but the air is charged with heat. The plane sluiced through a cluster of trees and dug itself into the earth. The good news, the members of the team tell one another, is that it wasn't in a residential area. No humans on the ground were hurt. They find two mangled cows and a dead bird among the chairs, luggage, metal, and limbs.

Families of the victims arrive in Denver by plane and car over the twenty-four hours following the event. The downtown Marriott has several floors reserved for them. At 5:00 P.M. on June 13, the NTSB spokesman, a man with acne-scarred skin and a gentle demeanor, gives an update to the families and media in the hotel banquet hall.

Family members perch on folding chairs. They lean forward as if the skin on their shoulders can hear; they bow their heads as if hair follicles might pick up what no other part of their body can. Pores are open, fingers spread. They listen fiercely, hoping that a better, less crushing truth exists beneath the facts being delivered.

There is a cluster of elaborate flower arrangements in the back corner of the room, which no one looks at. Red and pink peonies in giant vases. A cascade of white lilies. They are left over from a wedding held in the room the night before. This smell will keep several family members out of flower shops for the rest of their lives.

The press stands apart at the briefing. They avoid eye contact with the relatives during interviews. They develop their own tics: One man scratches his arms as if he's been attacked by poison ivy; an on-air reporter fixes and re-fixes her hair. They disseminate the updates in live television interviews and through emailed AP reports. They focus on the "known" passengers. A plastics baron, famous for building an empire and automating thousands of employees out of work. A Wall Street wunderkind, worth an estimated 104 million dollars. A United States army officer, three college professors, a civil-rights activist, and a former writer for *Law & Order.* They pour facts into hungry mouths; this news story has captivated the world. Every corner of the Internet has weighed in.

A reporter holds up a copy of *The New York Times* to a camera, to show the huge block headline, the kind normally reserved for presidential elections and moonwalks. It

reads: 191 DIE IN PLANE CRASH; 1 SURVI-
VOR.

The relatives have only one question when
the press briefing comes to a close; they all
lean toward it like a window in a dark room:
"How is the boy?"

The intact pieces of the plane will be
transported to the NTSB's facility in Virginia. They will put the puzzle back together
there. Now they are looking for the black
box. The woman who leads the team, a
sixty-year-old legend in the field known
simply as Donovan, is certain that they will
find it.

For someone with her experience, the
scene is uncomplicated. The debris is contained within a half-mile vicinity, and there
are no bodies of water or swampy ground,
just hard dirt and grass. Nothing can be
permanently missing or lost; it is all within
reach. There is charred metal, seats cracked
down the middle, splinters of glass. There
are pieces of bodies but no intact cadavers.
It's easy to look past the human flesh and
focus on the metal. Focus on the fact that
this jigsaw puzzle makes sense. Donovan's
team is made up of men and women who
spend their professional lives waiting for
tragedies to occur. They drive themselves

hard, mouths drawn under masks, taking inventory and bagging evidence.

A few days later, the allotted rooms at the Marriott have emptied: The families have left. The daily updates to the press have stopped. The NTSB team has found the black box and returned to Virginia. It has been announced that they will release basic findings within three weeks and that there will be a public hearing on the evidence in Washington, D.C., in approximately six months.

The news coverage has broadened; several stories focus on the boy's aunt and uncle, who have flown in from New Jersey to adopt him. Lacey Curtis, thirty-nine, is Jane Adler's younger sister, and the boy's only remaining blood relative. There's a photo of a woman with light hair, freckles, and plump cheeks, smiling tentatively. The only other information known about her is that she's a housewife. Her husband, John Curtis, forty-one, is a computer scientist who does IT consulting for local businesses. They have no children.

Information about anything and anyone related to the crash continues to be inhaled, so television and Internet pundits continue to speculate. Were the pilots drunk? Did the plane malfunction? Is it 100 percent certain that this wasn't an act of terrorism? Did one of the passengers go crazy and rush the cockpit? Was it the rainstorm? Google analytics show that, one week after the accident, 53 percent of U.S. online searches are related to the crash. "Why is it," an old news anchor growls, "that out of all the terrible news in this terrible world, we care so much about this one downed plane and this one little boy?"

He's been in the hospital for a week. A woman on crutches enters the room; she's the head of public relations for the Denver hospital and has been appointed to update the family on everything that's not directly medical.

"Susan," John Curtis says in greeting. He's a tall, bearded man, with the pallor and potbelly befitting a person who spends most of his life in front of a computer screen.

"Has he spoken today?"

Lacey — pale, with a coffee stain on her blouse — shakes her head. "Not since we told him."

"Have you decided if you'd like us to refer to him as Eddie or Edward?" Susan asks.

John turns to his wife, and they share a

look. The look — haggard and thready — suggests that they have not slept for more than an hour at a stretch since receiving the phone call. The plane had crashed in the middle of a week when Lacey and John were not speaking to each other, because she wanted to move on with their quest to have a baby and he did not. And now the fight and the silence feel irrelevant. They have been bucked off the horse that was their life. Their nephew is lying in front of them, broken, and he is their responsibility.

"This is for strangers, right?" Lacey says. "They don't know him, or us. The press should use his given name. Edward."

"Not Eddie," John says.

"Fine," Susan says.

Edward — for that's his name now — is sleeping, or pretending to sleep. The three adults look at him, as if for the first time. The bandage circles his forehead; thick moppish hair slips out beneath it. He has sheer white skin and dark circles beneath his eyes. He's lost weight and appears younger than twelve. There's purple bruising on his chest that flowers beyond the neckline of the loose hospital gown. Both of his legs are in casts, but his right one is raised in traction. His feet are covered in orange socks, bought in the hospital gift

43

shop. White letters spell DENVER!!! on the soles.

There is a soft stuffed elephant beneath Edward's arm that Lacey finds difficult to look at. The moving company hired to transport the Adler family's belongings across the country stopped at a motel in Omaha the night after the crash. They emptied the truck in the parking lot, pulled every single box onto the asphalt. They opened the one that read EDDIE'S ROOM. They fished the stuffed elephant out of the box and mailed it to the Denver hospital with a note that said: *We thought the boy might want this.*

Susan says, "The plan is still to airlift him in two days, now that he's stable. A private plane has been donated for the trip, so you can both ride with him."

"Everyone is being so kind!" Lacey says, and then blushes. She has so many freckles that the blush simply serves to join them together. She has taken to wringing her freckled hands, as if the repeated motion might somehow change this unacceptable reality.

"A few other things," Susan says. She leans into her crutches. "Have you been online?"

"No," John says. "Not really."

44

"Well, just so you know, several Facebook pages have sprung up, devoted to either the flight or to Edward. There was also a Twitter account called @miracleboy, with Edward's face as the avatar, but that's been taken down."

John and Lacey blink at her.

"The content is mostly positive," Susan says. "Condolences, sympathy notes, that kind of thing. You've both been in the news some, because people were curious about who was taking Edward in. I just didn't want you to be surprised if you happened upon it."

"*Mostly* positive?" Lacey says.

"Trolls," John says.

"Trolls?" Lacey's eyes look impossibly wide.

"People who write provocative comments online, to try to get an emotional response," John says. "Their goal is to upset people. The more people they upset, the more successful their trolling is."

Lacey wrinkles her nose.

"It's considered an art form by some," John says.

Susan gives an almost inaudible sigh. "In case we don't have another chance to talk properly before you leave, I wanted to remind you about the personal-injury and aviation lawyers. They're going to land on you like vultures, I'm afraid. But they're not allowed to approach you until forty-five days after the crash. So please disregard, or sue, anyone who does. You know all the medical bills are being covered by the airline. There's no rush to settle. You'll get Social Security death benefits first, then life-insurance money, if either of Edward's parents had a policy. It will take time to sort out the rest, and I don't want you to let anyone convince you that any kind of legal action is urgent."

"Okay," Lacey says, but it's clear that she's not paying attention. The TV in the corner is on mute, but the bottom of the screen runs a banner reading, MIRACLE BOY BE-ING RELEASED TO HOSPITAL NEAR RELA-TIVES' HOME.

"People *can* be terrible," Susan says.

Edward shifts on the bed. He turns his head, exposing a smooth, bruised cheek.

"There are family members," she continues, "from the other passengers on the plane who wanted to see Edward, but we kept them away."

"Jesus," John says. "Why do they want to see him?"

Susan shrugs. "Maybe because Edward was the last one to see their loved ones alive."

46

John makes a small noise in his throat.

"I'm sorry," Susan says, her cheeks pinkening. "I should have phrased that differently."

Lacey sits down in one of the chairs next to the window. A beam of sunlight creates a halo effect around her exhausted face.

"One more thing," Susan says. "The president is going to call."

"The president?"

"*The* president. Of the United States."

John laughs, a quick burst into the particular air of this room. Charged air. Air that is waiting for the next word from the boy on the bed. Air that shushes everyone who enters, separating those who have lost from those who haven't.

Lacey puts her hands to her unwashed hair and John says, "He'll be on the phone, Lace. He won't be able to see you."

The nurses bustle the boy awake by drawing blood and taking vitals right around when the call is due to come in.

"I'm here," Lacey says. "So is Uncle John."

Edward's face contorts.

Lacey feels a shot of panic. *Is he in pain?* And then realizes what his face is trying to do. He's trying to smile, to please her.

47

"No, no," she whispers. Then, to the room at large: "Are we ready for the call?"

When she turns back, Edward has stopped trying.

A brand-new phone has been installed next to the bed, and Susan is there to press the speaker button.

"Edward?" The voice is deep; it fills the room.

The boy is horizontal on the bed, looking small and damaged to the grown-ups that surround him. "Yes, sir?"

"Young man . . ." The president pauses. "There's not much I or anyone else can say that will mean anything to you right now. I can only imagine what you're going through."

Edward's eyes are wide, flat.

"I wanted to tell you that the whole country is sorry for your loss and that we're rooting for you to pull through this. We're rooting for you, son."

Lacey nudges Edward's arm, but Edward doesn't say a word.

The deep voice repeats the words, slower now, as if convinced that the repetition will make a difference. "The whole country is rooting for you."

Edward is silent on the plane ride to New

Jersey. Silent in the ambulance, which has blacked-out windows to keep the press from snapping pictures of him. He speaks only when medically necessary for the remaining two weeks in the New Jersey hospital, as his lung mends and his leg comes out of traction.

"You're healing beautifully," a doctor says to Edward.

"I keep hearing a clicking sound."

The doctor's face changes; an invisible dial inside him spins and lands on the clinical setting. "How long have you been hearing it?"

The boy considers. "Since I woke up."

The neurologist is summoned. He orders new tests and an MRI of Edward's brain. He has white eyebrows and no other visible hair, and every day he cups Edward's face in his hand while he stares deep into his eyes, as if there's information there only he can read.

The neurologist calls Lacey and John into the hall. "The truth is," he says, "that if ten different people went through exactly the same trauma as this child — were banged around, pitched at a tremendous velocity, and then jolted to a stop — they would all have different symptoms." He raises his white eyebrows for emphasis. "Traumatic brain injury is invisible to most of our measuring tools, so I can't tell you with any certainty what Edward is going through or will go through in the future." He focuses his attention on Lacey. "Imagine I grabbed you by the shoulders and shook you as hard as I could. When I let go, you might not be technically injured — no muscles pulled, et cetera — but your body would feel the trauma. Right? That's how it is for Edward. He may have odd symptoms over the next few months, even years. Things like depression, anxiety, panic; his senses of balance, hearing, and smell may all be affected." The doctor glances at his watch. "Any questions?"

John and Lacey look at each other. Everything, including language, seems to have splintered and fallen apart at their feet. *Any questions?*

Finally, John says, "Not right now," and Lacey shakes her head.

The nurse wakes the boy up in the middle of the night to take his blood pressure and temperature. She says, "Are you okay?" The bald doctor always leads with, "How's the pain?" When his aunt arrives each morning, she smooths his hair off his forehead and says, in a low whisper, "How're you doing?"

Edward is unable to answer any of these questions. He can't consider how he's feeling; that door is far too dangerous to open. He tries to stay away from thoughts and emotions, as if they're furniture he can skirt past in a room. When the nurse leaves the TV on the cartoon channel, he watches it. His mouth is always dry, and the clicking in his ear comes and goes. Sometimes he is awake but not awake, and hours go by without him noticing. He'll have a breakfast tray across his lap, and then the light's fading outside.

He doesn't like his daily walk, which isn't actually a walk, since he's in a wheelchair. "You need a change of scenery," the nurse with dreadlocks tells him each weekday. The weekend nurse, who has blond hair so long it almost touches her bottom, doesn't say anything. She just loads him into the wheelchair and pushes him into the hallway.

This is where the people wait. The hall is lined with them. Sick people, also in wheelchairs, or standing weakly in doorways. The nurses try to shoo them back into their rooms. "Don't clog the corridor," a male nurse shouts. "This is a fire hazard. Give the boy some space."

An old man makes the sign of the cross, and so does a dark-skinned woman with an

IV in her arm. A redheaded teenager, the age of Jordan, nods at him, his eyes curious. So many eyes stare at Edward that the scene looks like a Picasso painting: hundreds of eyeballs, and then a smattering of limbs and hairstyles. An old woman reaches out to touch his hand as he passes. "God has blessed you."

The worst are the criers. Edward tries not to look, but their sobs thunder like organ notes and suck up the available air. It feels unkind that they are shoving their emotions at him when his own sadness and fear are so vast that he has to hide from them. The tears of these strangers sting against his raw skin. His ears click and people hold handkerchiefs to their mouths and then the nurse reaches the end of the corridor and the mechanical door slides open and they are outside. He looks down at his busted legs, to avoid seeing the lethal sky.

They release Edward from the hospital when he can bear weight on the less damaged leg and therefore use crutches. His head and ribs have healed, and the bruises on his chest and legs are yellow now instead of purple. The staff gather in his room to say goodbye, and it is only then that Edward realizes he doesn't know any of their names.

They are wearing name tags on their chests, but it makes his head hurt to read. He wonders if this is another symptom. Perhaps he will never put a name with a face ever again, and the only names he will know will be the ones he knew before the crash. This thought is oddly comforting, as he shakes hands with the bald doctor and the blond nurse and the one with the dreadlocks too.

He rises out of the wheelchair at the front door of the hospital and is handed crutches. He walks slowly to the car, between Lacey and John. He's conscious of his aunt and uncle's presence in a new way. The last time he saw them before this was at Christmas-time, when they'd met for brunch at a restaurant in Manhattan. He remembers listening to his father and uncle discuss a new computer-programming language. He'd sat between his mother and Lacey and had been so bored that he built a house using his silverware and napkin. The women had skipped from one seemingly pointless conversation to the next: neighbors, the ice cream Lacey made once a year from an elusive Canadian berry, a handsome actor on his mom's television show.

If asked, Edward would have said that he loved his aunt and uncle, but it had always been clear that they weren't *for* him, or Jordan. The grown-ups got together for the grownups. The gatherings were designed to allow his mother and aunt to share a teary hug goodbye and promise into each other's hair: *We will see each other more often.* Edward can picture his brother across from him at that brunch, steepling his fingers and trying to weigh in on the technical conversation his dad and John were having, as if he were also a grown-up. The image of his brother is so painful that Edward's vision cuts out entirely for a second, and he stumbles.

"Steady," John says.

"Goodbye, Edward," voices say.

"Good luck, Edward."

A car door swings open in front of him. Only then does he see, on the far side of the car, across the street, a small crowd of people. He wonders dimly why they're there. Then someone in the crowd calls Edward's name, and others clap and wave their arms when they see that they have his attention. He studies a poster-board held by a little girl. His head aches as he absorbs the words: *Stay Strong.* The sign beside it says in block letters: MIRACLE BOY!

"I don't know how they found out your release date," John says. "It wasn't in the papers."

54

Lacey rubs his arm, and since he is precariously balanced on his booted foot, this almost throws him over.

"It's like they think I'm famous."

"You are famous, kind of," John says.

"Let's leave," Lacey says.

They climb into the car and drive past the waving, poster-bearing crowd. Edward stares at them through the window. He offers a small wave, and a man pumps the air with his fist, as if Edward's wave was what he'd been hoping for. The clicking noise starts up inside Edward then, a reminder of the staccato beat he used to time piano notes with. He sinks back into his seat and listens to his body. He can't remember being invaded with sounds like this ever before. Beneath the sharp clicks there is the thud — a blurrier, messier sound — of his own heart.

They drive toward a house Edward has visited sporadically over the course of his life, but always with his parents and brother. Now he's going to live there. How is that possible? He tries to recall the name of his aunt and uncle's town. He watches the cars and trees wash past the window. They seem to be driving too quickly, and he's about to say something when he spots a graveyard. For the first time, he wonders what happened to the bodies.

An icy sweat coats his skin. "Please pull over."

John swerves to the hard edge of the highway, and Edward pushes open his door, hangs his body out, and throws up onto the gray dirt. Oatmeal and orange juice. Cars hurtle past. Lacey rubs his back. He pretends, as he does every time her face isn't directly in his line of vision, that she is his mom.

He can't stop vomiting; his body coils up, releases.

He hears her say, "I hated when the nurses told you that you were going to be okay." Lacey's voice is more strident than his mother's; she's his aunt again.

"You're not okay. Do you hear me, Edward? Are you listening? You are not okay. We are not okay. *This is not okay.*"

His body has paused, and he's unsure whether the violence will continue. When he realizes he's done, that his body is scraped clean and pulsing with emptiness, he sits up. He nods his head. And somehow, that statement and that nod loosen and break apart the air between the three of them. There is a note of relief. They have somewhere to start, even if it is the worst place imaginable.

9:05 A.M.

The spiky buildings of Manhattan can be seen out the window, the raised right arm of the Statue of Liberty, the swipe of a bridge across the river. The passengers shift in their seats, searching for positions comfortable enough to occupy for six hours in the sky. Top buttons on shirts are undone. Shoes removed. Passengers with the gift of being able to fall asleep anywhere, anytime, do so now. There's no need for consciousness, after all. On the ground, people's bodies are utilized, but on a plane, a person's size, shape, and strength have no utility and are in fact an inconvenience. Everyone has to find a way to store themselves, in the most tolerable fashion possible, for the duration of the flight.

Florida peers past Linda and the sleeping woman with the blue scarf. She has a hunger to see the city before it disappears behind clouds. Different locations have different energies, and for her, New York is glittering eye shadow, Basquiat graffiti, and strangers with bold dreams. She sees herself dancing in bars, slow-walking across cacophonous streets while men hoot at her womanly goods, wringing all the life she can out of her days in that snap-crackle-pop city.

Florida lived in New York during her twenties and early thirties, but she never pictures only one period of time; she has to think of them all, layered on top of each other like a Mexican dip. She's lived many lives, in many bodies, so her memories are oceanic — a body of water she swims regularly. She tried to count her lives once and reached thirteen before the project bored her. Some lives she entered as a walk-in, which meant she'd entered the body of someone whose soul had departed after either a physical trauma — like a car accident that left the person in a coma — or an attempted suicide. Those entries were innately exciting, and therefore her favorite kind. There was nothing like waking up in a new adult body, suffused in someone else's aura. She was always a little disappointed when — as in her current life — she entered in the traditional manner, as a baby.

The plane climbs, and Florida finds herself remembering her most recent wedding, only seven years earlier. Two dozen friends on the piece of Vermont land she and Bobby had recently bought. The five acres were pristine then, a meadow dipping down to a stream, with a forest on the far side. They'd only just started to plan — Bobby was in charge of this, a fact Florida would later regret — and were several months from building their home. Florida's friends had traveled up from the East Village, and there was a tent with Christmas lights and a local band. They danced in the smoky blue air to Pinoy music. Florida drank wine and shook her ass and tits and hair and sang along, her hand in her husband's. It was one of those magic evenings when happiness shone out of every heart and face, and Florida felt knitted together by love.

The memory makes her sigh now, wedged into an airplane seat. She feels the plane rise beneath her. She glances at Linda, whose eyes are closed. She's keenly aware of the irony. This girl is running toward a husband, while Florida is running away from one.

The plane hits thirty thousand feet, and Mark Lassio remembers something from the night before, something he'd blanked out until this moment. He was at a club, celebrating a buddy's birthday — more a colleague than a buddy, actually — when he caught sight of an ex-girlfriend across the room. His most recent ex-girlfriend, who hated clubs, who hated to dance, who was, in fact, highly skilled at hating. She was certainly better at hating than she was at bond trading, which was her job. It was something she and Mark had had in common; they delighted in ranting to each other. After sex, they would lie in bed and take turns going off. They trashed co-workers, friends, bosses, politicians, their families, everyone. It was the best part of their relationship — there was a childlike joy to it, like flying downhill on a sled — and Mark felt a prick of true disappointment when his therapist insisted that it wasn't healthy.

His ex had noticed him a second after he spotted her. She stood by the far wall; a crowd of people were dancing and making out between them, and the music was a collection of beats pitched at a volume designed to shake the words out of your head. He shouldn't have been there at all; he was trying to stay clean, and he could smell the goddamn cocaine in the air. Sharp and tangy, like sliced lemon. Mark searched her face, and a question yawned open inside him. *Maybe? Could we? Did we once have?*

She met his look. She had dark, almost black, eyes. She shook her head and mouthed: *No.*

He mouthed back: *Fuck you,* and started to dance, something he rarely did anymore. He was off the beat at first and had to rejig his movements to match the thumping noise. He bounced on his toes and threw his arms over his head, and when the crowd yelled along to a refrain that he couldn't make out, he yelled too. A guy nearby gave him a startled look, then grinned and they crashed palms in a high five.

Veronica's voice issues from the PA, and Mark cranes to see her, but she's not in sight. She announces that the plane has reached a sufficient altitude that approved electronic devices can be used. He pulls his laptop out of the seat-back pocket at the same moment the woman sitting next to him pulls out hers. They give each other a weak smile.

"Deadline," she says.

"Life isn't life without them."

She screws up her face as if she's actually considering his words. This annoys him.

"Hmm," she says.

Mark wants to stop talking, but he also wants this lady to know that he's on top of everything. He says, "You have two boys. I was on the security line with you."

His seatmate — who's maybe forty-five, not that much older than he is but from a totally different place, probably the suburbs, definitely the marriage-and-kids lifestyle, which is another planet from the one that he lives on — looks startled. She squints at her laptop, which has powered up. "I do."

"I have a brother," he says. Then he thinks, *Sure, that makes sense. This lady looks a little like Mom, and the boys are Jax and me.* He remembers being with his family on a plane, heading to visit his grandparents. He and Jax are punching each other in the arm and splitting a Twix bar. His mom looks stressed, like this lady looks stressed, though he didn't understand why until he grew up and started to rattle like a boiling pot about to lose its lid. His mom, quiet with thin lips, who always seemed to be turning away from him, took too many sleeping pills when Mark was eighteen and never woke up.

"I'm not sitting with them, with the boys, because I have work to do," the woman says.

Mark takes this as a request to buzz off. He turns his attention to his own screen, which is covered with detailed graphs and tables depicting market trends, losses, and indices of change. He scans the scalp trade. He processes the S&P numbers, the CME exchange, the latest bids. He's looking for the same thing he looks for every minute of every day: opportunities invisible to everyone but himself.

Linda slides both hands into her purse and wriggles the pregnancy test up her sleeve. She waits as long as she can before asking Florida to move.

"You have to pee?" the woman asks.

When Florida stands, her clothes chime. She steps into the aisle, and Linda sidles by. She hurries toward the bathroom and finds herself making accidental eye contact with a soldier sitting in an aisle seat.

"Hi," Linda says, more a squeak than a word.

He lifts a massive hand in greeting, and then she is past him, feeling even more flustered than when she first stood. There's a line for the bathroom, which she joins. In front of her, standing sideways in the aisle, is a tall, messy-haired teenager, the one she saw getting patted down earlier. He's wearing earbuds and jiggling slightly to unheard music. When he rolls his shoulders, even though the movement is slight, its carefreeness makes something inside Linda ache.

He looks a little like an ex-boyfriend, one of the early ones. She remembers running her hands through wild hair like his and then brushes the memory away, because the boy in front of her is most definitely underage. She'd observed him with the TSA officer and thought: *Why not just go through the machine?* She'd never understood people who took a stand. So what if the security machine was pointless? What was the point in making a fuss and irritating the people in charge? The airport wasn't going to redo its security system because of the opinions of one teenage boy, after all. She couldn't see the gain.

She fingers her sleeve and feels the crackle of the plastic wrapper. She used to hide test answers in the same spot during high school. She wonders if that piece of skin, right above the wrist on her right arm, is tired of bearing witness to her failures.

"Are you all right?" the boy in front of her asks. "Ma'am?"

"Me? Yes?" Linda wonders what her face was doing, to pull a teenager out of his own orbit. She tries to smooth her features.

"You don't need to call me ma'am," she says. "I'm only twenty-five." But as the words leave her mouth she realizes that, to this boy, twenty-five is *ancient,* and definitely ma'am-worthy.

The boy smiles politely and walks into a vacated bathroom.

Twenty-five is actually very young, she thinks, in the direction of the closed door.

When Linda was a teenager, she and her best friend decided twenty-five was the oldest acceptable age for a girl to be single. Gary is thirty-three, which is the perfect match for her age. It takes men longer than women to mature; by thirty-three, he's slept with enough people (nine, he told her, though she assumes that number is lower than the truth) to settle down. She has slept with enough men (sixteen) to want to stop forever. Guy number nine burned her with a cigarette in the middle of an orgasm; number eleven cheated on her with the high school math teacher, who was a man; number fifteen spent their rent money on meth. Only guy thirteen had a decent job and money in the bank, but his way of showing affection was to criticize. For her birthday, he gave her makeup, and for Christmas, weight-loss pills. She broke up with him before Valentine's Day, but she'd left that relationship second-guessing every facet of herself.

A bathroom becomes available, and Linda scoots inside. She closes and locks the door, which activates the fluorescent lighting overhead. There is only one place to stand: directly between the toilet and the tiny vanity mirror. She pulls the test out from under her sleeve. She puts the top between her teeth and gives a little tug, splitting the wrapper.

She pulls down her white pants, then her underwear, and squats over the toilet seat with her arm between her legs. She takes a deep breath and pees on what she hopes is the stick. She remembers the teenage boy telling the TSA officer that he didn't like the pose people had to take inside the screening machine — something about it being degrading? — and wonders what he would think of *this* pose. Her thighs shake, and the plane trembles too.

In first class, Crispin Cox tries to ignore the twinges in his abdomen. Instead, he thinks of his first wife, Louisa, the one who never gave up. That's her tagline in his head: *the one who never gives up.* They've been divorced for thirty-nine years, much longer than they were married, and yet every few years her lawyer contacts his lawyer with some drummed-up excuse to take more from him. More money, more stock, more real estate. Sometimes in the name of their kids, sometimes for herself. And goddammit if she doesn't win half the time.

The nurse, next to him, says, "The doctor said that you were in stable condition, sir. But you seem to be in a fair amount of pain. Can you rank the pain on a scale of one to ten for me?"

"I'm fine," Crispin says. "I just need another pill."

Why does he remember Louisa so well — he could repeat verbatim their dialogue at Carlino's that night, when she wore her hair the way he liked and a peacock-blue dress — but he can't remember where they honeymooned, or the occupation of his youngest son, the bright, squirrelly one? His life is there, with all its characters, but clouds keep passing across the view. What he sees, what he recalls, changes every hour.

The nurse centers the pill on his open palm.

He says, "Stop looking at me like that."

"Sir, I'm just trying to do my job."

"Exactly," he says. "You're looking at me like I'm your goddamn job. I'm no one's job — never have been, never will be. Can you get that through your thick, mulish head?"

The nurse looks down, as if her feet have suddenly caught fire and she needs to watch the flames. *Jesus, some people are so weak. Blow on them and they fall over.* He pictures Louisa again and thinks: *She never looked away when I yelled.*

The flight attendant with the world-class hips is in front of him. Where did she come from? The pain is abruptly worse. A wave crests.

"Can I help out here at all?" she asks, in a smooth voice. "Would you like a beverage, sir, or a snack?"

But the pain is stuck, the wave fixed, and he can't speak. Next to him, the nurse is mute. She might even be crying, for Chrissakes. Crispin forces his hand into the air, hoping the gesture will make the flight attendant disappear.

"I'd love a beverage," a man across the aisle says, and Crispin closes his eyes, the pill safely beneath his tongue.

The plane gives a gentle bounce; Veronica places her hand on a seat as she swivels. It's quiet on the aircraft; only the overhead vents can be heard clearing their throats. The passengers are pulled into themselves; the long flight has only just begun, and they need to get used to this new space, the silver bullet in which they will spend most of the day. They resign themselves to the new

68

normal, one by one. The prevalent question is: *How should I pass this time before my real life resumes?*

Jane hides her smile while listening to her seatmate flirt when the flight attendant returns with his drink.

"Where are you from?" he asks.

"Here's your Bloody Mary, sir."

"Mark, please."

"Mark." Veronica readjusts her hips. "I'm from Kentucky," she says. "But I live in L.A. now."

"I'm from Baltimore. I live in New York, though. I couldn't live anywhere else. How long have you been in the flight industry?"

"Oh, five years, I guess."

He's nervous. Jane sees his knee bouncing beneath the tray he's lowered over his lap. She tries to block the scene out. She has to write. She has to finish polishing this script, which means rewriting most of it, before they land. She can do it; she's good at focusing when there's a gun to her head. The problem is that she doesn't want to. If she was sitting next to Bruce, and he wasn't annoyed at her, he would ask: *What do you want to do?* He always goes back to the origin, to the essential question. His brain never gets tied up with tangents and obligations and feelings, like hers does. Sometimes his head tips to the side while he's looking at her, and she knows he's thinking: *Do I still love her?* And then, every time so far, thankfully: *Yes.*

She's in first class because she spent weeks obsessively packing their apartment instead of writing. She knows which box Eddie's elephant is in and the exact location of each of Jordan's prized books. She numbered the boxes in the order they should be unpacked in L.A. She'd wished, while packing, that there was a competition she could enter for moving a family cross-country with the greatest efficiency, because she would win first prize. When Lacey offered to drive to New York last week to help pull things together, Jane had laughed.

"Forgive me for trying to be helpful," Lacey said, offended.

"Oh, I know. I'm sorry, I was laughing because of me, not you."

The exchange fogged up with bruised feelings and their long history of poking and prodding each other, and though they both tried, neither was able to clear the fog before they hung up. Lacey and Jane have different operating systems, which often lands them in trouble. What they care about overlaps, but there are key divergences. Lacey has always, always wanted to fit in, which she believed required a husband, two kids, and a nice house in the suburbs. She wanted her life to look "right." This has simply never interested Jane much, as a concept. When she wanted something — a relationship, a baby, a job — she tried to get it. She rarely looked to her right or left to check on the progress of other women. She had been amazed once, at Lacey's house, to find that her sister subscribed to thirteen different women's magazines. There were subsets, her sister explained. Cooking, housekeeping, fertility, home decor, beauty. "What?" Lacey had said, in response to the look on her sister's face. "I'm not the weird one here. You are."

Lacey keeps score in her relationships in a way that is anathema to Jane but that she can use, in a moment like this, to help smooth away any wrinkles between them. *I'll phone her as soon as we get to the house,* Jane thinks. *Lacey will be touched that she was the first person I called from the landline. That's the kind of thing that matters to her.*

She notices that Veronica is gone and Mark looks forlorn, the Bloody Mary cupped in his hand. His mood settles like a fine mist over her skin, and she starts to type.

■ ■ ■ ■

The test instructions say that it takes three minutes for the results to show. The white stick stares blankly at Linda. She would like to pace, or even leave the room during this period, but that's not possible. She has to stand still. Perhaps because her body is stuck, her brain goes scattershot.

She remembers when she drank alcohol for the first time — Jägermeister — the night before the SAT. She arrived at the gymnasium to take the test on two hours' sleep, with what felt like a brain full of discarded engine parts. Six weeks later, her homeroom teacher, who'd always told her that her father was wrong, that she was smart and had a bright future if she'd only fight for it, went dead in the eyes when Linda told her how badly she'd scored. Linda saw her decide, in that moment, to move her hope and attention to a different, younger kid.

The bathroom lighting is terrible. Her skin looks yellow in the small mirror. And what was she thinking, wearing all white for a day of travel? She sticks her tongue out at the reflection and sees the scar from when she got it pierced at the age of thirteen.

Another terrible decision. Linda had done it simply because a girl she admired had gone goth. Within two days, her tongue had swelled so badly that she was having trouble breathing, and her stepmother had to drive her to the ER. The incident delighted her stepmother, who henceforth liked to insert the memory into unrelated conversations. "You almost lost your tongue, you know. Then where would you have been? You'd have had even less chance of landing a man."

"I landed Gary," she says, to the mirror and her stepmother.

But she secretly shares her stepmother's skepticism, and always has. She worries that the only reason she and Gary have lasted an entire eleven months is because they've been long distance, and now that distance is about to disappear. They'd visited each other, sure, the most recent visit being six weeks earlier, but visits were short and therefore sweet. There wasn't time over a long weekend for crankiness or bad moods or long-held insecurities to arise. Day-to-day life in the same location would reveal all of Linda's flaws.

They'd met at a wedding — Gary had gone to college with the bride; she had once dated the groom — and ended up servicing each other's acute loneliness later that night. Linda had assumed it to be a one-night stand, but Gary texted her the following day on his way back to California. They'd chatted by phone and text over the next few weeks. When he told her that he studied whales, she'd felt a surge of annoyance and almost hung up. She thought he was making fun of her lack of education; he had a PhD, and she'd never even gone to college. He obviously thought she was so dumb he could claim to have a fantastical job and she wouldn't know better. More than that, the lie felt barbed, specifically tailored to take *her* down. She'd been obsessed with whales as a child. Posters of the giant mammals had covered her bedroom walls, and most of her treasured books had concerned sea life. It felt like Gary was mocking both the twenty-five-year-old and twelve-year-old versions of herself.

"You mean you're unemployed," she'd said, in her meanest voice.

"I'm emailing you information on my program."

They were still on the phone when she opened the link and saw video clips of bearded men in windbreakers on a boat in the middle of the ocean. She saw that one of the men was a sunburned Gary. The next clip showed a whale's hump passing the ship. Then classrooms and cubbies stacked with scuba gear, which is when she closed her laptop and started to cough.

When the coughing ended, Gary said, "Linda?"

"I had something in my throat," she said.

Linda assumed she and Gary were just friends, because she felt none of the obsessive worry she normally experienced when she was interested in a man. Her day improved after she spoke to him, and he provoked the hiccuppy giggle she'd tried to suppress her entire life. *Hideous,* her stepmother had once muttered, when Linda laughed in front of her. They've never talked about children; Linda has no idea how Gary feels about having one. He had a crummy childhood; he'd said that he would rather kill himself than go through that again. Her secret hope is that they can make a life, together, that will heal the broken paths behind them. *When I'm with you, I feel fixed,* he told her once, and though she wasn't able to utter the words at the time, she felt the same way with him.

There's a loud buzz, and the speaker in the ceiling announces the commencement of the beverage-cart service. Linda is aware, suddenly, of being thirsty.

"Hello?" The bathroom knob rattles, and a man's voice says, "You okay in there?"

"Yes!" Linda says, and grips the test in her hand like a spear. A pink plus sign wavers in the middle of the white. "Yes!" She slides the bolt open and lurches into the aisle.

When Edward arrives at the house, he's shown to the nursery. John had moved the crib to the attic and replaced it with a single bed with a dark-blue bedspread. The bookshelf, filled with cardboard books that babies can safely chew on, remains. The walls and curtains are light pink, because Lacey had been convinced, each time she got pregnant, that it would be a girl. A rocking chair sits beside the window.

The boy and his uncle stand in the doorway for a moment. John looks confused, like he's forgotten why they're there. Edward wonders if he can turn and shuffle away without the man noticing.

This isn't my room, he thinks. *It can't be.*

John says, "Would you like to see the lake?"

He walks toward the window, so Edward follows on his crutches.

West Milford was built on the edge of a

seven-mile lake. During the town's heyday in the late 1800s, three enormous steamboats operated on the water, carrying visitors from trains to one of the many resorts. With the advent of airplanes, tourism changed. People still came to Greenwood Lake, but it was only families from New Jersey and New York, many of whom bought summer homes there. John's parents had met as eight-year-olds playing beside the lake, and both had summered there throughout their childhood. It was a safe town, though most suburban towns were safer then. Kids ran free, skidding into the house only for meals and bedtime, lake-wet and suntanned.

In the 1970s, the lake lost its widespread appeal. If families could afford a summer house, they bought at the New Jersey shore or on Long Island. The hotels didn't do enough business to stay open. John and Lacey bought a house there shortly after getting married in 2002, because they could afford a nicer place in West Milford than closer to the city, because there were enough businesses to support John's IT work, and because the lake reminded Lacey of Canada. They have a nice view from the second floor of the house. The nursery looks out over the vast, flat water, as does John and

Lacey's bedroom.

"When you're feeling better, maybe we can go swimming there," John says.

The new place inside Edward, the one that revealed itself after the crash, starts clicking. He remembers overhearing his mother tell his dad that Lacey had had another miscarriage. He hadn't known what the word meant and had looked it up in the dictionary.

"We can fix the room up more," John says. "We will, definitely. You decide what color you want the walls, and I'll paint them. Do you have a favorite color?"

"No, thank you," Edward says.

He turns and maneuvers slowly out of the room, then down the stairs. That night he sleeps — or, more truthfully, doesn't sleep — on the couch in the living room. He hates being out of the hospital. He hadn't anticipated this feeling, but then, he finds it impossible to anticipate any feeling now. It turns out that the hospital, with its beeping machines and routine and constant parade of medical staff, had been holding him together. His body now hurts in a new way; the dullness has been extinguished. He can sense the metal rod that replaced part of his shinbone, and his skin feels weird and rough to the touch. The hair on his head — which doesn't even have nerve endings — somehow aches. At 2:00 A.M., on his second night in West Milford, he sits upright on the couch with his hands on his thighs. The pain shimmers beyond the boundaries of his body. It seems impossible that he can survive this.

The next morning, there's a knock at the front door. John has already left for work, and Lacey hasn't yet come downstairs. Edward blinks his eyes — two hot, dry stones — and hauls himself up on his crutches to answer. A woman and a girl about his age are on the front steps. The woman is dark-haired, with light-brown skin. She's holding a red thermos. The girl is half hidden, peering out from behind her mother. Edward can only see one eye behind a pair of glasses, staring at him. His brain clicks, rattles almost, then stops. For a second, Edward feels okay. Clear, normal, unbroken. The sensation, gone almost immediately, is jarring.

"Hello," he says, to the girl.

"I'm Besa," the woman says. "And this is Shay. We live next door, so you'll see a lot of us. I brought this coffee for your aunt, but it looks like you need it more."

She holds the thermos out, and Edward hugs the warm cylinder to his chest. The smell reminds him of a café near his family's apartment that pumped coffee-scented air onto the sidewalk in order to lure people inside.

"I'm —" He hesitates. This is the first time he's had to introduce himself. Eddie is gone. He's glad his aunt made the decision she did in the hospital. "I'm Edward."

Besa gives a warm smile, which triggers a memory of Edward's mother smiling, and then triggers a wave of fear. He has the sudden desire to lie down at this woman's feet. Is every mom he encounters going to remind him of his own? If this is the case, he's doomed.

Besa says, "We know who you are, *niñito.*"

Shay steps out from behind her mother, a small frown on her lips. "I'm two months older than him, and you said I had to wait until I was eighteen to have coffee."

Besa puts up her hand. *"Cállate, mi amor."*

Lacey appears then and leads them into the kitchen. Edward lowers himself into a seat at the table and pours an inch of coffee into the thermos lid.

"Do you like it?" Shay asks.

The coffee tastes like he imagines fresh pavement does, burning and sticky, but he nods and tries to pull himself straighter in his chair. Shay is an inch taller than him, with shoulder-length brown hair and a dimple in her left cheek.

"Have you gone outside yet?" Besa asks. "Into town?"

"He needs rest," Lacey says. "He's not ready."

"Good," Besa says. "Because this place has gone *completamente loco.* West Milford is small, Edward, and everyone knows everyone, and nothing as exciting as you showing up has happened in decades, if ever. Did your aunt tell you the town painted this house while you were in the hospital?"

Edward tries to make sense of this. "How does a town paint a house?"

Lacey says, "The town council did. They wanted to be helpful." She pushes her chair back and walks to the counter. "They felt bad and wanted to help but didn't know what to do. It's so silly, because John painted the house last summer. It didn't need it at all."

"Everyone at camp is talking about how you're here," Shay says. "I'm practically a celebrity because I live next door to you."

Camp, Edward thinks. The word sounds familiar, but it takes his brain a moment to figure it out. Summertime. Children. Arts and crafts. He and Jordan did a science camp every summer, at the Museum of Natural History.

"Do we all want pancakes?" Lacey says, in a bright, let's-change-the-subject voice.

He's staring into the coffee when he hears the girl say, "I met your brother once."

He thinks he's misheard her. When the sentence replays inside his head, he sags slightly in his chair.

But Besa seems to have heard the same thing. She says, "What are you talking about? You never met his brother."

"I met him here," the girl says. "Well, on the lawn. I think I was six. I knew your family was visiting that day, and I was pretending to cut my lawn with my toy lawnmower. Jordan came outside by himself."

"I didn't know this." Besa sounds offended.

"Mom, I was six. I probably told you and you forgot. Also, it wasn't a big deal. I didn't even remember until" — she pauses — "recently."

"Jane loved to bring the boys here." Lacey's shoulders straighten. "She needed to give them a break from the hubbub of the city."

Edward says to Shay, "Did you talk to him?"

"A little. When he came outside, he

jumped down the steps, from the top to the grass. For some reason I was really shocked by this. Maybe I gasped, because he noticed me."

Edward tries to picture this: bright sunshine, green grass, the five cement stairs in front of his aunt and uncle's house.

"Jordan said something like, *You've never seen anyone jump before?* And I said that I hadn't seen anyone jump like *that.* He laughed and ran to the driveway. Then he climbed on top of your parents' minivan."

"Wait a second." Lacey frowns. "Don't tell tales, Shay. We don't need that around here."

"Jordan did things like that," Edward says. "That's something he would do."

Shay gives a small nod. "He waved at me, and then he jumped off the car roof."

"Dios mío," Besa says.

"Oh," Lacey says, then pauses. In a different tone, she says, "I remember. He hurt his knee. . . . He wouldn't tell me how, but I gave him a bag of frozen peas to put on it."

Edward doesn't remember any of this. He doesn't remember Jordan going outside without him. He doesn't remember the frozen peas, or this girl, or his brother with a limp. There is a cracking sensation in his

84

chest, as if small bones are breaking. Why can't he remember?

"He didn't seem hurt to me," Shay says. "A grown-up called him right after he jumped, and he went back inside."

She pushes back her chair and swipes her mother's cheek with a kiss. "I have to go, Mamí. The bus will be here any second."

"Que tengas un buen día."

"Adiós," Shay says, and then she's gone.

Edward takes another gulp of coffee to try to block the lump in his throat. He coughs into his napkin. He can feel Lacey's desire for him to eat, but there's a force field around food that he can't seem to penetrate — the smell, the solidity of it is impossible. He returns to the couch. Lacey switches the television on, but he can't focus on the images. He listens to the hum of Lacey and Besa's voices in the kitchen. When he passes the door once, on the way to the bathroom, he hears his aunt say, "Instead of a baby, a twelve-year-old boy." Edward keeps his eyes on his feet, to make sure he doesn't fall.

When the sky dims, and John comes home, Edward returns to the kitchen table. His uncle ruffles his hair; Lacey puts a dollop of buttery mashed potatoes on his plate and says, "Please, Edward?"

John says something about a lawyer, and

Lacey says that it seems to be a bad season for tomatoes. His uncle and aunt pass bowls of food back and forth to each other, more often than is necessary, Edward thinks.

"I wish I liked salad," Lacey says.

John makes a face. "Nobody *likes* salad."

Edward can tell, without knowing how, that this exchange about salad is a standard in their marital repertoire. It's a back-and-forth they repeat in order to recognize themselves, within their marriage and their lives. The same way John says, *Lace, you okay?* when he enters a room, without seeming to expect or need an answer. The way Lacey reaches up to check her hair a few times an hour. The way his aunt places the condiments in the door of the fridge, and John moves them to the top shelf.

"Did you have to take me in?" he asks.

Their faces turn to him. Lacey's freckles darken. A line crosses John's forehead.

"I mean, is it the law, because you're my only relatives?"

"I don't know if it's the law," Lacey says, and looks at her husband.

"There was no question," John says. "There was no other possible outcome. We're your family."

"Yes," Lacey says, but as her freckles lighten, Edward realizes she's on the verge

86

of tears. He sees John notice this too and press his hand over hers.

"My leg hurts," he says. "May I be excused?"

"Of course," John says.

Eventually, the square of window over the couch grows dark, and then darker. John stands in the doorway of the living room and says, "It's bedtime, kiddo. Can I help you upstairs?"

Edward says the same thing he's said the last two nights: "My leg . . . The stairs make me nervous. Would it be okay if I just stayed down here again?"

"Sure." Moments later, Lacey appears with blankets and a pillow and murmurs *good night* into his ear. Edward listens to their footsteps on the stairs, and then their bedroom door clicks shut. He stands up, walks to the front door, opens it, and hobbles outside.

He crosses the lawn and his aunt and uncle's driveway. He's slow in his movements. It's ten o'clock. The nighttime air feels soft against his cheek and makes the hairs stand up on his arms. Edward registers that the suburbs' night sounds are very different from the city's. Here, there is a wall of quiet set in front of warbling creatures, rustling leaves, and distant car engines. He drags across another lawn and climbs the front steps of a house that looks, in the shadows, almost identical to the one he came from.

He knocks on the door.

After a pause, a woman opens it. Besa squints into the darkness.

"Edward? Are you okay?"

He says, "Can I come in and see Shay?"

Another pause, and a memory cracks through Edward's mind. This is how memories appear now, like a burglar bursting through a locked door without warning. It's a few weeks before the flight, and he and Jordan are in the elevator of their building. They'd snuck out of the apartment without their dad noticing, and they're grinning at each other. They know that when they hit the lobby, the doorman will be shaking his head. He'll say, *Boys, your father called. Back upstairs now.* But as the elevator swooped down, he and his brother played air guitar.

Edward thinks, *Jordan should have been the one to live, not me.*

Besa looks over her shoulder and calls out, "Shay, *mi amor,* are you decent?"

Shay's voice travels from upstairs. "Why?"

Besa doesn't answer. She leads him past the living room and up a set of stairs. Through an open doorway, he sees Shay leaning against pillows on a bed. She's wearing pajamas with pink clouds on them and holding a book.

"Hi," he says.

She straightens with a bustle of motion. She gives the same squint her mother used at the door, this time from behind glasses.

"Um, hi?"

"Shay," Besa says, "maybe you can tell Edward about your day at camp." She has her hand on Edward's shoulder, and the sensation is both wonderful and terrible.

"Why would I do that?" Shay says.

Edward is aware that Besa is staring at her daughter, trying to deliver a message without words. And he knows — maybe, a little bit — why he came here. To be with another kid, to have a break from the intense, watching, worried eyes of adults.

Besa says in a bright, we-will-make-this-work tone, "Have you ever been to camp, Edward?"

"This is weird," Shay says.

Besa hurls a sigh at her daughter.

"You don't have to talk to me," Edward says. "Not if you don't want to."

"I'll need to go to sleep soon."

He swivels his head from side to side and locates an armchair by the window. "I could sit there for a bit." He feels his body slow-ing down. He swallows. Then takes a breath. "Just for a few minutes," he says.

Shay and her mother exchange another long look, complicated with twists and beats. Edward makes his way to the chair. He feels like he's pushing through water. His crutches drag across the carpet. *Why would they make the carpet this fluffy?* he thinks.

Besa says, "I'll give Lacey a call, so she knows you're here."

"I'm going to say again, for the record, that this is w-e-i-r-d," Shay says.

By the time Besa leaves the room, Edward is asleep.

When he wakes, it is to white light so glaring that all he can do is blink. He doesn't know, during the blinking, who or what or where he is. Only when he has adjusted to the light, and his brain has stopped panicking and throwing switches, does Edward see that he's alone in Shay's room. There's a green blanket draped over his lap. He can feel that he's alone in the house; the walls, the open doorway, everything suggests emptiness. He just sits there, for a long time.

When he knocks on his aunt's front door and she opens it, he says, "Are you mad at me?"

She gives him a funny look. "I don't think

I could be mad at you," she says. "Come inside and rest. You have a doctor's appointment this afternoon."

When Edward has lowered himself to the couch, Lacey helps him lift his hurt leg onto the stack of pillows on the coffee table. Something occurs to him, and he says, "Am I stopping you from going somewhere? I mean, do you have a job you're not going to, because of me?"

She straightens the corners of the pillows around his foot. "No. I used to have a job," she says. "But I stopped working when I got pregnant. I was on bed rest. Last year."

"Oh."

Lacey looks around the room, and Edward thinks, *This was her space.* There are magazines stacked on the lower level of the coffee table. The ones in his line of vision are about either pregnancy or babies. His aunt had spent her days alone in this house planning to get pregnant, or trying to stay pregnant. Edward's head clicks, and he wishes he could get up and leave the room, the same way he left the nursery upstairs, but Shay's at camp, his leg prickles with pain, and he has nowhere else to go.

"I'd been thinking about looking for another job. Something," Lacey says. "I just hadn't gotten around to it yet." She pauses, as if to catch her breath. "Can I get you anything from the kitchen?"

"No, thank you."

He watches a soap opera in which a woman weeps over whether or not to have an abortion while her mother wonders whether or not to leave her husband. He feels aware of the hours in a new way. He has a vague understanding of how they pile on top of each other to make days, and how seven days group together into a week. And the weeks collect until there are fifty-two, and then it is a year. The flight was on June 12. That means it must be late July now. Time is passing.

The doctor is a throat-clearer. He enters the room making the noise of a bullfrog and continues for a solid ten seconds while standing in front of Edward and Lacey. When he finally stops, he looks pleased with his performance. He says, "You've lost eight pounds since the event."

Event? Edward thinks, confused for a split second. Then he understands.

Lacey says, "That's not good."

The doctor repeats: "That is *not* good."

There's a photographic mural of a butterfly on one wall. Edward wonders if the doctor regretted the mural once it was put up.

The butterfly, at that swollen size, doesn't look beautiful. Its scale and strangeness make everyone stand as far away from it as possible.

"Buy him ice cream, candy bars, whatever he wants," the doctor says, and issues an emphatic honking noise. "This is no time for nutrition. He's a growing boy, and he didn't have the weight to lose. He needs calories. Lose one more pound and I'm going to put you on an IV, Edward. That means re-hospitalization."

In the car on the way home, his aunt says, "Please think of something you might be able to eat."

Edward feels barren on the inside. There's nothing alive in him. Food seems not only unnecessary but irrelevant.

Lacey pulls into the parking lot of an oversized convenience store. She turns the engine off but keeps her hands on the steering wheel. She gives Edward a look he hasn't seen before. "Please don't do this." Her voice is pinched. "If Jane knew how badly I was doing at taking care of you . . ."

Edward says, "No, Aunt Lacey." He scans the air for more words and sees only *convenience, store, chips, beer, sale, parking.*

She is out of the car, away from him, and he scrambles to follow.

Inside the store, she says, "We're going to walk up and down every aisle. If the food doesn't disgust you, put it in here."

He looks at the stacks of chocolate bars. Crunchy, caramel-filled, nut-buttered, dark chocolate, white chocolate, milk chocolate. He chooses Jordan's favorite: a Twix bar. Lacey's shoulders drop slightly when he places it in the basket. Chips: ranch, barbecue, nacho cheese, dill pickle, jalapeño, salted, baked, ruffled, flat, sour cream and onion. He chooses a bag of his mother's favorite: salt and vinegar. The next aisle is Fruit Roll-Ups, meat jerkies, and a coffee setup. Nothing goes in the basket. Then there's a long row of cereals. Edward thinks, *Maybe without milk it would be okay.* He can't bear the idea of food that changes form in any way. Sloshing is intolerable, and he doesn't want anything with bubbles. Soup, stew, smoothies, and sodas are out. Ice cream melts, and that makes him uncomfortable too.

He chooses the cereal with the least colorful box. "Is this enough?" he asks his aunt.

"It's a start."

When they get home, she spreads the food out on the coffee table. Then she leaves the room and comes back with a plate and spoon. Edward sits on the couch and watches. His leg is throbbing, even though it's elevated on a pillow. The muscles and tendons above his knee pulse, as if they themselves are a heart.

Lacey unwraps the Twix first. She breaks off a section and puts the piece on the plate. Then she opens the box of cereal and puts a spoonful of the O shapes on the far side. Then two potato chips.

The aunt and nephew regard the plate in silence.

"I want you to eat all of this in the next hour," she says. "Then I'm going to replace these amounts. Understood?"

Edward nods. He switches the television on; there's a talk show with a table full of women interrupting each other. He starts by nibbling the edge of a potato chip. When his mouth feels like sawdust, he scrapes a small amount of chocolate off the bar with his front teeth. He remembers cramming potato chips in his mouth with his brother, to see how many could fit. He remembers sitting at the dining room table with his family, the sun setting behind them, Bach playing on the stereo. Then he bites an O in half and wills himself to remember nothing, think nothing, until all that exists is a flatness — a flatness he now identifies as himself.

10:02 A.M.

The plane weighs 73.5 tons. The wingspan measures 124 feet. It is constructed of metal sheets, extrusions, castings, ingots, bolts, and wing spars. It has 367,000 individual parts and took two months to build; 280,000 pounds of thrust are required to power this bus through the sky.

Bruce peers past Eddie, out the window.

"I was about your age when I took my first flight," he says. "We were going to a funeral for an uncle, whom I'd never met. And when I saw what the clouds looked like from the sky, I wanted to get out of the plane and dance on them."

Eddie looks into his cup of orange juice. He seems annoyed, but it's not real annoyance. Bruce has noticed that as Jordan becomes a more combative teenager, his younger brother tries, at moments, to project similar anger, irritation, or indignation. He's not much good at it, though;

neither his heart nor his hormones are in the right place.

"This is my third flight, Dad," Eddie says.

This time, Bruce thinks, *I want to understand the composition of the clouds. I want the clouds contained and understood. When did that switch happen? When did I go from wanting to dance to wanting to write dimensions down in a notebook?* He scans his adolescence: his thirteen-year-old self, a shyer version of the twelve-year-old. Each year he sank more deeply into awkwardness and silence. But there was a jolt of excitement when he realized, much later than he should have, that inside himself was a brain that aced tests easily, that he could use, really *use,* to make sense of the loud noises and strange customs and unpredictable people around him. Math was the deepest pool in sight, so he dove in. Numbers and equations led to theorems and binomials and n-dimensions and monster groups, and then, in his twenties, he began to use math to tie together pieces of the universe that no one had thought to tie together before.

He looks over his shoulder. Jordan is slowly making his way down the aisle, his head bouncing to a beat.

"You should push harder in your career," Jane has told Bruce during fights. "Why do

I need to carry us? Why is college tuition —
probably three hundred and fifty thousand
freaking dollars, you know — *my* responsibility while you make up mathematical
constellations and hang pretty beads from
them?"

Jane has no understanding of his work,
but he doesn't blame her for that. Only
about seven people in his own field understand what he's doing. That's the way of
pure math; you need a PhD in the subject
to even have a hope of crawling into the
specific rabbit hole that a mathematician
inhabits. And an individual project — a
lifetime of work — may very well appear to
non-mathematicians to be pointless, a piece
of exquisite but inapplicable math work. It
could turn out to be extremely valuable but
not until years after your death, in a field
you couldn't have dreamed into existence.
Pure math is the stuff of dreams, strands of
gossamer built to be thrown to smarter men
in the future.

One example Bruce sometimes cites,
when non-mathematicians ask about his
work, is Sir William Hamilton. The Irish
mathematician had a revelation while out
for a walk in 1843 and carved the resulting
equation into Dublin's Broome Bridge with
a penknife. That equation marked the

discovery of the quaternion group, which proved useless in his lifetime but one hundred fifty years later helped to create video games. The French mathematician Pierre de Fermat's "Little Theorem," as it was known, served little purpose when it was developed in 1640 but became the basis of RSA encryption systems for computers in the twenty-first century.

"Why not just do normal math?" Jane said. "The kind that has actual applications. The kind that helps scientists build things." *The kind,* she might as well have said out loud, *that makes money.*

Tenure at Columbia would have solved a lot of problems. It would have kept them off this plane, in New York. Bruce sighs and checks over his shoulder again. He knows Jordan is taking his time on purpose. The boy thinks it's good for his father to sweat a bit.

Jordan *schzoom-schzooms* and *zump-zumps* down the aisle. The music in his ears tells him to *tump-tump,* so he does that too. There is a girl with a peace sign drawn on the back of her hand, probably around his brother's age, watching from a window seat. He offers her a wave. He wants to enjoy this brief unleashed moment. Buckled in beside his father means they'll argue, and he'll start thinking about L.A. and wondering what that will be like. And he'll miss Mahira.

It had started from nothing. One day, he'd been in the deli buying a soda, and she'd given him an unhooked smile, one that told him she liked him and had liked him for some time, and he smiled back, and before he knew it, he was kissing a real live girl in real live time. Every time he went in the store and her uncle was out, they would go to the back supply room. They stood among cans of beans and boxes of toilet paper and kissed, kissed, kissed. They barely spoke. Their language was composed of smiles and welcoming looks and brushing the hair off her cheek and about twenty different kinds of kisses ranging from *hello* to *I want you (though I don't really know what that means)* to *I want to figure out what your lips taste like.* He never would have guessed that kisses could be so variant: in speed, depth, ferocity. He could have kissed her for hours and never been bored. He saw Mahira only once outside the deli, in a Chinese restaurant; his father was with him, and her uncle with her. They had to limit their communication to smiles.

When he told her he was moving, Mahira looked away for a second, then turned back and met his lips differently. And for his final three visits to the storeroom, they shared a new kiss, one that said, *I'll miss you,* and *I'm scared that we're growing up,* and *I wish this could continue forever, but I know that even if you weren't leaving, it could not.*

Jordan sighs, *tump-tump,* and says, "Excuse me."

His father slides out so he can slide into his seat, and he is back to being a term in the equation that states Eddie + Jordan = Bruce. Jordan tips his head back and closes his eyes, the music still playing in his ears. He's pleased that he never told anyone about Mahira. She is his alone. His secret history. He figures that the more times he opts out of security machines, the more girls he kisses, the more of himself he will own, the more of an unknown quantity he will become, and the equation, the one his father has built his life around, will no longer be true.

Directly across the aisle from the Adlers, Benjamin slides the free magazine back into the seat pocket. He tries to change his position, but there's not a lot of room to do so. He's uncomfortable; his side aches where the bag is taped to his skin. After surgery, the drugs were the only upside to the weeks

101

spent in the hospital. Benjamin had never taken anything stronger than ibuprofen before, but while pumped with pain medication during the day and sleeping pills at night, he was able to exist in a delicious haze. He thought about the fight with Gavin, but his thoughts were not tethered to reality. He watched it like a play: a massive black guy circling a skinny blond white one.

This flight, the final one home, has unfortunately woken him up. He's drug-free, and the return to sobriety makes him feel painfully aware of every niggle in his body and every thought in his head. He has flashes of panic, even reaching to his belt to see if he's armed. How is he supposed to bear himself nonstop?

He's being sent back to L.A. for one more operation, and then he'll be assigned a desk job. He is no longer allowed to work in the field. He catches himself hoping, now that the drugs have cleared his system, that he will die on the next operating table. That would be better, far better, than folding himself into a desk chair every day. Besides, he is a stranger to himself now, and he's not at all sure that this stranger deserves to live.

The clouds outside the windows are a shade

darker than before. Inside the cabin feels darker too, beset with memories of soft-lipped girls, permanently sleeping mothers, shy teenage boys, and clashing fists. Florida can almost see the scenes, the missing people, the dense minutes and hours and years that sit behind each person on the plane. She inhales and lets the choked air fill her lungs. The past is the same as the present to her, as precious and as close at hand. After all, if you think about one memory for most of a day, is that not your present? Some people live in the now; some people prefer to reside in the past — either choice is valid. Florida operates her lungs, pleased by the fullness.

When Linda sits back down, Florida pats her hand. "You remind me of someone," she says. "I've been trying to remember who."

"Oh?"

"Might be one of the revolutionaries I took care of in my store in Cebu. In the Philippines. They were mostly boys, but occasionally I'd get a feisty girl who had faked her way into battle." Florida pictures the crowded back room of that store. She sold or traded rice and beans out front and hid the wounded under blankets in the back. She held secret meetings of the Katipuneros in her bedroom late at night. The wounded or sick soldiers came straight from fighting the Spanish, but they were no more than children. They called her Tandang Sora, and she whispered the same truth in each child-soldier's ear: *You are special. You are meant to survive, to go on and do great things.*

Florida is proud of this memory; she lived that life well. There are other lives, in which her opinion of herself isn't so high. The one she's sitting in right now, for instance, feels like it's gotten away from her.

Linda stares. "When was this? I thought you said you lived in Vermont."

"Oh, a couple hundred years ago." Florida studies her seatmate. "There was a girl I treated for pleurisy; I think it's her you remind me of."

Linda looks at her like she's crazy. Florida sighs. Sometimes she explains, sometimes she doesn't, but this girl looks like she needs all the help she can get. "This isn't my first life," she says, "or my first body. I have a longer memory than most people. I can remember most of time."

"Oh. I've heard of people like you."

Florida is unfazed by Linda's distrustful tone. Even her parents in her current life, two Filipino doctors who immigrated to

Atlanta, Georgia, only to become a dry cleaner and a housewife, didn't believe their daughter's tales of past lives. She had been only too happy, in the middle of high school, to leave them and the South by attaching herself to a boyfriend who had a drum set and a dream of the big city.

Linda is chewing her lower lip. She's a pretty young woman who seems to have mastered how to make herself ugly. She wears too much makeup and has an over-expressive face. Her mouth is rarely still, her eyebrows shoot up, her cheeks draw in and then push out. Her face contorts, as if it's striving for something.

Florida pats her hand again. "You'll be okay. You want to marry this man in California, right? So you get off the plane and you marry him, and, *voilà,* you have a new life. A new life is what you're after, isn't it?"

Linda says, in a small voice, "I'm not a hundred percent sure he's going to propose."

Florida smiles. "Sweetheart, no one is one hundred percent sure of any damn thing. If someone says they are, they're a liar." She shifts in her seat hard enough that the bells on her skirt jangle. Bobby used to say it sounded like she was wearing tiny alarm clocks. She'd respond: *Who am I trying to*

Benjamin hates being strapped in this seat, mired in his own thoughts. He's unable to do the physical movement necessary to quiet his brain. He doesn't think about the gunfire during his last patrol; the night he was injured makes sense to him. He'd grown sloppy in the weeks following the fight with Gavin. Distracted. He'd basically stopped sleeping, which made everything worse. He was shot during patrol because his reflexes were gone, which made him an easy target. Benjamin actually saw the shooter, positioned between two branches. Looked the man in the eyes and received his bullet. That information computes. There's nothing there for the ants to chew on.

Instead, he thinks about Gavin. Gavin was a white guy from Boston who had showed up in his platoon six months earlier. Benjamin knew by looking at him that he'd been to college and probably joined the army to piss off his parents. There were plenty of guys like that, amid the lifers like him. Gavin, if he stayed alive long enough, would do his tour and get out. Probably become an accountant — a guy who drives his kids to soccer games. He wore wire-rim glasses and had white-blond hair.

In general, Benjamin stayed away from white guys. The army, like everywhere else, segregated itself, and Benjamin preferred hanging out with people who looked like him. The truth was that no one — black, Latino, Asian, or white — was clamoring to be his friend. He knew he had a reputation for being uptight and a little scary. His grandmother, Lolly, had once told him that his "resting face" wasn't particularly friendly.

One night, he and Gavin were both assigned latrine duty. The bathroom was disgusting; there were dark, unidentifiable stains on the walls and sticky floors. There had been talk of their platoon moving to a new location, and the uncertainty translated into a lack of motivation for this kind of work. Benjamin and Gavin walked into the room with buckets and mops and a gallon of toxic-smelling cleaning solution; they both paused just inside the doorway, and Benjamin's jaw set. When he looked at Gavin, he saw the same determination on his face. They went at it, and after three straight hours, they had deep-cleaned the entire room.

"Motherfucker," Gavin said at the end, covered in sweat and grime. "We fucking

107

did this."

He held his fist out to Benjamin, and Benjamin, grinning, met it with his own.

"We sure did," he said.

They became friends that night, and it was no big deal — just nice, but nice meant something to Benjamin. They had actual conversations, mostly because Gavin asked Benjamin questions and seemed interested in the answers. Benjamin told Gavin that he barely remembered his parents and that Lolly wasn't his *real* grandmother — she had found him in a stairwell at the age of four and taken him in. Gavin told Benjamin that his father wanted him to take over his dental practice and that teeth made Gavin queasy, so he joined the army to escape the future that had been mapped out for him before he was even born.

Gavin was friends with everyone, so his friendship with Benjamin was a small part of his military life, but it was a significant part of Benjamin's. Gavin liked to smoke pot — there were weeks of no activity on base, and in times of boredom, the captain looked the other way on things like marijuana and video games — and when he smoked, he told the kind of knock-knock jokes usually favored by nine-year-olds. Benjamin never smoked, but he made sure he was around when Gavin did, and he laughed hysterically while the other guys groaned.

The first-class flight attendant walks by his seat and gives him a smile. *Boom chicka boom.* Benjamin can hear her soundtrack so clearly she might as well be carrying a speaker on each hip. In his neighborhood, she'd have a line of men following her down the street, dancing to that beat.

He glances around at the rows of civilians with their untucked shirts, beer bellies, and pointless chitchat. The flight attendant is neat, pulled together, and in uniform, which he appreciates. The mess of everyone else's appearance, and of their non-military lives, confuses him. *Pull yourself together,* he wants to tell the old lady next to him and the rumpled dad across the aisle. How hard is it to tuck in your shirt, straighten your posture, lose ten pounds?

Benjamin clenches his jaw. He's not made to sit still. If he could only take a short break to run sprints, do push-ups, or even just stride someplace with a sense of purpose. He touches his side now, checking that the bag is in place, that he's still contained by his own body.

July 2013

That night, when John and Lacey go upstairs, Edward is finally able to unfurl — his sadness, his blankness — into the empty living room. He's not tired; he feels terrible and awake the same way he did ten hours earlier. *I must be missing hormones,* he thinks. *Something to do with the word "endocrine."* There is a cycle that normal people ride: They wake up with the light, rub their eyes, get hungry, eat cereal, go about their days, and then, with sunset, begin to wind down. They eat again, watch TV, yawn, and climb into bed.

Edward sits in the middle of the couch, wired and surrounded by shadows. He hears the upstairs sink run, and the toilet flush; John is getting ready for bed. Edward had told himself that he wouldn't do this again, but nonetheless he stands up, leaves the house, and hitches his way across the lawn.

110

When Besa opens the door, he says, "I'm sorry."

"Nonsense," Besa says. "We'll just have to find something more comfortable for you to rest on than a chair." She leads him up the stairs.

Shay is wearing a T-shirt and sweatpants this time. Her hair is in a ponytail. She nods when she sees him. "I was thinking about you at camp today," she says. "I'm glad you came over."

"You are?" His voice squeaks with relief. This means she won't send him away.

Besa has disappeared; they are alone in the lamplit room. Edward sinks down in the chair. He balances his crutches carefully against the bookshelf beside him.

"I don't know why I didn't think of it earlier." Shay is on her knees on her bed. She looks excited. Edward identifies this emotion as if it's an answer on a test. *That's a nimbus cloud. That's the pancreas. That's excitement.* He feels around inside himself and touches the four corners of his flatness.

"You've read *Harry Potter,* right?"

He nods. Jordan was given the series as a birthday gift and then had the idea to take the books out of the library as well, so he and his brother could read them at the same time. They lay in their bunks for hours, for several weeks on end, mowing through one book after another. Jordan would call out from the top bunk: *Holy cow, Eddie, are you on page 202 yet?* The brothers had long conversations about whether Snape was in fact a bad person. They had once, after splitting a nearly full gallon of apple juice at the kitchen table, gotten into an argument so intense — Jordan insisting that Snape was the key, even the genesis, of all the evil in the books, Eddie saying he was essentially good — that their father had to send them to opposite ends of the apartment until they calmed down. "No more sugar!" Bruce had yelled. "And what the hell is a snape?"

Shay bounces lightly on the mattress and studies Edward. Her gaze makes him uncomfortable.

"I'm going to blow your mind," she says. "Are you ready?"

The sinkhole inside him grows deeper, and he can taste weariness in his mouth. "I guess so?"

"You're just like Harry Potter."

He looks at her, not sure what to say.

"Okay, listen. As a child, Harry survived a terrible attack that no one should have been able to survive, right?"

Edward can see that an answer is expected of him. "Right."

"Voldemort killed Harry's parents but couldn't kill him, even though he was a baby. Nobody understood how it was possible. And the fact that he survived scared a lot of people — it freaked them out." She blinks behind her glasses. "I heard a doctor on TV say that there was a zero percent chance of survival from your plane crash."

Edward swallows. Like a dutiful student, he follows her train of thought. Voldemort equals plane crash. Dead parents equal dead parents. Harry equals him.

"My uncle said they think I survived because of where my seat was in relation to the fuselage and because it ejected out of the wreckage. . . ."

Shay shakes her head.

Edward stares at the girl: her glasses, her one dimple, her determined expression.

"Do you have any scars from your injuries?"

He does. He has a horrible one extending down the middle of his left shin. He pulls up his pant leg. The line is jagged, pink, and raised.

"That's disgusting," Shay says, sounding delighted. "So you have a scar like Harry Potter too. *And* you were taken in by your aunt and uncle. Also, remember how Aunt Petunia was jealous of her sister being a witch? Lacey was totally jealous of your mom. My mom made me go and sit with Lacey when she was on bed rest last year, and she used to brag about your mom's achievements, but in a sad voice."

There is a dark window behind Edward's head, and he can feel the silence on the lawn and streets. When cars pass, they creep by, as if afraid they might hit a child or a deer. He feels faintly nauseous, considering her words. Or maybe it's her excitement that's making him seasick, as if he's stepped onto a rocking boat. Either way, he knows he won't be able to eat in the morning.

"You probably have special powers. You must be magic, to survive that crash."

"No," Edward says, without hesitation.

"Harry didn't know he had special powers either," Shay says. "He lived in a cupboard under the stairs at the Dursleys' house for eleven years before he found out." She looks at the clock on her nightstand. "I have to go to sleep in three minutes in order to get eight hours' sleep. And I need eight hours. Are you going to sleep here or go home?"

"Here," Edward says. "If that's okay."

The light is off before he finishes the sentence.

Edward's therapist is a skinny man named

Dr. Mike. Dr. Mike wears a baseball cap and has an ornate clock on his desk, which is decorated with gold and silver flowers. Edward studies the clock hands when there's a lull in the conversation. The timepiece seems to operate by its own system of measurement. This is his fifth visit to this office, and the clock freezes for entire moments, then leaps forward to catch up with the surrounding world.

"Anything new?" Dr. Mike says.

"No," Edward says. "Well. My aunt and uncle are upset because I'm losing weight."

"Are you upset about it?"

Edward shrugs. "No?" He doesn't like these sessions. The doctor seems like a nice enough man, but his job is to excavate Edward's brain, and Edward's job is to fend him off, because his brain is too sore and tender to withstand even the lightest touch. The job is exhausting.

When the silence has gone on too long, he says, "I know I need to eat."

Dr. Mike moves a pen from one side of his desk to the other. "My wife is pregnant, and her physician told her that physiologically and medically speaking, there are three different kinds of humans: men, women, and pregnant women. I think the same idea applies to you, Edward. There are grown-ups, children, and then you. You don't feel like a kid anymore, right?"

Edward nods.

"But you won't be an adult for years. You're something else, and we need to figure out what you are, so we can figure out how to help you. My wife needs extra folic acid, more sleep, and has a higher volume of blood in her body than she did before she was pregnant. Your head clicks, you don't like food, and you've found a way to dull your brain to protect yourself."

"My next-door neighbor thinks I'm magic. She thinks I'm like Harry Potter."

Dr. Mike touches the brim of his hat, a gesture Edward remembers as being a signal in baseball to slide, or run to another base, or tag a player out. He can't remember what the sign means, and for a second he panics, as if he's about to let his entire team down.

"That's interesting."

Right away, Edward regrets sharing what Shay said. His new friend — he guesses Shay is a friend; he sleeps in her room every night, what else can he call her? — would not approve. The idea sounded ridiculous in the air, and Shay is not ridiculous.

He uses what energy he has left to try to change the subject. "Why does your wife have extra blood?"

Dr. Mike regards him from beneath the brim of the cap. "Why can't you bear the texture of bananas, even though you loved them before?"

"I don't know."

"Exactly."

Edward wonders if Dr. Mike has some kind of unusual baldness on the top of his head — there is hair around the side of his head, below the cap — or perhaps a terrible scar that requires the hat. He wonders if it would be rude of him to ask.

He says, "Am I supposed to tell you what I am?"

"No," Dr. Mike says. "We'll figure that out together."

When night falls, Edward dims further with the sky. The flatness inside him becomes a cloak, and so he feels no reaction, and no sense of responsibility, as he hobbles out the front door of the house, down the steps, across the lawn, and up the neighboring stairs.

Besa opens the door, but this time doesn't step aside to let him pass.

Edward looks up at her. Besa is short, with wide hips and thick dark eyebrows. She works from home, translating novels from Spanish to English. John's nickname for

Besa is *Spitfire.* He told Edward that Besa's husband left when Shay was a toddler. Edward said, *He left?*

He moved away, John said. *He isn't part of their family anymore.*

This had made Edward think of all the ways of leaving: through doors, windows, in cars, on bikes, trains, boats, planes. Leaving was different than what his family had done. Leaving was a choice.

"Edward, *mi amor.*"

He squints at Besa. "Yes?"

"I want you to know that I'm happy you like Shay. She's never really had any friends. Politeness bores her, the same as it does me. I try to get her to say the things a young girl is supposed to say, but . . ." She sighs. "My heart is not in it. She never liked dolls. She always ends up insulting people. She used to get in fistfights with other girls. I've left her to her books probably more than I should have. She's been lonely."

Edward says, "I like her." Even though *like* has nothing to do with it. Shay feels like oxygen to him. He doesn't *like* oxygen; he requires it.

Besa moves to the side. "I just want to make sure you don't feel grateful to *us.* You've been a blessing already. I knew from day one that you would help your aunt.

118

Poor Lacey was making herself sick, trying to have a baby. Now she has someone to care for."

Edward almost shakes his head, disagrees, but then doesn't bother. He feels like his arrival did the opposite of helping his aunt; his arrival interrupted Lacey, and now she's struggling beside him. Sometimes his aunt looks as gray in the face as he feels, and sometimes he can see her anger at John as clearly as lightning bolts across a room. Other times, she clings to her husband after he comes home from work, like a small child to a parent. Edward is a mess, so he recognizes Lacey. And he recognizes that he's part of her mess.

He pictures the nursery, with its baby books and rocking chair. His body had jerked backward when he'd entered on the first day. He'd wanted to leave immediately, somehow knowing that those four walls couldn't bear both Lacey's grief and his own. Children who were never born, and parents no longer alive. He follows Besa up the stairs, with the sensation that he's being followed by more ghosts than he can personally account for.

His mornings start on the couch with a plate, which includes saltine crackers now.

John added them to the plate one afternoon, and they have become the most tolerable food. Salt with a collapsing layer of cracker. Minimal amount of chewing necessary. After the first morning plate, he and Lacey leave for his physical-therapy appointment. In between appointments, his aunt walks up and down the stairs with baskets of laundry. She gives him a second plate of food at lunchtime and then sits with him to watch one of the afternoon soap operas. It's centered on a hospital, and Lacey tells him that she and his mother watched the same show every day when they were teenagers. "So you've been watching these actors your whole life?" Edward says, amazed.

"On and off. Your mother was head-over-heels in love with Luke." Lacey points at a bald, tired-looking man wearing a single earring. The love of his life, Laura, who is shown in flashbacks to be dewy and beautiful, is now sad-looking and plump.

"It's not the best commercial for the passage of time," his aunt says.

The soap moves slowly and doubles back to repeat itself often, which feels like the right pace to Edward. Characters sum up their problems and then fumble the solutions. Most of the scenes take place either in the rooms of the hospital or, for some reason, on the town dock. Edward and Lacey watch in silence, with a seriousness that would have amused Edward back when he was a normal boy.

When John comes home after work, Edward looks for lightning bolts from his aunt. John always wears an apprehensive expression when he enters the room, which Edward can tell irritates Lacey, even on her better days. After dinner, Lacey goes upstairs, and it's John's turn to sit beside Edward. He punches at his tablet or computer. He is rarely without a screen in front of him.

Edward holds another plate on his lap and counts in his head, like he did while playing the piano, to measure the time between bites. He's been able to eat only by changing the reasons. He used to eat because he was hungry, or because he loved a specific food. Now he eats to stay out of the hospital and to keep from worrying his aunt and uncle. He handles a saltine by the corner, and the metronome beats: *one and two and three and four.*

He's halfway through the contents of the plate when the flatness inside him pulls back, like a sheet on a bed, and he suddenly knows that his uncle's activity on the tablet has to do with the flight. Edward looks sideways, but, as always, John has the screen tipped away from his nephew.

"What are you doing on there?" Edward asks.

John's movements are usually slow; he appears to be paying only half-attention most of the time. But this is a direct question from his nephew, who hardly speaks and has perhaps not asked a single non-survival-related question of him since he woke up in the Colorado hospital. John sits up straight, and that throws off his balance. As a result, the tablet ricochets out of his hands and onto the floor.

John makes a loud gasping sound and dives for it.

Something about the exaggerated noise is funny to Edward. It tickles him, and he laughs.

John stops moving, on his hands and knees, on the floor.

Edward freezes too. The laugh fizzles, doused by the cold water of guilt, shame, and confusion. He pushes the plate away. He reaches inside his brain for the sheet and pulls it back up, tight.

John is still on the floor; he shifts to a seated position. He says, "I use the iPad for work, mostly."

"Oh."

"Edward," John says. "Laughing is okay. It's good, even. You have to go back to doing all the normal human things."

Edward's body is sore. He almost tells John about what the therapist said, that he's a different kind of human. He's not a boy. He's a bundle of cells and two eyeballs and a busted-up leg.

"I gained a pound," he says, and is surprised by the note of triumph in his voice.

There is an evening routine too. Edward shows up in Shay's room around nine and spends the first hour sitting in the chair by the window. At ten, they take turns brushing teeth in the bathroom, and then he unrolls a navy sleeping bag in the middle of her floor. By ten-fifteen, Shay has turned off the light.

"How was camp?" He's in the armchair, his bad leg stretched board-straight in front of him.

"Stupid. You're so lucky you don't have to go."

"I *can't* go. I'm not exactly up to running bases."

She looks up from the notepad in her lap. "Even if you were a thousand percent healthy, they'd let you do whatever you wanted. If you asked my mother for her car keys right now, she'd probably give them to you."

"No, she wouldn't."

"Do you want to try and see?"

He tries to imagine approaching Besa with this request. He shakes his head.

Shay looks disappointed. "Well, my point is that normal kid rules don't apply to you. Which you should be *grateful* for, because most kid rules are completely bogus and all about the grown-ups feeling like they have power over us. My camp counselor won't even let me read during lunch. She says it's because reading is antisocial, but I think it's because she's actually Joseph Goebbels."

"Who's that?"

"Nazi. Burned books." Shay returns her attention to the notepad and writes a few lines.

Edward watches her write in this notepad every night. He suspects she's taking notes on him and his potential magical powers, but he's scared to ask if he's right. He studies his damaged leg and waits for the scribbles to stop. He asked her about camp because he knows that's the kind of thing people ask each other. *How was your day? How are you feeling?* But he sounded stupid asking, and she sounded annoyed answering, and he can feel this other weird conversation running underneath, in a language he can't quite grasp. It's something about magic, their age, her lack of friends, the curve of their emotions, the crash of the plane, and whatever she's writing down.

When the scribbling stops, she says, "I see all your skeptical looks."

He tries to look innocent. "What?"

"There's no point to them. The reality is that I'm capable of seeing things that grown-ups can't. Which means I'll be able to see what's inside you before anyone else does."

The air in the room compresses, as if the electricity of the secret conversation and the real one have aligned for a moment.

The real Edward — not the one who's always trying to deliver the "correct" line of dialogue — says, "You're going to be disappointed when I turn out to be a normal kid."

"It's too late for that," she says. "You'll never be a normal kid."

This sounds true, and he feels a ping of relief.

"I'm not normal either," she says, as if answering a question he hadn't asked.

"Great," he says, and the wave of enthusiasm in his voice makes him blush.

She returns to the notebook, and Edward is aware that he's breathing easier. His chest has loosened. When the clock reads ten, he gathers his crutches and hitches to the bathroom.

They are in their bed and sleeping bag, respectively, when Shay says, "I wonder how long they're going to let you sleep here. I heard a lady in the grocery store asking my mom about it. It makes the grown-ups uncomfortable because we're not quite teenagers and not quite kids. They might try to end it soon. They're going to want everyone to go back to behaving" — she makes air quotes with her fingers — "in an acceptable way."

Edward stares at her. "How do people in town know where I'm sleeping?"

"Gossip. Osmosis. Who knows?" She must notice the look on his face then, because she says, "Oh, don't worry. You can keep sleeping here for as long as you like. I'll fight them off. I'm good at that. I can be deeply annoying."

An oversized envelope arrives in the mail. It's at least two inches thick. Lacey carries it to the sofa in the living room and sinks down beside Edward on the couch. She peels off the outside of the envelope, and the paper falls heavily to the floor. She pulls out a large blue binder.

"What's that?" Edward asks, at the same time processing the title on the front: *Personal Effects of Flight #2977 Passengers.*

"Oh dear," Lacey says.

There is a cover letter. It says that if they identify any effects belonging to the Adler family, they will send the items to them. Lacey flips the binder open to the middle, to a photograph of a gold charm bracelet with a description typed beneath it. There is a charm in the shape of the Eiffel Tower and another of a teddy bear.

"I don't understand," Edward says. "These *things* survived the crash? That many things?"

Lacey nods.

"They didn't melt? Or explode?"

She taps the binder with her finger. "Do you want to look through it?"

Edward's ears click, a staccato drumroll. "No, thank you. Not now."

Later, he hears his aunt and uncle arguing in the kitchen. John is angry that Lacey opened the book in front of him.

"Jesus," John says. "Our job is to protect him. Do you see how depressed he is? Dr. Mike says we need to be very, very careful."

Lacey's voice sharpens. "I don't want to lie to him. I think he should be able to see the information, so he can make sense of it

127

himself."

Edward's parents used to argue regularly, but this sounds different, sadder and more desperate, like John and Lacey are on the side of a mountain and underprepared in terms of both fitness and supplies. They sound keenly aware that one or both of them might lose their grip and fall at any second.

His uncle says, "Edward's not ready to make sense of anything. It's too soon."

"Of course he's not *ready*. Nobody's ever ready for anything this hard."

John's voice drops, as if in an effort to change the nature of the exchange. "Lace, calm down." A pause, and then, "You never call me Bear anymore."

But Lacey seems unable, or unwilling, to shift gears. If anything, she sounds angrier. "I don't need it thrown in my face that I'm doing a bad job. I don't know anything about children, and I think he can sense that. He doesn't even want to sleep here."

"You just need to be careful around him. For God's sake, that's why we turned off the phone."

This strikes Edward, as he realizes for the first time that he hasn't heard a phone ring in this house since his arrival. He wonders whose calls they're avoiding.

Lacey says, "That horrible man emailed again to say that they need DNA samples to identify the bodies. I'm supposed to call Jane's dentist and ask for samples."

Jane, Edward thinks. And it is only then that he realizes his aunt lost her sibling, just like he lost his. *Jane, Jordan. Jane, Jordan.*

"Forward me the email. I'll write him back."

"It's *my* responsibility. She was my sister."

Their voices stop. Either they leave the room or Edward's ears make an executive decision to block them out.

The summer pulses on, bleary and filled with too much sunlight for Edward's taste. He sees the throat-clearing doctor for his leg and weight, Dr. Mike for his emotions, and a physical therapist to make sure his gait returns to normal.

It occurs to Edward that no one alive knows or remembers his pre-crash walk. He doesn't either. He remembers Jordan's, though. His brother's stride had always been distinctive: long and leaping. Gravity seemed to have less hold on him than on other people; Edward could remember talking to Jordan while walking down the sidewalk, and mid-sentence his brother would be in the air. *He bounds,* his mother had once said.

Edward bends his knees and bounces.

"Whoa there, tiger," the physical therapist says. "What was that? I'd like you to focus on forward motion, please. Not elevation."

In the afternoons, his physical-therapy homework is to walk to the end of their block and back again. The first few days, Lacey walked with him, but now she waits on the front steps, because the therapist said Edward needs to relearn balance by himself. A small crowd stands on the far side of the street. A few teenagers, a nun, and some older men and women. They look like they're waiting for a parade.

Edward knows he's the parade. If they say something, he doesn't hear it. If they wave, he doesn't see it. He never looks in their direction; he concentrates on hitching a single crutch forward, one step and then another. His ear clicks, a metronome counts, and he can hear the clocks shuttling forward in every house he passes.

Worst parade ever, he thinks.

Edward sits on John's tablet by accident one evening. It's on the couch, covered by a blanket. Edward pulls it free and sees his reflection in the black screen. His uncle is at a meeting, and his aunt is in bed. His face looks older, and more true, as if this dark mirror sees the grayness within him. The face looking back at Edward wouldn't be out of place as a villain in a movie: serious to the point of malevolent.

His parents wouldn't allow him or Jordan to have a cellphone — the boys had texting pagers so that Bruce and Jane could reach them in case of an emergency. His parents both had tablets, though, which they let the boys use for educational games.

Edward presses the on button.

A four-digit passcode screen appears.

Am I going to do this? he thinks, with genuine curiosity. *Yes.*

He tries to approach the task the way his father would. His father talked about numeracy with such affection — as if the numbers were a collection of odd characters in the local bar — that when Edward fills his brain with numbers, he finds it to be a warm space. As he puzzles through the possible digits, he feels like he's using the DNA he shares with his father.

He types in Lacey's birth year: 1974. The screen shakes its refusal. He tries John's birth year: 1972. No. There is only one attempt left before it locks and an email is sent to John, checking if he has indeed been struggling with his own device.

Edward lays the tablet down. He regards it for a minute. *Numbers are never random,* his father would say. *They like patterns and meaning.*

Edward picks up the tablet again and types in the flight number: 2977.

The screen clears.

A wave of fear surges through Edward, and he stands up from the couch. He leaves the house, pushes through the muggy night air, and climbs the steps to Shay's house and Shay's bedroom. When he clatters into her room, she's at her desk. He hands the tablet to her as if it's a grenade without a pin.

She accepts it with appropriate gravity. Edward leans over her shoulder and types in the passcode.

They both watch the home page appear. In the lower-right corner, there is a red circle with the words *Plane Tree* beneath it.

She looks at him, and he nods. She clicks on the symbol, and a list of links appears:

relatives of victims
edward twitter
edward facebook
edward google alerts
notes

She says in a low voice, "Where did you get this?"

"It's John's."

The dimple in her cheek deepens with her frown. "Look," she says. "I can look up one of these things and read it, and tell you what it says. You don't have to look yourself. I wouldn't want to, if I were you."

Edward crosses the room and sinks down on her bed. In all his visits to this room, he's never sat on the mattress before. It's soft and creaks lightly under his weight. He wishes he could lie down, close his eyes, and sleep. But sleep, even in this room, is hard to come by. Edward spends every night reaching for unconsciousness as if it were a rock in the middle of a river, while a fierce current pulls him away. His fingertips sometimes brush the rock, and he manages a nap. Never a full night's rest.

He whispers, "Is there information about Jordan?"

He can see only the side of Shay's face. She taps at the screen. "John's created PDFs with links," she says. "There's a Facebook page that was created about Jordan after the crash. By a couple girls, it looks like. I don't think they knew him. There's a photo."

"I want to see."

She holds the screen up. There is Jordan, beaming in his bright-orange parka. He's outside the deli near their house. His hair is standing almost completely upright.

"I took that picture," Edward says.

Shay lowers the screen. "He's mentioned in the lists of people who died on the plane and as your brother," she says. "Online and in the newspaper articles about the crash. That's it." She takes a breath.

"What?" Edward says, and an unlikely stripe of hope crosses his chest.

"I just clicked on the Google search for your name, and there are over a hundred and twenty thousand results, Edward. One hundred and twenty thousand."

"Okay." He doesn't know what else to say.

"Jordan only has forty-three thousand results."

"Turn it off," Edward says. "Please."

She closes the case, and he's grateful for her immediate response. He knew there were people outside the house keeping watch for him; it hadn't occurred to him that the same might be true online, inside every phone, tablet, and computer.

He and Shay get ready for bed, taking turns in the bathroom. Edward's green toothbrush sits in a glass next to her blue one on the side of the sink.

When he comes out, she's already un-furled the navy sleeping bag in the middle of the floor. Edward folds down onto it, favoring his damaged leg. "I'll need to wake up early," he says. "To get the iPad back before John notices."

"Would he be mad if he knew?"

Edward considers this. "I don't think so."

"Do you think he and Lacey mind that you sleep here?"

He answers without thinking. "Lacey does."

Shay nods and takes off her glasses, which makes her face look different — bleary and vulnerable. It's the only moment of the day when she doesn't look confident, and it's a moment Edward watches for every evening. Before she can turn out the light, he says, "Where's your father?"

Shay reaches out for her glasses, but then her hand drops, and she looks in Edward's direction. It's clear that she can't see him, beyond a blurred shape and a collection of colors.

"My father," she says, and the two words sound awkward in her mouth. "He took off when I was two. I've never heard from him. My mom thinks he has a new family, some-where out West."

Colorado, Edward thinks, because that is

now the West to him. The white walls of the hospital, the lady on crutches, the swimming sensation in his brain. Maybe Shay's father saw the plane fall out of the sky. *He took off,* Shay said, while Edward's family descended.

Shay says, "If he didn't want us, then I don't want him."

"He must be crazy," Edward says. "To leave you guys."

"My mom said he only married her to piss off his own mother, who didn't want him to marry a Mexican."

Edward watches Shay's clouded face, hoping for more words, explanations, answers — something to fill the ever-emerging craters that make him up. But Shay switches the light off, and he's left alone in the darkness and quiet.

10:17 A.M.

There is a monotony to time in the air. Consistent air quality and temperature, limited collection of sounds, circumscribed range of motion for the passengers. Some people thrive within these restrictions and relax in the sky in a way they rarely do at home. They have powered down their phones and packed their computers in their luggage; they delight in being unreachable, and read novels, or giggle at sitcoms on the in-seat monitor. But certain driven individuals, who can't conceive of taking a break, hate being disconnected from their life on the ground and find their anxiety amplified.

Jane squeezes past Mark. There's extra legroom in first class, so he doesn't have to stand up, but she feels like he ought to, out of politeness. As it is now, she has to trail her bottom directly in front of his face. When she's upright and in the aisle, she glances back and sees that his attention is

137

fixed on the computer screen. This man, who's basically been in heat over the flight attendant since boarding the plane, hasn't even glanced up.

Jesus, she thinks. *I have the sexual allure of a grapefruit.*

She walks up the aisle and through the red curtain that separates first from economy. Every seat is full, and the passengers in this section all look mildly uncomfortable. Jane gives her birthmark a quick press. She wonders if it's possible to fly in first class and not feel guilty. Does her seatmate feel guilty? She decides probably not.

"Mom!" Eddie cries, and her eyes trace the sound to her three boys. One white-headed, two with curly handfuls of hair sticking out in every direction.

She waves to Eddie, and just like every time she sees him after an absence, she remembers him as a colicky baby, wailing in her arms, heaving sobs in his crib, being bounced on Bruce's shoulder. He barely slept those first three months, and that was the darkest time in Jane's life. She was hormonal, with leaking breasts, and she was failing, every single minute of every single day. She was failing to provide significant comfort to her baby, and she was failing to be the mother that Jordan had always known. The three-year-old gazed at her nursing nightgown and uncombed hair with a combination of fear and sadness. She was also keenly aware that she was failing herself — she'd always believed that she could kick the butt of any situation, and this proved she couldn't. She was not the woman she'd thought she was, nor the one she'd planned to be.

Her adult life had been a smooth trajectory until that point. *She* had decided what she'd wanted and gotten it, from stories published in a literary magazine, to Bruce, to a high-paying job writing for a television show, to her first baby boy, whom she'd strapped to her chest and carried throughout her days. Now she sat paralyzed on the couch, milk-stained, unable to sleep or rest or think, because of the unstoppable, strangled cries of an infant. But when Eddie did stop crying, he became a sweet, smiling baby, who crawled around the apartment after his brother. He snuggled more than Jordan had. Jane's depression was broken for good when she woke up laughing one morning because her baby was on top of her, dive-bombing her cheek with open-mouthed infant kisses. *Mwah, mwah, mwah.*

Jordan always drew the eye. As the older brother, he was faster, stronger, first in most things, but Eddie and Jordan operated as a team. Eddie was the one who calmed his brother down when he got angry that something wasn't going his way. Eddie loved to play the piano, so Jordan wrote compositions for him to perform. Eddie built Lego cities that stretched from the kitchen to the front door, guaranteeing that his parents would swear and rub bruised feet while walking to the bathroom in the middle of the night. When the Lego obsession started, Jordan checked architecture books out of the library in order to help his brother plan ever more elaborate metropolises. When Jordan started defying Bruce in small ways, like sneaking out of the apartment when he was supposed to be studying, or coming home from the museum ten or fifteen minutes later than arranged, Eddie went along as his partner in crime. When they were "caught" by the doorman or by Bruce himself, Eddie always immediately said, "I'm sorry, Dad," in his sweetest little-boy voice, which cut Bruce's anger off at the knees. Jane liked to think that Eddie's early rage and tears had emptied him out and he was going to coast, smiling, into adulthood, in the wake of Jordan's more turbulent boat.

"How are you guys doing?" she asks when she reaches their row. The three heads tip back to look at her, all sharing the same serious expression.

"You're going to get much better food in first class," Jordan says. "Can you save us your dessert?"

"Definitely." She smiles at the boys; she's a little scared to look at Bruce. It's hard to know how long he'll hold a grudge about her not getting her work done in time to sit with them.

"Any aliens in your script yet?" Eddie asks.

"No."

"Submarines?"

"No."

"Mutant monkeys?"

"Yes. There are several of those."

"Maybe your mother will write a love story," Bruce says.

This is his way of pressing down on her birthmark. She has a movie she's been wanting to write for a decade — a quiet, dialogue-driven piece that takes place during a single hour — but she keeps putting it off for these lucrative rewrite jobs. She feels a pang for that movie now. She pictures the fictional couple, about to kiss for the first time — a moment that won't exist until she writes it — and shakes her head. The man, with his arms wrapped around his beloved, turns his head and looks at Jane. *Please hurry,* his eyes say. *Time is running out.*

The PA system buzzes overhead, and a voice says, "This is your captain speaking. We'll be flying through a small rainstorm for the next twenty minutes, so there may be some light turbulence. We ask that passengers return to their seats until I turn off the fasten-seatbelt sign."

Eddie crosses his arms and turns toward the window. Jane knows, without seeing, that his eyes are wet with sudden tears. This move has been stressful for all of them, and he would have preferred to sit with his mother during the flight.

"I'm sorry, baby," she says, to his narrow shoulders. "I'll come back and visit in a few minutes."

"Dessert," Jordan says. "When lunch comes, don't forget to save your dessert."

She and Jordan perform an elaborate handshake they've been working on; it takes five seconds to complete, and part of the routine is keeping a straight face. No smiling allowed. He nods at her, pleased, when it's finished. She's relieved, as she is every time it's over; the handshake feels like a test that allows her to stay part of his inner circle. The problem is that she's retested at regular intervals, and one misstep might leave her stranded by the side of the road.

On her way back to her seat, she passes the large woman with bells stitched into her skirt. They both have to walk sideways to fit past each other in the narrow aisle, and it's impossible for them not to touch. For a second they are nose to nose, then their shoulders brush. The bells ring lightly below their waists.

"I like your skirt," Jane says. She knows *like* is the wrong word, but she's not sure what the right word is. She's embarrassed to find herself blushing.

The woman looks Jane up and down, surveys her buttoned cardigan and jeans, her chin-length hair. "Thank you," she says. "I saw you with your boys over there. They're adorable."

Jane smiles. "They used to be adorable. I don't know what they are now."

"Well, they look adorable to me."

"Thanks so much."

The conversation is clearly over, but Jane hesitates before walking away. In that moment of hesitation, she is about to say something more, but she can't think of a suitable line. Even when she's buckled back into her seat, she feels like she's still standing on that strip of orange rug, searching for words. *People pay me to write dialogue,* she thinks. *I'm a terrible fraud.*

■ ■ ■ ■

Benjamin watches the two women sway in the aisle. They're about six feet ahead of him. He can't hear their words, but he watches the mother's cheeks turn pink. He had overheard her conversation with the white-haired dad and two boys across from him. Nuclear families like theirs — white ones with a mom and a dad and two kids — always look like museum exhibits to him. When they speak, it sounds staged, as if they're reciting the script all happy families are handed at conception. He'd seen the youngest boy tear up when his mom walked away, and Benjamin hadn't been able to stop himself from thinking: *Are you for real? She's just going back to her seat.*

He knows the statistics, knows that these types of families exist, but he rarely saw them where he came from. And in the army, most of the soldiers came from circumstances that were less than ideal. No one talked about how happy their home life had been; Benjamin's story wasn't great, but he'd heard way worse. He had a sergeant once who liked to ask his men: *Who put that gun in your hand? You or your daddy?*

The two women separate, and the Filipino

lady's skirt jingles as she passes him. The dad across the aisle lays his hand on the older son's arm, and the boy laughs. Benjamin tries to identify what he's observing, and the word he comes up with is *ease*. They are at ease with each other. No one is on guard; there is no wariness or reserve. He can tell that the father has never beaten these boys. If violence is a stone thrown into a still pond, Benjamin has become adept at spotting the ripples, and there are none here.

Gavin grew up in a family like this one. That's why he was so loose with his friendship and his knock-knock jokes. His father was a dentist, who probably had soft hands and a nervous smile. Benjamin pictures a nice mom, the kind who bakes cookies and buys the most expensive tires for her station wagon. He can't help but think: *I would have liked to meet them.*

Florida watches the tired-looking mother walk away from her. She'd wanted to give her a hug, or at least a quick shoulder rub. The lady's whole being screams out to be touched. She's one of those people who live way too much in their heads and are too invested in their careful plans. Florida has seen her husband, the brainy Jewish guy, and she imagines they have semi-regular decent sex but don't spend a lot of time cuddling or making out. It's her belief that people sealed up that tight can often benefit from some medicinal loosening. They have no idea how to unzip their own boundaries; they need them removed on their behalf. If she had any mushrooms on her, she would have slipped them into the woman's purse.

The plane gives a single judder as she lowers into her seat.

"What's up, pussycat?" she says, at the same time reflecting that she wouldn't offer *this* girl any drugs. Linda's uptight too, but in a disheveled way. Her wires are crossed and split and her energy flow is a mess. Psychedelics would just loosen her death grip on normalcy, and seconds later she'd be screaming, naked, in the street.

Linda turns from the window and stares at Florida with wide eyes. "I don't know why I'm telling you this," she says. "But I don't have anyone else to tell, and I have to say it out loud."

"All right."

"I'm pregnant."

Florida regards the young girl. Bobby had wanted a baby. She'd had to sneak birth control in order to keep from giving him one. She'd known, by the time the subject

146

came up in earnest, that he wanted a child not to love but to mold in his image, to follow his orders. She'd folded as much of herself to him and his vision as she could, but he viewed the small parts she held back — her thoughts, her songs, her daily walks in the woods — as a criminal lack of commitment.

To survive after the breakdown of society, the failure of the dollar, or some kind of meteorological apocalypse, Bobby believed that he needed disciples. Florida believed that once she birthed a kid or two, he would phase her out. Phase her out of her own family, out of his plans, and hence his life.

Bobby had been working for an insurance company in downtown Manhattan when the Twin Towers were hit, and it changed everything for him. He'd quit his job, sold his suits, and worked as a waiter in Brooklyn, which is where Florida met him. She was a secretary at an acupuncture clinic and sang in an all-female blues band. She was drawn to Bobby because he talked about the importance of the truth; he was bright and well read, had a sexy little ass, and could explain exactly why capitalism was evil. He pointed out that the ninety-two-year-old woman in their neighborhood was being evicted from the apartment she'd lived in for fifty years, just so a new high-rise could be built and more money be made. It was the reason neither Florida nor any of her friends could afford health insurance — the industry had nothing to do with providing healthcare; it was designed to extract the maximum amount of money from each person. It was Bobby's verbal precision — she'd known countless handsome potheads who concluded arguments with *oh man, you know what I mean, right?* — and his fine ass that had sealed the deal.

They had shown up at Zuccotti Park together during the first week of Occupy and stayed in the park until Bloomberg — that tin-pot fascist — sent in the garbage trucks weeks later. Bobby was on several of the planning committees and was often sequestered in meetings. Florida cooked for the protesters and distributed blankets, toothbrushes, condoms, and tampons. She also joined one of the bands. This was her favorite part of that fall: so many good, hopeful, striving people, lifting their pure voices in song. She had always believed in the power of music, but now the proof was in front of her. People were changing, even shedding, their unhappy, enslaved lives to come to this park and sing about a better world. Their song was shaping their present, which created a full circle the likes of which Florida had rarely seen.

The plane gives a sharp bump, and Linda's knuckles whiten where she's gripping the armrest.

"I'm not ready for this," she says.

"This," Florida says. She thinks: *This is the subject that defines women. Having babies. Will you have them? Can you have them? Do you want to have them?*

"You'll be fine," Florida says, calling on her experience as a performer to shine confidence at the young girl, but her skepticism must have leaked through, because there it is, all over Linda's face.

The school is only three blocks away, but Besa drives them. "Wingnuts and fools are going to follow you around and say things to you." She addresses the rearview mirror. "They'll forget and leave you alone by Christmas, though, so please know that it's temporary. Reporters have the attention span of a fruit fly. The *religiosos* will be the worst; just smile politely while they tell you their fairy tales and then walk away."

Lacey is in the passenger seat. She looks odd to Edward, perfectly still, as if she's been turned to stone. When John was in the bathroom that morning, she'd leaned across the kitchen table and whispered, "Should I record *General Hospital*, and we'll watch it together after school?" He'd nodded, and she nodded back, her expression grave. He wonders what she'll do all day, alone in the house without him. He thinks he can see in the set of her shoulders that she's wondering the same thing.

He notices Besa glance at Lacey too. *Today is a big deal for them,* he thinks. *Them* includes Lacey, Besa, Shay, and John, whom they left behind in the driveway, waving at the car as if they were embarking on a perilous journey from which they might never return.

Edward thinks this to remind himself about normal people's behavior and to explain the weird charge in the air. A first day of school, even though he's never been to a proper school, feels no more broken or uncertain than any other day. His heart beats steadily in his chest; his head clicks; he breathes.

"You used to go to church, Mamí," Shay says.

"Before I came to my senses. I was brainwashed in Mexico."

Shay fidgets under her seatbelt. She and her mother spent three days arguing over her back-to-school outfit and finally reached a questionable compromise: Besa's choice of a pink ruffled skirt and Shay's choice of a blue baseball T-shirt. Shay had allowed her mother to braid her hair for the occasion, though, and Edward had watched the process on the front steps that morning. Besa's hands were deep in Shay's hair; Shay's head was tipped back, eyes closed, catlike in her pleasure. The mother and daughter were silent, a rarity, and peace had radiated off the scene.

Shay says, "You're making Edward nervous, and he shouldn't be, because the kids at this school are idiots. They're not worth the energy. I should know — I've been with them since I was five."

"I'm not nervous," he says, knowing that none of them will believe him.

"You were way better off being home-schooled," she says. "Getting to sit around all day reading books."

Edward shrugs. His father had explained to him and Jordan, very early on, his objections to the school system. "It's not awful," Bruce had said. "It's a mixed bag. But there are twenty-five kids in a class, at least, which means the learning is inefficient. If you're bright, you're slowed down by the fact that other kids can't move at your pace. And in part because there are so many kids, they run the schools like factories, or, dare I say, jails. You're put in lines, moved when the bells ring, allowed to run around in a high-fenced yard once a day. None of this is conducive to deep thinking or creativity. You start to go deep into a subject, and a bell rings to pull you out of it." Bruce rubbed his head, which was what he did when he was agitated. "Does this make sense to you?" Jordan, eight, and Edward, five, shrugged. But late at night, on a day long with math sheets, and piano practice, and their own thoughts, one of them would say into the dark, "I bet school would be better than this."

"I want to be in Shay's class," Edward says. He's wearing the gray pants and white button-down shirt that Lacey laid out for him. He didn't recognize the clothes, but he never does. Lacey bought an entire wardrobe for him after the crash, and she dresses him differently than his mother did. He used to wear bright colors, and cargo pants, and Jordan's hand-me-down skater T-shirts; now he wears pressed jeans, white T-shirts, and, apparently, slacks.

Besa's eyes are hard as they pull up in front of the school. *"Pobrecito,"* she says. "Don't worry, you and Shay will be together. We already took care of that."

The building — which houses the town's middle and high schools — is brick and enormous. They have pulled up by the middle school entrance; the older teenagers enter on the far side of the building and take all their classes on the top two floors. The middle school occupies the lower half of the building. Edward focuses on Shay's blue-shirted back and on keeping his balance — he no longer needs crutches, but his legs are not yet equally strong — as he makes his way inside. His expectation of what a school looks like comes from movies, and this one looks correct. A couple of offices by the front entrance, tile walls, rectangular lockers, and rows of classroom doors. It's very different from where Edward has spent his life learning: draped over the living room couch, reading on his bunk bed, working on math at the kitchen table while his dad cooked dinner.

He walks carefully, as kids pinball, laughing and talking, down the long hallway. There are warning calls from grown-ups to slow down, be careful, wait your turn. "Children!" an adult yells. "Calm your bodies!"

He's not talking to me, Edward thinks.

He feels his ears click, click, click. Then he's in a classroom sitting next to Shay, watching a teacher write the formula for the area of a triangle on a blackboard. He already knows this; his father taught it to him years earlier. A few minutes later, he realizes that he could teach this class; the math is as simple to him as breathing. Then another row of seats, in another classroom, with a female teacher dressed in lavender, who seems to look everywhere in the room but at him. Then a clamorous cafeteria, where Shay helps him with his tray and he nibbles at meatloaf that's the same color as his pants.

He has the sensation of being followed by a cloud of buzzing bees. He's bothered by the noise; it seems to descend from the ceiling and rise from the floor simultaneously.

Shay forks a Tater Tot and says, "Pretend we're in the Great Hall — everyone whispered about Harry on his first day there too."

"I haven't done anything to whisper about," Edward says.

"You've done as much as Harry had at that point."

When she sees he's still looking at her, she says, "You survived."

Oh, he thinks. *Right.*

He's on his way out of the cafeteria when there's a tap on his shoulder. He looks behind him and sees a brown-skinned man with a mustache.

"Principal Arundhi," Shay says.

"Good afternoon, Shay," he says. "Edward, may I have a word with you in my office?" He looks at Shay and says, "I promise to deliver him safely to his next class. Don't

155

worry, young lady."

Edward follows the man's back through the crowded hall, then up two sets of stairs, then down another hall. Here, the kids look swollen and distorted, and Edward realizes they're on a high school floor. The boys' voices are louder and deeper, and when two kids mock-tackle each other near him, Edward flinches. Students lower their voices, though, and straighten up when they notice the principal. Several say hello, then give Edward a look. Principal Arundhi turns in to a room with a mottled-glass door. When the door closes behind them, the clamor of the hallway is muffled.

The room and windowsill are lined with plants of various sizes, and more greenery hangs from the ceiling. Some have fat leaves, others are spindly and tall; two have small pink flowers. The air smells like moist dirt. The desk, in the center of this greenhouse, looks like a mistake.

Principal Arundhi smiles. "I like to bring nature inside. I'm a bit of a gardener." He puts his hands together in front of him. "Now, Edward, usually when we have a new student join us, I announce it over the loudspeaker on the beginning of the first day and ask everyone to help welcome the child. I didn't do that with you, because I

156

thought you wouldn't require, or desire, any additional attention. But I wanted to see if there was anything I could do to make you feel more comfortable here."

"I don't think so," Edward says, thinking: *I'm not comfortable anywhere.*

There is a pause while the principal looks over Edward's head, presumably at the orange-flowered bush on the filing cabinet. "You took a standardized test in the spring," he says. "Your father arranged for it, I believe. Your scores were very high — high enough for you to skip a grade."

Edward straightens in his chair. "I don't want to skip a grade. I'd like to stay with Shay, please."

"That's what your aunt and uncle thought you'd say. And so it shall be."

The man is looking at him expectantly, so Edward says, "Thanks."

"Let me ask you a question, young man."

Edward braces himself, knowing it will be about the crash.

"How do you feel about flora?"

It takes a second for Edward to understand what the man has asked him. "You mean plants?"

The principal nods. "The foundation of our ecosystem."

In truth, Edward's never thought about

157

plants before. His mother had a spider plant in the kitchen, but it had always appeared to him to be part of the furniture.

"Each year I ask a few students to help me with the care of these beauties." The man gestures around the room. "Perhaps you can be my first volunteer?"

"Okay," Edward says, because it seems to be the only possible answer.

"I'll let you know when your services are required. You can go now. But if you run into any problems during your schooldays, Edward, please know that I am here."

Lacey and Besa are waiting together in the car at pickup. They're first in line, parked right in front of the school doors, which is fortunate because the parking lot is jammed with cars and people. Besa sizes him up.

"They left you alone today, huh?"

He nods as he climbs into the back seat.

She waves her hand at the crowded parking lot. "You see how bored the lunatics in this town have been, that they're treating this like some kind of UFO sighting?"

She's not wrong. The entire town seems to be present, and every eye in the parking lot is on their car. This must be the most highly attended pickup in the school's history. Mothers, fathers, grandparents, aunts, and uncles have appeared. Relatives have traveled from out of town to collect their great-grandnephew on the first day of school. There are teenagers who have rounded the building or crushed their way through the middle school doors in order to collect younger siblings they generally have no time for. The crowd pretends not to stare but does so very badly. A couple brazenly gape. There are myriad cellphones pointed in Edward's direction. One young man is perched on a tree branch with an old-fashioned camera. There are whispers. *There he is. That's the boy. It's him.*

Edward notes the cellphones and cameras and remembers his total of Google hits. He thinks, *One hundred and twenty thousand and one. One hundred and twenty thousand and two. Three, four. Seven. Twenty-two.* He can imagine a photo of himself in these stiff clothes, looking skinny and drawn. New versions of this image proliferate. He imagines them being uploaded to Instagram, Facebook, Tumblr, Twitter.

"Don't they have anything better to do?" Lacey says.

"Fools," Besa says. Because of the traffic, the car can only inch forward. A woman who looks like a kindly grandmother holds her cellphone out and clicks it right next to

Edward's window. She offers him an apologetic smile.

Besa leans on the car horn, and the lady startles.

"That's my dentist over there," Lacey says. "I know for a fact that he doesn't have any kids."

Edward wants to say something, to let them know that he's all right, because he understands they're upset on his behalf. But this day seems to have completely drained his battery, and his jaw won't work.

"Hey," Shay says, as they finally burst free of the school grounds. "What about me? Isn't anyone going to ask about my first day of seventh grade?"

The tension cracks, and the three females in the car laugh. Lacey has to wipe her eyes, she's so undone. They laugh even harder when they pass a line of nuns, a block from the school. The row of black habits nods in the direction of the car.

At dinner, Lacey says, "A moving truck will be arriving next Wednesday."

John and Edward look at her. Dinner is lasagna and salad. Edward has gained back six of the eight lost pounds and has slowly started to eat normal meals. He experiences actual hunger sometimes and is always surprised by the gnawing sensation in his belly. He knows his aunt's cooking is organized around putting as many calories as possible into each of his bites. One morning at breakfast, John complained that the milk tasted funny, and she confessed that she'd added some ground cashews to bulk it up a little. John had looked at her like she'd lost her mind, and Edward giggled, his second-ever laugh in his new body.

"You're . . . we're moving?" Edward is unable to keep a note of horror from his voice.

"Oh no, I'm sorry," Lacey says quickly. "I should have phrased that differently."

"We're not moving." John puts a hand on Edward's shoulder.

"The boxes from the storage unit we rented in Omaha — that's where the movers stored your family's things while we figured out what to do with them — are being delivered here. The big items, like the furniture, are being sold, but the personal items are coming here Wednesday."

"Where are you planning to put them?" John says. "The basement would work, I guess. I just need to move some stuff around down there."

"I was thinking of putting them upstairs, in Edward's room." Lacey looks at her nephew. "If that's okay with you? It's so dark in the basement, and I think it's going to take some time to go through and organize."

Edward is confused for a moment, before making sense of the request. He's never slept in the nursery, and never will, but his aunt seems to need to believe that it belongs to him. He says, "Sure. That's fine."

"Maybe you'll want to go through the boxes with me," Lacey says. "Your personal things will be among them, of course."

"Maybe," Edward says. He thinks of the boxes, sitting on a truck right now, driving through the Midwest in the late afternoon. Driving in the wrong direction. The boxes were supposed to move in a straight line from New York City to Los Angeles. Instead, they made it halfway, stalled for three months, and are now headed back. Edward pictures the outside of the cardboard cubes, not the contents. He remembers them in neat piles in his New York apartment's living room, ready to be picked up. His mother had spent weeks meticulously packing and yelled at whichever boy she caught digging through a box in search of a particular shirt or book.

Edward dims his brain in order to stop picturing the boxes, and his mother, and asks to be excused from the table. In the living room, he notices John's tablet lying on the couch. His immediate instinct is to grab it, tuck it under his arm, and carry it over to Shay's house. Instead, he stands motionless for a minute, looking at it. His uncle is now alone in the kitchen, filling the coffeepot for the next morning. He's humming a show tune under his breath. John has started jogging in the mornings to ward off all the extra calories in Lacey's food, and has downloaded several Broadway shows to accompany his runs. Now he's liable to sing out a line from *Phantom of the Opera* or *Hello, Dolly!* while walking upstairs or pouring cereal.

"Don't cry for me, Argentina," he says to Edward, when the boy walks back into the kitchen.

"I don't think it's a good idea for me to go on the Internet right now." Edward stops, not sure how to proceed.

"I would agree with that statement," John says.

"But I was wondering if it would be okay, if you would let me know, every once in a while, whatever you think I should be aware of? I thought you might be able to decide . . ." Edward doesn't know how to say, *I know you're tracking the crash, and me, online,* without admitting that he'd stolen

163

his uncle's tablet once.

John leans against the counter, his arms crossed over his chest. "You want me to keep you roughly up to date about what's happening on the Internet in reference to you but without you having to know or see any of the specifics."

"I guess so, yes."

His uncle studies him for a moment, as if trying to figure out what he can handle. "I'm sure you've realized that because you've started school, and therefore reentered the public world, there will be a bunch of new photos and probably a video or two of you. I don't expect there to be more new content, though, Edward. Not of a factual nature. People will claim to have seen you places and claim to know you, just as they have done ever since the crash, but that's just fabrication."

"Where do people think they've seen me?"

John sighs. "All over the place. One man was convinced he was hiking behind you and a yellow Labrador on the Appalachian Trail for several weeks. You've been swimming in Lake Placid, at one of the art museums in New York. Sightseeing in Edinburgh."

Edward hears himself say, "Shay and I looked up Jordan on the Internet."

John is quiet for a minute. "There's not much on him, is there?"

"No."

"I'll do this," John says. "I'll let you know what's out there, within limits. But I want you to understand that there can't be information about you — that is true — that you don't already know. Your life takes place in your skin. No one else knows a goddamn thing, and the Internet is full of cowboys and sad people making stuff up." He pauses. "I love the Internet, or at least I used to, but it's not where you go for the truth."

Edward almost asks, *Where do you go for the truth?* But the question feels vast, unspeakable in his throat, so instead he says good night and goes next door.

There is a tree covered with pert green leaves outside the window in Dr. Mike's office. The trunk is a uniform brown, and robust. It looks tree-ier than the trees around it, as if it were made for a movie set by able craftsmen. The idea that the tree might be fake pleases something deep inside Edward. He himself feels half plastic, cobbled together, fabricated on an hour-to-hour basis to fulfill his role as "human boy recovering from tragedy." When he sits down in his usual chair, he watches the tree over the therapist's shoulder.

Dr. Mike says, "When you have memories, are they from the plane or before?"

"Before."

"List for me some things you remember. It can be anything. Snippets, whatever."

Edward closes his eyes for a second and sees his music composition book open on the piano. He says, "I was about to start learning a new movement on the piano. It was called 'Scarbo,' by Ravel."

"I wasn't aware you played the piano. Tell me about the piece."

Edward frowns. "I hadn't started yet. My teacher said he wasn't sure I was ready for it. It had really fast tremolos, a lot of octave jumps, and double-note scales in the major seconds in the right hand."

Edward looks down at his hands. The knuckles appear extra white under his skin. They don't look like the same hands that practiced piano for hours every afternoon. He feels certain that if he sat down at a piano now, he wouldn't be able to play *any* of the compositions he'd learned. His fingers feel different, and no music has played in his head since the crash. It's not something he's consciously thought about, but he realizes now that he'd been waiting for the music to return, like a dog that escaped its leash. But it hasn't, and it won't. It's gone. Eddie was musical; Edward is not.

Dr. Mike says, "So, you played seriously."

"I don't want to talk about it." Edward's voice rises at the end of the sentence. Since he usually operates at a monotone in this office, the sound startles them both.

"Don't tell my aunt and uncle," he says.

"They don't know that you play?"

"Played. If they knew, they've forgotten."

Dr. Mike looks like he wants to say something but then stops himself.

"I don't like this whole thing," Edward says.

"What whole thing?"

"Before was good. It's over. Why do we have to talk about it?"

"We don't have to right now," the man says. "I just don't want you to block all the memories out. The fact that they're good means they're powerful. We're building a new foundation here, and if you can let those memories in, and even, at some point, get pleasure from them, they can be bricks in the foundation. Good, solid bricks."

Edward sinks down in his chair and shuts his eyes.

He can only hear Dr. Mike, not see him, from his slumped position. "Are we done for today?"

"Yes," Edward says, "we're done."

A white rectangular truck is parked outside the house when they get home from school on Wednesday afternoon. Two burly-looking men struggle across the lawn, balancing an enormous box sideways between them. Edward reflexively turns his back on the sight.

Shay claps her hands together and says, "I want to help unpack."

"I'll help too," Besa says, in a similarly charged voice. "Between us, we can probably get most of it done today."

"Oh, well, I" — Lacey looks flustered — "I guess I didn't think about starting this afternoon?"

Edward nods. This is the hour when he and his aunt usually watch that day's recording of *General Hospital*. Luke and Laura's son, Lucky, is missing.

"We should take a thorough inventory," Shay says to her mother. "Write down the contents of each box."

"*Perfecto.* Then you can decide what to do with the items," Besa says.

Lacey and Edward exchange a look.

"Okay?" Lacey says.

Lacey and Edward helplessly follow the

168

mother and daughter inside. There are more boxes than Lacey was expecting, and they spill out of the nursery into the upstairs hall. Besa goes next door and comes back with a handful of what look like surgical scalpels.

"You don't have to watch," Shay says to Edward. "Not if you don't want to."

He nods but doesn't move. He watches her cut into a box with the number 1 written in Sharpie on the side. He'd watched his mother write that number.

"Kitchen supplies," Shay says, and pulls a piece of paper out of the box. "Oooh, a spreadsheet." She shakes her head with what appears to be admiration. "This is very well organized. Let's see. Coffee cups, drinking glasses, cutlery, dessert plates."

His mother's favorite mug will be in there, the one with a red balloon on the side, from a French movie that she loved. The tall glass with the chip that Edward preferred over the others. The smaller cups that they all put beside their beds, with water for the middle of the night.

Edward backs away. He passes his aunt, who is hovering behind the active figures of Besa and Shay. Lacey looks pale; her freckles stand out like tiny cries for help. She touches Edward's arm and glances at him with what he thinks is apology. *I might not have thought this through,* he can feel her thinking.

The flat sheet is pulling up over his insides. It starts low and rises over his abdomen, then his chest. Edward glances down at his pressed gray slacks. The buttons on his white Brooks Brothers shirt.

"Lacey," he says, and she startles at the sound of her name coming out of his mouth.

Edward realizes, in that moment, how rarely he addresses her. They sit side by side on the couch each afternoon, but they rarely speak. Edward likes his aunt, but she feels more unpredictable than John, and she reminds him enough of his mother to make him want to look away. There is a certain angle, rarely caught, from which she looks 80 percent like his mom. Most of the time, though, it's a frustrating 20 percent, a reminder only of what he's lost. When Edward needs something, he gravitates toward his uncle.

"Yes?" she says.

"I'd like the clothes in the boxes, the ones that belong to me and the ones that are Jordan's, please. I'd like to wear them, if you don't mind."

"Oh." Lacey scans him up and down, and her face changes. "You don't . . . I understand. Of course."

170

"I'm on it," Shay calls from the middle of a tower of cardboard. "I'll find the clothes, pronto."

That night, Edward lies on the sleeping bag in his own plaid pajama pants and his brother's red T-shirt. He has already put the clothes Lacey bought him into a bag; he will wear them only if he has to, every once in a while, to make his aunt happy. Otherwise, he will wear clothes that fit and suit him. Clothes already worn and that smell faintly of Jordan.

He listens to Shay read, so exhausted that he is unable to separate himself from the experience. They're making their way through the Harry Potter series; every night Shay reads a chapter aloud.

"Hey," Shay says, at the end of a paragraph.

"Hey," Edward says sleepily.

"Did your scar hurt when you saw the boxes?"

"No."

"Hmm." She doesn't look discouraged. "When you encounter something important, you'll feel it," she says. "I know you will."

Edward closes his eyes. He listens to Shay's voice; she's a good reader, her voice dramatic in the right places, lower when it's more effective. Jordan used to read to him too. Not regularly, but when he came to a particularly funny or scary passage of a novel, he'd repeat it aloud. The pajamas are so soft against Edward's skin that, when he lies perfectly still, he can pretend he's the same boy who used to sleep in a bunk bed beneath his brother.

One morning, his aunt says, "Was there a warm coat in those boxes?" This is how Edward finds out it's almost winter. He goes to the closet and pulls out Jordan's orange parka. It's far too big for him, but the long sleeves double as mittens, and the hood covers most of his face, which he likes. He tries to avoid knowledge of the seasons passing. First fall alone, gone. First winter alone, here. His birthday, Christmas and Hanukkah — his family celebrated both, to some degree — rapidly approaching. Dr. Mike tells him that the experience of time passing without noticing is called a *fugue state.* "It's common in trauma victims," he says. "They lose track of hours, sometimes days. They live their lives, but their brains don't seem to register the experiences. It's like the brain doesn't take note; it's not paying attention."

"I'd like to be in a fugue state every day."

Dr. Mike shrugs and says, "If I could give you one that would take you through the holiday season, I would."

This type of kindness makes Edward want to cry, but crying doesn't come easily to him. He has rarely cried since the hospital; his tears seem lodged in his head, unsure of which pipe to exit through. In their place is a sinus ache. He rubs the bridge of his nose now. "Can we stop?"

"No."

"No?"

"Last week you told me that Jordan should have survived instead of you. Why do you think that?"

Edward's whole body groans, though no sound comes out of his mouth. Leaves on the tree outside the window, which were bright red during his last appointment, have faded and are curling up on themselves. Some have already fallen to the ground.

Edward can feel Dr. Mike looking at him. "Because," he says.

"Because why?"

Edward thinks, *Why are you pushing me?*

Dr. Mike touches the rim of his cap. Edward knows now that this is not a signal; it's just a habit. The man does it without thinking.

He says, "I'm sorry, Edward. But I can't let you shut down anymore. Out there, yes. But not in here."

I could leave, Edward thinks. But he says, in a voice that sounds annoyed, "Jordan was a real person. . . . He knew who he was. People liked him. He was already doing things. Important things. Like he did at the airport when he opted out of the scanner. He stopped eating meat . . ." Edward trails off.

"You were twelve when the plane crashed," Dr. Mike says. "Jordan was fifteen. That's a crucial difference in age. Was your brother opting out of security checks when he was twelve?"

Edward thinks for a second. "No."

"You get to choose a lot of what you do when you're fifteen, Edward. You're still only twelve. Because of what you've survived, you're already more interesting than your brother. People want to talk to you, don't they?"

This is true. Edward visits the principal's office every Wednesday afternoon, and while he hoists an old blue watering can from one pot to the next, Principal Arundhi tells him the names and history of each plant. The short boy in his science lab told him, while they were dissecting frogs, that he wants to be an opera singer when he grows up. The school secretary, when he was submitting paperwork to the office, told him that she was born in Georgia and that she and her sister had fed two wild alligators every afternoon after school. "They liked Wonder Bread best," she said. The girl with the locker next to his told him that she has a six-year-old sister who has never spoken out loud.

Dr. Mike says, "They want to share something extraordinary about themselves, because you've experienced something extraordinary."

Edward doesn't say anything in reply, because he has no response. The doctor has told him something true. He will not waste time arguing the point.

One afternoon, Shay goes back into school to get a forgotten book, and Edward is left alone on the curb. The buses just left, and the parking lot is scattered with parked cars. It's almost Christmas break. Edward shivers in the orange coat — it's so large that it allows drafts from every opening. He bends over to itch his shin. The scar has reached a new stage of healing, and it's been bothering him. It looked like a pinched mouth when he woke up this morning. He scratches it gently so as not to disturb the delicate skin.

He hears a man's voice say, "Hi, Edward

175

— you don't know me, but my name's Gary."

Edward loses his balance and has to work to steady himself. Once he's re-rooted, he sees a middle-aged man a few steps away, wearing jeans and a thick sweater.

"My girlfriend was on the plane." The man blinks behind his glasses. He has dirty-blond hair and a beard. "I apologize for disturbing you," he says. "I drove here from California. I have a lot of respect for what you've been through."

Edward looks around. No one else is nearby.

"I wonder if you saw my girlfriend on the plane? I think you sat near her; I studied the seating chart. Everyone talks about how you survived because of where your seat was, and Linda's was nearby. A couple rows forward, maybe. On the other side of the aisle."

Edward swallows. He hears himself say, "What did she look like?"

"She was twenty-five, white, but maybe I don't need to say that. I had a professor once who said it was racist if you didn't mention that white people were white, since we always describe black people as black. She was blond." He is blinking wildly. "Wait a second, I'm an idiot."

176

He reaches into his pocket and pulls out his phone. He scrolls through it with his finger, and pushes it toward Edward with a velocity that makes the boy flinch for a second, before his eyes focus on a photograph of a blond young woman. She is smiling at the camera. She's sitting on a park bench, wearing a sweater that looks like it's made out of lace.

Edward feels something twist inside him. He remembers Dr. Mike saying: *When you have memories, are they from the plane, or before?* He has worked hard to remember only before, but this woman's photo makes that impossible. He does remember her. She sat a few rows ahead of them. She was on line with Jordan for the bathroom. She'd smiled at Edward while walking past their row, the same smile she has offered the camera.

Gary seems calmer now, with the photo in his hand. "I was going to propose that day," he says. "I was going to bring the engagement ring to the airport."

"I did see her," Edward says. He tries to imagine what a grown-up would want to hear. "She looked nice. She looked excited. And happy."

He sees from the look on the man's face that he has guessed correctly. "Thank you,"

Gary says.

Edward shivers, his hands buried deep in the parka's pockets. "Did you drive all the way here to ask me that?"

Gary nods. "They put me on leave at work, so I've just been sitting in my apartment, drinking Sprite, and making lists of all the questions I wanted answers to. I was driving myself crazy, and it occurred to me that you could answer one of my questions. So I got in the car."

Edward thinks, *That makes sense.*

"I'm not sure if this is rude to ask." Gary blinks rapidly again. "But I wonder if you're okay."

People have asked Edward if he's okay ever since he woke up in the hospital, and the question has always bothered him. Lacey, the nurses, the doctors, and his teachers — all asked it with expectation in their voices. He could see, baked into the words, their desire for him to say yes. Edward is surprised to find that he doesn't mind the question now, coming from this stranger in the parking lot. He can tell that Gary doesn't want a particular answer; all he's expecting is the truth, which is probably what frees Edward to give it.

"Not really," he says. He pauses, then asks, "Are you okay?"

Gary gives him a measured look, and says, "No."

They're both quiet for a moment in the freezing air.

The man says, "The thing is, I never thought I'd have a normal life on land, and get married, until I met Linda. I didn't want any of that until I met her."

He closes his eyes for a second, and Edward sees the lines of pain on Gary's face; they're the same lines — carved by loss — that engrave Edward's whole self, and the boy shudders in recognition.

"I'm glad to have spoken to you, though. This, right now, is the best I've felt in months." Gary nods, as if in agreement with himself. "I appreciate your time, Edward." He turns and begins to walk away.

"Wait," Edward says.

The man stops and turns.

"Are you going to drive back to California right now?"

"Yes," Gary says. "I study whales — they're waiting for me."

The whales are waiting for him, Edward thinks, and it's weeks before that sentence strikes him as strange. He watches the man duck into his car and drive away. When Shay comes outside, they walk home together.

Edward thinks, *I will tell her about this later.*

179

And he will. But during the walk home, his scar pulses, and the frozen air is sticky in his throat. He thinks of blond ladies and whales and he worries that if he tried to find words, he might dissolve into syllables, into the air particles, into the very cold around him.

11:16 A.M.

The solid gray sky grows heavier and starts to spit rain. The water is light, colorless, tapping the exterior of the plane. Wipers are activated in the cockpit, and the small oval windows that line the vehicle are washed. Rain is inconsequential to a commercial aircraft, but the fact that precipitation is beating the windows at full altitude means today's rain clouds are unusually high and dense. Clouds usually float at 2,000 to 15,000 feet. Planes fly at 30,000 to 40,000. Outer space begins at 300,000.

Passengers turn their attention to the weather. The raindrops and gloomy sky make some people feel sleepy, and they close the books they've been struggling with. They give their chairs a hard look, as if hoping to discover a magic button that might turn the narrow, unforgiving seat into something resembling their bed at home.

Benjamin closes his eyes and stops fighting the memory. This feels like giving up, and he hates to give up, but he's both exhausted and six-cups-of-coffee awake, and there's nowhere else to send his mind. The family across the aisle has gone silent; the father's asleep.

It was quiet for an entire month before the fight, which meant everyone in camp was bored out of their skulls. Weapons had been cleaned and recleaned; video games were played at all hours; guys even looked forward to midnight patrol, just to have something to do. There were rumors of an Afghan attack, but it never happened, and Benjamin had found himself standing at the edge of camp, staring into the woods, confusing trees with men. When there was wind, the branches waved like arms, and he grabbed at his weapon.

He and Gavin and another white boy, whom everyone called Jersey, were on the late-afternoon patrol. There had been more rumors that day, this time about three groups joining forces for an ambush. The mess had run out of fruit and vegetables and the delivery wouldn't arrive until the next morning, and Benjamin felt like he was composed of gummy cornflakes, oatmeal, and hamburgers. His tongue felt funny in his mouth.

"Stop sighing," Gavin said. "You're making me nervous."

"I'm not sighing." Benjamin was surprised by the comment, as if Gavin had told him he'd been picking his nose.

"Shut the fuck up," Jersey said. He was the kind of guy who never knew what to say and had figured out that *shut the fuck up* was a safe choice. He repeated it in varying tones depending on the occasion: sincere, ironic, angry. This time, he sounded bored.

"You *were* sighing," Gavin said. "All day you've been sighing. When we were brushing our teeth this morning, you were sighing into the mirror."

Benjamin stopped walking. He gave Gavin the look that he knew, from experience, scared the shit out of almost everyone. He'd learned it from Lolly; he'd seen her giving it to Crazy Luther on the corner. He had never seen the look on his own face, but he knew it was mean and full of threat. It was a look that ended conversations.

"I did not sigh."

Jersey whistled, the second of his three stock responses. His complete I-just-want-to-get-to-the-end-of-this-tour-alive repertoire was: *shut the fuck up,* a low whistle, and *motherfucker.*

Gavin didn't look intimidated. He said,

183

"You sighed."

Benjamin and Gavin stared each other down, the word *sighed* in the air like a bubble in a cartoon strip. Benjamin would have staked everything on the fact that he had not sighed. If he'd ever sighed, and he's not sure he ever had, it would have been in private.

"What did you say?" he said.

"Hey, motherfuckers," Jersey said, in a placating tone.

"I said you sighed. Maybe you were sad." Gavin kicked at the dirt. It hadn't rained in weeks. They'd been besieged by dry peace. "It's fucking sad out here, after all."

Benjamin felt his insides flood, like a bad engine, with hot red steam. He lunged at Gavin, grabbed him by the shirt, and threw him. The soldier went a fair distance and then rolled to a stop. His glasses were no longer on his face. Gavin clambered up, dropped into a sprinter's stance, and came at Benjamin. He moved like a small locomotive. He hit Benjamin in his midsection and knocked the wind out of him.

Benjamin sucked the air, incredulous. He moved outside himself. He thought, in some distant part of his brain, that he might be dreaming. In the dream, he lurched at Gavin, lifted him up, and then shoved him to the ground. There was a sound when Gavin's head hit the dirt.

In the distance now, Jersey was shouting, "Motherfuckers! Get your asses over here — Stillman's gonna kill Gavin!"

Benjamin dove as if he were a baseball player aiming for home plate. He pressed Gavin to the dry earth. He stared him down and tried to come up with words. Words that would intimidate him, get him to apologize. Get him to admit that Benjamin had never sighed, would never, ever sigh.

He stared at Gavin's blue eyes and freshly shaven chin, and the red warmth inside him rolled over into something new. Something powerful, something he had no control over. It felt like an internal wall had exploded into pebbles and rocks of every size. Each rock was a desire; he was a beach of itchy, terrible needs. He wanted fresh salads and nice sneakers and an end to this constant fear of death, and he wanted to touch Gavin's cheek to see how soft it was. He could do that. He heard the trample of boots shaking the ground as soldiers approached. Benjamin leaned forward; he was only inches from Gavin's face.

If the guys hadn't pulled Benjamin off Gavin at that moment, he would have done something weird. He knew it, and from the look on his face, Gavin knew it too. Benjamin got up quickly, forced his features into a forbidding expression, and took off. He hid in the forest for hours, shaking. When he crept into his bunk after midnight, he heard someone whisper through the dark tent: *faggot.* Two weeks later, sleep-starved, marching a few steps behind the rest of his patrol, he was shot in the side.

The man across the aisle is talking to Crispin, which is an unwelcome development.

"I read your book," the guy says. "Even saw you speak when you toured for it. You came to my college. You were a rock star, sir."

Crispin nods. It's amazing to him, in this body, that he used to tour the country and shout passionately from stages about hiring the right people, cutting dead weight, keeping a growing business light on its feet. There was a time when he used to have to cross picket lines to get to those speeches. Men and women pumped posterboards up and down that said things like: *People Before Profit* and *Another World Is Possible* and *Human Need, Not Corporate Greed.* Total claptrap, obviously. They were imbeciles incapable of seeing the big picture. Louisa used to delight in sending him slanderous press clippings in the mail. *Dear Asshole,* she would start every note.

This kid is staring him down with a look Crispin recognizes — hell, a look he invented. It says, *I'm hungry, desperate, and smarter than you are, so get out of my way.* That look exhausts him now; it punctures another hole in his leaky tire.

"How many ex-wives you got?" Crispin asks.

The kid's eyes darken. "One. I know you have four."

"Try to keep it at one," he says. "One good one. Four gets expensive. Try to figure your shit out sooner rather than later." He coughs, then lowers his voice. "I'm alone on this plane with a goddamn nurse."

The kid looks confused and then a little sympathetic. It's occurred to him that Crispin might be senile.

"You look like you're doing okay," the kid says, an obvious fucking lie.

Crispin returns the lie, even though he wants to close his eyes and rest. He's still competitive and doesn't want this punk kid thinking he's past everything. "You look like you're doing okay with that stewardess."

The kid's eyes light up like a Christmas tree; Crispin has rung the right bell. "You think so?"

Crispin nods. "Play your cards right, she could be ex-wife number two."

The kid laughs, and the sound is surprisingly familiar. It's the sound Crispin used to hear when he opened the door to his house after twelve hours at work. Peals of delight or conquest coming from the kitchen, the bedrooms, the playroom. One child or another would realize Daddy was home and throw himself at him. Soon he'd have all of them pinned to the floor, a mess of limbs and bare feet and bellies, and the laughter would be orchestral, every note of joy hit simultaneously. The *Dear Asshole* notes from Louisa had come later, when the house was silent every night, when he lived alone with a new wife.

Jordan watches his brother. Eddie is pressing his hand against the rain-splattered window, holding it there for a while, then pulling it away. He repeats this motion, over and over. Jordan looks at his watch. His father gave it to him for his thirteenth birthday, and it has several small squares filled with different measurements, including one that registers hundredths of seconds. Jordan times his brother for three minutes.

"What the hell?" he says.

His father is asleep in his seat. If he'd been awake, he would have complained about Jordan's use of language. Bruce has told the boys that he doesn't mind cursing, if it's used to good effect. Jane had once walked into a lecture on the subject in which Bruce was saying, "If you are furious, and you've exhausted your reasoned argument but still want to get a powerful emotion across, then you might say, *Fuck you.* What I object to is the use of these impactful words as fillers, such as when people say, *What the fuck are you doing?* That's lazy. How is *fuck* helping that particular sentence?" Jane had coughed in the doorway and said, "I'm sorry, it's okay to say *fuck you*?"

Eddie looks startled. He drops his hands to his lap. "What," he says.

"How did you do that?"

"Do what?"

"You held your hand to the pane for exactly twenty seconds, then pulled it away for ten. And then you repeated that over and over, exactly, never off by a second. It was never twenty-one or eleven."

"Huh," Eddie says. "I don't know. I wasn't thinking about it, just doing it."

Jordan regards his brother, who looks tired. Neither of them has slept well for weeks. They've never been to California

189

before and, barring a few educational vacations to Civil War battlefields and other historical sites, have never slept anywhere other than their bunk bed in their New York City bedroom.

"Must have something to do with playing the piano."

Eddie gives a small smile. The piano is the excuse, or the example, Jordan often reaches for, probably because it bothers him that he's not musical. His little brother, he knows, hears music during every waking hour. All of the music Jordan has composed is bombastic and irritable — railing at his own lack of aptitude. He'd been even more annoyed when he realized his father knew what he was doing. Bruce said one afternoon, looking over Jordan's shoulder while he was writing a composition, "All motivators are valid if they produce good work, son. And frustration can be a powerful motivator."

What he realizes now, for the first time, is that none of his compositions are any good at all. He thinks, *Eddie's the one with the talent. I'm the one with the anger.*

"Your eyes look weird and shiny," Eddie says.

"Screw you," Jordan says.

"Hey," Bruce says, rearing from his seat,

out of sleep, like a startled walrus. "Hey, what's going on here?"

The brothers are still looking at each other. Jordan's insides turn peaceful. The change is abrupt but welcome. He wants, suddenly, to lean forward and whisper all the details about his relationship with Mahira into Eddie's ear. He's wanted to do this for weeks; he's never kept a secret from his brother until now, and this is a secret that has shaped his daily life and mapped his thoughts. But somehow, from the first kiss, the secret has acted as a wedge. It's created space between him and Eddie where none has ever existed.

Jordan wants to cup his hands around Eddie's ear and start talking, but he doesn't open his mouth. He and his brother pull apart, and he knows the division, however slight, hurts them both. They're two toddlers rolling around on the rug, then two boys shape-shifting into men. One amorphous mass, then two boulders on opposite sides of the room.

"Oh, Dad," Eddie says, and he sounds sympathetic, as if soothing a child who could never possibly understand, "we're fine."

On January 1, Edward dresses in as many layers of Jordan's clothes as he can manage: underwear, long johns, socks, long-sleeve T-shirt, short-sleeve T-shirt, zip-up sweat-shirt, woolen hat, too-big red Converse sneakers. When he enters the kitchen, Lacey and John have their backs to him. They're standing by the window, talking in quiet voices. Quiet, but not calm. *Shoving voices,* Edward's brain decides. Lacey's tone shoves at John, then he, more weakly, shoves back.

"You didn't even ask if I wanted to come to the hearing."

"It didn't occur to me," John says. "Do you?"

A hard headshake. "I don't even know if he wants to be there, really. This is about you, and it's not healthy. Why are *you* go-ing?"

John is leaning against the kitchen counter as if he requires the structural support. "It's my responsibility to gather all the information, so I can protect him. I need to know what's coming his way. If I don't know everything —"

"You said you were protecting me. Last year." Lacey takes a choppy breath. "Which basically meant you stopped talking to me until I agreed to stop."

"This is different. There was no information then, no knowable reason. They didn't know why your body wasn't accepting the baby. There is knowable information now, though. That's why the NTSB is holding a hearing." He pauses, then says, "I wanted you to stop because the doctor said you might die."

"I did stop."

"Only because of what happened."

"But your *protection* didn't help me." Lacey bites off the last word, then turns quickly and sees Edward in the doorway. Her face shifts from darkness to surprise to a fake smile.

"Goodness!" she says. "Did you sleep all right?"

The false brightness on his aunt's face makes Edward feel terrible. He nods, even though he didn't sleep all right. He never does, and she must know that, but she wants everything to be different in this moment, and he wants to help her.

"John," Lacey says, "do you see how many clothes he's wearing?"

John shudders, like a toy robot coming out of sleep mode. He plays along, but his voice isn't full strength. "Maybe he's going out on an expedition."

Edward thinks: *This is the first day of a year that my parents and brother will never see. Don't you know that?* He looks carefully from his aunt to his uncle and sees that they haven't remembered. They haven't had this thought. Which means he's alone, skating on black ice that exists beneath only his feet.

"We actually wanted to talk to you," John says. "Just to fill you in on some news from the lawyers."

Lacey stands by the window, holding a hard-boiled egg; John is by the calendar on the far wall. Edward thinks, *Geometrically, in this room, I am in the middle of their argument.* He feels himself bend, like a reedy limb, under the weight.

"Would you like a piece of toast?" Lacey asks.

"No, thanks."

"So, the lawyers," John says. "Most of the logistics have been finalized, with the insurance companies, plural." He grimaces. "The majority of the victims' families will receive approximately one million dollars in recognition of their loss and suffering. You'll receive five million, because —" He stops for a second. "You get more. It will be put in trust for you until you're twenty-one."

Lacey lowers the egg to the table and taps it twice. Edward watches tiny cracks spread across the shell.

"This kind of talk reminds me of the hospital," she says. "Everything sounded absurd then too."

"It's a lot of money," John says.

Edward leans away from the table, as if the money has been physically piled in front of him. He remembers the hospital too — his bright sock elevated, a deep voice filling the air, and wondering why the president of the United States thought it was a good idea to have a conversation with a boy who'd recently fallen out of the sky.

"What I recommend," John says, "is that you put it out of your mind. You just turned thirteen." They had marked the occasion a few weeks earlier, by eating cake. It had been a quiet celebration; no one sang the birthday song, because Edward had implored them with his eyes not to do so. If the birthday *had* to happen, it needed to be quick, and muted.

"You won't be twenty-one for eight years,

195

and the money isn't even real yet. There's another period of red tape that needs to be gone through. We just wanted you to know, in case someone mentioned it at the NTSB hearing." John spreads low-fat butter across a piece of toast. "Not that I expect anyone to do so, but we didn't want you to be caught unawares."

"I don't want it," Edward says.

"I hear you," Lacey says. "Do you need any help packing for D.C.?"

Shay keeps him company while he packs, though he half-regrets her presence. She wants to discuss the upcoming hearing, and he does not. He decided he wanted to go, months earlier, but he doesn't want to think about it. *Go, not think,* some Neanderthal voice in his head repeats, whenever he starts to absorb her words.

"It's going to be like the courtroom scene in the movie," she says. "Where the identity of the murderer is revealed."

"Not exactly." Edward has all of his brother's T-shirts laid out on the couch. He chooses two and stuffs them in the bag.

"They're going to explain why the plane crashed, right? They have the black box, so they know everything that happened."

I was on the plane, he thinks. And this is

the first moment that he allows himself to place himself there, in the seat, beside his brother. It's only a flash of a thought, a fraction of a second, but it lays out the frame of the plane around him: the sky, the wing, the other passengers.

"God, I wish I could come," she says. "You know that all those relatives will be there. Gary might be there too. Your scar is going to go crazy." She clasps her hands. "I wouldn't be surprised if you see some sign of your powers. You'll be near the pieces of the plane and finding out the truth. It's like you're visiting the mothership."

Dr. Mike, in their session that week, had said, "You look checked out, Edward. You do know that you don't have to go to Washington, right?"

Edward had answered with language he knew Dr. Mike would understand: "I want to go." Even though *want* was not the right word. All Edward knew for sure was that he'd said he would go, and so he would go.

"Pay close attention," Shay says. "Take notes, if you can. I need to know everything so I can help you."

Edward nods.

"No one there can hurt you," Shay says. "No one can hurt you ever again. You already lost everything, right?"

This startles something deep inside Edward. He tries the words in his mouth. "No one can ever hurt me?"

"That's right," Shay says.

She claps him on the back right before he and John leave, like a colonel sending a soldier into battle. Lacey follows them out to the car, and when John goes inside for a minute, she gives Edward a tight hug.

"Wish me luck. I have a job interview today." Lacey smiles, but the rest of her face is anxious. "I have to do something with my days at some point, right? We all have to."

"Good luck," he says.

"I need to feel brave, so I'm wearing your mom's blouse. I want to get stronger, Edward. For me and for you."

Edward hadn't noticed, but now he sees that Lacey's wearing a shirt with tiny roses on it, which his mom had worn to work at least once a week. The familiarity of the garment makes it difficult for him to swallow for a moment, and he experiences a flash of anger — *that's not yours, that's my mom's!* But the anger dissolves almost immediately. He's wearing his brother's clothes, so how can he say it's wrong for Lacey to wear her sister's? Also, the idea that wearing the shirt gives Lacey some of his mom's bravery is interesting. It makes Edward wonder what

198

wearing Jordan's clothes gives him. He hadn't thought of it that way; the red sneakers, the parka, the pajamas, were simply a way of keeping his brother close by. Right now he's wearing Jordan's blue-striped sweater, and Lacey is wearing his mom's blouse. When Lacey pulls him in for a final hug, he thinks, *Who are we?* He steps away from the hug and the tangle of *Jane, Jordan, Jane, Jordan* and almost throws himself into the car.

The ride is four hours long and consists of gray highway after gray highway.

John glances at his watch when they pass Princeton and says, "Your aunt is in her interview right now. We should think good thoughts."

Edward shifts beneath his seatbelt, looking for a more comfortable position. "You want her to have a job?"

"I want her to be happy. And you're doing better, right? So, she doesn't have a reason to be home all the time."

Edward thinks, *I'm doing better?* The question feels unanswerable, and he has a memory of his father marking up one of his writing assignments and saying: *You have to qualify your terms. What does* better *mean? Better than what?*

The trees are stripped of leaves; the sky is

199

colorless. There are a series of warnings that they're about to leave New Jersey and then a sign that they're in Delaware. John gives Edward the choice of which Broadway soundtrack to listen to. Edward stares at the list of options, trying to figure out which one might be the least cheesy and awful. *"Rent?"*

"Excellent decision," John says, and they listen to impoverished young artists belt out their feelings for the rest of the drive.

They share a hotel room that night, where Edward lies in the dark and listens to his uncle snore. His body had ached during the car ride, as if gravity weighed more than it usually did. He'd hoped the sensation would stop when the car stopped, and for a while it did, but in the darkness it's returned. Edward wriggles beneath the papery sheets. The sensation reminds him of when he left the hospital and his body hurt in a new way, because it turned out the hospital had been an exoskeleton and without it he was vulnerable. He presses his hands against his forehead, trying to match the pressure with pressure. He's in a hotel bed, in a strange darkness, listening to a twitchy heater mixed with his uncle's wheezes. Edward feels unmoored, like he might be anywhere in space, anywhere in time, and anywhere is terrifying. When he manages to fall asleep, his body ejects him back into consciousness, into panic: *Where am I?*

In the morning, over oatmeal, John says, "I think we should have a signal, in case you want to leave in the middle of the hearing. We can leave, whenever you want."

"A signal?" He thinks of Dr. Mike and his baseball cap.

"Maybe you could say, *It's hot in here.* If you say that, we'll leave."

"What if it just *is* hot in there?"

John looks at him. "Then don't comment on it."

"Oh, okay. Good idea."

The hearing is in the National Transportation Safety Board's conference center in downtown D.C. They park several blocks away, due to closed streets. "Must be construction," John says as they walk. When they turn onto the block, the foot traffic is thicker, and they have to navigate through a group of people.

"What do you think?" John sounds like he's asking himself.

The hairs on Edward's arms rise. But before he has a chance to figure out why, a man — smelling of sharp aftershave — turns to him and says in a polite voice, "May I touch your arm for a second? My wife was on the plane."

Edward's first thought is that the man is lying. This is a man on a sidewalk, making things up. But someone else, as if released by the man's words, is talking to him. "Hi, Edward? I'm sorry to bother you, but I wondered if you saw my sister?" A woman is holding out her phone, with a photo of a curly-haired, smiling brunette.

"Oh," Edward says, and his voice lilts, as if trying to make the syllable sound like an answer.

"Her name is Rolina?" the woman says.

Another phone is thrust in front of him, though from a different direction, with the image of a middle-aged Asian man. A blue-eyed, scruffy-looking guy offers a printed photograph of an old woman with white curls and an annoyed smile. "Does my mom look familiar?" he says.

Edward directs his eyes where they're pointing. Screens, faces. He thinks, *I should respond,* but he can't. He feels like he's forgotten how to speak English.

He hears — the terms layered over one another — *girl, mother, cousin, buddy, boyfriend.*

Someone says, "I want to make a documentary about sole survivors. Can I interview you?"

John grabs Edward's arm and pulls him to the right, off the sidewalk and into a dry cleaner. John turns the lock on the door. "I have a Kickstarter!" the guy calls through the glass.

"Hey!" the man behind the counter says, but he goes quiet when he sees the cameras and faces at the window. "Is one of you famous?" he says. "You must be famous. You in movies?"

Edward turns away from the window.

"Can I have your autograph for my wall?"

"I don't think so," Edward says.

John calls the NTSB contact, and a security officer meets them at the dry cleaner, takes them out the back door, and uses his body to shield Edward from the crowd. Hands make their way past the officer and touch his arm, his shoulder. There are more phone screens, more photos of men and women. He's pelted with names.

Someone says, "What did it feel like to walk away from the plane?"

A lady with a strong Southern accent recites the Hail Mary, which is the only prayer Edward knows by heart. A homeless woman, who was a fixture at their local New York playground, used to shout the prayer all day long from her favorite bench. Sometimes Jordan would sneak up on Eddie while he was balancing an equation, or reading, and chant into his ear: *Hail Mary, full of grace, the Lord is with thee.* Edward can remember the last time this happened, his brother singing, and how he had taken off his sneaker and thrown it at Jordan's retreating back, both of them laughing.

A voice from behind Edward yells: "No one would give a shit about this kid if he was black. You people realize that? They think he's the second coming only because he's white!"

The security officer pulls open the door. John is in front, so he walks through first. Just before Edward enters, the officer leans close and says, "High five, buddy. It was badass, surviving that crash. Bad-ass."

Edward meets the man's hand with his own — because he can't see any alternative — and ducks inside the building. The beige metal door shuts behind him. He follows his uncle and a different security guard down two empty hallways. The officer points to a row of folding chairs on the side of the hall, tells them to wait, and disappears. John and Edward sit. There are no more footsteps, so Edward listens to himself and his uncle breathe. John seems to be inhaling and exhaling with deliberate slowness, as if to calm them both down. *Shay was wrong,*

Edward thinks. He could be hurt. This hurt.

"We're safe here," John says. "We're in the basement. The hearing is on the third floor. We're right around the corner from the elevator we need." He delivers this practical information with such relief that Edward realizes information is his uncle's favorite thing. Data, statistics, and systems keep the world straight for John.

His uncle continues: "The hearing, assuming it's on time, starts in ten minutes. We're not late. I was told it usually runs about an hour. Ninety minutes tops."

Edward says, "I'm not going to the hearing."

"What do you mean?"

"I don't want to. I thought I did, but I actually don't."

"Edward?" John says.

The boy wants to give his uncle an explanation, but he's not sure what to say, because if he says that something inside his body has changed, such a statement would alarm John. But it's true. It started yesterday in the car: a stripping of the flat sheet inside him. Walking through that crowd removed the last remaining threads. *Hail Mary, full of grace.* Edward realizes that he'd never been able to picture himself inside the hearing room. Had he known all along that he wasn't going to attend? If so, then why did he come here?

He feels newly aware, newly awake. He locates himself, like a blinking dot on a map, in this building, on this floor, on this metal chair with his hands on his knees. He's 100 percent in Washington, District of Columbia, a state that's not a real state. He's sitting beside his uncle. Edward understands — the knowledge arising with a surprising casualness — the real reason he doesn't sleep in his aunt and uncle's house. He can't bear to live with a mother figure, who's not his mom, and a father figure, who's not his dad. He had the real thing, and he lost it. Also, it's too difficult to try to pretend to be John and Lacey's kid, when their real kids never made it, and he's not even a kid; he's something else altogether.

Edward leans over and puts his forehead in his hands. He thinks, in the direction of his uncle: *I'm sorry.*

John clears his throat. "What they announce at the hearing today is public record. It will be published on the Internet and everywhere. I wanted to hear it first and take notes in case you had any questions about it. But now, if you want to leave, that's fine."

"You should go to the hearing," Edward

says. "I might have questions. Shay asked me to take notes, so you could do that. I can wait here. The guard is stationed at the door. I'll be fine."

John gazes at him with wide eyes. "Look," he says, "your aunt thought I was wrong to bring you here, even though you said you wanted to come. I should have listened to her. I'm too stubborn."

Edward doesn't like how upset his uncle looks, how upset he seems at himself. He says, "The hearing is about to start. You should definitely go."

"Would you feel better if I went to the hearing than if I didn't?"

"Yes."

When John leaves, Edward remains unmoving on the hard chair. He feels the plane seatbelt around his waist. His hands are cold, like they were when he pressed his palm against the wet plane window. He remembers pressing the window, then pulling his hand away. Edward feels the warmth of his brother's body next to his. It doesn't feel like a memory. He feels the tightness of the airplane seatbelt around his waist as he sits on the folding chair.

Edward can feel the heartbeats of the mothers, fathers, siblings, spouses, cousins, friends, and children upstairs. His body syncs up with their sadness. He's glad he stayed in the basement. The others are beating the plane windows with their fists, and Edward is down here because he doesn't belong with them. He belongs with the dead, the ones who didn't show up, the ones who know everything, and nothing.

After an hour, he hears real footsteps and looks up to see his uncle striding toward him. "The hearing just ended." John glances over his shoulder. "We should leave right away. We're going to meet the guard by the side door. Hundreds of people showed up, too many to fit in the room."

Edward nods, because this makes sense to him. He'd been listening to hundreds of heartbeats.

"Most of them came because they wanted to see you, which I think is outrageous." John waves his hand, as if to sweep those people away. "Someone from the hearing has a car and driver out back. She's going to take us to our car, so we can avoid the crowd." He leads the way toward the doors. "I took a lot of notes," he says, over his shoulder. "The commissioner spoke, and I took photos of the slides they presented. I'll show them to you when we get to our car."

Edward's head is shaking before his uncle has finished speaking. "That's okay. I don't need to see them. I don't want to hear about why the plane crashed."

His uncle flashes him a look. But Edward feels pleased, because after not knowing *anything* for sure, he knows this answer is correct. He doesn't want to learn any more details about the worst day of his life.

It occurs to him that maybe he came to Washington to figure out what he did want. Did he want to be part of the public drama surrounding the crash? Did he want to be swarmed on sidewalks? Did he want to be told that he's special and chosen? Did he want the kind of answers the hearing offered? He gives something approaching a smile as he follows his uncle out the door. The answer is no, on every count, and the answer is a relief. He feels like he's deliberately walking away from something — the plane, or the burning field where it broke apart.

They cross a sidewalk and step through the open door of a very long car. From the inside, Edward decides it's some kind of mini-limousine. There's a suited man in the driver's seat. Seated across from Edward is a thin elderly woman with a white bun and a velvet dress. Her hands are folded in front of her, her chin lifted. Although it never would have occurred to Edward that a person could sit with dignity — this woman does.

"Greetings, Edward," the woman says. "My name is Louisa Cox."

"Hello," Edward says.

"I'm glad we brought the Bentley, Beau," the woman says to the driver. "Its size is an asset."

"Yes, ma'am. The gentleman's car is not far away." He has already pulled out into the road, and as they ease away from the building, and the people, something eases inside of Edward, and he's afraid he might cry. He'd rather not cry in front of this fancy old woman, who is now carefully removing her gloves and smiling at him.

"I have three boys," Louisa says. "I can picture all of them at your age, sitting beside you there. They made a motley crew. I had them sewn up in blazers and ties, even though they wanted to wear jeans like yours. I should have let them. They looked like angry little CEOs, like their father."

"Thank you so much for your help," John says. "I had no idea . . ."

She waves her hand, and rings sparkle from the fingers. "It's my pleasure. Once we get you to your car, you can make a proper escape." She turns her attention to Edward, as if he's a lock she is going to unpick. He has the thought that it's not polite, the way she's looking at him.

"You were wise to skip the hearing, young man. It was a circus, and you would have become the main attraction."

Edward pulls a seatbelt across his waist, but the receiving end is buried in the seat beside him and it won't click. "Ma'am," he says. "Is this seatbelt broken?"

"You don't need a belt," John says. "We're only going a few blocks."

"I need a belt," he says.

Louisa reaches across him and releases the end of the seatbelt. He buckles it with a hard *click*. Edward gives her a grateful nod.

The car turns left and then right. Every street is one-way.

"I don't think I knew what to expect," John says. "It . . . it didn't occur to me that so many family members would be there."

Louisa gives a small smile. "My ex-husband was one of the passengers. Crispin Cox — perhaps you've heard of him? We've been divorced for, oh, let's see . . . nearly forty years."

Edward lays his hand over his seatbelt, to make sure it's doing its job. In his fully alert state, the world looks exactly as dangerous as it is.

"Your ex-husband spoke at my college,"

John says. "Many years ago."

"Crispin was an asshole," Louisa says. "He had cancer, but he would have beaten it and gone on to be an asshole for many more years."

"You didn't like him?" Edward says.

"Well," she says, "it was more complicated than like or dislike. But I did hate him, most days of the week."

"I see our car." John leans forward in the direction of their car, which they're inching toward. The sidewalk looks normal now, peopled only by men and women on their way somewhere, who have no interest in or knowledge of Edward Adler.

"I didn't hate my family," Edward says.

Louisa looks at him appraisingly. Her eyes are a vivid blue. "I'm sorry to hear that," she says. "It would have been much easier for you if you did, don't you think?"

John leans across Edward to open the car door, and then they are standing in the air, peering through the open window at the woman.

"It was a pleasure to meet you, Edward Adler. I believe I will keep in touch, if you don't mind."

"I don't mind," he says.

She waves her ring-laden hand, the window glides up, and the Bentley maneuvers away.

When they return to New Jersey, everything feels different. The air seems to have changed in Edward's absence; it's thicker and has a faintly sour taste. The milk Lacey hands him every morning is unpleasantly cold. Edward finds himself newly aware of germs, and he smells food — in case it's rancid, or overripe, or spoiled — before he puts it in his mouth. He's relieved to be back in Shay's room, but the sleeping bag feels like it shrank, and an inner tag irritates his scar when he rolls over in the night. Jordan's clothes no longer smell of him or of the cardboard boxes they lived in for months. They smell instead like Lacey's floral laundry detergent.

When Edward notices that the clicking in his head is gone too, he spends hours testing the new silence. He tilts his head slowly from side to side, jumps up and down, even thinks about his mother, but nothing elicits the familiar clicks. He wonders if the simultaneous departure of several symptoms — any trace of a fugue state, the flat sheet inside him, the clicking — could itself be considered a symptom.

Even Shay's face seems to have changed

in the few days he was away, and she's acquired a couple of new, unreadable looks. Occasionally, out of nowhere, in the middle of lunch or at their lockers, she'll give him a look, and he'll say, "I'm sorry."

"Stop that," she says each time. "Don't apologize; you didn't do anything wrong." But Edward knows she's still disappointed in him for not going inside the NTSB hearing. When he'd told her the first night back, her cheeks had flushed, and she'd said, "But that was going to be so *interesting.*"

He follows her down the school hallways and finds himself startling several times a day, when a door slams or the loudspeaker buzzes on. School is louder than he remembered, and one afternoon when a boy yells, "Fuck you!" right next to his ear and then gives him a look like, *Calm down, dude, I wasn't talking to you,* Edward has to stumble into the next empty classroom and find a chair.

In late spring, a letter arrives about the one-year memorial. Several families of the victims of Flight 2977 have formed a memorial committee, and the airline has offered to cover any costs. On the date of the crash one year later, a memorial statue will be erected in Colorado, at the location of the

214

tragedy. The land has been donated by the state. The memorial will remain on that ground forever.

A sketch of the planned tribute accompanies the letter. An artist is at work sculpting 191 birds out of metal, and the birds will be strung together in the shape of an airplane. A jet made of silver birds.

"How horrible. And beautiful," Lacey says, looking at the picture.

She had told John and Edward, when they returned from D.C., that she'd accepted the part-time job as the volunteer coordinator for the local children's hospital. She organizes the volunteers and makes sure there are enough people to read to sick children and hold brand-new babies. She said to Edward, with pride on her face, "I'll be working at the real *General Hospital* now."

Edward doesn't tell her that he wishes she hadn't taken the job, that it is another unwelcome change in his life. He doesn't tell her that he's noticed that the pregnancy magazines, which had lived under the coffee table since he'd arrived, are now gone. He doesn't tell her that he's noticed that she walks around the house differently, before and after work each day. She bustles from room to room, every step filled with purpose. She doesn't watch TV with him anymore. When Edward closes his eyes and listens to her quick steps across the kitchen floor, she sounds like a stranger.

"Do you want to go to the unveiling?" John says to him.

"No."

"Well, I have to say I'm relieved. The families will be there." John says this with a barely concealed horror that almost makes Edward smile.

"It's too much," Lacey says.

Even though the matter is settled, the three of them stand still — as sunset dims the room — and gaze at the image of a cascade of birds pointed at the sky.

That summer, Edward watches television during the day while Shay is at camp. His doctor said he could go to camp too, but there was hesitation in his voice that Edward capitalized on, because he can't imagine running bases, or gluing beads, or dodging dodgeballs. He finds that he enjoys being alone in the house. He talks to the characters during *General Hospital:* He tells Jason not to work for the gangster Sonny and tells Alan to be kinder to his daughter.

He has fewer doctors' appointments than the summer before, so he expands his television schedule and takes naps on the couch after lunch. A few times, presumably to make him leave the house, John takes Edward to work with him. They go into a mostly empty, cavernous office and move from one computer to the next, backing up the data onto drives. "They're in bankruptcy," John says, and nods at the huddle of men in the far corner, wearing wrinkled shirts and messy beards. "I set their computers up nine months ago, and they were so excited then. It's a shame."

Shay seems intent on making him leave the house too. A couple of days a week, after she gets home from camp, she insists they walk to the playground down the street. "You need fresh air," she says. "There's more to life than *General Hospital*."

He shrugs his skepticism, but he doesn't mind sitting on a swing beside her, listening while she tells him about something annoying that her mother, or a camper, said. He shades his eyes with his hand against the sunshine and watches toddlers dig in the sandbox with deadly serious expressions on their faces.

When eighth grade starts, they continue to visit the playground once or twice a week after school. Edward is unbothered by the resumption of school; he doesn't mind the routine of walking from one classroom to the next. He admires the two new ferns Principal Arundhi acquired over the summer and visits the man's office to water the plants every Wednesday afternoon. He sets the television to record *General Hospital* each day and watches it when he gets home.

It's mid-October when the actor who plays Lucky leaves the show, and a new actor immediately takes over the role. On the swings later that afternoon, Edward tries to explain the injustice of this to Shay.

"No one acknowledged the change at all, except to run a little announcement at the bottom of the screen. All the other actors just pretended it was the same Lucky, even though it was clearly an entirely different person. The new guy weighs about twenty pounds more than the real Lucky — he barely resembles him. It made it all look so fake."

"It's a soap opera." Shay kicks off the ground and swings forward. She always swings higher than he does. She pumps with her legs and never takes breaks, as if at any moment she might be judged on her form and trajectory. "Every female character on that show has had major plastic surgery. Monica can hardly move her face anymore."

He frowns at her, and thinks, *Is that true?*

"I don't care about the new Lucky," he

says. "I'm going to stop watching the show for good."

"The real Lucky might come back. His movie career might turn out to be a bust."

Edward almost growls at her with irritation. "No, he won't."

Shay turns her head to look at him. She swings by, a gentle blur. "I've been meaning to ask you. Did you not want to go to the memorial this summer just because you didn't want to fly there?"

Edward rubs at the dirt with his foot. He sways forward and back, with one foot touching the ground. "That was part of it."

She's surprised him with this question, and his chest aches as he considers it. He didn't let himself think about the memorial again after the conversation with his aunt and uncle in the kitchen. He'd tried, when he walked away from the hearing, to walk away from any thoughts related to the crash. But Shay asked him a question, and the answer is that he can't imagine entering an airport, or going through security, or buckling himself into a seat. That sequence of events feels unviable, opposed to a natural law. He could no sooner get on a plane than fly out of this playground by flapping his arms. He belongs on the ground. He has been grounded.

"The odds are impossible that anything like that could happen to you again," Shay says. "You'd basically guarantee the safety of a plane by getting on it."

"That's not how that works." He shifts his weight on the swing, and it creaks. "That's called the gambler's fallacy, you know."

"The what's what?"

"It's when gamblers convince themselves that because they've been losing for a long stretch, they're more likely to win any minute. But they're wrong — of course. The odds of flipping heads is still fifty percent, even if you've flipped ten tails in a row."

"That's interesting." Shay dips her head back as she arcs upward. "Because I always feel bulletproof when I'm with you, as if I'm safe by association."

Edward barely registers what she's said. He's been sucker-punched by memories of his brother. This happens sometimes, and he knows he has to ride the memories out. The only way out of it is through it. He remembers Jordan above him on the top bunk, his head half-buried in his pillow. He remembers Jordan's face when he wrote music, his brow furrowed in concentration. He sees Jordan beside him on the plane and knows that the smallest, truest reason he will never fly again is that the last airplane seat he ever sits in has to be the one beside his brother.

2.

"What do we live for, if it is not to make life less difficult to each other?"

— GEORGE ELIOT

2

11:42 A.M.

Just before lunch service, Veronica takes a short break in the front corner of the cabin, next to the kitchen. She always wishes, in this moment, for a cigarette. The yearning is strange, since she quit smoking four years earlier and doesn't miss the sensation of smoke filling her lungs, but something about leaning her hip against the metal counter and looking out the small port window makes her desire a cigarette every single time.

She wonders how long she'll be in L.A. — two days, three? She's been in the air for four days now, and though she hasn't yet received next week's schedule, she knows she's due a few days off. She wants to put on her new bikini and lie by the pool. She wants to drive her brother's convertible and wreck her hair with wind.

Wind is what she misses most, up in the sky. The airplane air isn't as bad as passengers say it is; she never likes when people spout opinions without bothering to gather the facts first. Airplanes take about 50 percent of the air collected in the outtake valves of the passenger compartment and mix it with fresh air from outside. The air is then passed through filters to be sterilized before it's introduced to the passengers. So the air on the plane *is* clean, and not worthy of complaint, but still, Veronica can taste the effort in it.

Every time she leaves an airport, she appreciates the unpredictability of each inhale. There might be a soft gust of wind, or the smell of popcorn, or the heaviness that precedes a rainstorm. She notices nuances in the air that everyone else is immune to, with the exception of submariners, probably, and astronauts. People for whom the earth is not enough; their freedom is off the ground. Veronica enjoys the unbridled nature of the outside world in small doses, but *this* is her home. She is the fullest version of herself at thirty thousand feet.

She straightens up, runs her hands over her hips. Hers have been the only hands on her body since her breakup with Lionel. She hasn't had sex in a month, which is a personal record. Usually she blitzes dry spells with the hot stoner on the first floor of her condo, or with her college ex-boyfriend, but she's been too busy, or distracted, perhaps, to have made that happen. She's aware that she's getting lonely, though; she gets a small charge now out of brushing up against a handsome passenger. Even the finance guy in first class — too slick and hungry for her taste, normally — is pressing something inside her. She shakes her head and pulls out the massive drawer stacked with lunch trays. She loads the cart. She chooses the slowest of her walks, the one that maximizes the side to side of her hips, and heads into the cabin. She asks for every look and then throws it like a coin into the till.

The economy flight attendant appears at Bruce's side. "We deliver special meals first," she says.

Bruce blinks at her. "Special meals?"

Jordan lowers his tray over his lap. "It's for me. Thank you."

"Why do you get a special meal?" Eddie asks.

"It's vegan," Jordan says. "Mom ordered lunch for all of us when she booked the tickets, and I told her to enter my meal preference." The tray the flight attendant hands him holds a pot of applesauce, a hummus sandwich, and a pile of cut carrots.

Bruce says, "You're vegan now?"

"I've been vegan for a few weeks. You just haven't noticed me avoiding the dishes you cooked with dairy." Jordan tugs the clear wrapper off the sandwich.

The move is hard for all of us, Bruce tells himself. *He's just expressing himself. That's what teenagers do. Stay calm.*

Bruce has always been the cook in the family, and when Jordan was a preschooler, the little boy showed up in the kitchen and asked to help prepare dinner. They had been partners ever since. At first, Jordan was given a butter knife, which he used to cut soft vegetables. He arranged food on plates. He tasted pasta to see if it was done, and sauces for saltiness. By the time he was ten, he was helping Bruce choose recipes. He received his own subscription to *Bon Appétit* for Hanukkah and pored over every copy, folding down the corner on recipes he wanted to try. Eddie became their taster, coming to the kitchen from the piano, or the book he was reading, to give the dish a thumbs-up. When Bruce pictured happiness, it was cooking in the kitchen beside Jordan while listening to Eddie play the piano in the next room. That scene repeated regularly and made Bruce thrum with joy. Every time, he thought, *I will not take this for granted.*

It was a year ago that Jordan had announced he was turning vegetarian for moral reasons. No more brisket, Sunday hamburgers, pasta Bolognese, steamed clams. Bruce hated the idea of one meal for Jordan and a separate meal for the rest of them, so he subscribed to the *Vegetarian Times* and cooked a meatless meal for dinner each night. Sometimes he made burgers for him, Eddie, and Jane, and a veggie burger for Jordan, or included a side dish with chorizo or pancetta — two of his favorites — which Jordan avoided. It had been hard, and Bruce had secretly hated it, but he'd made it work.

Vegan, though, was something else altogether. He says, "No egg or dairy? No cheese at all?"

"I should have gone vegan right away," Jordan says. "It was morally weak of me. Cows on dairy farms are horribly abused. They're impregnated using artificial insemination over and over again, and then their calves are torn away from them. And they're genetically manipulated to produce ten times as much milk as they're supposed to, so they spend their lives bloated and in agonizing pain. They die much earlier than they would normally." He shakes his head. "It's awful."

"Ew," Eddie says.

"And you don't even want to hear about what happens to chickens."

"That's correct," Bruce says. "I do not."

Jordan narrows his eyes, as if assessing the man beside him. "Would you describe yourself as a moral coward?"

Bruce hesitates, taken aback. He can hear his wife whisper: *This was your doing. You said you wanted the boys to be critical thinkers.*

Eddie knocks his brother's shoulder with his own. "Don't be mean to Dad."

"I'm not being mean."

"Jordan's correct," Bruce says. "The facts are on his side. As a society, we treat animals terribly."

"And," Jordan says, "you should note that humans are the only species that drinks the breast milk of another mammal. You've never seen a kitten drinking goat's milk, right? It's kind of gross that we drink cows' breast milk, when you think about it."

Bruce rubs his eyes with his hands. *What will I cook?* he thinks. Almost all of his vegetarian recipes rely on cheese or cream. He feels a heavy weight spread across his chest. He had seen a photograph of the kitchen in the California house, shining stainless steel and double the size of the kitchen in their New York apartment. He'd been looking forward to cooking there. He'd thought that a week of their favorite recipes, filling the new house with familiar smells, would help them all feel at home.

"I'm not saying *you* have to be vegan," Jordan says, perhaps picking up on his father's melancholy. "If you want to continue to make animals suffer unnecessarily, be my guest."

"Thank you," Bruce says. "Thanks a lot."

Linda regrets ordering the lunch tray as it lowers in front of her. The chicken sandwich blasts its chicken smell up her nose; no matter how she twists her head, she can't escape it. The carrot sticks are depressingly orange and bendy. The only thing she's pleased about is the cold can of Coke.

Florida, next to her, is eating a sandwich that she took out of her capacious bag. It smells delicious. She hums while she eats and flips through a ladies' fashion magazine.

"Sweetheart," Florida says, "you sound like a tire losing air. You need to calm down. Can you eat something?"

"No," Linda says. "I can't."

"It's early days in this *situation.*" Florida waves a hand at her midsection. "Anything can happen, so I wouldn't start getting upset about not being able to pay for college yet."

Linda's chest tightens. She's yet to make more than twenty-six thousand dollars a year. She was planning to look for work in California, but is it fair to take on a job when she's pregnant? Something else occurs to her. She says, "I'm not supposed to be around that much radiation."

"What do you mean?"

"I'm an X-ray technician."

Florida's face changes, and she pats the girl's hand. "Ah," she says. "Marie was a dear friend. What a firebrand she was. I lived two doors down from her."

Linda blinks. "Marie?"

"Curie. She discovered radiation with her husband? Surely you've heard of her, in your field."

"Oh God," Linda says. She thinks she might laugh, but that flash of amusement is swallowed by the muck of her anxiety. She is poor and jobless and has sworn off taking money from her father, and she's been saturated with radiation her entire career. Her baby will probably be born glowing like a flashlight.

"Of course, Marie died from the stuff. But she carried it around in her pockets and kept it in the nightstand table. Not a good idea, as it turned out."

It's raining outside the window. Linda wishes she were outside in the storm, away from this woman's curly straw of personal history, in the teeming wetness, where she could wash off the radiation and the film and the sonar of the last five years. She wants to be clean.

Benjamin waits on line at the bathroom. He was hoping to avoid using the airplane facilities — he'd drunk as little as possible since waking, with the plan of waiting to pee until California. Although, if he's honest with himself, he's done this every day since the surgery. He's permanently parched, to the point of dehydration. He hates to look at the bag stuck to his side. He hates to unscrew the top and do the awkward maneuver required to pour the contents into the toilet. He used to be the strongest man in the room, any room. Now he carries his insides on his outside, and his skin can no longer contain his organs. Everything's seeping out.

Benjamin feels someone join the line behind him. "Hey, man," a male voice says.

Benjamin looks over his shoulder and sees a rich white guy in a button-down shirt. "Hey," he says, in a tone that discourages further conversation.

But the guy is rolling his neck, eyes half closed, apparently unable, or unwilling, to read cues. He says, "I can't take all this sitting still."

"Sure."

"I could use the first-class bathroom, but I needed the walk."

Benjamin doesn't respond to this, just wonders if the guy knows that he sounds like a prick.

"Excuse me, gentlemen," Veronica says, and turns sideways to move past them. She pauses mid-step, left hip cocked like a gun, and says to Benjamin, "You all right with this? If you need my help, just let me know."

"I'm fine," he says.

She nods and keeps rolling down the aisle.

"You know her?" the white dude says, and his voice cracks mid-sentence. When he looks after the flight attendant, his expression reminds Benjamin of the wolf in one of the Sunday-morning cartoons he used to watch as a kid. His eyes are bugging out, and he's staring at her as if he's starving and she's transmogrified into a whole ham.

Jesus crap, Benjamin thinks, *I wish I*

wanted her. And he knows, in that moment, with the plane rocking gently beneath him and rain spilling against the windows, that if he had to choose between the flight attendant and this guy next to him, he'd choose the guy. He'd been telling himself it was just Gavin, an aberration, possibly a mental break, but the truth goes past Gavin, back at least as far as military boarding school when he was aware that he was glad there were no girls around. Girls had made him feel vaguely sad for as long as he could remember, and this flight attendant, with her boom-boom ass, makes him feel positively desolate.

"No," he says. "I don't know her."

"Your turn," the guy says, and points at the VACANT sign above the bathroom door.

"You can go first."

"You sure? You don't have to tell me twice." And now he turns sideways, to get by Benjamin. In the process their shoulders touch for a second, and Benjamin registers the jolt that runs through him. The jolt makes him think, *Fuck this,* and the *this* includes this Wall Street–looking dude, and Gavin, and the bag taped to his side, and the next operation, and this idea that he's supposed to go on feeling sad and following the same rules he's been following ever

235

since Lolly dropped him off at military school. *Fuck,* he thinks — feeling a new jolt, one that comes from deep inside — *this.*

Florida takes the last bite of her sandwich and rolls the cellophane wrap into a tiny ball.

"The trick is to add a little turmeric to the meat," she says, when she notices Linda looking.

"Is that a spice?"

The cellophane in her hand is from her kitchen in Vermont, as are the turkey and tomatoes. She stood in front of the kitchen sink, her favorite spot in the house, where the light streamed in the window and you could see the mountains at the end of the yard, and sliced that tomato. Bobby had passed through the room twice while she constructed the sandwich. He knew she was leaving but not for how long. She'd told him she was going to a wedding shower for a girlfriend in the East Village. The shower was real, and Florida had been invited. But she had a one-way plane ticket to Los Angeles in the bottom of her hiking boots in the back of her closet.

"Yes, it's a spice." Florida puts the small ball into her purse. "I'm going to California for the sunshine," she says, waving her hand

236

at the window. "I like to think that this rain is clearing the path for blue skies."

"Why *are* you going there? For a vacation?"

Florida shrugs.

"You know people there?"

"I have a couple old friends I can look up. I've never been, is the real thing, and there aren't that many places that's true of. I want to rollerblade on that twisty sidewalk that goes along the beach, you know the one you always see in movies?"

"Yes," Linda says.

"Well, I'm going to L.A. to do that."

"You're married, though, aren't you?"

Linda is looking at Florida's hand, so she looks at it too. There's a plain silver band on her left ring finger. She'd thought about taking it off, but she likes the ring, and she also doubts she'd be able to get it over her knuckle. She was thinner when she and Bobby married.

"I left," she says. "Before it got bad, though. I've had enough lifetimes to know to trust my gut. I left while he still felt affection for me. We were just on different paths."

Linda is quiet for a moment. "You mean he didn't want to rollerblade on the twisty sidewalk by the beach?"

Florida is surprised by the laughter that erupts out of her. The people seated around them are probably startled too; she's never been quiet in her mirth. Heads turn, ahead of them and across the aisle. Somehow, the woman on the other side of Linda continues to sleep. Florida is cackling now, bent over. Picturing Bobby at his worktable with his raft of blueprints in front of him. Each one detailing a survival plan in case of a different catastrophe: the collapse of the dollar, limited water supply due to global warming, an extreme weather event, a populist uprising that overthrows the government, and a fascist police state, among others. He had thirteen detailed plans, notated with complicated if/then scenarios.

"That's right," Florida says, wheezing. "He doesn't want to rollerblade, and I do."

And this seems like as great a truth as any for why she left him. She regards the girl next to her with a new respect. Perhaps she has some wisdom in her, after all.

Another truth is that those blueprints had changed over the course of their marriage. In the beginning, those plans were shaped to save everyone, or at least their friends and like-minded allies, but as the years passed in Vermont and they grew more and more isolated, the plans were revised —

subtly at first, and then brazenly — to save only them. Or even, she came to suspect, just him.

"I'm sorry it didn't work out," Linda says.

Florida smiles at the girl. "Everything ends," she says. "That's nothing to be sad about. What matters is what starts in that moment."

"This moment?"

"That's right."

Mark walks up and down the aisle a couple of times after using the bathroom. Sitting next to the lady who's typing in a plodding way, her forehead scrunched up, is stressing him out. He has the desire to fist-bump the soldier when the huge man passes him on the way back to his seat, but he worries that the gesture would seem racist somehow. He gives him a nod instead. He wonders if the guy thinks he looks down on him because he's a soldier and probably less educated than him. He doesn't, though, at all. He can tell this guy can handle himself; he looks like a pro. And Mark is a pro too. Crispin Cox was, for damn sure, during his prime. These men are his brethren. Race and class have nothing to do with it. *Do you know your shit? Are you deeply competent? Can you kick ass? Then ride with me, brothers.*

He's back in first class again. He almost sits down but decides to do another lap. That lady with the kids and the white-haired husband is not an ass-kicker. She's a worrier, not a warrior. She's a mom, and she's sapping his powers. Mark stops halfway down the aisle and closes his eyes. He tries to sense Veronica's location.

"Everything all right?" he hears her say from beside him.

"Oh, yes." And it is. He took a caffeine pill right before he left his seat, and he feels good. Great, actually.

She's looking at him in that wise, I-can-read-your-thoughts way some women have, so he decides, *What the hell, I'll say them out loud.* He speaks in a low voice, though, so no one else can hear. "I'd like to kiss you more than anything else on earth."

A pause follows. The air conditioners hum, and someone loudly opens a bag of chips and someone else emits a high-pitched sneeze, and in that pause, Mark is aware that this could go very, very badly. She could look at him with disgust, insist he return to his seat immediately, report him for sexual harassment, even sue.

But then she says, in her own low tone, "We're not on earth, sir."

Pyrotechnics detonate inside him. He says, "Even better."

June 2015

Two years after the crash, the physical therapist and the throat-clearing doctor give Edward's health the all clear, which means he has no choice but to attend summer camp with Shay. He finds that the counselors — kids only a couple of years older than him — don't care whether he runs bases, so he becomes the camp score-keeper. He sits on the bleachers, in the shade, and keeps track of runs. Arts and crafts turn out to be surprisingly enjoyable; there's something calming about sitting next to Shay in front of an assortment of glue sticks, pipe cleaners, markers, and googly eyes, with the freedom to create something ugly.

Edward is alarmed, though, by how the doctor's all clear makes the air loosen around him. By the end of eighth grade, teachers expect him to do his homework and speak up in class discussions. Lacey assigns him household chores for the first time

— washing the dishes and doing his own laundry — and on the nights she stays late at the hospital, he heats up a frozen pizza in the oven for himself and John. Besa asks Edward to carry heavy groceries from her car, and sometimes she gives him a skeptical look that seems to ask, *Do you still need to be with my daughter all the time?* The grown-ups are collectively nudging Edward in the back and giving him the side-eye. Their body language says: *The crisis is over. You need to move on, so we can move on with our lives.*

But how can the crisis be over when he still struggles to sleep, and has to wear his brother's wardrobe in order to feel intact, and will never see his family again? So, when Lacey asks him, with eagerness in her eyes, *Is camp fun? Do you like it?* he has to hide his irritation. *No, I don't like camp,* he thinks. His main sensation is relief that this new experience is not unbearable. Edward finds himself avoiding his aunt, and spending more time than usual at Shay's house. He understands the adults' desire for him to just be healed — how could they really understand what he's been through? But he feels like Lacey should know better.

When the summer ends, his aunt becomes visibly excited about him starting high school, which is completely mystifying, because Edward can't see any real difference from middle school. He and Shay still go to the same building, with the same principal. They simply take classes on the top two floors instead of the bottom. The only change that feels significant, to Edward, is that he's no longer exempt from gym class. He'd enjoyed spending that period in study hall, reading or doodling in a notebook.

The massive high school gym is in the back corner of the fourth floor — Edward finds the teacher in her office, right before the first class, and says, "I can't run that fast, and I lose my balance sometimes. I think it's best if I sit on the bleachers and watch. I could keep score for you. Or operate your stopwatch, if you want. Time kids, or whatever."

The gym teacher, a squat woman named Mrs. Tuhane with short brown hair and a whistle around her neck, doesn't even glance up from her clipboard. "This isn't a team, son — it's gym class. You won't be the only kid out there falling over. You have five minutes, and then your bippie better be on that yellow line, wearing the proper attire."

"But —"

"No buts."

After changing clothes, he finds Shay waiting for him outside the locker room. "I think we're starting a basketball unit," she says. "Have you ever played basketball?"

Edward and his brother sometimes shot baskets at the local playground. He shakes his head. "My father didn't think much of organized sports."

"Maybe you'll find that you like it. I like knocking the ball out of assholes' hands. That's legal in basketball, you know. It's in the rules." She gives him a sideways look. "You might find that you're good at sports."

"It's unlikely."

Shay shrugs.

Edward's legs are cold in his gym shorts. He's growing so fast that his arms and legs ache all the time. He doesn't want to be here. He says, "Stop expecting me to have hidden powers, okay? I'm not a freaking wizard."

"I don't expect that anymore."

He looks at her and knows it's true. The Harry Potter series is in the distant past, and that possibility — that childishness — is behind them. They're growing up. Edward — in his stretching body — is a disappointment to her, and to himself. He braces himself for a wave of sadness and is surprised by anger. When his voice comes out, it's mean. "I can *promise* you I won't be any good at basketball."

"Jesus," Shay says. "Fine."

His face burning, he follows her onto the court. He stands where the other kids are standing. When the class begins, he finds the acoustics of the gymnasium excruciating. The repeated shrieks of the whistle, the slamming of the basketball to the floor, the scuffling of feet, and the thudding of bodies into his. The volume of the room, the urgency of the noise, calls up memories he tries to run away from. His heart, as he crisscrosses the court, beats inside his ears. He averts his eyes so no one will pass him the ball. Once, when it bounces into his arms, his entire body seizes. He hurls it away, as if it's a grenade about to explode.

Twice the gym teacher yells, "Adler, you're headed in the wrong direction! Turn around!" Edward becomes convinced that the clock on the wall has stopped, or that he's fallen inside this hour, as if it's a pool of quicksand, and he'll never work himself free. Time has swallowed him whole. He will sweat and panic across this gym forever. When a kid bangs into him, Edward acts without thinking: He turns and shoves him in the chest. The kid — who Edward sees is

246

not a him but an Asian girl named Margaret, who'd helped him find his new high school locker — falls to the floor. Mrs. Tuhane says, "Adler, get off the court right now! Take a seat!"

That night, he says to John and Lacey, "You need to write a note to get me out of gym class. Just for a few months, until I'm stronger. It's too dangerous."

"Dangerous?" John looks at his wife. "Have they changed gym class since we were kids?"

"I'll fake a stomachache every time if you don't write me a note," he says. "I'm not doing that again."

"Honey," Lacey says. "Of course. We'll write a note."

When he enters Shay's room that night, he stares down at his feet. He can still hear basketballs pounding the floorboards in his head when he says, "I'm sorry I was a jerk." He registers that he sounds angry, even though he's not; he's just trying to speak loudly enough to be heard over the rattle of balls.

"What do you have against Margaret?"

He tries to think of a way to explain what it felt like on the basketball court, how his nerves were being lit on fire, one wick at a time. After gym class, he'd apologized to Margaret. She hadn't said anything in response, just glowered at him and walked away.

"At least you know there won't be any consequences for shoving her," Shay says. "Because you're you."

"They wouldn't do anything to a kid for shoving someone *one* time."

"They most certainly would. I got suspended for punching a boy."

Edward stares. "You were suspended? When?"

"Right before you got here. The kid's family moved away, so he's not at the school anymore." Shay closes the book she's holding. "He hummed under his breath during every class, which was profoundly irritating. I couldn't take it."

"So you punched him?"

"Well, I was bored before you got here, and I hate being bored. I had to entertain myself. I've almost run away every year since I was six. I always had a different plan, with different timing. I realized at some point that I was never going to actually run away, because it would kill my mother. But I still needed to make the plan, to distract myself."

Edward has a memory of standing on the

front stoop with Besa during one of his first weeks here. "Your mom told me that you used to hit girls sometimes, when you were little. She was thanking me for being your friend, and I assumed she was exaggerating to make me feel less bad about showing up here."

"She wasn't exaggerating."

"What were you trying to distract yourself from?"

Shay makes an exasperated noise, then says, "I don't know. My mother buying me dolls every Christmas, hoping I would play with them. Eating dinner at five-fifteen every single day. Do you know our chicken schedule? Because we have a chicken schedule. We eat fried chicken on Mondays, roasted chicken on Wednesdays, and barbecued chicken breasts on Fridays. It never varies."

Edward feels like he's walked into a different bedroom from the one he sleeps in every night. He remembers following Shay down the school hallway on the first day of seventh grade, watching her elbow a boy out of his way. He remembers her scowling at the people who used to watch him as if he were a parade. He can see this new version of Shay in the old one.

She shakes her hands out, the way athletes

do between competitions. "Look," she says. "I don't want to shut up anymore. I don't think you want me to."

"No," he says, even though he feels nervous. The air in the room is strange, like the still precursor to a hurricane.

"The plane crash, and you moving here, was obviously exciting," she says. "But now . . ."

He nods. He knows that *now* is different, and dissatisfying. The air is loose, and there is room for boredom along with other types of chronic mild discomfort. Edward pants slightly, almost bends over and puts his hands on his knees because today has worn him out, but he has to focus, because him being irritable at the world and Shay being irritated at him are two very different things. The second is unacceptable, and yet Edward can now see small signs of her disengagement over the past few months. Sometimes Shay turns out the bedside light early, even when she's not particularly tired. She chose to take a different elective from him at camp: Edward signed up for an additional session of arts and crafts, and she took wood shop. Once or twice she sat at a table full of other kids at lunch. He feels a trill of panic. He's losing her.

"I'm sorry I'm boring you," he says, and

hates how whiny he sounds.

She shrugs. "This isn't about you, Edward. For once."

There's danger in her expression. She looks out the window like she wants to jump and hit the pavement running. He knows that, somehow, his speaking angrily to her in the gym unleashed this. She'd been committed to taking care of him, and he'd told her to back off.

Oh God, he thinks. *What have I done?*

When she turns back toward him, her expression is fierce. "I have to tell you something."

"You don't have to right now," Edward says. "Tell me tomorrow." He has no idea what Shay's about to say, only that he can't bear anything more. He has a memory of watching his mom press her thumb against the birthmark below her collarbone. When Jane noticed her son watching, she'd smiled and said, *I press here when I want to turn back time.* Eight-year-old Edward had believed her and wished that he'd been born with a magical birthmark. He has the same wish now, again. Filled with dread, he wants to reverse away from this moment.

"I promised my mother I would say this, or else she said she would tell you, and that would be mortifying."

251

A car on the street honks loudly, and Edward feels the sound inside his body.

"You can't sleep in my room anymore. It's fine, though; nothing else will change."

His body temperature plummets; his skin is suddenly cold. "Why?"

"My mother made me promise when you showed up here, when you first started sleeping in my room, that it would stop when we stopped being kids. When I became a woman. Ugh." Her hands are over her face. She speaks between the spread of fingers. "That's what she calls it."

Edward looks at the clock on her bedside table. It's eight-seventeen. How is this day still happening? "What are you talking about?" he says. "You know I don't understand anything."

"I got my period."

With the exception of the trip to D.C., Edward has walked in the darkness from his house to hers every night since he met her. "So what?" he says, but he knows this is something Besa would care about, a milestone where she would plant — has planted — her flag.

"I know you don't want to sleep in the nursery. But there's a pullout couch in your basement. You should sleep there. I can help you set it up. You can sleep in my room for a few more days, until the basement is ready."

Edward blinks. He knows he has to reply, so he says, "Okay."

"We both knew it couldn't go on forever."

He thinks, *I didn't.*

The next day is Wednesday, so Edward shows up at Principal Arundhi's office after school. They circle the perimeter of the room, Edward with the blue watering can, the principal with tiny muslin bags filled with different plant foods. The bags aren't labeled, but he knows which bag is which. For a few of the plants, the principal massages the food into the leaves and then adjusts the heat lamps situated overhead. For others, he makes careful divots in the soil with his index finger and then gently tips the contents of a bag into the holes.

Edward has learned to pour water slowly and to watch the soil color to see if it's saturated. Dark brown is good; tar-black and muddy means he's gone too far. He focuses on controlling his pour. His hands have an uneven tremor, because he barely slept the night before. He'd lain awake on Shay's floor, trying to memorize the Y-shaped crack in her ceiling, trying to memorize the tiny squeaks she makes when she rolls over in her sleep.

"Can you name them, Edward?" The principal is three plants ahead of the boy. He sniffs the leaf of a plant and then tips his head to the side, as if considering the meaning of the smell.

Edward knows now that the entire room is filled not with many different types of plants, as he'd assumed on his first visit, but with various ferns. Principal Arundhi is not just an avid gardener but specifically an expert on ferns. He's even published a book, called *Ferns of the Northeast: Including Club-mosses and Horsetails,* which is showcased on the windowsill between two large flowerpots.

Edward sets down the watering can and picks up a spray bottle from the desk. The frilly plant in front of him does best when misted with water. "This is a crocodile fern."

"Good."

Edward names the next one. "Boston fern. Staghorn. Then a couple maidenhairs. A holly fern." He squints at the plant in the corner. It's two feet tall with strappy, leathery fronds. "That one and the one behind it are bird's nests."

Principal Arundhi nods affectionately in the same direction. "I've had the beauty in front since graduate school."

"Button fern. The ones up on the shelf are silver brakes, and that's a kangaroo paw."

"Excellent. And what do they all have in common that differentiates them from other plants?"

"They're vascular and reproduce via spores."

The man nods, his mustache pulled taut with a smile. "Fine work. You're a pleasure to teach."

When Edward's finished watering, he pulls on his backpack. Shay is waiting for him at home, to start setting up the basement. Edward shifts the straps of the backpack and draws slow breaths, willing time to slow around him.

Principal Arundhi turns from the oldest fern in the corner. "Is it four already? One other thing before you go, Edward. Mrs. Tuhane told me that you opted out of gym."

"My leg hurt."

"Hmm, yes. She told me about the class and what the note said. Can you hold this for a second? I want to fix its perch."

Edward thinks, *He knows I shoved a girl.* The principal places the lemon-button fern in Edward's hands and turns back to adjust the stand. The boy looks down at the plant. It's bright green and about six inches tall. Its fronds are thumbnail-sized. Holding it

255

to his chest, Edward stares directly down into the center of the fern. If a plant has a face, this is it. Edward can't help but think that the plant is regarding him with skepticism. *I agree,* he thinks.

"What do you think about that idea? Edward?"

He realizes, just as he hears his name being spoken, that the principal has been talking for at least a minute. He looks up quickly and hands the plant back to him. "I'm sorry?"

"Weight lifting," Principal Arundhi says, looking slightly annoyed. "During your gym period, you can lift weights in the weight room instead of joining your class. This will allow you to accommodate your injured leg and yet still get some exercise. It's much quieter in the weight room than in the gymnasium. I myself prefer it. And we can all afford to get a bit stronger, can't we?"

"Weight lifting?" Edward says. He has a hard time finding an association for the word at first. He pictures huge, oiled men in bikinis. His father would never have lifted weights, nor would John. Edward regards the principal, who has soft cheeks and a soft middle. Does the principal lift weights?

Then he remembers the soldier on the plane. Edward and Benjamin had introduced themselves outside the bathroom, and the soldier had appeared almost impossibly muscular. He definitely lifted weights; nobody would have ever messed with him. Benjamin must have felt safe everywhere, at his size. He would have *been* safe everywhere, except on that plane. Edward looks down at his own skinny arms and bony wrists. He feels the shape of the scar on his shin. He tries to picture himself wider, stronger, safer.

"I'll do that," he says, and his voice cracks. "Thank you."

At dinner, Lacey says, "Do you have a favorite movie?"

"Me?" Edward had been staring down at his plate, trying to come up with a way to consume just enough pork chop to keep Lacey from being disappointed. His appetite has dimmed since Shay's pronouncement. He can feel himself dimming inside, his lights going out, one by one.

You okay? Shay had asked him at lunch today. *Don't get weird because of this. Everything is fine. We're fine.* He'd said, *I know,* but in truth he feels like he's been handed notice to walk a plank and drop into shark-infested waters. Every minute, he's inching down the wooden slab. Tonight will be his last night on her floor. Tomorrow, he jumps.

"Yes, you, silly," Lacey says.

"What's yours?" He says this to buy time. He doesn't have a favorite movie. When he was little, it was *The Jungle Book*. Has he even seen a movie since the crash? He thinks, *General Hospital*?

"*Steel Magnolias,*" Lacey says.

"What about you?" Edward says to John. He's comfortable with this kind of conversational bobbing and weaving; he does it with Dr. Mike every week. Every time a question makes him uncomfortable, he redirects. This week, in an effort to avoid any mention of Shay or the fact that he's moving bedrooms, he told Mike about the book on investing that Louisa Cox's driver had dropped off at their house that week. Included was a note on very thick cardstock that said, *There are elements of a proper education that they never teach you in school. Read this book and then write back with your organized thoughts.* This was the second book the driver had delivered since the hearing. The first was a biography of Teddy Roosevelt, which Shay and Edward had read together, stopping every page or two to make fun of how besotted the author clearly was with the burly president. But now when Shay says, *Should we do our homework?*

258

Edward feels a wave of guilt that has nothing to do with the work assigned by his teachers but with the fact that he owes organized thoughts — on a book so boring he can't get past the first page — to Mrs. Cox.

Dr. Mike had been amused, though, and therefore Edward won. He doesn't always win with the therapist — Dr. Mike usually plays along for a minute and then comes up with a question that's even closer to the bull's-eye — but Edward is confident he can run a conversation with his aunt and uncle. They are unskilled; they have no chance.

"Blade Runner." John chews a bite of food and smiles slightly, as if the movie is a warm memory. "Seen it twenty-three times."

"Goodness," Lacey says. "That's not something to brag about, you know."

"Oh yeah?" John points his fork in the direction of his wife. "How many times have you seen Steel Magnolias, Lace?"

"That movie is a classic," Lacey says, in a haughty tone. She turns back to Edward. "I was thinking that if you liked Star Wars, or another big movie, we could get you Star Wars bedding."

Edward rolls the sentence through his head, trying to make sense of it. "Bedding?"

"Besa told me that you're going to sleep

on the pullout couch in the basement. I think we can make that a really special space for you down there."

Down there. Edward pictures the basement, which lies directly beneath them. He is near the end of the plank, and the wind is howling, and he hates himself for feeling this way. He knows he's more upset than he should be, at least about what's happening on the surface. He went to bed in one room; now he'll go to bed in another. The distance between Shay's bedroom and the basement is less than thirty yards. He will still walk to school with Shay every morning. He will still listen to her read books aloud. The surface news is bearable. But what might be below the surface, below the roiling water, distresses him.

Lacey is beaming at him from across the table. Edward puts down his fork, his appetite finished. The darkness inside him has taken over. He wonders what exactly Besa told Lacey. Did she say that Shay got her period? Or did she say something else, something Edward dreads is the actual truth: that Shay is simply sick of him, and now she has the necessary excuse to get him out of her room and, therefore, her life?

He lifts the metal objects Mrs. Tuhane tells

him to lift, straightens his spine when she tells him to, and tries to decipher the strange physical-fitness language she speaks. The weight room is directly off the gym; Edward can hear kids shuffling across the shiny floor. Balls being dribbled. A whistle demanding attention.

"You're going to squat, you're going to deadlift, and you're going to bench," she says. "These are compound exercises, which means they exercise more than one muscle group at once. If you learn to bench properly, you can shove away someone who's got a hundred pounds on you. You deadlift to your potential, you can lift a car off a trapped child."

"Really?" Edward says. He tries to picture himself lifting a car, his face red, his arms shaking with effort. The image is ridiculous.

"Really."

"What does the squat do?"

"The squat does everything. When you squat, you tax your entire system. You want big legs? Squat. You want big arms? You squat."

Mrs. Tuhane always looks intense, but right now she looks like she's channeling some great eternal truth. Benjamin Stillman must have done squats. He must have known what to do with every piece of metal in this room.

Edward squats with a wooden stick across his back, because Mrs. Tuhane says he's pitifully weak and not ready for a bar, much less actual weights. As he sinks down, he remembers Shay staring out the window, her expression fierce.

"Adler," Mrs. Tuhane says. "Squats don't end at the bottom. That's called sitting. You need to spring up with good form."

Spring up with good form, Edward repeats in his head, and tries to comply.

Shay reads a chapter of *The Golden Compass* out loud, and then at nine o'clock Edward stands up. He tries to think of something to say, to stop this from happening. But no answer comes, because the truth is: If Shay wants him gone, he should go. He barely heard a word she read from the book; he will have to skim the pages later to catch up. The muscles in his body ping and wobble, like hundreds of rubber bands, and he knows he'll be sore tomorrow.

He doesn't look at her. He says, "Okay, well, good night."

"I hope you sleep well. See you in the morning."

They're both speaking a little too loud, and Edward picks up his backpack and stumbles out of the room. He's relieved Besa is nowhere in sight. He lets himself out the front door, and then, in the middle of the walk to his aunt and uncle's house, in the shadows — a spot he knows Shay can't see from her window — he sinks to the ground. It's not a choice; his body just gives up and drops.

He thinks, *I have no home now.*

The New York City apartment, with his parents and brother, was home. After the crash, his body had led him to a place on Shay's floor, and he'd burrowed there, grown stronger there. He'd gone from sleeping near Jordan to sleeping near Shay, and that had been a comfort. His aunt and uncle's house, looming above him in the shadows, has never felt like what he needed. Edward has tipped off the end of the plank, and he's in the dark water, with the sharks circling.

He curls up on his side on the ground. The September night is surprisingly cold. He closes his eyes to match the dark water and the dark sky. He can't remember crying like this, since the crash, maybe ever. His cheeks become soaked, his shoulders judder. His tears raise the level of the ocean around him. Waves climb and then crumple into whitecaps, and he wonders if he'll see

Gary or his whales.

Only when someone shakes his arm does Edward realize he's fallen asleep.

"Oh my God, Edward! Are you hurt?" His aunt's pale, panicked face is above him. Then her face turns away and she screams, "John! John, come! John!"

Edward thinks, *She sounds scared.*

Lacey grips his shoulders. "Can you speak, Edward? Do you know where you are?"

He nods, even though the movement takes immense effort. His body feels like it's been soldered into a solid entity. He finally gets his mouth to say, "Yes."

Then his uncle is there too, bent over Edward. John's wearing his old plaid pajamas. "What happened?"

"I don't know. Look at him. Should we go to the hospital?"

"Let's get him inside first."

John half-lifts Edward to his feet, then puts one of the boy's arms around his shoulders. Lacey does the same on the other side. On his feet, Edward is higher up than he remembered, and he wonders if he's literally coming apart, with his head floating away. His only hope — as the three of them lurch forward — is that Shay is fast asleep and nowhere near her bedroom window, so

264

she can't see his aunt and uncle dragging what's left of him into a house.

People fly despite knowing that a certain percentage of airplanes crash every year. They "know" that fact yet find ways to qualify, and therefore soften, the knowledge. The most common qualification is the fact that it is statistically more dangerous to travel in a car than in an airplane. In absolute numbers, there are more than five million car accidents compared to twenty aeronautic accidents per year, so, in fact, flying *is* safer. People are also helped by etiquette; because commercial air travel is public, a kind of group confidence comes into play. People take comfort in one another's presence. Sitting side by side, shoulder to shoulder, they believe that it is impossible for this many people to have taken a foolish risk at the same time.

The floor shudders beneath Crispin's feet as he inches back to his seat. The round trip to the bathroom has probably taken twenty minutes. He had to rest on the toilet seat for a long time, just to summon the strength to walk back. He'd thought, *I felt fine a month ago. I felt like myself. I don't know who the hell this guy is.*

Right before the flight, Crispin's lawyer, Samuels, who is as old as he is but so fit he decided to take up powerlifting in his seventies, called to say that Crispin was on the annual *Forbes* list of the top hundred richest individuals in America.

"Huh," he'd said into the phone.

"Congratulations, Cox. You're a beast."

"Huh," he'd said again. What he was really doing was registering that he felt nothing. He'd been on the list for twenty years, and in the top half for the last decade, ever since he sold his company, and he'd looked forward to the announcement by *Forbes* every year. Noted the date on his calendar, answered the phone with alacrity on the day. Whooped and pounded the desk with the news.

"Cox, you feeling okay? I know the docs in L.A. are going to fix you up in no time."

"Call Ernie and tell him I want to redo my will when I get there."

"Will do."

"Why am I leaving everything to the kids? They hate me."

267

"The Met is hoping you might think of them, obviously."

"Fuck them." Crispin was on the board for decades — he enjoyed the meetings, filled with New York heavy hitters and much of his social group — but he almost never walked through the rooms to look at the art. It had been a fun sparring ground for him and Louisa, since they were both involved in the institution. She had majored in art history in college and fancied herself a collector. For one stretch in the mid-nineties, she had been president of the board and had banned him from meetings.

"What's your plan?"

Crispin holds back from saying, *I'm not sure.* He never says, *I'm not sure.* Uncertainty is weakness, and he has a policy against it. He says, "I might just dump the whole mountain on Louisa. That would really mess with her head. The damn woman has spent her life trying to get my money. I could just hand it to her on a silver platter." This idea makes him chuckle.

There's a pause on the other end of the phone, because Samuels is Louisa's lawyer as well. He's choked with professional discretion. "As you wish, Cox. I'll alert Ernie."

Now, as Crispin sinks gratefully into his

seat, he sees the raindrops outside as his fortune, sinking to earth. This is a woebegone idea, because the money — without him attached to it — has no meaning. Just green and white paper rectangles that he spent his whole life, his whole self, socking away. He would love to mess with Louisa, but she doesn't need the cash — wouldn't even notice the addition in her day-to-day life. As a friend of his once put it, "You can't eat any better than you do now." He and Louisa both eat as well as is humanly possible.

He's always given a crap about his money and about what it takes to get more. The numbers mattered to him until his lawyer's phone call this morning, and if that has fallen away, what's left? Across the aisle, this kid, who looks high as a kite, is banging away on his keyboard like every letter he hits is going to make a real difference. And maybe it will, maybe it does.

Maybe it did.

The pain is a collection of marbles now, rolling around his abdomen. As he falls asleep, he thinks, *I should have taken my kids camping when they asked.*

Bruce rubs his head — a nervous tic that he's not sure counts as a tic, because he's always aware when he does it — and stands up.

"Just going to say hello to your mother," he says. "Be good."

Eddie says, "Dad, we're not five."

Jordan says, "Tell her thank you for the dessert, but it had dairy in it, so I gave it to Eddie."

Bruce sighs, because in the dream he was just having, Eddie *was* five. The little boy was sitting on his lap, on the couch, and Bruce was reading *Winnie-the-Pooh* to him. Eddie was leaning against his father's chest, and the sensation of that weight — the complete trust and lack of inhibition with which the boy relaxed every ounce of his body into his father's — was one of the things that made parenthood unmissable.

Bruce had read Eddie that book twelve or thirteen times, from start to finish. He knew that all children liked repetition, but Eddie more than most. Once he learned to read, he read some of *Winnie-the-Pooh* to himself almost every night in bed, and he'd watched his favorite movie, *The Jungle Book,* countless times. "At least he has good taste," Jane used to say when Bruce worried aloud that he wasn't reading enough *other* books. "At least he likes the classics."

The twelve-year-old Eddie is made up of

spindly limbs. His chubbiness is gone. He's awkward in his hugs; he feels, in his father's arms, like a sapling at risk to the elements. Putting his hands on the piano keys seems to be the repetition Eddie now craves, and he no longer needs or wants his father to read to him.

Bruce pushes the first-class curtain to one side and sees that the seat beside Jane is empty.

"Sit down," she says. "I don't know where he went."

Bruce eases down next to her. "That guy doesn't look too good," he says, indicating the old man sleeping across the aisle.

"Apparently he's a famous baron."

"Baron," he says, and smiles. "Why would he fly commercial? If I were a baron, I'd have my own plane."

"He's actually a hornswoggler, a bamboozler," she says. "And that goes double for my seatmate. I can just tell."

"How's the script going?" Bruce tries to make sure his tone isn't too weighted. He wants to have a conversation, not a fight. He has missed his wife from the far reaches of economy class.

She seems to sense what he's thinking, as usual. "I'm sorry," she says. "Again."

She fits her hand over his and presses. Her

skin is soft, and the pressure makes his mouth form a smile. He can be furious with her and still be aware that he loves her at the same time. It took years for him to be able to accept the absence of logic in their love. Frustration plus a bad mood plus a particular smile of hers equaled a shot of joy in his belly. He hopes that his boys find this same kind of unbalanced logic in their own futures. He remembers the look on Jordan's face in the Chinese restaurant and wonders, for a fleeting moment, if it's possible that his older son already has. But then he dismisses the thought as absurd.

"What?" Jane says. "Please think out loud."

"We should sign Eddie up for the Colburn School in L.A."

Jane raises her eyebrows. "Really?"

"Don't you agree?"

"Yes, of course. I think he's talented, and he loves the piano. But that will remove him from your curriculum."

"Not entirely. I can still make sure he gets his math and reads history."

"Jordan will be lonely."

"I know. We'll have to figure something out. Maybe he'll like spending even more one-on-one time with his dad."

This is a joke, but they both get it and

don't bother to smile.

Jane leans her head against his shoulder.

"Where is this guy?" Bruce says.

"He's probably following the first-class flight attendant around. I think he's in love."

"Is she pretty?" He tries to picture the woman and recalls a tight bun of hair but nothing else.

Jane narrows her eyes. "You honestly haven't noticed?"

He nods at her computer. "Are you almost done with this?" He can hear an accumulated frustration seep into his voice and is disappointed in himself. This response is so pedestrian; he wants to be better, as a husband and a man.

Jane straightens and looks at the screen. At the rows of letters lumped into words, the screenplay format of open spaces and spatterings of dialogue. "No," she says. "But I will be by the time we land. I promise."

Veronica has done this twice in her career. It's nothing she makes a habit of, but she has best practices to execute. She tells Mark to go to the back left bathroom — the one most hidden from sight from the rest of the plane — in ten minutes' time. After she sees him do this, she turns on the FASTEN SEAT-BELT sign, to keep as many people as possible in their seats. Then she flips on the overhead speakers at the highest volume, filling the air with a staticky buzz. The head of every waking passenger tips back to look at the ceiling, where the speakers reside. She switches the noise off and ducks into the bathroom.

The dimensions of the room are so small that she and Mark are pressed together immediately. The door lock turns on the fan and light, so they're doused in fluorescence, a mirror two inches behind her head. The back of Mark's knees are pressed into the toilet rim. It smells surprisingly fine, though; the air vents are doing their job.

"No talking," Veronica whispers.

Mark cups the back of her head, his fingers lacing through the bun at the nape of her neck. Veronica gasps a little at her own hunger. She wants to pull the bobby pins out of her hair, but she has to return to work within six minutes or she will definitely be missed, and she must look exactly the same as when she entered the bathroom.

She shimmies her skirt up and shimmies her pantyhose down.

Mark undoes his belt.

There is a tapping noise, not on the bathroom door but from the sides of the plane, and in the back of Veronica's mind, she thinks, *What is that?*

Chip, chip, chip, goes the knock, or the air-conditioning unit, or the loose duct, while Mark molds his lips to hers — he's a surprisingly competent kisser — and she grabs his ass to pull him in.

And then there's roaring in her head and she's as red as her lipstick and coursing with everything that makes up life, and when Mark Lassio whispers in her ear, *I might need you,* she blows the words away like kisses.

Jordan nudges his brother, then leans in close. Their father is still gone.

"What?" Eddie says.

"The first-class flight attendant and a guy just went in the bathroom together."

Eddie screws around in his seat and looks toward the back of the plane. "Why would they do that?"

Jordan's laugh is almost a cackle. "To have sex, probably."

Eddie looks horrified. "In the plane bathroom?"

"I don't think anyone else noticed. She distracted everyone with that overhead noise, so no one would look."

"Why did you look?"

"I was counting how many rows of seats

were on the plane, so I was facing that way."

Eddie contemplates this, his face serious. "Maybe he's sick, and she went in there to help him."

"Maybe. He looked pretty healthy, though."

Eddie shudders. "That's gross."

"Well, I'm not going to go in that bathroom again, that's for sure." Jordan thinks of Mahira and grows hard in his pants. He lowers his tray so his brother doesn't see.

He notices his dad headed toward them, down the aisle. He thinks of his dad and mom having sex, and the erection dims.

"Still," Eddie says, in his careful, considered way, "it's kind of cool to think that having sex is so great that you don't mind doing it in a bathroom."

Jordan nods and feels deeply grateful for the comment. Grateful that his brother is beginning to join him in the land of erotic dreams and uncomfortable underpants.

Crispin opens his eyes and doesn't know where he is. Well, he knows he's on a plane. That's obvious. But to where, and when? He's been on hundreds of flights in his life; there were entire years when he seemed to spend more days in the air, en route to meetings and conferences and lavish vacations, than he did on the ground. He could afford to buy a fleet of these planes if he wanted to, but he'd always refused to fly private. Commercial flights were one of the few places he got to sit among his customers, to observe how they thought and behaved. He'd always considered his time in the airports and on planes to be invaluable market research.

"What year is it?" he asks the woman next to him.

She's wearing a white cardigan that's buttoned right up to the top. "Give me your wrist," she says. "I want to check your pulse."

"Absolutely not. Answer my question."

"It's 2013."

"I was born in 1936. That means I'm . . ." He shuts his eyes, but his brain refuses to make the computation. He suspects that this woman is a nurse, probably his nurse.

She takes his arm, as if she has some right to it, and places two fingers on the inside of his wrist. He lets her, because, along with the ability to subtract, his physical strength is gone.

"Thready pulse," she says, under her breath.

He nods, or maybe he doesn't actually nod but he nods on the inside, in agreement. He is thready. He's threading in and out of whatever and wherever this is.

"Are you cold, Mr. Cox?"

Yes, he thinks. *I am freezing cold. And I am no longer young. And I am alone in the sky, headed to where I do not know.*

When her seatmate returns, Jane is amused by the difference in energy between him and her husband.

The skin on Mark's face appears chapped and ruddy, as if he's been out for a walk in rough weather. He fidgets and clicks the end of his pen on and off. Bruce had sat quietly beside her. She'd had to look in his eyes to guess his thoughts; there were no external clues.

"I think it's hailing," she says, indicating the window.

"That's crazy. It's summer."

She nods and stares out at the gray blur of cloud and precipitation. She wonders if the weather is trying to warn her off. *Turn back,* it might be saying. *Write your love story. Live smaller, on less. You could move near Lacey, like she's always wanted. Raise your babies together.*

But it had turned out that Lacey wasn't able to have babies. Jane had been surprised, each time, by how upset *she* was when her sister miscarried. She'd hidden her sadness from Lacey, of course, but when her sister became pregnant again, Jane felt her body flood with excitement. There would be a brand-new person in their family, and a baby for her boys to dote on. She became almost dizzy with joy at the prospect. *A new baby to love.* Balancing the rush of hope, though, was fear at what her sister might lose in the process.

Jane had said into the phone: *There are other ways to make a family. Do you want me to research adoption agencies, or surrogacy?* But Lacey had refused to stop trying to get pregnant, and Jane certainly wasn't going to move next door to her sister to watch her kill herself. Besides, she would hate the suburbs, the Super Bowl parties, the weird looks people would give her family for their homeschooling and dangerous opinions. Bruce would alienate people by showing up uninvited at local education meetings to debate the merits of the mass education of children.

"Goddammit," Mark says. "I can't focus."

"It's because it's the middle of the flight," Jane says. "I always get hopeless in the middle. When you still have hours in front of you and hours behind you. You feel stuck."

Mark turns to look at her. "That makes sense." He clicks his pen and says, "How long have you been married?"

She smiles with surprise. "Let's see . . . sixteen years."

"Fuck. That's a long time. And you never cheated?"

What a strange conversation, Jane thinks. *But perhaps people in first class are always more open with each other, because they assume they have so much in common?*

"No."

He shakes his head. "Fuck."

"Are you married?"

"I was once, for about ten minutes."

"Was that a fun mistake?"

"Ha." The laugh is a bark. "Yeah, it kind of was. Too much cocaine, though."

"Ah." Jane has never taken cocaine, never married the wrong person, never fallen for a flight attendant. She feels a pang of regret. She would not like to be this man, with his scratchy energy, but she wishes she had perhaps taken a detour or two in her own journey. She has always moved with deliberation.

Now that Jordan seems to have his fists raised at the world, she wishes she could say to her son, *I can relate. I spent one November in Seattle protesting the WTO.* But

280

she can't. Her version of fist-raising has been to read articles in *The Nation* and nod emphatically. *There can be merit,* she thinks, *in a life of messiness.* She and Bruce live a tidy life. Even her greatest ambition — writing a small, personal, intimate film — is neat and tidy.

Mark rubs his eyes and looks around, no doubt for the flight attendant.

Jane cranes her head too, in an effort to help.

Edward checks the tree outside Dr. Mike's office. Its gray bark is traced with deep rivulets. The branches look like they'll never grow leaves. A bird alights on a branch and almost immediately helicopters away.

Dr. Mike says, "Can you tell me what's going on in there? If I know what the problem is, maybe I can help."

Edward has stopped trying to control his thoughts, so each one is a small surprise. He hears the ornate clock on the desk tick forward and thinks, *I miss Jordan more than ever.*

"Edward?" Dr. Mike says.

"I know they want me to come here twice a week," he says. "But I think that's a waste of your time."

"You collapsed outside your aunt and uncle's house."

"Three months ago. It really wasn't a big deal."

"If it had been colder outside, you could have frozen to death. It is a big deal."

"I wouldn't have died."

"How do you know?"

Edward watches the branch, hoping the bird will corkscrew back to its spot, but the air and the tree remain still. The empty space feels appropriate, though. Edward sleeps in empty space now, alone. He walks around all day, alone, even if Shay is with him. He considers telling the therapist that even though Shay is still his friend, their deeper connection — which he'd always known was his oxygen — has been slowly dying ever since he told her to back off in the gym. Shay is so strong that when she has to, she will break free and find air elsewhere, but he knows that he's not strong like her and that this was already his second chance. Edward understands that when whatever's between him and Shay finally dies, what's alive inside him will be done too.

Dr. Mike would want Edward to tell him all this, but Edward is disinclined to talk. He keeps his eyes on the window and has the sense that the tree is watching him in return.

John stays up every night now, until Edward

is in bed in the basement. He sticks his head through the door, checks to make sure his nephew is lying under sheets on the pullout bed. "Everything okay?" John says, and Edward nods and rolls over.

An hour later, when he's sure his aunt and uncle are asleep, Edward gets up, pulls on sweats and his Converse — his orange parka if it's really cold — and goes outside. He walks around the block several times, careful to stay out of view of Shay's bedroom. He counts the houses he passes, the number of windows, the patchwork of stars overhead. He craves motion and likes the near-darkness of the night sky and the black air between the trees. Sometimes, when the numbers begin to jumble in his head, he walks with his eyes closed. He never lets himself sit or lie down, though, in case he falls asleep and freezes, thus proving the grown-ups' fears valid.

At some point, when something inside him has eased, he returns to the basement and the pullout bed. The basement isn't quiet, but the noises are completely different from the noises in Shay's room. Perhaps because he's at the bottom of the house, the structure seems to shift and wheeze above his bed. He can hear the rasp of dry leaves through the closed windows. At least twice every night there's a loud *crack,* which makes him sit upright in bed, and stare into the shadows.

Inside, he doesn't want darkness. He keeps the light on in the adjoining bathroom, and a diffuse glow from the streetlight travels through the high basement windows. The only positive to having his own bedroom is that he doesn't have to be quiet in order not to disturb Shay. He doesn't have to pretend to sleep. He can cough, hit the mattress with his fist, talk to himself. He can roll from one side of the bed to the other. Eat a granola bar at 2:00 A.M. because his stomach is rumbling.

He hears Mrs. Tuhane's shrill whistle, recalls overhearing Shay — her voice spiky, excited — talking to a girl in French class about maybe going to a party this Friday down by the lake. Edward is staring through the high, narrow windows when the sky lightens and another day begins.

Mrs. Tuhane is obsessed with what she calls "form" and has him move his right foot a centimeter, push his hips back an iota, extend his arms until they are 100 percent straight. The football captain — a stocky red-haired kid — enters the weight room during a session. He grins at the sight of

285

Edward in a deep squat.

"Nice look, Adler," he says, and takes a photo with his phone. Mrs. Tuhane tells the kid off and orders him out of the room, but Edward knows it's too late. The image has already been texted to his friends. By the end of the day, kids on the football team drop into a squat when they see Edward, their faces mocking great concentration.

When Edward and Shay turn a corner and a shy boy with hair the color of wheat lowers into the squat position, Shay says, "You? Why are you doing this? You're not an asshole. You're better than this."

The boys goes pale, stands up, and runs away.

Edward sits through his three afternoon classes with his notebook open and a pen in his hand, but never writes anything down. His teachers seem to be talking from a great distance. He and Shay walk home from school, and he pretends everything is normal between them. He knows Shay's irritable because she senses something is wrong too, something beyond Edward moving out of her bedroom, but she can't put her finger on the glitch. *What's between us is dying,* he thinks. *We won't be friends for much longer.*

She says, "Did Arundhi ask to see you too?"

"No. Why?"

"Hmm. I think my grades dropped. He's probably going to give me a talk about needing to do my best to get into college."

"No, too young. Not college." Edward is too worn out to speak in full sentences. "Something else. My grades dropped too."

"Well, he wouldn't give you that talk, because you can get into any college you want, even if your grades suck. All you have to do is write about the crash in your personal essay."

Edward shakes his head. He has a sudden wish for it to be the middle of the night, when he walks with his eyes shut under stars. He doesn't want to be in daylight, itchy inside his skin, listening to Shay talk about things she knows nothing about.

He closes his eyes for a few steps now and then has a thought that makes him open them. "How come none of the kids at school like me?"

"What are you talking about?" Shay pauses. "Some of them like you."

"I've hardly spoken to them." How has this not occurred to him before? He's lived in this town for two and half years, and he's been so relieved that most of the students leave him alone that he's never thought to wonder why. He pictures the football captain, his awful friends, Margaret, the girls with the scented ChapStick whose lockers are near his own. Then there are the kids who never look at him — as if on principle — and turn away whenever he approaches.

"Oh," Shay makes a face. "They're total idiots, and you should ignore them. They think you're lucky. Some of them are jealous."

He thinks he must have misheard. "Lucky?"

Shay gives him a sideways glance as they step onto their street. "There are three kids in our grade who have a parent in jail. A bunch are on food stamps and, you know, everyone has some sad story. But you got famous for yours."

Edward breathes the cold air.

"Also," she says, in an apologetic tone, "it doesn't help that they see you as a privileged white boy who's going to be loaded, when you get the insurance money."

Lucky. Edward tests the word inside his head, as if considering its weight.

"Like I said, you should ignore them."

He feels himself darken further on the inside, a lightbulb that's burning out. Nothing she'd said was incorrect. *Maybe I'm an*

asshole, he thinks. None of this has occurred to him before.

That night when he finishes his neighborhood walk, Edward circles the house in the
shadows. He's thinking about the sneer on
the football captain's face, and the possibility that he might be an asshole himself, and
these thoughts demand motion. There's
another thought too, one that's been following Edward for weeks, which is now tapping
him on the shoulder. Tomorrow is his
fifteenth birthday. Tomorrow, he'll turn the
same age his brother was when he died.
Edward rounds the four corners of the dark
house, again and again. He notices the
garage on one of the laps and heads over to
circumnavigate that shape too.

The backyard is long, and the garage,
separate from the house, is set far back. It
abuts the hedge, and beyond the hedge are
the woods. Edward has never gone near the
garage — John and Lacey both park their
cars in the driveway. He'd never given the
structure any thought. Never wondered
what it was used for, what was inside. He
realizes that he's limited his environments
since he moved here. The kitchen, the living
room, Shay's room, the playground, school.

In the darkness now, with grass dampening his sneakers, he feels a small satisfaction at taking himself to a new place, even if it is just a garage. He walks around the building, then stops to peer through the windows. He can see only his own reflection, ghostly and serious. He wonders what his aunt and uncle keep inside, since they don't use the space for their cars.

There's a door on the side, and he tries the knob, expecting it to be locked. It's not; when he twists, the door swings inward. As he steps inside, the dark room looks like an extension of the backyard. Chunky hedges, a house-like structure in the center, rectangles of varying shades of darkness, tangles of uncut charcoal-colored grass. Edward stays next to the door. His vision improves slightly, and he sees that there's a flashlight plugged into the socket right beside him. This is John's handiwork — every room in the house has the same feature, in case of emergency. Edward pulls out the flashlight and switches it on.

In the center of the room is a workbench, with tools hanging off hooks on the sides. The setup looks too neat to be in regular use, and Edward wonders what his uncle builds here. He tries to imagine John sanding down an old table, but the image makes no sense. Stepping closer, he sees a stack of laptops, and smiles. Of course — this isn't for building or fixing furniture; the workbench is for constructing and deconstructing computers. He's never seen his uncle anywhere near the garage, but John's an early riser, so he must come here before Edward and Lacey are awake.

In the corner, there's a faded green armchair of the kind usually owned by elderly ladies. Beside it is a bookcase. Edward points the flashlight at the shelves and sees that it's filled with what must be the complete works of only two authors: Zane Grey and Louis L'Amour. Edward double-checks, to see if there are other writers represented, but there aren't. *John comes out here and reads Westerns?* For some reason, Edward is certain that all of this belongs to John, not Lacey. The house is Lacey's; Edward knows this in his bones. This has to be where John keeps the messy odds and ends that his wife won't allow inside.

Edward sinks down in the green armchair, to see the world from John's seat. He's glad he came inside, glad he found a small distraction to delay his return to the basement. He would like to delay going to sleep tonight, and therefore delay waking up fifteen. There's a round table beside the armchair, with a stack of different-colored folders on it. By his feet are two large army-style duffel bags. Edward shifts one with his foot, and it moves easily. Whatever's inside the bag is very light. He shines his flashlight down and sees that both duffels are locked with padlocks.

He pulls the top folder onto his lap and opens it. There's a sheet of paper covered with John's neat handwriting, which Edward associates with the grocery list on the kitchen counter: *the nice apples, turkey breasts, soy milk, chocolate-covered almonds.* But this isn't a shopping list; it's a list of names, and beside each name is a number and letter: 34B, 12A, 27C. Only five of the names have no accompanying numbers.

Edward's fingertips begin to sweat against the sheet of paper.

There will be 191 names, he knows without counting. It's the flight list. The five names without accompanying seat numbers are the two pilots and the three flight attendants. Edward scans the list, looking for his own name. It's not there, but his brother's and father's and mother's names are written in John's neat script. His mother's row number is different from the rest of the Adler family. *You should have sat with us,* Edward thinks.

There are other documents below the flight list, and some of the papers feel different than the top one, thicker in consistency. He doesn't lift the top page, though, doesn't look further. He sits with the folder open on his lap, the flashlight in his hand. Edward remembers sitting in the NTSB basement hallway beside his uncle and thinks: *So, you're still gathering information.*

He watches himself return the folder to the table. His body, as much as his brain, knows that he can't do this alone. He plugs the flashlight in next to the door, and runs across the backyard in the direction of Shay's house. He throws pebbles — the smallest he can find, for fear of waking Besa or breaking the glass — against Shay's window until she appears, her hair wild, her glasses on.

"What in the world?" she says, once she's pulled the window open. Her voice is barely loud enough to reach him; she doesn't want to wake Besa either. "Are you okay?"

"I have something to show you," he says back, and he feels a wave of relief when her face lights up.

"Hey," she says, "happy birthday."

"Oh." He glances up at the night sky, at the punched-out stars in the black blanket. "It's after midnight?"

She nods, and he can tell, even though they haven't spoken about it, that Shay understands that this birthday is different, and more complicated. She's downstairs two minutes later, wearing sweats, and Edward leads the way to the garage. He feels ridiculous and exhausted, but also giddy, as Shay whispers questions from behind him.

"What made you look in the garage?

"Why were you up at this hour?

"If you were going for walks, why didn't you get me? I totally would have come. . . ."

Inside the garage, he points the flashlight at the chair, then the bookcase, the stacks of folders, and the locked duffel bags. He spots a small matching green footstool tucked under the armchair, which he pulls out for himself, while Shay sits down on the chair.

He points at the top folder, and Shay puts it on her lap. She looks down and then up again at Edward.

"What?" he says. "Go ahead, open it."

"No." She says the word slowly, as if the syllable is a surprise to her.

"No?"

"I'm not going to open it unless you promise me something." She pulls herself up straight. "You have to promise to stop

294

being weird. You have to be normal with me from now on. You can't go back to being all icy and far away tomorrow morning." She pauses, then says more quietly, "I can't take it anymore."

He looks into her eyes, startled. He realizes that they seem unfamiliar and that he hasn't looked at her eyes for a long time. He's been looking at the ground, looking away, scuffling inside himself. Edward understands, in that moment, that it's been *him* all along, and not her. When Shay had said things were normal between them, she meant it. He'd convinced himself something between them was broken, when in truth the broken thing was him. Edward's cheeks grow hot. He, alone, had almost destroyed the most important part of his life.

"I'm sorry," he says. "I promise."

"Good." She nods. "I've missed you, you weirdo." Shay opens the folder, and he watches her scan the flight list. "Is this what I think it is?"

He presses his hands to his hot cheeks.

She whispers, "You're not here. What was your seat number?"

"31A."

When she's done reading, she lifts the top page aside and reveals a photograph of a blond woman. The woman is leaning forward slightly, smiling at the camera as if she's trying to please whoever's behind it. It's a different photograph than the one Edward saw in the school parking lot, but he still recognizes her. He says, "That's Gary's girlfriend."

"Oh," Shay murmurs. "Poor Linda."

Next there's a photo of an unsmiling Benjamin Stillman in uniform, but Edward stays quiet. He's never mentioned the soldier to Shay and has no idea how to explain who Benjamin is. How can he say, *I only met him for a few minutes, but I think about him at least once a day and want to get strong because of him,* without sounding stupid, or crazy?

The following photos are of his family. His mother. His father. Jordan wearing the parka that Edward's wearing right now. Then there's a photo of the large woman who had bells on her skirt. She looks like she's dancing; her arms are in the air. The photographs are so immediate — especially of his family — that Edward feels slightly seasick. It's a relief when strangers appear. Many of the people look a little familiar but he can't place them. Maybe he walked by their row on the plane. Maybe they stood in line together for the bathroom. His eyes fall on the rich-looking guy with the slicked hair, whom he does recognize. The man is smiling widely, but he looks a little angry, or mean, like he's about to tell the photographer what's wrong with him or her.

Shay turns the photo of the rich guy over, and that's how they discover that there are notes on the back of each picture. His name: Mark Lassio. His age, presumably at the time of the crash. A list of the names of living relatives, which in his case is only one, a brother named Jax Lassio, with an address in Florida.

There are more than a hundred photographs in the folder, including two official-looking headshots of the pilots: one smiling under a salt-and-pepper mustache; the other, younger pilot somber but handsome. Edward feels their faces take up space inside him, as if the plane is being peopled within his skin. His arms are the wings. His torso, the body of the plane. The men and women file in, one by one.

When they've looked at every photo, Shay closes the folder. They sit in the dimness without talking, and then Shay says, "I bet John started putting this together after you came back from D.C."

"What?" Edward's hand rests on the folder. There's so much within it, and for the moment he's within it, and so what

Shay's saying doesn't make sense.

"That's when he and Lacey stopped sleeping together, so that timing makes sense."

Edward looks at her. "What are you talking about?"

"Haven't you noticed that John's been sleeping on the bed in the nursery?"

Edward pictures the nursery, with its stacked boxes and single bed. "I don't . . . I never go up to the second floor. How do you know where he's sleeping?"

Shay swoops her hair up and twists it into a bun with mystifying speed and accuracy. Edward notices, not for the first time, that she has breasts now, the shape of which are visible through her sweatshirt. He blushes, and looks down.

"Lacey told my mom. First she said it was because of an argument, but then she said it was actually because John snores. But that can't be the real problem, because my mom says with the sleeping pills Lacey takes, there's no chance she could hear him."

Edward scans the shadowy room. He'd thought this was a place where his uncle read novels and examined circuit boards, but there's a darker exploration taking place. The shadows stretch toward him, swollen with potential secrets. "Lacey takes sleeping pills?"

"The doctor gave them to her after the crash. Big horse pills. My mom worries that they're too strong." Shay notices the look on his face and gives him a comforting smile. "Don't worry. I know you don't notice things. I'll be better from now on about pointing them out to you."

A week earlier, a student had brought cupcakes to French class to celebrate their teacher's imminent maternity leave, and Edward had been confused because he somehow hadn't noticed the teacher's gigantic belly or registered any talk of her upcoming departure. With a cupcake in his hand, as the news sank in, he wondered how he'd been able to miss something so obvious.

"Lacey does always go to bed early," he says, trying to catch up.

Shay nods. "She takes a pill right after dinner."

Edward presses his palm against the folder, which contains the names and faces and numbers his uncle has gathered. He thinks of all the faces at school that dislike him. He wonders how much else he's missing and feels sympathetic to his uncle's instinct to do research and take notes.

"If it makes you feel better," Shay says, "you notice things I don't. What do you think brought you out here tonight? I think you were drawn here somehow. You sensed that there was something meaningful going on."

Edward shakes his head, dismissing that idea, even though at the same time he's pleased that she can still imagine something special within him.

"Lacey must be upset that John's doing this." Shay pokes the duffel bag closest to her. "What do you think's in these? It must have to do with the flight."

That hadn't occurred to Edward. He looks at the enormous bags with suspicion.

"We should open them. There are more folders too. Let's wait till tomorrow, though. You're looking a little crazy around the eyes. No need to rush."

Edward tries to appear celebratory the next night, when he finds that Lacey has tied a balloon to the back of his chair at the kitchen table. "Hey, big guy," his uncle says. "Fifteen, huh? You kids are really growing up."

Edward works his face into a smile. He wonders if his aunt or uncle is going to mention that this was Jordan's age. Probably they won't, and then he'll be left wondering if they don't remember or if they simply don't know what to say about it.

Shay gave him a pep talk before dinner: "I know you hate your birthday, but try to suck it up for John and Lacey."

Edward had nodded. Despite the unease this particular birthday delivers, he is sustained by a sodden gratitude, because what's between him and Shay has been revived. He's thankful that the folder in the garage made him reach out to Shay and therefore stopped him from blowing up his own life. Earlier today, Shay had looked at him and said, with apparent relief, "You're being normal again."

Edward twirls spaghetti around his fork and tries to casually observe his aunt and uncle. Next to him, Shay appears to be doing the same thing. Edward checked the single bed in the nursery that morning, and it was clear John had slept there. His pajamas were folded over a chair, and the bedsheets were mussed. However, Lacey doesn't appear to dislike her husband. She passes John the bowl of spaghetti and smiles when he makes a dumb joke about fifteen being the processing speed of his first computer.

It occurs to Edward that he hasn't seen Lacey throw a lightning bolt at her husband in a long time, nor has she clung to John like a needy child. She's become steadier, but also more distant. Shay's theory of marital unrest blames John for having a creepy hobby — collecting information on the crash — but Edward wonders if it's actually Lacey who has changed and therefore thrown the balance off between them.

"How did you guys meet?" Shay says.

"Us?" Lacey looks surprised. "Oh gosh. We met in an Italian restaurant on the Upper East Side. We had a friend in common, and he introduced us. Then we had a big group dinner and sat next to each other."

"It was snowing," John says.

"It *was* snowing. We got married so quickly after that." Lacey smiles. "Your mother told me I was crazy, but we were both ready to be married."

Shay narrows her eyes at Edward, and he can hear her thoughts: *It was snowing. Lacey's smiling. I think they still like each other.* But this isn't convincing enough for Edward. He remembers how his parents would sometimes start fighting in the middle of what seemed like a normal conversation. The vein on the side of his dad's forehead would pulse, and his mom's voice climbed a few octaves higher. Edward and his brother would look at each other in surprise, as if to ask, *Did you see that com-*

ing? If he couldn't understand the patterns of his own parents' marriage, what hope does he have of doing so with his aunt and uncle? Besides, he's Jordan's age now, and his brother wouldn't keep quiet.

He says to John, "Why are you sleeping in the nursery?"

The question makes everyone freeze. Lacey has her napkin pressed to her mouth; Shay and John are mid-bite. Edward notes the pause with a flicker of satisfaction.

John's cheeks darken. "I sleep there when my snoring bothers Lacey."

Lacey's napkin is gripped in her fist. "Why do you ask?" Her voice lifts at the end of the question, as if trying to force a lighter tone.

Edward says, "I guess I wondered if everything was okay."

This comment removes the air from the room again, and Edward knows, in the silence, that everything is not okay. Lacey and John exchange a look.

Shay clears her throat and says, "There are nose bands I read about that apparently stop snoring. I think you can get them in the pharmacy."

John says, "Thank you, Shay. I'll look into that."

"Where people sleep doesn't *matter.*"

303

Lacey points a look at Edward, which makes him half-remember saying something similar in the first few months of his stay, when she was unhappy about him sleeping at Shay's house.

"Now cake," John says, as if it's a command.

They sing "Happy Birthday" while his uncle carries the multilayer cake over and gently places it in front of Edward.

"Make a wish," John says.

Wishes are dangerous, pointless, and part of why Edward hates his birthday. He wishes he could ask his uncle if what he's gathering in the garage is helping him, but Edward feels like he needs to find that answer for himself. He thinks, *Are you doing this to protect me? Is it working?*

When Shay compliments the cake, Lacey says, "It was my grandmother's recipe, which Edward's loved since he was tiny."

"Yes," Edward says, but the truth is that she has him confused with Jordan. It was Jordan's favorite cake, and their mom had made it for Jordan on *his* birthdays. Edward's favorite dessert — what he'd had for his birthdays while his parents were alive — was an ice cream sundae. But Lacey had been so pleased that she remembered his special dessert that he could never tell her the truth. He forks bites of his brother's favorite cake into his mouth. He ate it on his thirteenth and fourteenth birthdays too. He will, he assumes, eat it on his sixteenth.

John yawns and stands up.

"What are you doing?" Lacey says, with disapproval in her voice.

John looks around him, surprised. "I'm sorry," he says, and sits back down. "That was rude. I didn't mean to rush you."

"You're tired," Edward says.

His uncle frowns, and something about his expression makes Edward understand that insomnia and nighttime disruption don't belong only to him. In the dark, flat middle of the night, Edward had assumed that he was the only one awake, the only one who wasn't allowed rest. But now teenagers are crossing lawns and John is choosing between beds, and Edward is another year older, another year distant from his family.

Edward and Shay return to the garage at midnight, when all the grown-ups have been in bed for over an hour, so they deem it to be safe.

Shay taps one of the duffel bags with her sneaker. "I estimate each one weighs about ten pounds. Maybe fifteen? They're not as heavy as they look. And whatever's in them is packed with some kind of paper. They crinkle."

"It might just be his summer clothes, or stuff for Goodwill."

"Then they wouldn't bother to lock the bags. Nobody does that. Something important must be in them."

They take their seats: Edward on the footstool, Shay on the chair. Their plan is to finish going through the folders tonight — Shay wants to take notes on the contents — and turn their attention to opening the bags tomorrow. One folder contains pages of information on the Airbus A321 aircraft. There are diagrams of the plane, measurements of the wingspan, the engines, and the fuel capacity. The history of that kind of plane, and its frequency of use by different airlines. There are photographs of the underbelly of an Airbus A321, photographs of it from above, and one of it in the air. At the bottom of the folder are photographs of the crash scene. Edward can't make his eyes focus on them. He hands them to Shay, and she puts them back in the folder.

The other folder contains printouts of social-media mentions of either Edward or the flight. The top half is from a Facebook account called *Miracle Boy*. The avatar is the only photograph taken of Edward in the hospital. He has a bandage around his head and is looking to the side. Edward can barely recognize himself in the image. Most of the posts are URL links for news articles about the flight, but there are also posts with writing, which were cross-posted to the Twitter account with the same name. *I am scared. I'm lonely. I miss my mom. I don't know why I'm here. Maybe God did save me, but I'm just a kid.*

"Who would write this?" Edward whispers. "How could they think it was okay to do?"

"I saw these in the beginning," Shay says. "Online. I didn't know you yet, obviously, and I wondered if you were writing them in the hospital."

"I could hardly swallow," he says, "much less set up a Twitter account." But part of him thinks, *Did I?* His brain is undependable, with no fact solid enough to bear his weight. He imagines himself lying in the hospital bed, his leg in a cast, typing his feelings into an iPad.

Shay holds the flashlight between cupped hands, as if it were the contents of a prayer. She shakes her head and whispers, "We've gone through everything. We should go."

Before they leave the garage, they reread

the flight list — they are both trying to memorize the names — and check for new photographs in the first folder. John has added one since yesterday. It's a photo of a red-haired woman wearing a white coat, with a stethoscope around her neck. She looks at the camera with an expression that suggests pausing for the photo was an inconvenience. Her name is written on the back: *Dr. Nancy Louis.* She's survived by her parents, who have a Connecticut address.

Edward recognizes her. The memory, which is tied to so much else, makes his throat tighten.

"You knew her?" Shay says.

"No," he says, but that *no* hurts, and so does the last glance he gives the doctor before putting back the folder, and heading out the door, and across the frozen lawn.

The next morning after math class, Margaret appears at his side and says, "It's been bothering me, so I had to check. You didn't get in trouble *at all* for shoving me, did you?"

Edward looks down at her. He's grown three inches in the last six months and is constantly surprised to see the tops of his classmates' heads when he walks down the halls. "No," he says. "I'm really sorry. It was

308

a mistake. I kind of freaked out; that's why I'm not in gym class anymore."

Then he sighs, because the football captain is approaching. He spots Edward and shows all his teeth in what Edward assumes is intended to be a smile, then puts his hand up for a mandatory high five. Edward raises his hand and slaps the kid's palm. When he turns back to Margaret, she's looking at him with disgust. "He's not my friend," Edward says.

"How many APs are you going to take when we're juniors and seniors?"

"I don't know." He looks at her in surprise. "Do you already know that?"

"Seven."

"Wow." Edward doesn't know what else to say. He hadn't known there were that many AP classes on offer. He wishes he hadn't pushed her in gym class, and he wishes he wasn't having this confusing conversation now. He's aware of sweat lining the back of his neck.

"There were eleven Asian people on your flight." Margaret says this in a lower voice. "One of them lived in the same town as my auntie."

Her words travel directly inside Edward, to the place where the flight roster is now imprinted, and where he had assumed by the spelling of certain names that eleven people were Asian. Margaret has just given him a confirmation that feels like a puzzle piece locking into place, and he's grateful. He understands now that this was why she approached him; this is what she cares about.

"I know their names," he says, in the same low tone she used.

He thinks for a second that Margaret's going to demand that he recite them for her, but she nods, apparently satisfied, and walks away.

12:44 P.M.

Flight 2977 trails in the jet stream of all the aircraft that came before it. The men who strapped flapping metal wings called ornithopters to their arms, the gliders, the hot-air balloons, the aerial steam carriages, the Ezekiel Airships, and many more. All of the people on this flight were born during the age of commercial air travel, and so everyone, to some extent, takes for granted the fact that they are able to sit in the sky.

Benjamin is reluctant to sit when he leaves the bathroom. He can't tolerate hours folded into a cramped seat. He stands near the back of the plane, out of the way. He looks at the small window to his right, at the branches of water etched on the glass. The branches fade as he watches — under his gaze, the rain stops. The sky, as if taking a breath, lightens.

He feels something shift inside him in response to the change in the sky, and he

311

thinks, for the first time, about the reality of his life after this plane ride. Lolly will meet him in the airport. He stops there and thinks, *Maybe that's enough.*

He hasn't lived with, or near, his grandmother since he was twelve. Maybe he can turn the focus of his life to thanking her. Even if he didn't deserve to be saved — in the hallway of the apartment building where his parents squatted or on the dry dirt of the Afghan field with blood gushing from his side — Lolly saved him when he was four years old. She fed, clothed, and bathed him. Read to him. Yelled at him, when he talked back or when he stopped talking.

He was eleven when he found out she'd gotten him a full scholarship to military school. He'd gone mute, to punish Lolly and to keep himself from crying. Lolly had seemed more offended by the silence than anything he'd done to date. She shouted at him, morning, noon, and night. *Open your mouth, child! Don't you ghost around! If you want to be in this life, you got to speak up! I'm doing you a favor! I'm getting you out of this place!*

He'd kept his mouth shut but thought: *I love this place. This place is home.*

Maybe he can devote himself to the service of this old lady. He could clock in and out of the desk job, recruiting new grunts and completing their paperwork, and spend his money and free time on Lolly. They could go to the movies. Lolly likes jigsaw puzzles — she always has one spread out on the kitchen table; he could buy her a brand-new one every week, so she doesn't have to keep redoing the frayed, incomplete sets she bought at the dime store. They could drive to the ocean, which is only a few miles from where she lives but which no one in their neighborhood ever visits, as if the great blue sea isn't there for them.

One of the boys from across the aisle — the younger brother — walks toward him and then comes to a stop.

"Are you waiting for the bathroom?" the boy asks.

Benjamin shakes his head.

"Oh," the boy says, and sticks his hands in the pockets of his jeans. "Can I ask — are you in the army?"

The kid is skinny, with a worried expression and a mess of dark hair. He's probably about the same age Benjamin was when he was dropped off at military boarding school. Benjamin didn't know shit at that age. The oldest boys made fun of him that first semester, and though he knew their intentions were mean-spirited, Benjamin couldn't make sense of the insults. They were mock-ing him, but which part? Luckily, he had a growth spurt over Christmas break and came back thirty pounds heavier than any kid his age, so they left him alone.

But he'd never figured out that interper-sonal language. He'd done well on every academic test but remained stupid socially. If he had been savvier, he would have put himself on the officer path and found his way to West Point. Mostly white boys went there, but to make their numbers, the army was always on the lookout for enterprising young men of color. But Benjamin never shook the right hand, or even knew the right hand to shake. He kept his mouth shut throughout high school and was funneled directly into basic training afterward. It shouldn't be a surprise that he'd confused his own thoughts to the point that he had no idea who he was or what he wanted. He pictures Gavin and feels a deep ache.

"I'm leaving the army," he says, and the sadness inside him morphs into incredulity. He says it again, but more loudly. He wants to hear what the words sound like in the air. "I'm leaving the army. I'm on my way home."

The boy nods, like this makes sense. Does this make sense? How can this make sense?

He has no expertise, no experience outside the military. He can handle a .50-caliber rifle better than almost anyone, march impeccably in formation, and walk through a forest wearing a seventy-five-pound pack without making a sound. Are those skills applicable to civilian life?

The boy says, "It must be really stressful, knowing you could die at any time."

It is, Benjamin thinks, as if this too is a new idea.

He considers the boy. It feels like so long ago that he was that young. "You're in school?"

"Kind of. My dad homeschools my brother and me."

Benjamin gives a smile so small no one else would identify it as such. "What's your name?"

"Eddie."

"I'm Benjamin."

"I should . . ." The boy points at the bathroom door. "It was nice to meet you. Sir." He adds the last word as an afterthought.

"You too, Eddie." Benjamin watches the boy walk into one of the bathrooms and lock the door.

Linda tracks the mousier flight attendant as

she makes her way down the aisle with a trash bag. *Hurry up,* she thinks. *Please hurry up.* She's trapped by the foul-smelling, untouched food on her tray. She wants it gone. She wants the gray sky gone and a blue sky in its place. She wants Florida, and her encroaching mass, gone. She wants off this plane. She imagines her moment of exit: seeing Gary waiting with a bouquet of flowers in the center of a crowd of strangers. It's the moment featured in nearly every romantic movie. The girl exits the plane looking lipsticked, dewy, well rested. The man's eyes light up at the sight of her.

Linda looks down. Her clothes, so crisp when she put them on, now look dingy and faintly gray. Her hands are chapped from the dry air. Her hair — she puts her hand up to touch it and immediately brushes against a rough spot — is undoubtedly not at its best. She imagines Gary's eyes widening in dismay. The flowers wilting.

"What do you think she does for a living?" Florida says.

"Who?"

Florida points to the sleeping woman on Linda's right, who is still draped in a blue scarf.

"I envy people who can sleep like that," Florida says. "I've had insomnia for as long as I can remember."

"She must be really tired," Linda says. "Maybe she works two jobs and never gets enough rest."

Florida narrows her eyes, as if making a mathematical calculation. "Nope. Her shoes are expensive. My guess is that she's over-tired from trying to satisfy multiple boy-friends. It's exhausting to lead that kind of secretive life, not to mention have that much sex."

Linda laughs, an openmouthed hiccup.

"Sweetheart," Florida says.

"What?"

"You should laugh more. What a wonder-ful sound."

"Shhhh," Linda says. "You'll wake her."

They both grin up at the flight attendant, who has just appeared beside their seats with the garbage bag. Linda lifts her tray toward her, permeated with relief.

Mark hates coming down: off drugs, off running a Spartan Race, off sixteen straight hours of tracking patterns in the market. It was the coming down that made him finally kick cocaine last year. The headache, the scratchy sensation *inside* his skin, the dry eyeballs, the sluggish brain — the fact that these symptoms were the aftermath of every single delicious high became intolerable. He loved getting high, had no access issues — the dealer was one of the assistants in his office, a popular young kid with a bright future — and Mark operated, if he did say so himself, magnificently while intoxicated. He'd seen sloppy users — hell, he saw them every day at work. Guys rubbing their noses, with obnoxiously large pupils, talking so fast they had to repeat themselves three times in order to be understood. No one could even tell when Mark was coked; he prided himself on this fact. Well, his brother could tell, but Jax was a special case and he hardly ever saw him. Mark worked hard on not thinking about him. Thoughts of Jax felt like coming down, and he had built his post-cocaine life around avoiding that feeling at all costs.

Mark feels, buckled into his seat, on the verge of that sensation now. He's at the top of the mountain, still coursing with sex and adrenaline and a feeling of holy-shit-did-that-really-happen? He has to either keep his engine revved at this level or knock himself out so he can remain unconscious for the decline. He doesn't have the necessary narcotics in his carry-on to engender that kind of blackout, so his only alternative is to keep going.

He looks around.

"Are you all right?" His seatmate gives him a look of maternal concern.

Jesus, he thinks. *No way. Just no. Don't push that shit on me.*

He stands up. He'd like to spar with Crispin again, but the old man's eyes are closed and his skin looks translucent. His veins are visible through papery skin. Mark shudders. *Sickness, old age, decline — unacceptable.*

He finds Veronica in the galley kitchen, next to the cockpit door. Actually, he notices — his senses so acute he can't help but process everything — that he's surrounded by doors. The massive plane entrance is six paces behind him, the cockpit door to his left, and the first-class bathroom directly to his back.

"Hey," he says, in what he hopes is a charming voice. He goes for an equally charming smile, but both efforts feel like a throw at a dartboard. It's hard to hit the bull's-eye. He gives himself an 80 percent chance now of having missed both marks.

Veronica is crouched down in the corner, folding what look like cellophane squares and placing them in a container. When she hears Mark's voice, she stands and turns in one movement, and her grace takes his breath away.

His mother used to drag him and Jax to the ballet when they were boys, and though Mark complained, he'd secretly loved watching the singular moments of beauty. A ballerina pirouetting. A leap, which ended in another dancer's arms. This was the loveliness — the magic — Veronica brought to a small galley kitchen in an airplane thirty thousand feet in the air.

"I'm grateful for you," he says, and then he thinks, aghast: *I'm grateful for you? Jesus Christ, you fucking idiot.*

"What did you say?" She looks genuinely confused.

With his slow-motion, super-detailed vision, Mark sees the coolness that had been on her face when she turned, the certainty that she was about to shut him down and send him away, be replaced with this confusion, this vulnerability.

He sees another door. They are now on all sides. He's just got to push through this one, and he certainly knows how to push.

"You have a job to do," he says. "I appreciate that. And I promise I won't bother you again. I would simply like to take you to dinner tomorrow night. In L.A."

She looks at him, her red lipstick perfect, her eyes divine.

"Please say yes," he says. "To one date."

She doesn't speak right away. He can tell she is a master of pauses. He waits, with a patience unfamiliar to him.

"Yes," she says finally. "To one date."

"One date," he repeats, and the engine in his chest whirs. He's surprised to realize he's truly grateful to this woman. The coming down has been postponed. He will coast on this win, until he's seated across the table from her tomorrow night.

Jordan stares at the open book, willing his mind to focus. His brother and father are working on a sudoku puzzle and keep passing it back and forth in front of his face. He wants no part of their geekery, and he knows that his father would never disturb him while he's reading. He's in a safe zone, and the book is good — *A Prayer for Owen Meany* — but he's unable to concentrate. His brain keeps peeking forward, toward L.A.

He hadn't fought the idea of the move, unlike Eddie. His brother had cried and begged to stay in New York. "This is our home," he'd said. "We can't live out there. Los Angeles has earthquakes. Everyone drives in cars. We'll have to wear sunscreen." Their parents had promised Eddie a piano in their house, and lots of books, but he only gave up arguing when more of his belongings were in moving boxes than out of them.

The idea of sunshine, the beach, and girls in bikinis sounded fine to Jordan, though it was hard to understand the logistics. Did kids his age really show up by the ocean on weekends with towels and a packed lunch? Everyone lived in houses with lawns. There would be no deli on the corner. There would be no Mahira. Jordan realizes that he'd assumed, when he'd kissed her the last time, that a new Mahira would magically appear in L.A. and at every other step in his future.

He rereads the same sentence for the fourth time and thinks, *But they won't actually be her lips.* How has this not occurred to him before? He doesn't want to kiss just any girl. It has to be the right one — at least he assumes this is true. He has, after all, never kissed anyone other than Mahira. Jordan straightens in his chair, in order to be taller than his brother and father. The L.A. sunshine suddenly looks white and bland. The bikinied girls look white and bland. Mahira had chosen him, and he had been lucky. What if his luck has run out or was tied to New York City and her?

"Dad," Eddie says, "remember how you told us that every whole number can be written as a product of prime numbers?"

Bruce nods.

"Why is that? I mean, that's super weird, isn't it? That it works for every single number?"

Their father regards Eddie. "You're asking me why it's true?"

I want to turn this plane around, Jordan thinks. He feels punctured, stupid, young. He can feel the falseness of his actions. He drew attention to himself by opting out in the security line. He drew attention to himself by ordering a vegan airplane meal. He drew attention to himself every time he flouted his father's curfews and rules. He hadn't kissed Mahira; she had kissed him. It had been *her* idea, not his, and it was the one part of his life that had been secret and genuine. Otherwise, apart from her, he is a blowhard, a showman, playacting at real life. Jordan misses her in a new, more acute way. The feeling twists like hot metal in his chest. She had been at the core of him — maybe she was the core of him? — and he hadn't appreciated that until now.

"That's a great question," Bruce says. "But I don't know the answer. I mean, why is anything true?"

Jordan shuts his novel.

"You tired, buddy?" his father says.

He thinks: *I'll text Mahira when I land. I'll tell her what I feel.*

"Look," Eddie says, excitement in his voice, "the rain has stopped."

JANUARY 2016

Edward and Shay end up having to wait to open the duffel bags until after the holidays, because Besa is — as Shay puts it — batshit crazy about Christmas and New Year's, which means she more or less stops sleeping for the duration, so they can't safely visit the garage. At 2:00 A.M. Besa was likely to be in the kitchen baking polvorones de canela or mulling wine. She would move to the living room at some point, take a short nap on the couch, and then commence with wrapping presents or redecorating the Christmas tree. Before her cousins arrived on New Year's, she draped the dining room walls with red, yellow, green, and white streamers — each color solicited a different kind of luck — and baked buns called pan dulce. At midnight on New Year's Eve, she opened the front door and swept out the previous year's bad luck with a broom.

"Is she like this every year?" Edward

asked, because he had no memory of Besa attacking the holidays in this manner. Shay nodded wearily, while building a tall stack of cookies to bring to her room, where she hid for as much of each day as possible.

Edward's sleep worsened over the holiday period, which he attributed to a diet of mostly sugar and the frustration of not being able to visit the garage. Dark circles appeared beneath his eyes, and his aunt told him that if he didn't look less terrible soon, she would bring him to the doctor. In an effort to wear his body out, Edward forced himself to eat kale, drink Sleepytime tea before bed, and lift the dumbbells he kept in the basement. Each day he considered stealing one of Lacey's sleeping pills, thinking that they would solve the problem, but the strength of the pills scared him. He worried that if he swallowed one, he might never wake up.

On the first Monday back to school — even though he's relieved that life has returned to normal and he and Shay can visit the garage that night — he's half-asleep through every class. He trudges to Principal Arundhi's office when the final bell rings, to see how the ferns fared over the break. He picks up his watering can from its usual spot inside the door.

"Happy New Year, Edward," the principal says.

"Happy New Year." The words are hard to get out of Edward's mouth; they jumble like marbles for a moment in his throat. He realizes how little he's spoken that day.

While studying the stem of a spider fern, the principal says, "I've been meaning to ask you, what would you think about joining the math club?"

Edward blinks. "Me? Uh, I guess I've never thought about math club."

"You're a fine natural mathematician. Perhaps you should consider it."

"No, thank you."

"How about debate, then, or is there a sport you like? I fancied fencing when I was young, but I've never been able to muster enough interest for a fencing club here." The principal's mustache droops for a moment, as if in memory of that failure.

Edward focuses on watering in a slow, steady circle around the periphery of the fern, and then a smaller circle at the base of the stem.

"I just think, Edward, that it might be good for you to join a group of some kind. To broaden your circle. Humans need community, for our emotional health. We need connection, a sense of belonging. We are

327

not built to thrive in isolation."

"I'm not isolated," Edward says. "I have my aunt and uncle. And Shay."

"I myself belong to a botanical club that meets twice a month. We help each other with our research, share information, and eat very fine cookies."

Edward says, "Shay thinks I can get into any college I want, as long as I write about the crash in my essay. Do you think that's true?"

The principal turns to face him. "She said that, did she?"

He nods.

Principal Arundhi smooths his mustache. "And you object to that idea?"

"Of course. It's not fair. It would mean that I got into college, regardless of my grades or how hard I worked, just because something bad happened to me."

"Some might call that affirmative action." The man smiles. "If it offends you, Edward, then I suggest that you study harder and improve your marks — I've heard about the erratic nature of your homework."

"I don't want to join a team."

The older man regards him. "Then you should not do so. Please don't think I care about your résumé, or the depth of your college application, when I speak of things like this. I am thinking, more or less, of my ferns."

Edward wonders if his lack of sleep has now landed him in a spot where he's not processing information correctly. "Your ferns?"

"Well, any living thing. A fern either grows or it dies. I would like" — he stops for a moment, considering — "I would like to do anything I can to ensure that you keep growing."

Edward feels the kindness of the man across the room and at the same time thinks that his team, his community, is in the folder in the garage. It is the 191 people who died on the flight. It's the men and women whose faces stare from the photographs, who ask questions of him that he can't answer. *Why did you survive, and not me?*

"Sir, can I be done for the day?"

The principal continues to study him, his face sad. It is a kind of deep sadness that Edward recognizes, and he feels a shard of his own sadness rise to the surface.

"When in doubt, read books," Principal Arundhi says. He speaks quickly, as if worried this might be his last opportunity to share his thoughts. "Educate yourself. Education has always saved me, Edward.

Learn about the mysteries."

The boy looks at him, and believes him. Believes that education saved him, believes that he had once been a person who needed to be saved. "Thank you, sir," he says, and turns to leave.

On the way home, Edward can identify different blades of grass within the clumps. Stratus clouds blanket the sky, and he can identify where one cloud ends and another begins. In his fatigue, he's seeing the boundaries that separate one thing from another. The gnarled tree on their corner is made of so many pieces: roots, branches, micro-branches, the distinct wrinkles on the bark. Edward thinks of the outer façade — the bark — of his school, with so many internal parts making up the organism. Chairs, lockers, children young enough to cry when someone insults them. Teachers, janitors, all the noise, the moving herd of growing humans. The students who hate Edward, who feel worse off than him, even though his whole life fell out of the sky. Edward finds that he's not mad at their hatred. Maybe it *is* worse to have a father in jail, to live in a town that's mostly white when your skin is brown, to find homework difficult even when you try your best. How would he know?

There are no cars in the driveway. Lacey is at the hospital, John at work. Shay will be in her bedroom, reading or doing her homework. Edward decides to go to the garage now, even though it's daytime. He'll ignore the duffel bags; those are a mystery to be solved with Shay. *I can lie on the floor,* he thinks. *No one will see me.* He has a desire to be near the photographs. But he's hungry, so he goes inside to get a snack first. He and Lacey both gasp when he thunders into the kitchen.

"Goodness!" she says.

"Your car's not here." Edward says this in a tone of accusation, while taking in the picture of his aunt sitting at the table in her work clothes — nice slacks and one of his mother's cardigans — and holding one of John's beers. Lacey never drinks beer.

"I got dropped off by a colleague. There was a retirement party for someone at work, and I drank a few glasses of champagne."

"Oh." Edward stands still, not sure what to do.

"Join me," Lacey says.

He gets an apple from the fruit bowl on the counter and then takes his normal seat across from her. He bites the apple and chews, more for the activity than the taste.

They sit in silence for a moment, and it occurs to Edward that this is the time of day when he used to come home and find his aunt waiting for him on the couch, with their soap opera cued to play. Neither of them has watched *General Hospital* for a long time. It had felt like a mutual hibernation, those hours spent side by side watching the most predictable of dramas. Edward wonders if his aunt ever misses that hour in the day; he sometimes does.

"Did you sleep better last night?"

"Yes," he lies.

"Good, good." Lacey's voice is slower than usual, and her posture less straight. She says, "Did I ever tell you that when I hold babies in the nursery, I sometimes think about you as a baby? You were a memorable baby, because you cried so much. Did your parents tell you about your colicky phase?"

Edward presses the apple to his mouth and nods.

"One day, I remember, your mom left Jordan with your dad and came out here. She hoped that the car ride, or the change of scenery, would soothe you. It didn't, though." Lacey gives a half smile. "Jane lay on the couch and slept, while I walked you in laps around the house. You screamed the whole time. I didn't mind, though. You seemed okay, even though you were crying. Like you'd been set on some kind of anger mode and you needed to yell yourself out of it. It was your mom who needed help, and I hardly ever got a chance to help her. She was always trying to help me."

Edward attempts to picture this. A younger, exhausted version of his mom sleeping on the couch where he'd logged so many miserable hours. Lacey holding him to her shoulder, lap after lap. His mom had told him about his colicky phase, many times, but never mentioned a field trip to New Jersey. She'd always seemed to bring up his crying jag in order to retell the happy ending, about how she had woken up one morning to find Edward dive-bombing her cheek with kisses.

"I didn't know she brought me here."

"It's funny now," Lacey says, as if to herself, "to think that Jane and I ended up sharing that baby."

Sharing. The word has a bitter taste in Edward's mouth.

Lacey rubs at her eyes, in the manner of a sleepy toddler. "The lady who retired had been working at the hospital for thirty years, in an administrative job. She and her husband are going on a trip around the world.

Isn't that something?"

Edward nods, because a response seems required.

"I was thinking that retirement is kind of like having someone you love die. It makes you focus on how you want to live your life. It makes you start over. Or feel like you should." She looks at Edward, appears to really notice him. "Your mother always wanted to write a movie. That's what she would talk about when she was tipsy. Did you know that?"

"She was writing a movie on the plane."

"No, not that. That was a dumb rewrite job, which she hated. She had an idea that she loved, that she took notes on for years. I was jealous of how much she cared about that idea. Sometimes I feel like I should write Jane's movie for her, but then I remember that I'm not a writer."

Edward tries to look sympathetic. He doesn't know what to say. He both hates having this conversation with his aunt and experiences her words as a cold glass of water sating a thirst he didn't know he had. *Say more about my mother,* he thinks. He knows that if he says that aloud, the moment will end, and no more truths will be revealed.

Lacey picks at the label on the beer bottle.

"If you saw the lady who just retired, you never would suspect that she was going to travel the world. She looks like she would never leave this town." She yawns. "Do you know where your uncle is?"

"At work?"

Lacey shrugs, and pushes the bottle away from her. "I never know with him these days. I'm going to take a nap. Will you wake me up for dinner?"

Edward nods and is surprised that as she leaves the kitchen, she bends down and kisses his cheek. It's a gentle kiss, and she ruffles his hair on the way up. He's surprised partly because Lacey rarely kisses him but also because the moment separates, the way the individual clouds did in the sky and the threads of grass did on the ground. He sees — and feels — two separate realities.

Lacey kisses his cheek the exact same way his mother had kissed Edward's cheek when she was alive. The kiss feels deliberate and intentional; Lacey can't write her sister's movie, but *this* is something she can do. But she also kisses his cheek the way Lacey would have kissed the cheek of the baby she had so badly wanted. Edward knows this, even though he can't explain how. The word *cherish* enters his brain as if on a foreign breeze, and then departs. His aunt is gone too, and Edward is left alone at the kitchen table, holding an apple core.

At midnight, he and Shay are seated on the cold floor of the garage, in front of the duffel bags. They're wearing their winter coats and hats, because this room isn't much warmer than the outdoors, but when Edward shivers, it's with anticipation. He and Shay exchange a look that says, *We're finally here.*

Shay has researched the combination locks on the bags, because the Internet is her domain. Edward has a laptop now, for schoolwork, and a phone. He hardly uses the phone, but sometimes Mrs. Cox texts him, since one of her sons taught her how. In the middle of math class his phone buzzes with the sentence: *You will need to visit Europe before you turn twenty, while your mind is still impressionable.* On a Saturday evening: *I recommend keeping a list of the books you read, as well as notes on them. I forget everything I don't write down, so notes are important.* Mrs. Cox had also texted him on his birthday to say that she was gifting him several Series I savings bonds.

Edward uses Google for academic information when necessary, but he has never searched for the flight, or himself, or his family. Shay teases him that he uses technology like an old man, but of course she understands. When there's any information to be gathered, like now, she gathers it. And according to the Internet, the lock is both old and cheap, which means that if you no longer remember the code, the best thing to do is cut it off.

"We can't cut the lock off without John noticing," Shay says. "I remembered this morning that I actually have a lock-picking book. I found it in the back of my dresser." She pulls her bag toward her. "I don't think it will help with this kind of lock, though. Why did John have to use such cheap ones?"

"Why do you have a book about lock-picking?"

"Oh, well, when I was planning to run away from home, I was going to break into houses and sleep in people's closets while I made my way across the country. That way, I'd have shelter when I needed rest."

Edward likes the image of a small, determined Shay with a lock-picking book under her arm. "Across the country to where?"

She shrugs. "Who knows? I told you, I knew I'd never actually do it."

He reads the truth in her shrug. That younger version of Shay was planning to find her father. Out West. He wonders whether it would be for a reconciliation or to tell him off. He guesses a little of both.

He points the flashlight at the bag closest to them. The lock is a horizontal row of four dials with numbers. The correct four-number combination will open it.

Shay flips through the book in her lap. "I think we have to just try every possible combination."

Edward looks at her. "There are ten thousand."

"You should do it, then. I'll get frustrated."

Edward leans forward and spins one of the dials. It takes a few rotations for him to get a feel for the traction between the numbers and the wheel beneath them. He's looking for the telltale stickiness that signals the correct digit.

"I wish John had put in carpeting," Shay says. "This could take forever, and my butt is cold."

Something occurs to Edward. "Wait a minute," he says. He stares down at the lock. These four digits were programmed by his uncle, which means they're not random. "I have an idea." He spins each of the four dials until the lock reads 2977.

There's a loud click, and the lock mechanism opens quietly and falls into Edward's waiting palm.

"You did it," Shay whispers. She leans forward and unzips the length of the duffel bag. This seems to take a long time, and Edward watches. He's aware that part of him had not wanted the bags to open. He'd wanted them to remain in the corner, a mystery that enticed Shay but a mystery unanswered. *I wonder,* instead of *I know.*

"It is full of paper," Shay says.

The bag is stuffed with envelopes. Shay picks one up, and Edward reads the handwritten name above the address.

Edward Adler

The letter is unopened. The address is unfamiliar: It's a P.O. box in town. Edward's heartbeat notches faster. Who would have written to him? Shay pulls another letter from the bag. It's also addressed to him, at the same address.

Edward reaches past Shay and pushes his arm into the bag, creating space so he can read several addresses at once. The handwriting is different. The color of the envelopes, the color of the ink, all varied. He picks one out at random and sees that the postmark is for a date two years earlier.

"They're all addressed to you," Shay says, in a quiet voice.

Same name, every envelope. So many en-velopes.

Adrenaline ignites Edward's brain and he feels his thoughts shoot forward, beyond his control. He figures something out and says it at the same time. "They don't get mail here at the house. I've never seen any lying around. I guess I figured Lacey got it while I was at school? But all the mail must go to that P.O. box."

Why? he sees Shay think.

"Because of how upset they got about the binder — they had a big fight — and be-cause of whatever this is," he says, and waves his hand at the paper rectangles, the stamps, the printed dates. "I guess the other bag must be full of letters too?"

"Do you want me to open one?"

"Wait."

She studies his face in the dim light.

He thinks, *I know the impossible is pos-sible. I've seen it, been inside it.*

"What?" she whispers.

When he speaks, his voice is small too, as if they're trying to communicate below a larger, louder conversation, as if to speak now they need a new register. "What if the letters are from my parents and brother and everyone who died on the plane?"

She looks startled. "You mean from their

ghosts?"

"Things don't always have to make sense. Do they? Maybe if you're open to things not making sense, you get to see more?"

He can read Shay. He always can. Now she looks sad, worried. She knows he wants these letters to be from his parents and brother. She wants the letters to be from them too. But she hasn't seen the impossible herself. She wasn't inside the plane when it fell out of the sky. She only saw the aftermath on television, watching beside her mother on a couch.

"I don't think things always make sense," she says, her voice so soft the words join the dust atop the shelves around them.

He nods. "Open one."

1:40 P.M.

There is no true silence on an airplane. The engines drone; air swooshes from vents overhead. There are occasional coughs, stifled conversations, the hiccup of the beverage cart's one bad wheel, the clipping shut of the bathroom door, small children and babies putting up an intermittent, righteous wail of protest. The seatbelt and cramped quarters say, *Be still.* The air says, *Listen.* More passengers are asleep now than at any other point during the flight. Some cover themselves with a jacket or blanket; like turtles, they withdraw into their shells. Another camp seems to flaunt their vulnerability. They sleep with their faces tilted back, mouths slightly agape. An arm might dangle into the aisle, as if hoping a stranger will reach out and clasp his or her hand.

Veronica sways down the first-class aisle. "Beverage?" She speaks in a singsong whisper, so as not to awaken the sleepers. She

342

makes eye contact with everyone who's conscious, because eye contact is a crucial ingredient in ensuring that first-class passengers feel special, like they got their money's worth.

She gives Mark a quick glance, though, and no more. The woman seated beside him asks for a bottle of water.

"Of course."

She turns to check on the old man and his nurse. The vibe in this row has been off-putting since the flight began. The man clearly has that kind of over-the-top wealth that's led him to expect service from everyone he encounters. Veronica saw his nurse crying earlier and slipped her an extra bag of roasted nuts while he was in the bathroom.

There have been many occasions when Veronica's been treated like a second-class citizen, so she understands the bad taste it puts in your mouth. She knows roasted nuts won't erase that taste, but she hopes the gesture tells the woman that she's not alone. Veronica has had her ass pinched and slapped too many times to count. The same goes for men telling her to smile, as if the arrangement of her features, or her mood, is any of their damn business. She's had guys casually lean into her as they pass her in the aisle, so their hard penis presses against her hip. She's regularly referred to as "sweetheart," "darling," and "baby." She's paid the same salary as Luis, even though she's the chief flight attendant and he's only been in the industry for six months. She's been leered at by men floating in a sea of vodka tonics, and she's had her work — which she excels at — criticized by men who seem to be simply looking for a sport to pass the time.

Veronica knows how to handle these situations, of course. Not allowing men to diminish her, shining her light straight at them, is perhaps her greatest gift. She feels for women who seem unskilled in this particular art. The nurse is clearly one of those women.

Veronica straightens her skirt as she returns to the galley kitchen. She's a little off-balance — it's not like her to dwell on the unpleasant aspects of her job. She needs to get back on her game. But when she closes her eyes to regroup, she sees Mark's. They have the sheen of dark blue velvet, filled with shimmer and shine. His eyes startled her in the bathroom. Perhaps it's that unexpected beauty that has her shaken. She'd thought she was offering her beauty to him; she hadn't anticipated receiving any in return.

Crispin is filled with a sensation he can't identify, one he hasn't experienced in decades. Since childhood, perhaps. The feeling flickers through him, like candlelight bouncing off walls. The light travels down twisting dark hallways inside him.

Crispin grew up in a small house in Maine, the middle of thirteen children. There were no hallways in his childhood home. Two steps and you were in the kitchen; two more steps, the bathroom; two more steps, the main room. Crispin slept in a small bedroom with his five brothers. The oldest boy was a religious bully who regularly tackled Crispin to the floor, then perched on top of him and read the Bible aloud. Crispin, his cheek pressed against the rough floor, muttered swear words in return. He spoke quietly enough that his mother couldn't hear but loudly enough to make his brother's ears go red. That was the memory he returned to, in the rare moments when he thought of his own youth. Pinned against the wooden floor, spitting curses while his brother furiously preached.

Where are these hallways? They're rough, dusty, belonging to a house inferior to any

Crispin has inhabited as an adult. He had always hired decorators, and he married women with inherent style. Crispin had never been able to create anything beautiful himself, but he knew beauty when he saw it. His hallways had lush wallpaper and wainscoting. They were well lit with fancy sconces and chandeliers.

The candlelight and rough interior keep bringing him back to Maine, before his family had a television, when they all sat around the radio in the evening, listening to Jack Benny and the news. Crispin always scooted closest to the radio; the smooth voice vibrating through the speaker was the only hint he had of life outside his town, his neighborhood, his snowy state, and he wanted out. He'd wanted out from the moment he could string the words together. Most of his brothers and sisters would marry their high school sweethearts and work at the local factory. The brother who sat on him started a landscaping business. Crispin knew a trap when he saw it, though. He found, applied for, and won a scholarship to boarding school. He moved out of the house at the age of fourteen and never went back.

The light wavers; perhaps the person holding it is tired. The steps slow. The rush seems to be over. There is a crushing feeling, which puts Crispin back on the floor, his brother's weight grinding him down.

Florida surveys the rows around her. People are settling down, clocking out. The airplane is humming at a deeper frequency, as if it too has moved into some kind of REM sleep. Florida feels herself expand into the quiet. Her attention spreads out, and she allows herself — her thoughts, her feelings — to unpack. She wonders if Bobby has figured out that she's gone farther than a baby shower in New York City. She threw her cellphone into a garbage can at the airport. She's not scared of him, but his intensity is formidable, and she'd rather not leave an easy trail. She'd married a man hot with potential, who made her scream with joy in bed, but she'd ended up living with a stranger, a man she couldn't predict. It was her lack of judgment that disturbs her the most.

She had screwed up, not him. It made her sad that her vast experience, even her marathon dances with men, hadn't left her any the wiser. She had long nursed a theory that she improved with every incarnation. She remained human, and flawed, but she was more evolved. She knew what was what. She knew what mattered. She knew, at a deeper level each time, that what mattered was love. But love was what she had misread, mistaken, and misplaced in this life. Florida glances at the sleeping women beside her. The woman with the blue scarf and the expensive shoes. Linda, her blond hair swept over her face, her mouth slightly open. She looks like a little girl. A little girl having a baby of her own.

Florida pictures herself rollerblading down the twisty boardwalk. She doesn't have a plan for her new life, but she has possibilities. She can join a band. Creating music with other people always nourishes her, and she needs nourishment. She could read tarot cards. She's not a great card reader, but she's good, and customers always walk away from her readings with satisfaction and insight. She pays real attention to the person who sits across from her, and real attention is hard to come by. Florida looks deep into their eyes and finds their inevitable goodness. Sometimes that goodness is a pebble; sometimes it's fireworks.

More intangible, and yet the foundation of her California plan, is to love. Not men specifically. She will not marry again. She refuses to bicker, or ride moody silences, or eat broccoli because he likes broccoli and wants her to do the same. She will quite simply love everyone who crosses her path, starting with the girl beside her. She will act as a mama to Linda, who badly needs one, and a grandmother to her baby.

When Linda told her that her boyfriend was a scientist who studied whales, Florida had a rare glimpse into her own future. She nearly always traffics in her past, but occasionally she has a vision that stretches forward, like the steel cables of a suspension bridge, toward a land she hasn't yet touched. She pictures herself, Linda, and Gary on a boat in the middle of a gusty ocean. A low horizon and whitecaps are visible in every direction. They're wearing bright-yellow slickers and rain hats. They stand side by side, pressed against the railing, staring in the same direction. There is a whale fifty yards from the boat. It breaches the surface, sprays water at the sky, and dives back down again. The three humans gaze at the spot where it disappeared, in a state of perfect wonder. They wait, and don't mind waiting. Moments later, as if to reward them, the animal of impossible size and beauty leaps into the air.

JANUARY 2016

The ripping of the envelope sounds violent in the quiet garage. The sheet of paper is white, thick; Shay unfolds it carefully.

Dear Edward,

I hope you are well and are recovering from your injuries. God has certainly blessed you with your life.

My daughter, Nancy, was on the flight with you. She was our only child, and her death cratered her papa and myself. She was grown — forty-three years old, but grown makes no difference in my heart. She was still my baby, my red-headed girl.

She was a doctor — a brilliant physician — but her hobby was photography. I want to ask you for something. I want to ask you to please take photographs for her. She took pictures of everything: her nursing staff, her cat, Beezus (who

350

lives with Papa and me now; that cat is as devastated as we are), buildings, nature, you name it. It was her passion.

It will heal my heart to know you are taking photos for her. That the camera wasn't put down but passed on. I hope it's not asking too much, but I figure everyone takes pictures occasionally, right? I am simply asking you to do so with more deliberation.

I wish you well, Edward. Thank you.

Sincerely,

Jeanette Louis

Shay looks up from the letter, her eyes wide. "The doctor in the folder."

Cratered, Edward thinks.

"Another one?" she whispers.

This one is on gray stationery, from the husband of a woman on the plane. Her death left him alone with their three children. He asks Edward to please write to each of the children, telling them that he met their mother during the flight. *I know you probably didn't meet her. Who gets to know strangers on a flight? But my kids won't know that. They'll believe you. Please tell them that she told you how much she loved them and that she knew they would be okay. In the letter to Charlie, add that his mom wanted him to keep reading. Tell the little one to keep her sweetness. And tell Connor that she wouldn't want him to drop out of the science competition.*

There's a photo with the letter. Shay holds it up. Three black kids standing in height order. The two older boys wear striped sweaters, and the littlest one, a girl, wears a matching striped dress. They're smiling for the camera.

"Mierda," Shay says.

Edward wraps his hands around his skull, as if palming a basketball, fingers spread. His head is pulsing.

"A few more, and then we stop for tonight," Shay says. Edward knows that she wants to keep reading in the hope that they can end on a better note. Whatever that might mean.

The next letter is from a mom whose daughter died on the flight. Her daughter's dream was to honor her Chinese heritage by walking the Great Wall of China. *Please, Edward, find it in your heart to fulfill this dream for my daughter.*

It turns out that almost all the letters ask Edward for something. The next letter requests that he write a novel. The one after that implores him to move to London, hopefully into an apartment overlooking St.

James's Park. A mother whose son had aspired to be a stand-up comedian wants Edward to open a comedy club in their small Wisconsin town and name it after the dead young man.

Shay's face looks how Edward imagines his own does: stricken. He thinks, *Can we bear this?* He has to force his voice out of his throat. "How many letters do you think there are?"

"If the other bag is full of them too, then hundreds." Shay is still holding the photograph of the three kids in matching outfits. "Why didn't they email you? Why did they write real letters?"

"Because John gave me that obscure email address. It's all numbers and hyphens. So no stranger could find me that way."

"Do you want to tell him or Lacey that we found these?"

Edward tightens his fingers on his skull. He says, "Do you think they're all like this?"

Buy a camera. Write letters to children who lost their mother. Go to China, England, Wisconsin.

"I hope not," Shay says into the darkness.

When Edward finally makes his way to the basement, it's three in the morning. He moves mechanically through brushing his teeth, switching off lights, climbing under the sheets. He closes his eyes out of a sense of duty and routine. He no longer has any hope of sleep; he lost hope days earlier. But as soon as his eyes are closed, something is different. The darkness inside him has taken on a new shade; there's a richness to it. It's slippery, like velvet. Edward can barely keep his feet under him; he's sliding toward sleep like a child downhill on a sled. He hasn't experienced this feeling since his family died, and it's accompanied by an explosion of relief. He thinks, the thought blurred: *the letters.* It has to be the letters; nothing else has changed. It doesn't make sense, but he's too tired to care. He's too relieved to care. He sleeps, and he can feel, as he disappears, his cells buzzing in celebration.

His dreams that night feel like actual experiences. Edward climbs a mountain on the other side of the world and then skypes with a victim's family from the top. Then he's balanced on a mossy rock, throwing a stranger's ashes into a stream in Oregon. He swims in an Olympic-size pool to try to beat a specific record. He sweats through the sheets, several times over. He sees himself bent in prayer, a position he has never taken in his life.

Edward wanders from class to class the next

day, not hearing anything anyone says to him. More than once, Shay has to take him by the elbow and change the direction he's walking. He lets her do so but thinks, *It makes no difference if I sit in English or social studies.*

They wait only fifteen minutes after all the bedroom lights have been extinguished before crossing the lawn to the garage that night.

When they're inside, Edward unlocks the duffel bag. Shay says, "I think we should have rules."

"Rules?"

"Maybe we should only read ten letters a night, or for an hour or something like that. They're . . . intense. And I think once we read a letter we should take it. We have to leave the bags here, obviously, but I can stuff them to make them look full, once we've read a bunch. I want to log the letters, and then we can respond to them if we decide to."

"You don't think John will notice?"

"He never opened any of these letters. My guess is that he was going to leave them in the bags forever. Or maybe give them to you when you were older?"

Edward has stopped listening. His arm is already plunged deep into the bag. He pinches his fingers around an envelope, pulls it out.

Dear Edward,
Sunrise was at 4:55 A.M. today, and I haven't seen Linda or Betsy for a week. There have been no spottings of a baby blue whale worldwide for over a year. It's possible that my colleague and I are following the last blue whales to ever live, and that is a sobering thought. Maybe that's why I didn't get off the boat after the last trip. I'm supposed to take a break — hand my notes to another scientist to keep up while I see movies and eat burgers. But I didn't want to. And if I'm really honest, I worry that if I take my eyes off these girls, they might disappear for good. Which is, I know, stupid. But I've let my life onshore die off since my Linda died, so the only place I'm even possibly of use is out here.

Anyway, Edward, I hope you're well. I appreciate having someone to write letters to. Best wishes, sincerely,

Gary

"Oh, that's nice," Shay says, clearly relieved. "Hi, Gary."

"Hi, Gary," Edward says.

The next letter asks him to visit a home in Alabama, to hug the bedridden mother of a man on the plane. Edward tries to imagine bending over the bed of a frail, dying stranger and gathering her in his arms. When he finishes the letter, he hands it to Shay. She brought a notebook to the garage to take notes and then compile all the requests into a spreadsheet.

The following two letters ask Edward to take on the vocation of the deceased: He should become a nurse, and then a violinist. A woman asks him to pray for her husband every night before bed. This letter is accompanied by hand-copied psalms, which he assumes he is also supposed to read before bed.

"You can't do this many things," Shay says.

"Maybe I can?" In the middle of every single letter, Edward thinks: *I have to do that. I have to play the violin. I have to smile more. I have to learn to fish.* At the end of each letter, he feels like he's already failed.

Dear Edward,
My mother met you recently in Washington. Apparently she gave you and your uncle a ride to your car. She'd wanted

my brothers or me to come to the hearing with her, but we all said we were busy. I think we're just programmed to say no to her now, no matter what the question is, as punishment for the perceived crimes of our childhood.

My youngest brother is in rehab, so he was legitimately busy. What was I doing that afternoon? Reading William Blake. I'm torturing my mother by making her pay for my second PhD in poetry. I tell her that it's her fault, since she gives talks all the time about how vital the arts are, even though she really means as a hobby for rich people, not as a vocation for her own children.

When I read poetry, I forget about both of my parents, and that's what I tried to do on the afternoon of the hearing. I try to forget about the crash, try to forget that I come from two ruinous human beings. But it has bothered me, the idea that I should have been in that car when you got in, because I should have accompanied my elderly mother to that kind of event. Also, I know you are the last person to have seen my father alive, assuming you walked by his seat or saw him in his wheelchair in the airport. There is some poetry in the idea of sharing your presence.

You're probably wondering why I've sent you this letter. Since my father died, I've made myself write something every day. I want to make things, not just study them. Ideally, I write a poem, but on the hard days I write correspondence. And today I wrote to you, to connect the living dots between me, my mother, my father, and yourself.

Regards,
Harrison Cox

"Will you tell Mrs. Cox that her son wrote you?" Shay says when she's read it too.

Edward shakes his head. This letter belongs in a different category, one shared by the school secretary who told him about feeding alligators as a girl or Edward's lab partner telling him that he wants to be an opera singer when he grows up. These are secrets, confessions, and therefore sacred. He will hold them to his chest.

Edward is staring into the duffel bag, his eyes bleary, when Shay says, "Stop. We have to stop. We've read way more than ten letters."

Edward notices that her fingertips are ink-stained, as he helps her to her feet. He feels older, or heavier, than he did when he entered the garage, and Shay looks changed too, in a way he wouldn't be able to describe. They walk together out of the room and carry all the words they've ingested into the dark night.

"I didn't think you'd last this long," Mrs. Tuhane says to Edward's reflection in the mirror.

Edward has just sat down on the weight-lifting bench. Her words startle him, because to his recollection, this is the first thing the coach has ever said to him that's not a directive. He wishes Shay were here to translate, because although he'd like to be able to respond to this comment properly, he has no idea what the coach is talking about.

"Um, at what?" he says.

"I thought you'd quit, run crying back to the principal about this being too hard. I would have bet money you were headed for study hall within two weeks of entering this room."

Edward shakes his head, still confused. "But isn't this mandatory?"

Mrs. Tuhane slides a small metal plate onto either end of the bar Edward is about to press. "I'm giving you a compliment, kid. You've been at it for months. You're tougher

360

than I thought. And you're getting stronger."

Edward looks at his skinny frame in the mirror.

She seems to read his mind and scowls. "It doesn't matter if you can see the muscles. I don't give a damn what you can see. You've rewired your brain. You can bench a hundred pounds. You're objectively stronger. Now, stop wasting time."

Edward lies back on the bench and wraps his hands around the bar. Before school, he'd read a handful of letters that he'd smuggled into the basement. One was from an elderly woman in Detroit, who said one of her twenty-seven grandchildren had died on the flight and that he had always secretly been her favorite. She'd been wondering if all the passengers on that plane had simply been too good, in one way or another, for this earth. She wondered what Edward thought about this theory.

"Press," Mrs. Tuhane says, and he lifts the bar up.

Another letter was from a woman who claimed to have kissed Edward on the cheek outside the NTSB hearing in Washington, though he can't remember anyone kissing him that day. Another was from a mother who said she regretted how critical she had been of her daughter. *I told her that she should stop eating carbs, or that her hair was unflattering. Now I think, why did I care how she looked?* Then there was a stretch of letters that contained what felt like inappropriate demands.

Please don't waste a minute, don't waste this gift you've been given.

Make sure you live a meaningful life.

Live every day in the memory of those who died.

These are Edward's least favorite kinds of letters — the ones that tell him how to live his own life.

"Besides," Mrs. Tuhane says, "your metabolism is a burning furnace at your age. I predict that if you keep lifting with this regularity, you'll gain twenty pounds of muscle your senior year. Bring it down now, slow."

Edward lowers the bar to his chest. He thinks of himself three years from now, with a wider chest and thicker limbs. He thinks of the unopened letters in the duffel bags — his name etched on each one — and lifts the bar up and down until all of him aches.

During dinner, Edward notices that his aunt and uncle seem withdrawn. He doesn't know where Lacey keeps her sleeping pills,

362

but Edward has the desire to go find the bottle and flush them down the toilet. *You have to earn sleep,* he wants to tell her. Even though he knows he didn't earn it; the letters gave him sleep as a gift.

His unspoken allegiance is to John, who looks distracted and checks his phone twice during the meal, a habit Lacey hates. His wife narrows her eyes and focuses on Edward while telling them that she had a slow day at work, which meant she got to spend an extra hour holding babies in the nursery.

"Have you ever smelled a newborn?" she says to Edward.

"I don't think so."

"You'll have to come to the hospital with me one day to smell one. It's indescribably wonderful."

I have too many letters to read, he thinks, and leans his weight imperceptibly toward his uncle. If Lacey is strong now and cloaked in the mantle of his mother's bravery, where does that leave her husband and nephew?

"It's true," John says with intensity, several beats too late, "about the newborn smell."

Edward and Lacey look at him, and an expression of alarm crosses John's face. Edward, who is sensitive to yearning and mixed-up time zones, is able to chart the three of them in this strange moment. Lacey is staring at her husband as if he'd accidentally hit her. As if he'd said something she'd hoped with all her heart that he would say a few years earlier — when holding their baby in her arms was her deepest desire — but that this version of herself no longer needs, and so she experiences the statement as a betrayal. John, lost and panicked, gazes at Lacey and Edward, thinking, *Dear God, have I messed everything up?* And Edward, living inside the correspondence in the garage, which means living inside questions and a deafening desire for answers, feels every atom of their shared vulnerability and wonders if any of them will be okay.

When Edward leaves the house after dinner, he finds Besa waiting for him in the driveway.

"Oh. Hi?" he says.

"I would like to know what you and my daughter are up to."

It's cold, but neither of them is wearing a winter coat. "We've had a lot of homework lately," he says, and shivers.

"Don't insult my intelligence, *mi amor.*" Besa has always called him *mi amor,* but Edward has sensed a slight dimming in her warmth toward him in the last year. He now towers over her, and annoyance flickers across her face when she cranes her neck to look at him. Shay said to him once that her mother loved all children but distrusted men. And Edward is uncomfortably aware that he now looks like a young man.

He tries to make his features appear trust-worthy. "You should ask Shay, Besa."

She regards him from beneath her eye-brows. "You know I already have. Would I be coming to you first?"

Edward sighs. Lying to Besa is unthink-able. She demands truth with every line of her face. He tries to come up with some-thing that at least feels true. "We're working on a project. We're trying to help people."

She glares at him, an expression that makes her look so much like her daughter that Edward almost smiles.

"In the middle of the night? You think I don't hear you two scurrying around?"

"Oh," Edward says. "Well, the project —"

"Are you and Shay having sex?"

The look on his face must be answer enough, because Besa's face softens with relief. She leans forward and presses her hand against his cheek. "I'm sorry, *pobre-cito*. I didn't mean to give you a heart at-tack. I have my fears, but of course I was wrong."

Edward is unable to speak, and his face

feels like it's burning up. Besa laughs and takes his arm. She leads him toward her house. "I'm glad you're working on a project. It's for school, I assume? Shay needs to keep her grades up in order to get a scholarship. A project for extra credit would be wonderful. We don't need to mention any of this to Shay, do we?"

"No," Edward croaks, as she deposits him inside her house.

He has to stand at the bottom of the stairs for a few minutes, trying to manage his heart rate and temperature, before he's able to enter Shay's room. He's relieved to see that she's at her desk, with her back to him.

"Just finishing one," she says, without turning.

He sits down on her bed to wait. When she turns, she hands him a large envelope. She says, "Are you okay? You look sunburned."

"I'm fine. How many responses are in here?"

"Just one today."

We can't ignore the letters from or about little kids, she'd said the morning after they opened the first duffel bag. They'd agreed that she would compose and type responses, which Edward would then sign. Shay had started with the second letter they'd read, from the dad asking Edward to write specific messages to his three children. She had written and rewritten those three letters over the course of several days. *I can't make a mistake,* she'd said. *This is important. I need to say the perfect thing.*

Edward pulls the new letter out of the envelope and scans the page. She's written to a nun in South Carolina, who said the beauty of Edward's salvation kept her from leaving the church.

"I know it's not a kid, but the nun seems sweet," Shay says. "And she's extremely old. Is that okay with you?"

"You're in charge of who gets written back."

"The nun claimed that she knew you were truly saved by God because of how your hair looked in the photos of you from the hospital."

"My hair?"

"Apparently Jesus had dark, shiny hair that looked wet, like he had just been anointed. And your hair looked like that too."

"My hair looked wet? That's gross."

"She believes it proved that God had anointed you and thereby saved you from death."

Edward almost laughs at this, but can't

muster the effort to force the sound up his throat and out his mouth.

"I'm going to skip school tomorrow," he says. "Lacey's going to the hospital all day for some training thing and I need to get through the rest of the letters. I feel like I can't breathe half the time."

"Fine, I will too."

He'd expected this and is prepared. "If we both skip, it will seem too obvious. We might get caught. I barely have any absences, so I can definitely get away with it if I'm alone. Besides, you need to keep your grades up." He blushes when he says this, remembering Besa's accusation in the driveway.

Shay's dimple deepens in her cheek, rarely a good sign. The fact that he has planned an escape on his own — even a tiny one — rankles her.

Edward meets her gaze. He has no choice. He has nothing against school at this point, but it's a waste of time. Time he should spend reading; each letter feels like a page in a book that he won't fully understand until he reaches the end. It feels imperative — in a way nothing else in his life has — that he read every word. The attention he brings to the letters seems to be changing him; Edward can feel strands inside himself gathering, trying to find a shape in which he will be able to meet the eyes of the people in the photographs.

2:04 P.M.

The plane is two-thirds of the way to Los
Angeles. The passengers' consciousness
reaches forward, searching the final stretch
of tunnel for a glimmer of light. Shoulders
loosen and headaches fade, because more
onboard hours lie behind them than ahead.
Hope returns with thoughts of logistics, car-
service pickups, and whom to text the moment the wheels touch the ground.

Jane looks up from her screen.

She's just rewritten a scene in which two
robots get into a fight, and the only pleasure
she has been able to salvage is changing the
gender of both robots to female. *Girl power,*
she thinks in disgust. She'd pictured the
robots as herself and Lacey. Sisters, which
means they love each other straight to the
bone but have spent their lives circling each
other, testing the air between them with
jabs. Jane is the seventh credited writer to
work on this script; it's only by personal-

370

izing the writing that she can endure it.

The cockpit door opens, and Jane has a clear view into the darkened space. A flash of windshield and a panel of blinking lights punctuated with levers, the shoulder of the co-pilot. The pilot, a gray-haired man with a salt-and-pepper mustache, smiles at Veronica, says a few words Jane can't hear, and then steps into the bathroom. The door pulls shut behind him.

Jane returns to her computer screen, writes three lines of dialogue, erases them, and tries again. She's getting somewhere, she thinks. She glances up then, because a spiky cry has filled the air. Jane cranes around. She thinks: *A baby? Mine?* Then: *Don't be ridiculous; they're not babies anymore. They don't need me like that.*

"Is there a doctor on the plane?" This issues in the same pitched voice, and even though passengers are now standing and Veronica is in the aisle, Jane is able to see that it's the nurse, wearing her whites. She's hunched over the old man beside her. He looks terrible, or not terrible exactly, but wrong. His skin seems to have gone rubbery — his eyes are closed, and he's whiter than the wall of the plane.

Jane's hands are off her computer; without thinking she presses on her birthmark. She presses hard, as if it's a button that will reverse the clock, even if only by a few minutes.

"Shit," Mark says.

He's backed up slightly, so he's halfway into Jane's seat area. They're both half-standing now, peering through the cluster of people at the agitated nurse, who is holding the old man's wrist as if it's a musical instrument she can't figure out how to play.

"He looks bad, doesn't he?" Mark says.

Veronica's voice comes over the loud-speaker: smooth, calm. "Two things, ladies and gentlemen. First, please notice that the fasten-seatbelt sign is on. We're anticipating turbulence, so kindly stay in your seats. Second, if there is a doctor on the plane, could he or she please report to first class?"

Jane thinks, *I want to go to the boys.* She has the image of rushing into the back of the plane, past the ill man and the nurse, giving her space over to Mark, who seems to want to reverse as far away from the scene as possible anyway.

A stocky redheaded woman appears with a gray backpack. She takes the old man's wrist from the nurse and puts her other hand to the side of the old man's neck. She waits, as if for news.

"Doctor?" Veronica murmurs.

Everybody in first class is watching. The nurse, with nothing left to hold on to, looks bereft.

Finally, the redheaded woman lays the arm across the old man's chest. She stands up. She speaks quietly to Veronica, but her voice carries.

"He's dead."

"Dead?" Veronica gasps the word. "You're sure?"

"Yes."

Jane reaches for the seat back in front of her, because she's lost her balance. There is a dead man across the aisle. The only other dead bodies she's seen were her parents, but that was two decades ago, and she had been prepared by terrible diagnoses and then visible declines. Their dead bodies had been in coffins. Her mother had been wearing her favorite pink lipstick, lying with her hands folded on her waist.

It takes a moment for Jane to realize that Mark has grabbed a seat in the opposite direction and Veronica has gone wavy in front of her. There is another spiky cry, but the nurse is in her seat, as silent as a stone. The old man is slumped in his chair.

"Turbulence," someone calls, and Jane is, for a split second, appreciative that what is happening isn't inside her body, because if this shaking, pitching, and blurring were taking place solely within her own skin, that would mean something had gone terribly wrong.

Edward pretends to go to school in the morning. He eats breakfast with his aunt and uncle. He uses the upstairs bathroom, so he can check to see if his uncle slept in the nursery. The sheets are rumpled, and a fat novel — *Last of the Breed,* by Louis L'Amour — sits on the bed stand. Edward blinks at the scene, and for a moment the bed and the letters and the lake outside the clear-paned window all feel the same, like a row of books on a shelf. Formed with equal weight and density. Why should one of these items make him happy, or unhappy? They are neutral. Beds are made to be slept in. Letters to be read. *I'm either becoming Zen or more depressed,* he thinks.

He waits on the sidewalk for Shay, as usual. He waves at Besa, and they walk together down the block. Shay has her haughty face on and says little during their walk, but he knows that she'll cover for him at school.

"Thank you," he says, when they reach the corner.

"You have to show me everything you read, obviously."

"Obviously."

He watches her walk forward. He waits until she's successfully crossed two sides of the intersection, and then he enters the forest that lines the back of the houses on their block. He knows John and Lacey are leaving the house now, and he can arrive home unnoticed by this route.

When you visited us when you were little, you and Jordan played back there, his aunt had said once, of the forest. *You thought it was wonderful, because you'd never been in proper woods before.* Edward has no memory of this, but as he picks his way over tree roots, he tries to imagine himself and Jordan as boys, running loops around the fat tree trunks. Jordan is in the lead, and Eddie follows, laughing. The two boys examine a bug in the dirt, then find two big sticks and pretend they're swords.

Edward stops when he reaches the hedge that backs up against the garage. He doesn't question the sight of the boys in front of him. He feels like his imagination, perhaps fueled by the contents of the letters, has

376

been butting up against reality lately. In his daydreams, he often sees Gary, his blond beard flecked with gray, taking notes on the deck of his research boat. In the gym a few days earlier, Edward thought he'd seen Benjamin Stillman lifting weights in the mirror. The soldier was dressed in his uniform, the same one he'd been wearing on the plane. He was deadlifting an enormous amount of weight. He'd looked real, to the extent that Edward almost dropped the dumbbell he was holding. He spun around, while Mrs. Tuhane barked, "Adler, pay attention!" But, of course, no one was there.

Edward watches Jordan, who appears to be about nine years old. This was the boy who jumped off the top of a car to impress Shay. His black hair, always untamable, shoots in several different directions. Edward has no problem recalling every plane of his brother's face, even as his parents' faces and voices zoom in and out of focus. He doesn't know why Jordan remains perfectly distinct while his parents blur, but perhaps it's because he'd always considered his brother to be part of him. They are inextricable, even now. Edward smiles because his brother is smiling at the sword in his hand.

A question appears in his mind: *What can*

I do for you?

Immediately, it seems strange that this didn't occur to Edward earlier, that it took an avalanche of letters from strangers to reveal this as a possibility. Lacey had kissed his cheek *for* her sister, which surely means Edward can do something for his brother. He can look at a day — today — and think, *If Jordan were here, what would he want to do?*

Edward's not sure where to start, but he's hungry again, so he decides to start with food. He squeezes through the hedge and checks that John and Lacey's cars are gone before heading to the kitchen. He can eat the way his brother would choose to, which means the meal Edward carries from the kitchen to the garage is almost exactly Jordan's last meal on the plane: carrot sticks, a small pot of applesauce, and a hummus sandwich.

When he opens the door to the garage, a voice says, "What, you didn't bring any food for me? So rude."

Shay is sitting cross-legged on the cement floor, next to the duffel bags. "Don't be mad," she says. "We won't get in trouble, I promise. I'll lie my pants off if I have to."

Edward frowns, but it's just to register his skepticism. He's not mad.

378

"Besides," she says, "we'll get twice as much reading done together."

He settles down beside her. "Hand me a letter."

She unzips the second duffel bag, which they're two-thirds of the way through. Shay's spreadsheet is next to them, to write down the different requests.

They both read for a few minutes, then Shay says, "Don't tell me you weren't happy to see me."

He says, truthfully, "I'm always happy to see you."

He opens the folder, as if to cross-reference the letter he'd just read with a victim's photograph. Really, he just wants to glance at the photo of Jordan. It seems possible to Edward that he'd made the decision to stay home today, to be *here,* because of Jordan. His brother would certainly have played hooky. The fully formed motivation had simply followed in the wake of the action. *What would Jordan do? What can I do for Jordan?* He is the age his brother was when he died, and Edward feels — hopes — that he's entered his brother's orbit in a new way.

He reads a series of letters with more demands on how he should live. *Fulfill every dream. My son was afraid to fail and so never joined a band. Don't be afraid to take risks.*

My daughter was lazy and put her dreams off because she thought she had nothing but time. Then she got on a plane to visit her sister in Los Angeles. She told me she would start working hard after her trip. Think of how much your mama must miss you, and make her proud.

I'm sorry for rambling — I've been in the Jack Daniel's — but my lady was the love of my life and she was in pastry school because she had a gift for pastry. I wish you could have tried her beignets. They were fucking fantastic. Figure out what your gift is, Edward Adler, and then blow that shit up. You owe my lady that.

Usually, Edward experiences these kinds of letters as a crushing weight on his chest. Today, though, eating his brother's sandwich, with Shay at his side, he feels a shot of Jordan's crinkly, excited energy. Jordan was always looking for the opportunity to say, *Fuck no.* To defy their dad's expectations and curfews, to opt out when everyone else was opting in. Edward never had that inclination, but he feels like he's ingesting it with the hummus. *Fuck no?* he thinks, and it's the first time he's considered it as an option. *Fuck no,* to the people telling him how to live.

He pulls his phone out of his pocket and

writes a text to Mrs. Cox. *I'm really sorry, but I haven't read the investing book. I tried to, but the subject isn't interesting to me, so I couldn't get through it. Shay and I have really enjoyed the biographies you've sent, though. I hope you're not disappointed.*

When he sends the text, Edward immediately feels lighter. He's felt guilty about his silence over the book since he received it. He pulls another letter out of the bag.

Hey, Edward,

My mother died a long time ago of depression and my brother, Mark, even though he crashed in your goddamn plane, would have died of depression eventually too. All I ever knew was that I wasn't going to go that way, and that's why I surf and smoke and don't own anything that doesn't fit inside my van. If I don't love it, I don't keep it.

Mark left me all his money in his will, even though we hadn't spoken in three years, which was a kind of fuck-you to the way I've chosen to live my life. He wanted to saddle me with millions — after I paid off his ridiculous debts — so I would have to buy a house and a Benz and some fancy vases to fill my empty shelves. He wanted me to be like him,

381

which just means rich and miserable and always in credit-card debt, but I'm not doing that. I'm giving the whole fuck-load away. The insurance money too. Well, after I fix the back left tire on my van and buy a new board.

My girl is a Buddhist, and she's always saying thank you to the beach and to the waves and the sunset. I used to think it was all woo-woo bullshit, but I like listening to her talk. I've caught myself thanking a tree once or twice. I've decided that even though it's bullshit, it's the good kind.

Anyway, she tells me to say thank you to Mark, because his death set me free all over again. Made me realize how important my chosen life is. But I think instead I'm going to say thank you to you, kid. Thank you for receiving this letter. Thank you for your life, and for being the one that was saved.

I've enclosed a check for the amount I got from the will and the insurance guys. I want you to have it. You can keep it, or give it away, whatever you want. I don't care what you do. You deserve it, man, after what you've been through. And I got no use for it at all.

So, thank you, and peace, brother.

Jax Lassio

The postmark on the envelope says that he mailed the letter almost two years earlier, and there's a check enclosed, made out to *Edward Adler,* for *$7,300,000.*

"Uh," Edward says.

"What?" Shay takes the letter from him. She reads quickly, and her mouth falls open.

He studies the rectangular check and the numbers written on it.

"Hold it up to the light," Shay says. "They always do that in movies. I don't know why."

Edward lifts his arm. Framed by the window, it's still a check, with the same impossible number of zeros.

"Holy shit," Shay says. "Holy shit. Do you think it's a joke?"

"No." Edward flips open the folder and finds Mark Lassio's photograph. The man's brash grin makes him look like someone who expects to be on magazine covers. Edward remembers Mark leaving the bathroom before the flight attendant. He hadn't been grinning, but he'd looked satisfied, as if that had been another magazine spread, as if he was where he wanted to be. *Gross,* Eddie had said to Jordan. How was it possible that Edward was now in a net that contained that man and his brother?

"You don't even need the money," Shay says, behind him. "This is insane."

When the school loudspeaker summons Edward to the principal's office the next afternoon, Edward assumes Principal Arundhi figured out that he'd skipped school. On the way through the halls, Edward looks for Shay, wanting to tell her that this was her fault; they are a package deal, so the double absence was glaringly obvious, and they have been caught.

Principal Arundhi meets him at the door. A watering can dangles from his hand at an odd angle, as if it were a cigarette, and his suit looks like it's been slept in.

"What's wrong?" Edward says. This has to be more than him missing school; the principal looks like a seam that's been picked apart.

"It must be a virus. Six ferns have died in the last three days. Six. I've removed the affected plants." The principal gestures to a blank stretch on the windowsill. One of the hanging pots is gone as well. "I'm hoping that will end the transmission. I see no signs of illness on the others." He looks at Edward blankly. "All I can do is take care of the ones that remain."

"Can I help?"

"Yes."

Principal Arundhi looks like he's not going to say more, as if specifics aren't necessary, only the promise of help. Edward says, "How?"

"I'd like you to take the kangaroo paw home. I don't know where the virus started. My home, as well as this office, might be infected. Please take him home with you just until I get everyone back in good health."

Edward looks at the old fern in the corner, ensconced in its bright-yellow pot. It is Principal Arundhi's oldest and favorite plant. "But what if I kill it?"

"I trust you, Edward," the principal says. "I trust you completely."

When Edward gets home, he sets up a station in the basement. He places the yellow pot on a card table directly beneath the window that gets the best light. Beside the fern is a bag of plant food and a spray bottle filled with room-temperature water. Edward checks the soil and mists the leaves.

Shay is hopping up and down on the other side of the basement. "I'm still trying to calm down," she says, when he gives her a

385

look. "Seven million dollars."

"I know," he says.

"I googled and it looks like you *can* deposit a check that's two years old, as long as the money is still in the originating bank account. Will you please stop obsessing over that bush?"

"Fern," he says. "And, no, I won't."

"You could buy about twelve houses in this town with that money," she says. "Or maybe an entire island somewhere! What are you going to do?"

Edward has the check in his back pocket. He didn't know where to put it, so keeping it on his person seemed safest. He touches the pocket now reflexively. He imagines himself surfing next to Jax, whom he pictures looking like a longhaired movie star. They pass the check back and forth in the middle of the waves.

"I can't deal with it now."

"I know. You can't deal with anything until you finish the letters." Shay sounds exasperated, and out of breath from the jumping.

"That's right." Edward presses the soil with his finger. He wonders if the plant knows it's in a new location and is confused. He wonders if it misses Principal Arundhi.

Shay stays for dinner that night, and when they slide into their seats in front of plates of pork chops, broccoli, and mashed pota-toes, Edward says, "I guess I should tell you guys that I'm eating vegan now."

Lacey wrinkles her nose, as if he's said a word she's never heard before. "Vegan?"

Shay says, "I'll eat his pork chop and his mashed potatoes, if you made them with milk. Don't worry, nothing will go to waste."

"Why the change?" John says.

Edward tells the truth. "I'm doing it for my brother." He pauses, and it occurs to him that his aunt and uncle probably hadn't been up to date on his brother's eating habits. He says, "Jordan became vegan a few weeks before he died."

Both his aunt and uncle flinch, and he knows it's because he used the word *died.* He has always said *the crash* when referenc-ing the loss of his family. They all have. His-tory is divided into before the crash and after the crash.

"You don't need to cook any differently," he says. "I'll eat whatever vegetable you're eating and make myself a sandwich."

John says, "I'm sure we could stand to eat more vegetables around here."

"I don't want you to change anything." Edward hears the stridency in his voice, but can't help it. He's annoyed that he had to tell them at all, and he's annoyed that

387

they're having a response. This choice, this idea, belongs to him and Jordan, and no one else.

"That's nice that you're doing that for your brother," Lacey says, but she sounds unsure.

Stop worrying, and stop taking sleeping pills, and pay attention to your marriage, Edward wants to say but does not.

At midnight in the garage, Shay divides a small handful of unread letters between them. Edward opens the one on the top of his pile.

Dear Eddie,
My name is Mahira. My uncle owns the deli you went to all the time with your family. I don't know if you know about me? Jordan said he didn't tell anyone, but maybe you didn't count as anyone. So, maybe I need to tell you that we were together, that he was my first boyfriend. I can't speak for your brother's feelings, of course, only my own. I loved Jordan.
   The minute he told me that your family was moving to the West Coast, I decided I would go to college in Los Angeles. I didn't tell him that, in case it

didn't happen, but I knew we weren't really saying goodbye. I want to study physics, and there are some excellent programs out there. I'd pictured that entire future. I'd pictured meeting you, his brother. I'd imagined you and me becoming friends while standing on a beach.

I'm eighteen now, and I told my uncle that I needed to take a year off before college. So I'm working in the deli while my uncle visits family in Pakistan. Why am I telling you any of this? I think because I want to tell Jordan. I wish I had told him my — our — future before he got on the plane. I thought I had time. It's strange to be young and run out of time, isn't it? I also wanted to write in order to tell you that your name always made Jordan smile. If I were you, I would want to be told that.

I wish you well, Eddie,
Mahira

Edward reads the letter over and over, on a loop. He might have kept reading the page until it was time to leave the garage, but Shay notices and says, "Is that one okay?"

He hands it to her.

When she looks up, she says, "Did you

know he had a girlfriend?"

"No." The word echoes inside him, as if he's become an empty well.

"Did you know this girl at all?"

He shakes his head. "I probably saw her in the deli, but I don't remember."

"Seven million dollars and a girlfriend," Shay says, in a hushed voice.

Edward pictures his brother running around tree trunks, jumping off the roof of a car, holding his arms outstretched for airport security. He feels an ache spread through his center, like the fault line before an earthquake. He thinks: *What can I do for you, Jordan? What does this mean? How can I help?*

The answer is immediate: *Go see the girl.*

■ ■ ■ ■

3.

■ ■ ■ ■

"We contain the other, hopelessly and forever."

— JAMES BALDWIN

2:07 P.M.

The frozen rain hitting the aircraft causes a glitch. The pitots (named after the early-eighteenth-century French engineer and inventor Henri Pitot), which look like small steel Popsicle sticks on the outside of the plane, freeze. Pitots aren't supposed to freeze — even at arctic temperatures — a critical fact that will be brought up in the NTSB hearing seven months later. While frozen, pitots are unable to do their job, which is to assess the aircraft's speed. This is unfortunate, but planes are embedded with backup plans. If one engine fails, there is another of equal power. In this case, the failure of the pitots triggers the autopilot system to disengage. The plane is no longer on cruise control. The pilots need to check the sensors on the dashboard, and assess the speed and balance of the plane themselves.

The rain has stopped, but the weather — an incredibly sensitive ocean of air and moisture — is still very much at play. Pockets of air pressure swirl around the plane like flocks of migrating birds. When the senior pilot reenters the cockpit after using the bathroom, he sinks into the left seat and studies the radar. He allows the co-pilot to continue to be in charge of the instrumentation.

The pilot says, "Rotor turbulence. Bigger than it looked on the radar." He stares at the screen. "Pull a little to the left, to avoid draft."

The co-pilot, a man twelve years the pilot's junior, looks worried. "What?"

"Pull a little left. We're on manual now, yes?"

The co-pilot nods and banks the plane to the left. A strange aroma, a burnt smell, floods the cockpit. The temperature also increases.

"Is something wrong with the AC?"

"No," the pilot says. "It's an effect from the weather."

The sound of slipstream becomes louder.

"It's okay," the pilot says. "Accumulation of ice crystals on the exterior of the fuselage. We're fine. Let's reduce speed."

An alarm sounds for 2.2 seconds in the cockpit, to remind them that they're not on autopilot.

■ ■ ■ ■

Jordan has felt clear, for some time now, that he no longer *needs* his parents. He lives with them because it's customary for kids to live at home until the age of eighteen, but he knows he could easily get a job, continue to educate himself with books, spend unsupervised hours with Mahira, and live on his own. He can picture his apartment: a light-filled, high-ceilinged studio with a loft bed. When he envisions himself living there, he's wearing glasses and holding a cup of coffee, even though he has perfect vision and caffeine makes him sweat.

Now he watches the doctor disappear behind the first-class curtain. He knows he and his brother and father are thinking the same thing: *Is something wrong with Mom?*

"There's a sick old man up there," Bruce says. "It's probably . . ."

The air seems to leave his mouth sideways, and the rest of the sentence is lost as the plane hops to the right, like a stone skipping across a pond.

The physical jolt shifts something inside Jordan, and a new truth yawns open: *I do need them. I need all three of them.* And while the plane hesitates, as if deciding its next move, his apartment now has a bunk bed to share with his brother and another bedroom, for his parents.

MARCH 2016

Edward keeps his eyes closed for most of the bus ride into New York City. The letters have all been read and categorized by him and Shay. It's the first Monday of spring break, and they were able to leave their houses undetected because Lacey is at work and Besa is spending the day with a cousin. Edward is rimmed with irritation, though, because he has to make this trip, because *this trip* is a thing at all. Edward would have bet his life that he and his brother had no secrets. And yet Jordan had kissed a girl. He had loved a girl, a stranger. Jordan had either not wanted to tell Edward or not trusted him with the truth.

Halfway through the ride, Edward's eyes fly open, as if they need light, the way his lungs need air. "I'm skipping that practice PSAT next weekend."

"Okay," Shay says.

"You're going to take it?" He feels antagonistic. The bus is curling around the long entrance loop to the Lincoln Tunnel.

"I don't know what I want to do with my life, so yes."

"I don't know what I want to do with my life either."

She shrugs. "Well, you don't have to take stupid tests. I'm a normal person."

He feels jittery, over-caffeinated, though he hasn't had any soda. They're in the tunnel now. He didn't tell his aunt and uncle where he was going. It won't have occurred to them that he's gone any farther away than Shay's house. After all, he never has before.

This is his first trip back to New York City. He doesn't want to say that out loud.

Instead, he says, "The first summer, you told me that I wasn't normal and that you weren't either."

"Look," she says, "if I want to have a chance to do something great, I need a college degree." She has the window seat, and he can see half of her face and her reflection, which looks like it belongs to a young woman, not a girl.

They take a taxi from Port Authority to the deli. The Upper East Side unfolds around Edward as they climb north in the grid of Manhattan. His family's life was

398

carpeted over the surrounding streets. They pass their dry cleaner, the brick-fronted library, the run-down grocery store where they bought most of their food, and then, a block farther, the fancy supermarket where his father bought meat and cheese.

They pass an antiques shop where his mother once bought a clock. She kept it on her dresser and said it reminded her of her grandmother in Canada. Then a mailbox, which Edward remembers leaning against while his father slid in his April tax checks. He remembers his dad banging the little blue door open and shut while complaining about the unfairness of having to pay for wars he didn't believe in. "If I could designate where my money went," his dad had said, "I'd pay my taxes with enthusiasm."

Edward tightens his seatbelt, as if in protection against the memories.

"Do you have a plan?" Shay says. "Are we just going to meet her?"

Edward shrugs. All he knows is that he has to lay eyes on Mahira, for two reasons. First, because Jordan would want to see her. Second, because she is the only living person — other than him — who deeply, specifically, loved his brother. He lost Jordan, and she did too.

He says, "We don't have to stay long."

The taxi is stopped at a red light. Edward considers that he is going to visit a truth — a person — he hadn't known existed. Mahira's letter had opened a door inside the life he'd lived. It's as if he's discovered a new room off his family's kitchen, with Jordan's girlfriend inside. Were there other doors he'd simply never noticed? The idea is unsettling, but also compelling. He can't recover what he knows he lost — his family — but perhaps he can recover things, people, that he didn't know were there in the first place?

The taxi pulls over at 72nd and Lexington. Shay pays the driver, while Edward stands on the sidewalk. His face must look alarming, because her eyes widen when she joins him. "It's going to be okay," Shay says. "I'll help."

Thank you, he thinks, and watches her turn and walk through the deli door. He watches his new life walk into his old life.

The deli is rectangular and narrow, with one long row of shelves in the center. The space is clean and well lit. Edward used to buy chocolate Yoo-hoos from the refrigerator in the corner whenever he had pocket money. He came here with his dad for emergency items — toilet paper, deodorant, milk. This was where he and Jordan bought illicit candy — almost always Twix for Jordan, and Haribo gummy bears for him. It was the first place they were allowed to walk without supervision. Bruce would send them to the deli for a specific item and set the timer on his watch for fifteen minutes. Their task was to get home before the timer went off.

Edward stands just inside the door. A longing for his brother comes over him, smothering in its intensity. How can he be standing *here,* alone?

No one is behind the counter. There's a boy wearing a soccer jersey standing at the rack of magazines in the corner. Edward wonders if Jordan had known this kid too. Anything is possible. Judging by his size, the kid would have been in early elementary school when they'd lived in the neighborhood. Perhaps his brother had babysat him and never told Edward about the job.

"I checked," a girl's voice calls from the back of the store. "That magazine didn't come in yet. Maybe tomorrow."

"Okay," the boy says. "Thanks." He skips past Edward and Shay and pushes out the front door.

Edward looks at Shay and then does a double take. She has two cans of soup balanced in one hand, a loaf of bread under her arm, and a bag of pretzels.

"What?" she whispers. "I thought we should buy something, so we don't look weird."

"Trust me," he says. "We look weird." But he's grateful to her again, for coming, and for being nervous with him even though she can't parse all of his specific anxieties.

He feels a shift in the air and sees a girl walk out from the back room. She sees him at the same moment and stops.

She shivers. It's a full-bodied motion, as if she's just climbed out of a freezing lake. "Eddie Adler?" she says.

He nods.

"You look like him."

"I'm sorry." But he feels pleased to be told this. No one has compared him to his brother for a long time. He studies her. Shoulder-length black hair, heart-shaped face, skin a few shades darker than Shay's. *Jordan loved you,* he thinks.

"I got your letter," he says. "I didn't know. About you and my brother."

She nods, calmer; she's reined herself in. "I figured not." She looks at Shay. "I'm Mahira," she says. "Can I take those items? You look uncomfortable."

Shay walks forward and awkwardly places the food on the counter. "I'm Edward's friend," she says. "Shay."

Mahira's forehead wrinkles. "Edward?" she says. "I thought you went by . . ."

"You can call me Eddie," he says. "If you want."

The door bangs open behind them, and they turn in that direction. A man in a UPS uniform drops three large boxes on the floor. He says, "See you tomorrow."

"Tomorrow!" Mahira calls, and the man is gone. But almost immediately the door swings open again, and a woman pushes a stroller into the deli. She talks to her baby in a low singsong voice and heads straight for the shelf with the diapers.

Shay says, "Um, do you live here?"

"In the apartment upstairs." Mahira points at the ceiling. She says, "And you're in New Jersey now. Are the aunt and uncle you live with nice? Is it okay?"

"Yes," Edward says. "They're nice."

The woman with the stroller is at the counter now, and Shay and Edward shuffle out of the way. She shoots them a quick glance while fishing her wallet out of her bag. The look seems to say: *What suspicious behavior are you teens up to?*

Edward looks at the baby in the stroller and finds the baby staring back at him. He has giant blue eyes, fat cheeks, and is completely bald. Still staring at Edward, the baby sticks most of his hand in his mouth and makes a blowing sound. He pulls his fingers out and grins.

"You're very cute," Shay says, in a polite voice.

The woman finishes paying, stuffs the package of diapers under the stroller, and shoves the baby away from them, out the jangling door.

"Maybe I'll close up for a few minutes so we can have an actual conversation without half the neighborhood walking in," Mahira says. "There's a busybody who comes at the same time every afternoon and buys a pack of gum; I think she's reporting on me to my uncle. It would be good to avoid her."

She flips the sign on the door from OPEN to CLOSED and turns two heavy locks. "You're fifteen now?" she says.

Edward studies the locks. He wishes the door was still open. He would like escape to be an easy possibility, as opposed to an awkward challenge. He nods. "You were fifteen when you were dating my brother."

Dating my brother. The words sound impossible in the air.

Mahira walks to the counter and leans against it. "You do look like him," she says. "But your voice is different. Your eyes too."

Edward feels an ache that runs the length of him and he knows it's on behalf of Jordan. His brother should be here now. If he *were* Jordan, he would walk up to the counter and hug her. Should he do that for his brother now?

He glances at Shay. Shay is solid. Shay is real. She's standing by a rack of different-flavored potato chips. She's watching the two of them with the same face she uses while studying for a test.

Mahira says, "Are you wearing . . . Was that your brother's coat?"

Edward looks down at the orange parka. It fits him perfectly now but is worn on the elbows and seams. Lacey has been threatening to replace it. "Yes," he says. "I have all his clothes."

"Of course. That makes sense." Her voice is level, but her eyes change, shine.

Edward wants to make this a normal conversation, between normal people. Even though he knows that's not possible. "You said in your letter that you're taking a gap year?"

Mahira nods. "I think I'm going to start at Hunter in the fall; it's only a few blocks away, and it's cheap. I'm a science person," she says. "I always have been, and it's important to my uncle that I become an engineer."

Edward has no idea what kind of person he is. He feels lit up with pain and somehow knows that Mahira feels the same way. Jordan stands between them, a repository of longing created by their proximity. Not a ghost, a longing. *Me plus Mahira equals missing Jordan,* Edward thinks. But the word *missing* doesn't say enough. The name *Jordan* doesn't say enough.

The shimmering Jordan, carrying all of their loss, says to Edward: *Stop talking about bullshit.*

Edward says: "How did you find out about the crash? Where were you when you found out?"

He has been careful to collect this information from the people in his life. Edward thinks of it as plotting points on a graph, arresting the location of each person during a single moment. John saw news of the crash on Twitter almost immediately. He'd been in the middle of an IT job at a retail company, but when he saw the headline he packed up his bag and phoned Lacey from the parking lot. He wasn't sure it was the same flight, and he stayed on the phone with Lacey while she checked her last email with her sister, the one with the information about their travel plans. Shay had been

406

reading the third book of *Anne of Green Gables* on her bed when she heard the phone ring and heard her mother call out in Spanish. She and Besa had watched the crash footage on the television in the living room with the volume turned up so they could hear the reporter over Besa's sobs. Mrs. Cox had been at the 92nd Street Y, listening to a talk on the legacy of Eleanor Roosevelt, when her chauffeur had tapped her on the arm. She'd followed him into the lobby, and he showed her the news on his phone. Dr. Mike had been in a session when the plane crashed and didn't find out until later, when he turned on the radio in his car.

"Oh." Mahira turns her face, looks toward the back storage room. "I was on my way home. I always walked past a big sports bar on the corner of Eighty-third. It has televisions covering all the walls, and they're usually tuned to two or three different games. Football, soccer, ice hockey. But" — she hesitates — "that day, all of the screens were showing one side of an airplane lying in a field. I stopped because the image was so unusual, especially for that place. I walked into the bar, which I'd never done before, and the bartender told me what had happened." She stops talking for a second, then puts her hands out in front of her, as if about to receive something: coins, a gift, Communion? When she drops her hands again, puts them on her thighs, she says, "Back at home, at the deli, the news said that one boy had survived."

Edward processes this. "You would have thought it was Jordan."

She doesn't respond. A new reality blossoms in Edward's brain. Jordan is the one who survives, and instead of going home with Lacey and John from the hospital, he insists on recuperating with Mahira, in the apartment above the deli. Edward can picture him lying in a single bed, one of his legs in a cast. His face is contorted with pain, but he's looking at Mahira. He's going through the loss with her and finding comfort in that. When the plane crashed, he didn't lose everything.

"I'm sorry," Edward says.

"You and I were supposed to meet on a beach in California." Mahira smiles, but the smile has effort behind it. "Do you want to hear something strange?"

Shay, who hasn't spoken in some time, says, "Yes, please."

"I've been going to get my tarot cards read by a woman who works a few blocks from here. She has a purple lamp in her window and a chime hung in the doorway. It's absurd, and I don't believe in any of it, but I can't seem to stay away."

"What does she tell you?"

Mahira's cheeks turn a faint pink. "Part of it is fairy tales. She talks about Jordan and our love. I guess that's why I keep going. I haven't had anyone else to talk to about it. My uncle won't hear his name mentioned."

"Jordan," Edward says reflexively.

"Jordan." Mahira says the name in the same tone she used with the UPS guy — deliberate, authoritative. She says his name the same way she called out the word *tomorrow*.

There's a pounding on the door, and they all jump. The silhouette of a figure is visible through the marbled glass. A fist is raised again, then dropped. The person walks away.

Edward wonders what the tarot-card lady would talk to him about. He likes the idea of someone talking to him about his and his brother's love. He says, "Can you tell me why you and Jordan were a secret? Why he didn't tell me?"

She shakes her head. "We never talked that much, to be honest. I was afraid long conversations would ruin everything, that I might say something stupid. I kept thinking

409

I would talk soon, ask questions soon, tell him everything soon."

"You thought you had time," Shay says.

"Yes."

Edward thinks of the letters, all the people asking him questions, wanting to believe they could find a solution, or resolution, to their heartbreak. The lonely girl in front of him and the ache of those letters make his own chest hurt, and he hunches slightly.

"I should reopen the store," Mahira says.

"No problem," he says.

But they stand in silence for a few more moments, before they break apart.

When they enter the garage that night, Shay says, "Why can't you talk to John in the house, over breakfast, like a civilized person? We don't even know how early he comes out here in the morning. We may have to wait for hours and hours."

"I have to talk to him here. Away from Lacey." Edward sits down on the footstool, which he thinks of as his footstool. The chair belongs to Shay.

"You've turned bossy lately. I'm not sure if I like it."

Edward smiles. "You can go to sleep until he gets here."

"Oh, I will." Shay wriggles around in the

armchair, as if looking for the most comfortable spot. She says, "Did you almost kiss Mahira today?"

Edward freezes for a second, and his cheeks flush. "I thought about it. For Jordan." He takes an uneven breath. "I'm not sure what I can or should do, for him."

"I saw you considering it."

"How? What did that look like?"

She smiles and shrugs. "I couldn't describe it in words."

He meets her gaze, and there's something new there. Edward used to think that what had happened had happened only to him, but he knows Shay has been changed, and he knows the writers of the letters have been changed too, so the ripple effects feel possibly infinite. He is on the lookout for the infinite now, in Shay's dimple.

There's a pause, and she turns off the flashlight. Shay says into the darkness, "Good night."

She turns away from Edward and curls up in the chair. He remains upright on the stool. The air between him and Shay is charged, the atoms swollen with new possibilities. He knows — somehow — that they both imagined kissing each other. He had imagined tilting his head to the side, and leaning in. Their lips touching. He thinks of the air between him and Mahira that afternoon, the shimmering presence of his brother, the loss of what was.

Edward's science teacher recently told them about the Large Hadron Collider in Switzerland, the largest machine ever built. *It's investigating different theories of particle physics,* the teacher had said. *The scientists think they're on the brink of understanding what happens in the air between two people. Why some people repel us, and others attract us, and everything in between. The air between us is not empty space.*

Edward's entire body is aware of Shay's body only a few feet from his own. He doesn't try to find a comfortable position; he intends to stay awake until his uncle arrives in the garage.

He stares into the darkness and finds himself replaying the visit to the deli. His grief for his brother is bigger at the end of this day, a fact he wouldn't have thought possible. But Edward used to miss Jordan only for himself. It had been *his* terrible loss. Now he also mourns what his brother has lost. Jordan will never sit this close to a girl again, with his entire body tingling.

The sky is purple-ribboned when John opens the garage door. He stops in the doorway and regards the scene. The tired-eyed teenage boy, and the sleeping teenage girl.

"Good morning," John says, in a cautious voice.

"Hi." Edward stands up from the stool. "Don't worry," he says. "Nothing's wrong. I just wanted to tell you that I looked in your folders. I found them by accident. And then we opened the duffel bags too and read the letters."

John's face registers surprise, and something else too. Maybe fear? "You opened the locks on the bags?" Then, "I was going to give them to you when you were older. I know they're yours. It's just that I read a few, when they first started coming, and I thought it was outrageous that people were writing letters like that to a young child."

"That's what we assumed."

John sighs, the sound of a small boulder rolling down a hill. "Those aren't even all of them."

It takes a second for this to sink in. "There are more letters?"

"Not many. But there are a few recent ones in the back of the hall closet. They still come in now, at a slower rate. I collect them every Friday from the post office."

Shay shifts on the chair. When she has resettled into sleep, Edward says, "Why did you use a P.O. box?"

"We set it up after we got that binder of personal effects in the mail. We thought it would be safer not to have mail coming straight to the house. We didn't want you to stumble into anything we hadn't had a chance to check out first."

Edward looks at his uncle. He has the thought that he's just a person who happens to be older than him. He doesn't know better, or more, than Edward does. John and Lacey are playing the roles they've been assigned: husband, wife, aunt, uncle. When Shay had pushed him to tell John and Lacey about the letters, he'd resisted because he wanted to first figure out what he wanted to do, before asking the grown-ups. Built into that was the assumption that John and Lacey would have a solid answer, a solution to the problem. But he sees now and understands that's not the case.

He says, "Are you and Lacey going to be okay?"

John gives a pained smile. "She's been frustrated with me. Understandably." He shrugs. "When you have a long history with someone . . . Nothing is as linear as you think it's going to be. Lacey and I have always mistimed getting upset when something challenging happens. I go cold at first, and she falls apart. Once she's pulled herself together, I'm usually okay, but this time . . . It's a kind of marital glitch."

"It's complicated," Edward offers, because he wants to help.

John gestures with his hand again, this time seeming to refer to everything: the photographs, the letters, middle age, marriage. "If you live long enough, everything is complicated."

Edward thinks of the history that already winds, nonlinear and intricate, between himself and Shay. And the history that continues to pulsate between Mahira and his brother, even though Jordan is dead. He listens to the light rustle of Shay's breath and says, "It would have been better, I think, if you'd showed me everything from the beginning. I think it's important . . . to see everyone who died. They matter as much as you or me, and I want to remember them."

Edward watches his uncle consider this. "That's interesting," John says. "Maybe I should have shown you everything, but I didn't feel like I could." His uncle looks old, draped in the pastel light of dawn. "You need to understand that my biggest fear, our biggest fear . . ." He hesitates.

"What?" Edward says.

John turns his head slightly, so he's looking at the sunrise, not his nephew. He says,
"That you might, well, decide not to live.
Dr. Mike said it was a real concern, and
you starved yourself when you first got here,
and then you collapsed outside. You were
deeply depressed."

Edward blinks, trying to understand. "You
were worried I would kill myself?"

"We based all our decisions on preventing
that. I didn't want you around anything that
might upset you further. Lacey thinks I was
too hardcore about it and that by protecting
you from the crash, I ended up obsessed
with it." He rubs his hands over his face.
"Women are smarter than we are, you
know."

Dr. Mike had said something to Edward
once, during a session, about taking suicide
off the table as an option. Edward hadn't
responded, confused by the comment. But
now, with this idea in front of him, Edward
can see that fear in the careful attention of
Principal Arundhi, in Lacey's sleeping pill
prescription, in the new lines on John's face.
He shakes his head. "I never would have
done that."

John shrugs, as if to say: *Maybe, but I
couldn't be sure.*

The weariness in his uncle's eyes makes

Edward realize, for the first time, why John had needed to save him at all costs. His uncle — with all his will, attention, and care — had been unable to save anyone else. The babies Lacey had carried. Jane and Bruce, and his oldest nephew. And so he had been willing to wreck his own life, even his marriage, to make sure he didn't lose the nephew who came to live in his house.

"I wouldn't have done that to you" — Edward looks at his uncle and then over at Shay; this applies to her too — "because I know what it's like to be left behind."

He's winded by the sentence, as if the truth has taken something from him. He feels a flash of fear, but then sees the look on his uncle's face. John opens his arms, and Edward steps forward.

2:08 P.M.

The co-pilot, spooked by the alarm, or the turbulence, or by the experience of flying the plane by hand — most pilots train for manual takeoff and landings, not midair flight — makes an irrational decision. He pulls back on the side stick to put the airplane into a steep climb. The pilot, from his vantage point, doesn't have a clear view of the co-pilot's right arm, and it doesn't occur to him that his colleague would make such an unwise decision.

"Steady," the pilot says.

"Roger that."

Almost as soon as the co-pilot pulls up, the plane's computer reacts. A warning chime alerts the cockpit to the fact that they're leaving their programmed altitude. The stall warning sounds. This is a synthesized human voice that repeatedly calls out, "Stall!" in English, followed by a loud and intentionally annoying sound called a cricket. A stall is a potentially dangerous situation that can result from flying too slowly. At a critical speed, a wing suddenly becomes much less effective at generating lift, and a plane can plunge precipitously. But the pilot believes they are following the correct protocols, so he's not overly concerned by the stall warning. The co-pilot, who is still pulling back on the side stick, is now covered with a cold sweat and breathing shallowly. He tries to hide his panic.

The floor buckles beneath Veronica, then re-forms. "Return to your seat," she says to the red-haired doctor. She gives the dead old man a look, then gives the nurse a kinder one. "I'll be back in a few minutes," she says.

She trips toward her seat, which is around the corner from first class. She falls onto the hard horizontal rectangle and tugs the strap across her chest. She pictures the white features of Crispin Cox. She considers that there is no breath in his throat, no blood coursing through his body. She's never had anyone die on a flight before. What is the protocol? She's read all the protocols, and for this situation, the first step is to alert the pilot. She will do so as soon as she can get to the intercom. Then, if possible, the dead body should be moved to an empty row of seats, away from other passengers. That's not possible on this flight, which is full, but she did read that sometimes the corpse is gently placed into a closet until the flight ends. There is a closet in the back of the plane that might work, if she emptied out a few containers.

She imagines herself and Ellen carrying the body through the entire plane to get to the closet. Her with her hands under the old man's armpits, Ellen holding his feet. Luis waiting by the closet to help.

The plane gives a hard cough, and the nose wavers. Veronica shifts her attention to the grumbles and clanks of this colossal machine, which she knows as intimately as her own body. She thinks, *What are you trying to tell me?*

Edward has only two responsibilities that feel real to him now: reading new letters as they arrive, and taking care of Principal Arundhi's fern. Edward has had the plant for nearly four months. The fern appears to be thriving, bright green and placid on its table beneath the basement window. Edward takes photos of the kangaroo paw and shows them to Principal Arundhi, to reassure him of the plant's good health. The principal's office looks more like an office now and less like a greenhouse. The virus had turned out to be a long, truly nasty one, which came in three waves. It has finally lost its grip on the ferns, but thirteen died in total. There is only a spattering of plants on the windowsill and the side table.

"I have to rebuild," the principal says. "I'm considering purchasing some orchids. Marvelous plants, orchids. Don't you think?" He sighs, and Edward can see that his heart's not in the rebuilding. He's just saying the words. Principal Arundhi asks Edward to hold on to the kangaroo paw for a few more weeks, just to be safe.

Friday is the only day of the week Edward bothers to keep track of, because that's the day John brings home new letters, if there are any. Shay is now pen pals with the nun in South Carolina. Edward writes to Gary and asks him questions about whales. He and Shay both text with Mahira. All the children have been replied to. They have, Edward thinks, responded to the letters on the edges: *the very old, and the very young.* In the center are hundreds of requests that Edward has come to picture as a stretch of quicksand. He hasn't decided what to do about them, but he knows that if he fulfills the wish of one letter, he must fulfill them all. And that, as depicted by Shay's spreadsheet, is technically impossible. It would have him living in multiple parts of the globe, working as a doctor, a librarian, a chef, an activist, a novelist, a photographer, a classics professor, a clothing designer, a war reporter, a sommelier, and a social worker, among other careers. He would be mapping out wishes that oppose one another, in locations multiple time zones apart.

The letter he read this morning was a very short, almost incomprehensible note from the wife of the co-pilot. In it, she tells the story of how she and her husband met in college and how sorry she is that he made a mistake in the cockpit. She ends with: *My husband killed 191 people. Can you imagine what it's like to be me?*

Out of all the letters Edward has read, this is the only one he's certain shouldn't have been sent. Her husband killed his family. How could she think it was okay to write and ask him for . . . what? Validation? Empathy? He should be angry at her, he thinks, but he's not. She had nothing to do with what happened, and she was left behind too. Besides, whether Edward likes it or not, he *can* imagine what it's like to be her. He can imagine the crush of guilt, the fractured metal airplane that must lie on this woman whenever she tries to sleep.

He's in the middle of the main hallway at school; he looks around at the throng of teenagers. Social studies begins in three minutes; they're studying the French Revolution. He knows his peers in that class are hoping to ace this semester so they have a better chance of being accepted into AP History next year, not because they're interested in history, but because the best colleges expect students to take at least three advanced placement classes. There's an exit door at the end of the hallway, and Edward slips through it.

He walks toward the main street, feeling the school drift, cloud-like, behind him. He feels bad that Shay will be confused, and concerned, when she realizes he's not in social studies, and then not in school at all. But he keeps walking anyway. When he's on the next bus into the city, he texts Mahira for the address of the tarot-card reader.

Aren't you supposed to be in school? she texts back.

Yes.

Ha. She sends the address and then adds, *Remember, it's all bullshit.*

He takes a taxi to the location, which is on a tree-lined side street on the Upper East Side. Edward climbs out of the taxi on the corner and has the thought that he's traveled more miles in the last six months than in the prior three years combined. It's as if he turned his brother's age and Jordan shoved him into motion. He's propelled now, toward what he does not exactly know.

Edward spots the purple lamp in the window first, before he sees the street number over the door. It's a ground-floor window in a medium-sized apartment building. There's a small white sign with black lettering in the lower right corner of the window. The sign reads: FUTURES TOLD BY MADAME VICTORY, BUZZER 1A.

This is bullshit, he thinks, and feels a searing hopelessness again. He stands on the far side of the street and decides, *I'll write back to the co-pilot's wife when I get home. I'll tell her that I understand.* This decision allows Edward to move, to cross the street, climb the steps, and ring the buzzer.

He hears a click, and pushes through the building's two front doors. He finds himself in a lobby with a green rug and wallpaper covered with leaves. The door to his left is partly ajar. He pushes it the rest of the way open.

"Hello?" he says. He's in what looks like a dingy dining room. There's a round wooden table with four chairs around it. A bureau against one wall. A tapestry against the far wall in the style of the Renaissance; it shows a unicorn on its hind legs inside a corral. Flowers decorate the air around the corral. Edward remembers watching an animated movie about a unicorn when he was very young, and becoming, for a time, obsessed with the mythical animal. Part of his obsession stemmed from the fact that his parents, who prided themselves on separating fact and fiction for the boys, seemed uncomfortable when he asked if unicorns were real. *Maybe?* his mother had said. *Maybe they were real, a long time ago?*

"One second, sweetheart," a woman's voice says. Edward hears bells and looks toward the window, where a metal wind chime is quivering. Had the woman's voice set it off? He gets goosebumps on his arms, and then she's in front of him.

She's tall — at least six feet — and has a colorful wrap around her hair. She has tan skin, brown eyes, and a generous smile. She's wearing a bright-yellow skirt and a zipped-up hoodie sweatshirt.

"Sit down, handsome," she says, waving at one of the chairs. "Fifteen minutes with Madame Victory costs thirty dollars in cash, just so you are aware."

"Okay," Edward says, but he hesitates before sitting down, because his body is on high alert. The chimes still ring from the corner, though less wildly now. He can't quite decipher the message his body is sending him; he's experiencing it as a surge of adrenaline: *Be careful; danger; leave.* But he sinks into the chair, anyway.

Madame Victory sits down across the table. "Would you prefer a tarot-card or a palm reading?"

"I don't know."

She looks him in the face for the first time. He has trouble meeting her eyes but also can't look away. The adrenaline in his body hasn't faded. The chimes clatter as if a two-year-old were playing with them. Edward shifts in his chair, trying to find a comfortable position. She's doing this to him; he knows that, but he doesn't know why. His brain thinks, *Do I know you?* But of course he doesn't know her.

"Hmm," she says. "I'd like to look at your palm. Give me your hand please, darling."

He extends his arm, skinny despite the weights he lifts. He's shaking slightly. It occurs to him how intimate this is, offering your hand to another person. When she takes his hand, her skin is dry and warm.

"You are familiar to me," she says.

"My friend comes to see you." He's aware, of course, that Mahira is not his *friend,* but whatever she is has no tolerable name. His dead-brother's-girlfriend-whom-he-never-knew-about? The other-one-who-loved-Jordan?

Madame Victory nods, as if she already knew that. She studies his hand. She touches the middle of his palm with her index finger. "Eddie," she whispers.

He wonders if perhaps he heard her incorrectly. "Excuse me?"

She doesn't repeat herself, so he says, "Did Mahira tell you I was coming?"

"Mahira?" She shakes her head. She touches the mound under each of his fingers and thumb. "I don't usually ask my clients this," she says, "but, sweetheart, what would you like to hear?"

"What do you mean?" He's confused. "I thought you were going to tell me my future. . . . Are there other options?"

She doesn't respond. Bent over his hand, she doesn't look at him.

"I want to know what to do," he hears himself say, and, like the decision to write to the co-pilot's wife, the statement is a relief. He wants to know what to do.

She taps the center of his hand. "That's easy. The same thing we all must do. Take stock of who we are, and what we have, and then use it for good."

He replays this in his mind. He listens to it through, more than once, then says, "But you could tell anyone that."

She smiles. "Indeed I could. I would like to tell everyone that. Unfortunately, everyone does not come to see me. But you did, and you are of an age, and a history, that makes my advice particularly relevant."

Edward feels his phone buzz in his pocket,

and knows that school has ended for the day. Shay is texting: *Where are you? Are you okay?* He says, "There are these steps for what you're supposed to do: You figure out what you want to study, and then go to the best college you can get into. And then go to the best graduate school. And then get the best job."

This makes Madame Victory's face light up, and Edward watches as the light shines out of her skin and she starts to laugh: a giant, warm, bubbling sound that fills the room. She tips her head back, puts her free hand on her belly. The wind chime in the corner weighs in. Edward can't help but laugh in response. He hears himself give a new chuckle, one he hasn't heard himself make before.

When her laughter slows, the light dims slightly, and she says, "You're very cerebral, Eddie, aren't you?"

"Edward. Could you please tell me how you know my name?"

"What you need to realize, sweet boy, is that the thicket you're trying to walk through isn't cerebral in nature. It's not a math puzzle you can reason out. You need a different kind of wisdom to extract yourself."

"What do you mean?"

"It's been fifteen minutes," she says, in a changed tone.

"I'll pay for another fifteen."

"Impossible today, I'm afraid. I have a standing appointment. You may come again, if you like." She is still holding his hand; now she covers it with her own, and a feeling of warmth travels into his skin and up his arm. "I am tempted," she says, and it sounds like she's talking to herself, "to give you some mushrooms."

"Mushrooms?" Edward pictures the button mushrooms that grow between the roots of the tree in John and Lacey's backyard.

Psilocybe semilanceata," she says. "They would open you up to the different kinds of wisdom I mentioned. But, no, I'm not going to do that. You're capable of opening up on your own, Eddie. I trust you to see yourself all the way there."

"I don't understand," Edward says.

She smiles. "Understanding is overrated."

Madame Victory is standing now, so Edward stands too. The chimes ring out in the corner. He pulls his wallet out of his pocket.

She shakes her head, then comes closer. He can feel the warmth he'd felt from her hand coming off her entire body. She smells of cinnamon. "I won't charge for the first

430

session. It's a gift."

Madame Victory takes his arm and walks him to the door. Just before she opens it, she leans in and says into his ear, "There was no reason for what happened to you, Eddie. You could have died; you just didn't. It was dumb luck. Nobody chose you for anything. Which means, truly, that you can do anything."

And then the door is open and he's moving through it and then he's standing in the middle of the lobby, which he realizes has been decorated to look like a forest.

2:09 P.M.

The pilot raises his voice for the first time. "Check your speed!"

The plane is climbing at a blistering rate of seven thousand feet per minute. While it's gaining altitude, it's losing speed, until it's crawling along at only 93 knots, a speed more typical of a small Cessna than an airliner.

The pilot: "Pay attention to your speed. Pay attention to your speed."

The co-pilot: "Okay, okay, I'm descending."

Pilot: "Stabilize."

Thanks to the effects of the anti-icing system, one of the pitot tubes begins to work again. The cockpit displays once again show valid speed information.

"Here we go, we're descending."

"Gently."

"Yes."

The co-pilot eases the backward pressure

on the stick, and the plane gains speed as its climb becomes more shallow. It accelerates to 223 knots. The stall warning falls silent. For a moment, the pilots are in control. But they're not communicating well, so the pilot doesn't know that they're a hair's breadth away from total disaster, and the co-pilot doesn't know that if he never again pulled back on the stick, everything would be fine, and they would land in Los Angeles on schedule.

Mark can't see Veronica. He is in his seat, fumbling for the loose buckle. Jane is making a funny breathing noise next to him.

"It's just turbulence." His voice comes out choppy, knocked around his throat by the jerks of the plane. "Planes never crash because of turbulence. I read that somewhere."

"I know," she says. "I just wish I were back with my family."

Mark remembers being on the plane with Jax and his mother: nine years old, sharing candy bars with his brother, fighting the urge to kick the seat in front of him. Always a struggle to be still.

"I'm a writer," Jane says. "I have a habit, I guess, where I see all the possibilities in a situation. No matter what, there's always at least one that's terrifying."

"Don't do that," he says. "Focus on what's in front of you."

But his own attention is split between hoping to see Veronica's face, and the deal he's been prepping for in L.A. He's come up with a closing strategy that's complex and imbued with a shade of caution, and therefore not his usual style. He can feel his skills sharpening and his capacity growing with each heartbeat. With this deal, he'll prove his colleagues wrong for thinking he couldn't work at the highest level without cocaine. He'll prove the press wrong for thinking he was a flash in the pan. If men like Cox are leaving the world stage, he's ready to take over. And then Veronica will fuck him; every woman alive will want to fuck him. This — this turbulence, the dead hero across the aisle — none of this can stop him. He cannot be stopped.

Out of nowhere, Shay will whisper in Edward's ear, "Seven million dollars," while they're at the grocery store or trying on sneakers at the mall. Each time, he makes a face and says, "Not yet." The check is stored in the original envelope from Jax and is safely underneath Edward's bed with the other letters. After school each afternoon, he either lifts weights in the gym or runs a loop around the lake with Shay. If the weather is mild, they end their run at the playground and sit on the swings until their breath returns to normal. Edward does his math homework every day — a first — because a new math teacher had been hired midyear, and the work is finally both challenging and interesting. Deep inside a difficult problem, Edward can sense his father looking over his shoulder, offering strategies.

Edward doesn't know what he's waiting

for, until it arrives in the mail. It's one of the Friday letters John brings home from the post office. Edward takes it from his uncle in the front hallway and opens it. He normally waits until he's alone with Shay, but something about the slant of the writing on the envelope makes him slide open the flap, even though it's almost dinnertime and John's standing right in front of him.

Dear Edward,
You should know that Jax talked about you often. The idea of you made him happy. You freed him when he sent you the money. It was important to Jax that it be yours. I have the letter you sent him asking if he was sure, if he wanted it back. He never wanted it back.

He got really into big-wave surfing, so we moved near a famous break point in California last year. He loved it, but he died three months ago. He wiped out on a wave and then disappeared. They found him a couple hours later, with his board leash trapped under some rocks.

The lawyer told me there might be a problem depositing the original check because of Jax's death, so I've enclosed a new check for the same amount. Please don't write back and say you're sorry, because there's nothing to be sorry for. This was not a tragedy. Dying on your couch watching TV by yourself is a tragedy. Dying while doing something you love with every part of your body is magic. I wish you magic, Edward.

Tahiti

Edward looks up from the letter.

"Are you crying?" John says, and at the same moment Shay walks through the front door and Edward says to her, "Jax is dead."

Shay puts her hands over her mouth. "No. What happened?"

John says, "What's going on?"

"Hold on." Edward goes downstairs and gets the first letter from Jax. He hands it to his uncle, who reads it. Then he hands him Tahiti's letter and the new check.

When John has studied all three, he walks toward the kitchen, and the teenagers follow. Lacey is cooking at the stove. She has earbuds in and is humming. She removes them when they all troop in. The atmosphere in the house has changed since Edward confronted his uncle in the garage. They're all on the same page, even if that page is in the middle of an ongoing story with an uncertain end. There has been a softening between Lacey and John. A few days earlier, Edward had overheard his aunt call his uncle "Bear" and watched John blush with happiness.

"You won't believe this," John says to her now.

He fills her in, and she punctuates each piece of paper she's handed with a small "Oh my."

They gather around the kitchen table. The two letters and the check are now on the table, and because of their shapes and location they look like two placemats and a napkin.

"You told me the details once," Edward says. "Am I right that each victim's family got one million dollars from insurance and that I'll get five million when I turn twenty-one?"

"That's correct," John says.

"So Benjamin Stillman's grandmother got one million dollars, for instance."

Lacey scrunches up her face at the name — she hasn't memorized the roster of the plane like the other three have — but doesn't say anything.

Edward has been working with his uncle to complete the information in the folder. The collaboration had been John's idea. He'd approached Edward one afternoon and said, "I've been thinking about what you said in the garage. I think we should finish documenting everyone on the plane, to make sure everyone is — as you said — *seen.* I like that idea very much." He gave his nephew a shy look. "Would you help me finish the job?"

Edward told John everything he knew about the passengers on the flight. About the red-haired doctor going into first class to help someone. About his conversation with Benjamin. About the woman with the bells on her skirt, and Gary's girlfriend. Even about Mark and Veronica sharing a bathroom. While Edward talked, John took notes and added the information to the back of the relevant photos.

When John wrote the description onto the reverse of Florida's photograph, he'd said, "You know, I was in touch with her husband, and he told me that Florida believed in reincarnation, believed that she'd already had hundreds of lives. The husband — I believe his name was Bobby — sold his house after the crash and bought a camper, and now he's driving around the country looking for her in her new incarnation."

Edward's first thought had been that if they could find a photograph of Florida in her new body, they could add that photo to the folder too. Then he shook his head, and when he looked at his uncle, he saw that John was thinking the exact same thing. They shared their new smile — one that had emerged when they started working together — which confirmed their mutual craziness and the fact that they didn't care.

John says, "Lolly Stillman got a million dollars, yes. Why do you ask?"

The four of them are standing shoulder to shoulder, looking down at the correspondence, the check, the arrival and exit of Jax Lassio. Edward feels his shoulders soften with relief at having handed over another secret to his aunt and uncle. He no longer has any interest in secrets.

Before bed, Edward sprays the fern and checks the soil, adding a tablespoon of new dirt from the bag underneath the table. Principal Arundhi had told him that he wanted Edward to keep the kangaroo paw forever. "Ferns aren't meant to be bounced around," he'd said, with a mournful tug on his mustache. "You've cared for him long enough that you're now his home."

Edward brushes his teeth, flosses, puts on the sweatpants he wears as pajamas. He checks the fern one last time before climbing into bed. In the slow motion of these movements, an idea arrives in his head, fully formed. He could use Jax's money to give Principal Arundhi several truly rare and expensive ferns, to refill his collection. The idea makes Edward smile into his pillow.

The letter from Tahiti had saddened him, but it had also been a relief. It felt like a piece of punctuation in a run-on sentence. Edward can move forward. The truth was that he'd always been uncomfortable with the money from Jax, mostly because it made no sense. Jax must have known that Edward had been given insurance money after the crash; he must have known that Edward didn't need money. After the crash, it was perhaps the last thing Edward did need. But Jax had chosen to give it to him anyway. Maybe Edward can give it away in the same spirit? Just give it away simply because, and to whom, it feels right?

Ferns for Principal Arundhi feel right. Maybe Edward could even arrange for a greenhouse to be built behind the man's house and filled with plants. Edward starts to smile and finds that he is already smiling. It occurs to him that Mrs. Cox, in particular, would think this was pure insanity. She believed that money was a building block to create more money, a tool to be utilized in building a life of prosperity. She believed in philanthropy — giving to specific, prestigious entities like museums — but she would never condone this kind of frivolity. And, though he would never criticize her directly, Edward knows from the delight bubbling through him that he, and this frivolity, are on the right track.

Who else can he give to? Who else feels right, even if it doesn't make sense? Edward could give to the people who suffered from the crash but weren't compensated by the airline and insurance company. He could pay for Shay's college tuition, which Besa can't afford. Mahira's too. He could give Gary money for his whale research — Gary wasn't Linda's spouse, so he never received a check. He would like to give Benjamin's grandmother money, even though she received an insurance payment. She could give the amount away however *she* saw fit.

He can hear Shay's voice say: *Don't forget about my nun and the three kids in the second letter we read.*

Who else? What else?

His body grows heavy on the mattress; his eyes are closing. He's falling asleep. His last thought is that he has to find a way for the gifts to be anonymous and untraceable to him. Otherwise, he is an asshole.

2:10 P.M.

The plane has climbed to 2,512 feet above its initial altitude, and although it's still ascending at a dangerously high rate, it is flying within its acceptable envelope. But the co-pilot once again increases his backward pressure on the stick, raising the nose of the plane and bleeding off speed. None of the pilots who later study Flight 2977's black-box recording can believe that a trained pilot repeated the mistake at this point. But he did.

The stall alarm sounds.

"Pay attention," the pilot says.

"Okay."

Maybe the pilots ignore the alarm because they believe it's impossible for them to stall the airplane. It's not an entirely unreasonable idea. This is a fly-by-wire plane; the control inputs are fed directly to a computer, which in turn commands actuators that move the rudder, elevator, ailerons, and flaps. The vast majority of the time, the computer operates within what's known as "normal law," which means that the computer will not enact any control movements that would cause the plane to leave its flight envelope. The flight-control computer under normal law will not allow an aircraft to stall.

But once the computer loses its airspeed data, it disconnects the autopilot and switches from normal law to "alternate law," a regimen with far fewer restrictions on what a pilot can do. In alternate law, pilots can stall an airplane. And the co-pilot, by pulling back on the stick, is doing exactly that.

"What's happening?" the old lady next to Benjamin asks him. "What in the world is going on?"

She looks up at him with wide eyes. Her left hand is gripping his arm, a fact he doesn't think she's aware of.

"It's turbulence, ma'am. It happens."

The plane gives two hops, a sound like hard suitcases being slammed against the ground. Benjamin whistles slightly, under his breath. He thinks, *I do not want to die with this old white lady hanging on my arm. Please, God.*

"I have fourteen children," she says.

"Fourteen?"

She's happy to have surprised him. "Well, only nine are still alive."

"I'm sorry to hear that."

"Do you have a mother?" she asks.

Bam. The plane hops again. "No, ma'am. I don't."

"Oh." She looks disappointed.

He glances at the family across the aisle. Little Eddie looks terrified, gripping his brother's hand. Benjamin feels a small localized softening inside him, and thinks, *Poor kid.* The thought almost makes him tear up, and he realizes that his sympathy extends beyond the child across the aisle, back in time to himself, when he was Eddie's age. *Poor kid.*

He says, "A family that big must have been a lot of work."

"It was. You're a man, so you'll never know work that hard. It's reserved solely for the women."

The plane skitters sideways, and he thinks, *We're off course.*

"My oldest daughter is picking me up at the airport. I'm going to live with her. I have a plan."

"It's good to have a plan."

"This is going to be my retirement," she says. "I'm going to put my feet up, read magazines, and drink gin and tonics." She purses her lips. "I could use one now."

Benjamin glances again at the family across the aisle. He thinks of Gavin, eyes smiling behind his glasses. He thinks of resigning from the army, folding his uniform into a trunk and locking it shut. He thinks of fitting together puzzle pieces at the kitchen table with Lolly. Kissing a man behind the 7-Eleven down the street.

At school and at camp he woke to: *Boots on the ground, soldier!* He had one commanding officer who liked to mix things up by entering the barracks predawn and shouting: *Where's the enemy?*

These had been his wake-up calls, his alarm clocks, his calls to action for most of his life. *Where is the enemy?* he wonders. He feels a great sadness. This old lady's idea of putting her feet up is anathema to him. He will stay alert. He will keep his boots on the ground.

446

JULY 2016

The summer before tenth grade, Edward and Shay are counselors at the town's day camp. Edward is put in charge of the oldest group of campers, and on the first morning he stands in front of a cluster of twelve-year-old boys. He's about to introduce himself and call attendance, when something inside him judders.

He looks at one boy, and then another. He meets their eyes, one set brown under a mop of hair, one set blue. About half of the boys have arranged their hair to hide their faces, but Edward looks past these carefully arranged curtains. Their eyes hold something. He doesn't know what it is, but he can't look away.

"My mom said you were in a plane crash," one boy says.

"Yes, I was."

"Did it hurt?"

"Yes. It hurt a lot."

The boys laugh at this. Edward realizes that these boys are the same age he was when he crashed. He was broken open when he was twelve, but there's something broken open in these boys' eyes too.

"Is something wrong?" a boy asks.

"No. Get in height order."

They bustle into motion, bumping each other with their backpacks. He doesn't need them in height order. He's just buying time. He watches them shuffle and duck into place.

Is it the age?

Is it the moment in time right before you leave childhood?

He swims with them that afternoon. If he could have kept them out of the lake, he would have, but swimming is a nonnegotiable part of the camp schedule. He lectures them on safety before they enter the water. "No roughhousing. Focus on your stroke. You know who your buddy is, right? Keep an eye on him and no one else. We'll swim to the yellow buoy and back. No detours, no distractions. You hear me?"

Within fifty yards he's confident that all the campers are capable swimmers, which is a relief, but that doesn't mean there can't be an accident or mistake. He powers past the boys on the flanks, checking their faces

448

to make sure they're not struggling. The boys pivot their wet heads toward him and smile.

That night he says to Shay, "I think I want to be a teacher. Seventh-grade math, probably."

She laughs, then notices his expression. "You're serious?"

"I think so."

"So many kids with braces and acne," she says. "Everyone is a mess at that age. Do you remember my stupid bangs?"

"Kind of."

"Why would you want to spend your life with twelve-year-olds?"

"Maybe I can help them. When I was twelve, you watched me. You had a notepad just for writing down what you noticed, remember? Maybe everyone needs that kind of attention at that age. I could get a notepad."

She considers him, the dimple deep in her cheek.

He thinks, *She's still carrying that notepad.*

Edward spends the next weekend helping John turn the nursery into a home office. The single bed and rocking chair have been donated, and they paint the walls the specific shade of off-white that Lacey selected.

449

John and Edward mumble expletives while trying to force an Ikea desk into shape with hex keys and various screws and bolts. Behind them, Lacey pushes the green armchair from one corner of the room to the other, trying to get a feel for which position promotes the best feng shui. When a corner is finally chosen, the bookcase, packed with Westerns, is set carefully beside it.

The garage was cleaned out a few weeks earlier. The letters have all been collated; the ones Edward wants to keep are stored beneath his bed in the basement. John closed the P.O. box in town, and all mail now comes to the house. Cleaning out this room is the last step.

They're exhausted and sweaty when the room is done, but Edward, John, and Lacey bunch in the doorway. They regard the new space with amazement, as if it is a total surprise, and not the result of their labor.

On a Friday evening near the end of the summer, Shay and Edward walk down to the lake after dinner. The teenagers settle, cross-legged, onto the soft grass. They're in sight of where Edward swims every day with his campers. It's a particularly beautiful summer evening, and the lake shines like a coin under the setting sun.

"Two weeks until school," Shay says.

Edward studies the shimmering lake, with trees darkening behind it. "The first day I got here," he says, "John brought me up to the nursery and showed me this lake out the window. And then I didn't see it again for a long time, because I never went upstairs. But I remember him saying that we might go swimming in the lake when I felt better, and how that felt about as likely as going to the moon."

Shay wraps her arms around her knees. "You were so weak and skinny back then, you could hardly walk to the end of the block."

"I swam in the lake almost every day this summer." Edward feels no sense of accomplishment at this. Just wonder at left turns and moonscapes in his life. Tarot-card readers, heartbreaking letters, a new friendship with his uncle, lake swims. It's all equally unexpected.

"I didn't tell my mother we were coming down here." Shay lies back onto the grass.

"She wouldn't care."

"I care."

Edward smiles at the fact that Shay doesn't want to share *any* life experiences — big or small — with her mother. Life continues to be a tug of war between the two women, a battle Edward doesn't understand but enjoys watching. His brother had shared a tension with their father too. Had Edward simply been too young to engage in this primordial battle? He can only imagine turning toward his mom and dad, embracing them. He missed the chance to experience a more complicated relationship, and right now he feels another sting of loss.

"I don't know what temperature the air is," Shay says, "but this is the perfect temperature."

Edward puts his hand out, to assess the air himself, and decides she's right. He lies down on the soft grass. "Shay?" he says.

"Yes?"

He can't see her. He's looking up at the dimming sky. "I love you."

"I love you too."

He laughs, because they've never said this out loud before, and that strikes him as ridiculous. He knows that he's always loved her, and will always love her, even if another plane crashes or a car hits her or she has a heart attack or he gets cancer or an aneurysm ruptures their brains or global warming evaporates the water supply and causes them to join resource militias until they die of hunger or thirst.

"I'm really tired," Shay says.

"Me too, because of that dumb race. I canoed those kids for three hours."

"Is *canoed* a word?"

"Not sure. But I canoed them."

They're both quiet for a while. Maybe Edward dozes off, though he feels highly aware of his surroundings. He can sense the geometry of the lake — both its surface area and depth — and the moon, which is pinned halfway to the horizon. He can feel the loss of his brother, as if that loss has the solidity of one of the trees behind him. Edward breathes in, and when he exhales, he can feel his molecules travel into the air around him. *Maybe I am a little asleep,* he thinks. He's aware of Shay beside him. Her molecules are mixing with his; he's not just himself; he's made up of her too. Which means he's composed of everyone he's ever touched, everyone he's ever shaken hands with, hugged, or high-fived. That means he has molecules inside him from his parents and Jordan and everyone else on that plane.

The letters always referred to the weight he had to carry, and he'd thought of it that way himself: He had to carry the burden of so many lost lives. He had to make it up to the people who died. It was him pulling 191 dead people, like a fallen parachute, in his wake. But if the passengers are part of his

453

makeup, and all time and people are inter-connected, then the people on the plane exist, just as he exists. The present is infinite, and Flight 2977 flies on, far above him, hidden by clouds.

He told John the truth in the garage, that he would never leave anyone behind, but now that idea has expanded. He sits beside his brother on the plane, and lies on the ground beside Shay. Jordan argues with their dad about harming animals, and he kisses the fifteen-year-old Mahira, and the older Mahira loves him from behind the deli counter, right now.

"Shay?" he says.

"Mm-hmm."

"I used to have this crazy idea . . ." He pauses. "And I guess I still do, that as long as I stay on the ground, the plane will stay in the sky. It'll keep flying on its normal route to Los Angeles, and I'm its counterweight. They're all alive up there, as long as I'm alive down here."

"The twelve-year-old you is up there too?"

Eddie, he thinks, and nods.

"I can see that," she says, her voice sleepy. "That makes sense."

He grins, his eyes still closed, because Shay can see it too. He pictures his mother pressing a finger against her comet-shaped birthmark, in her first-class seat. His dad, making the surprised expression he made when he thought about his math problem. Edward pictures himself, in the future, teaching twelve-year-olds in Principal Arundhi's school and trying to convince them that they're okay. Future-Edward is wearing a handsome tweed blazer, and he's telling the kids to help others when they need help, and to accept help when they need it themselves.

Edward remembers watching Madame Victory double over with laughter, her face shining with what looks like joy. He hears her say to him, *Nobody chose you for anything.* He hears the camper's question: *Did it hurt?* He can feel Shay's fingers in his own. Moonlight beams through his eyelids and he can see, as if it's the lake in front of him, the pain and loss he's been swimming in for years. In the moonlight, though, the pain is revealed to be love. The emotions are entwined; they are the two sides of the same gleaming coin.

He and Shay walk home slowly that night. They weave around fat trees and cross quiet roads. When they reach their street, Edward stops in front of his aunt and uncle's house. He looks up at the window of the room that was supposed to be a nursery, but never was, and never will be. He can remember standing at that window, held up by crutches, etched with pain. He moves his gaze higher, where — beyond his field of vision — a young boy sits in a plane, with no idea what's about to happen.

2:11 P.M.

The co-pilot says, "I'm in TOGA, right?"

TOGA is an acronym for Take Off, Go Around. When a plane is taking off or aborting a landing — "going around" — it must gain both speed and altitude as efficiently as possible. Pilots are trained to increase engine speed to the TOGA level and raise the nose to a certain pitch angle at this critical phase of flight.

The co-pilot wants to increase speed and climb away from danger, but he's not at sea level; he's in the far thinner air of 37,500 feet. The engines generate less thrust here, and the wings generate less lift. Raising the nose to a certain angle of pitch does not result in the same angle of climb but far less. Indeed, it can — and will — result in a descent.

While the co-pilot's behavior is irrational, it is not inexplicable. Intense psychological stress tends to shut down the part of the brain responsible for innovative, creative thought. When frazzled, people tend to revert to the familiar and the well rehearsed. Though pilots are required to practice hand-flying their aircraft during all phases of flight as part of recurrent training, in their daily routine they do most of their hand-flying at low altitude — while taking off, landing, and maneuvering. It's not surprising, then, that the co-pilot reverts to flying the plane as if it were close to the ground, even though this response is ill-suited to the situation.

The plane now reaches its maximum altitude. With engines at full power, the nose pitched upward at an angle of 18 degrees, it moves horizontally for an instant and then begins to sink back toward the ground.

The pilot: "What the hell is happening? I don't understand what's happening!"

Linda says, "I need to use the bathroom."

Florida says, "Are you crazy, girl? You're not getting up from that seat."

"The doctor just went to first class and came back." Linda shuffles her feet in the three spare inches of room she has to move. She knows she sounds like a petulant toddler. She feels like one. When the plane shudders, the bells on Florida's skirt ring like an alarm. Linda is uncomfortable in her seat, the belt is pinching her side, and she feels like she might have a blister on the back of her heel. She's trapped, and the motion of the plane makes no sense. She's never been in turbulence this bad. She wants to call Gary and ask him if he's ever been on a flight this rough.

Florida fixes her with a look. "That lady went up there because someone died."

"That's not true. Why would you say that?"

"She came back too quick to have saved anyone. When she got up there, she saw there was nothing left to fix."

Linda wriggles, trying to find comfort. This is crazy talk, too crazy to even engage with. No one died on this airplane; that just didn't happen. There's no way she's trapped on this flying metal bullet with a dead person. There's no way her baby's earliest history includes this.

She's going to complain when she lands. To whom she's not sure, as she would never want to disrespect the pilots. Someone, though, has made a mistake, and now she's pregnant and alone, listening to a chorus of tiny bells.

Edward has one particular exchange with Dr. Mike that will replay regularly in his head for the rest of his life. It doesn't happen during a normal appointment. They run into each other at the interstate shopping center on a Saturday.

Edward and Shay had walked there that morning because Shay had an appointment to dye her hair bright pink, in order to irritate Besa. "You should remember me like this," Shay said to Edward, right before she went into the salon, and Edward had taken her seriously. The teenage girl in front of him was five and a half feet tall, with the lean body of a runner. She was wearing jeans and a snowboarding jacket, even though she'd never snowboarded or skied in her life. Her straight brown hair was chin-length. Shay looked like the woman she would become, with kind eyes that turned fierce if someone crossed her. She rarely wore her glasses, because she preferred contacts. And her dimple was still the barometer Edward used to assess her mood.

"Got it?" Shay said.

"Got it."

"Okay, well, here goes nothing."

Ninety minutes into the hair appointment, with at least another hour remaining, Edward is wandering around the stores when he sees Dr. Mike. They smile at each other in surprise, and Edward notices that he's now taller than the therapist by several inches. Edward accepts when Dr. Mike offers to buy him a tea or coffee.

After ordering their drinks, they stand by the window in the fancy coffee shop. Perhaps because of the unexpected meeting, or perhaps because Edward turned sixteen a few days earlier and the age — which his brother never reached — feels uncomfortable, he makes a confession. "I feel like I should be over it by now," he says. "Everyone else has forgotten about the flight. Mostly, anyway. But I feel like I still think about it all the time."

Dr. Mike stirs his coffee for a long minute. People straggle past the window. Three bearded men in a row are hunched over, reading their phones. A pregnant woman walks slowly next to a toddler with an Afro.

461

Edward feels his heart beat in his chest, feels the warmth of the tea seep through the cup into the skin of his hand.

The man says, "What happened is baked into your bones, Edward. It lives under your skin. It's not going away. It's part of you and will be part of you every moment until you die. What you've been working on, since the first time I met you, is learning to live with that."

2:12 P.M.

Because the co-pilot is holding the stick all the way back, the nose remains high and the plane has barely enough forward speed for the controls to be effective. Turbulence continues to buffet the plane, and it's nearly impossible to keep the wings level.

The co-pilot says, "Dammit, I don't have control of the plane. I don't have control of the plane at all!"

"I'm taking the controls. Left seat taking over." The pilot begins to hand-fly the plane for the first time.

"It doesn't make sense," the co-pilot says, slack in his seat. "I've been pulling back on the stick since we went on manual."

"What?" The pilot's eyes widen. "You've been pulling back on the stick — no!" He pushes the stick forward, but it's too late to correct. The plane's nose is pitched up, and it's descending at a 40-degree angle. The stall warning continues to sound.

"We've lost control of the plane!"

"We've totally lost control . . ."

When the plane lurches, Florida thinks of the television cartoons where a vehicle is balanced on the edge of a cliff, and then the wind shifts, or a tiny bird lands on the hood, and the vehicle plummets. She wonders why that moment, when animated, is considered funny.

She places her warm hand over Linda's cold one, so they are gripping the armrest together.

"Hold it together, baby," she says. "We can do this."

"Okay," Linda whispers.

Florida is startled to see a stranger on the other side of Linda, staring at them with a panicked face. The blue scarf has dropped and an Indian woman has appeared. She doesn't speak, just stares at the two of them as if waiting to be told her fate.

Florida can sense the rumblings of a scream in this woman and wants to avoid it. "I'm Florida," she says. "And this is Linda. We're here to help each other."

The woman nods. She's probably fifty-five. She says in a soft voice, "I overslept. I woke up thinking I must be in the wrong place. On the wrong plane."

464

"We're on our way to Los Angeles," Linda says.

"Los Angeles," the woman says. "Los Angeles is correct. Thank God."

She turns and looks out the window. There's nothing to see but a bank of gray clouds. She looks back at the two women. "But?" she says.

The question is vast.

"We don't know," Florida says.

"We don't know anything," Linda says.

The plane is now falling fast. With its nose pitched 15 degrees up and a forward speed of 100 knots, it is descending at a rate of 10,000 feet per minute, at an angle of 41.5 degrees. Though the pitot tubes are now fully functional, the forward airspeed is so low — below 60 knots — that the angle-of-attack inputs are no longer accepted as valid, and the stall-warning horn temporarily stops.

The two pilots discuss, incredibly, whether they are in fact climbing or descending, before agreeing that they are descending. As the plane approaches 10,000 feet, the nose remains high.

"Climb, climb!"

Veronica, strapped to her seat, tries to stand.

The plane is at an angle she's never experienced before. She wishes she were back in the bathroom with Mark, her body coiled around his. *What have those idiots in the cockpit done?* She has an urge to reach toward her passengers, to try to calm, to assist.

Mark is sliding out of his chair — his seatbelt was loose, and now it's gripping him not at the waist but under his armpits. He's looking at what must be the ceiling. He thinks about Jax and their last stupid argument. He realizes that he wasn't done. He's not done.

Jane sinks into herself; she cups her hands over her face. The shaking of the plane means there's no way to move her body back to her family, so she joins them inside her mind. She imagines she's sitting on Bruce's lap. She can feel his legs beneath hers. She looks into his eyes, because there are no words left for them to share. Then she kisses her boys, kisses and kisses and kisses them the way Eddie kissed her as a baby.

As the plane nears 2,000 feet, the aircraft's sensors detect the fast-approaching surface and trigger a new alarm. There's no time left to build up speed by pushing the plane's nose forward into a dive.

The pilot: "This can't be happening!"

"But what's happening?"

"Ten degrees of pitch . . ."

Exactly 1.4 seconds later, the cockpit voice recorder stops.

Bruce thinks about his math, the six years on a problem he has not yet managed to perfectly express, much less solve. He has an entire duffel bag full of his journals and notes packed into the hold of this plane. He can picture the page where he had a breakthrough last August; he can remember the bottle of Malbec he opened for himself and Jane that night. He'd thought that the breakthrough meant he was closer than he actually was. He should have known better. He had stepped into a clearing, and mistaken it for the edge of the forest.

That knowledge had set in over the following months and had been compounded by the announcement that he hadn't been awarded tenure. This setback plus the failure had crushed him, though he'd tried to hide that from his wife. He'd asked himself: *Why do you care so much?* The answer came immediately: *because of the boys.* He wanted the boys to see him labor — which they had — but then achieve something of note. He wanted them to be proud of him. He wanted to have done something worthy of their pride.

The plane is plummeting. He holds his boys' hands in his own and thinks: *I need more time.*

Dear Edward,

My name is Lyle. I used to be a volunteer paramedic in Greeley, Colorado. I was part of the team that was closest to Flight 2977's crash site. I was working at ShopRite when the call came in. I'm a butcher by trade — I come from a long line of butchers. I was cutting up a chicken, thinking it was a little too tough to make good eating. Funny what details get stuck in your mind.

That was my last day at ShopRite. Last day as a paramedic too. I couldn't go to work afterward. One doc said I was depressed; another called it PTSD. I feel lame even mentioning it, after what you must've been through. But if I tell you my story, then there's no point in leaving stuff out. So, I suffered some and eventually decided to move away, even

469

though my family had been in northern Colorado for as long as time. We even predated Columbus. I live in Texas now — I need big open spaces, even though the ones here are drier, less green. I'm still a butcher.

I'm writing to you because I can't shake the memory of that day. You rise up out of my dreams, shouting like you did from your place in the wreckage. If you've already stopped reading, if you've torn me — I mean, this letter — up, I totally understand. I wish I could do the same.

There were only four volunteer paramedics in our town, though of course the size of the crash meant the call went out wider, to more districts. But we were the closest and the first to report to the scene. I came in my car. Olivia and Bob were in the ambulance. There was another guy, and for the life of me I can't remember his name. The fire truck, a fancy one that cost so much money the county had been fighting over the purchase for years, was on our heels. The chief was thrilled, no doubt, at the chance to really use the thing.

When we got there, it was like driving up to a Hollywood movie set. To see a section of a plane lying in the middle of a dairy field I've driven by hundreds of times looked about as horrifying as seeing a whale beached there. My first thought was, *We've got to get it back up in the air.* That seemed like as reasonable a goal as any.

Before this, the most serious emergency I'd reported to was a heart attack suffered by an old guy in his bed. His wife called 911, we showed up, and he survived. We'd taken a training course but nothing that touched anything like this. Olivia was super. She yelled at us to break into separate quadrants. She told us to look for people to help. I went to the far left, near the tail, which had splintered off from the rest of the plane. I climbed over cracked metal and puddle-jumped seats and unrecognizable objects for at least an hour. Coughing because of the smoke. I could hear other people yell, "Hello, hello?" I hoped my colleagues were having better luck than I was.

I was trying to figure out how to quit in an acceptable way — basically hightail it back to my car — when I heard you. . . .

Edward does everything he can to avoid the memory of the crash, but sometimes it comes over him like a sickness, and once it begins, there's no escape. It descends in the darkest hour of a sleepless night. Occasionally, it sneaks in when he catches his breath a certain way, or when a loud noise makes his heart sputter.

Without warning, the plane tips downward inside him.

He grips his father's hand and Jordan's. They make a rope with their arms, and Eddie stares at the rope as the overhead compartments bang open, and bags fall through the air. He's not sure if the plane is pointing up, or down.

"I love you, boys," Bruce says, in a fierce voice. "I want to be here with you. I love you."

"I love you too," Eddie says.

"I love you," Jordan says.

It's unclear whether they can hear each other, over the hissing, the cannons of sound around them. Maybe a door is open somewhere. Maybe up is down.

"Jane!" Bruce shouts, into the din.

The people around Eddie make noises he's never heard before, and will never hear again. There is a deafening crack, like the world has split in two. He sees teardrops on his arm. Are they his, or Jordan's?

The noise is so loud, the pressure on his face, on his skin, so great he can't keep his eyes open. He, and everyone, falls.

. . . I didn't believe your voice at first, Edward. I was certain I was hearing things. But the same sentence rang out, over and over, and I moved toward it, as if it were a magnet.

"I'm here!"

"I'm here!"

I pulled aside a metal sheet; it felt like opening a door, and there you were, furious, as if offended at the wait. You made eye contact with me, and shouted: "I'm here!"

I stared at you, this tiny boy with a seatbelt still around your waist, until you yelled again. Then I stepped forward and picked you up, and you held me around the neck, and I felt like you were saving me in the same moment that I was saving you.

We walked back toward the others, while you repeated, quieter now, but with the

same level of insistence: I'm here. I'm
here. I'm here.

■ ■ ■ ■

EPILOGUE

■ ■ ■ ■

JUNE 2019

Edward and Shay drive across the country with the windows down on the Acura, a second-hand car they bought with Jax's money.

Edward has used the money to execute most of the ideas he'd dreamed up that night in the basement. It will pay for Shay's and Mahira's college and post-graduate educations — Mahira has been gifted the amount through a charity that supports the education of girls of color, so she doesn't know it came from Edward. Lacey, it turned out, had great administrative skills from her work at the hospital and was very helpful at coming up with creative covers for distributing the funds. She'd liaised with Principal Arundhi's botany club, passing the money on to them with the caveat that the principal never know where it came from. The club had designed and built a freestanding greenhouse where they could hold their meetings and showcase their personal collections, including the preeminent assemblage of ferns on the East Coast. Lacey had also founded a small charity devoted to survivors of tragedies, in order to make gifts to other people Edward designated, including Gary and the whale-conservation fund that employed him, Lolly Stillman, the nun, and the three children whose photograph Shay is never without.

The Acura's air-conditioning system is temperamental, so they try not to use it even though it's often ninety degrees outside. They take highways and drive fast. Shay's hair — brown again — blows back from her face, and when she drives and it's her turn to choose the music, they listen to hip-hop. She often beatboxes along, which makes Edward cackle with laughter. When he's behind the wheel, he's less consistent. He chooses according to his mood: sometimes a podcast, sometimes Bach, sometimes no music at all.

High school graduation was two weeks earlier, under a white tent on top of a hill. Principal Arundhi had handed out the diplomas, and Mrs. Cox and Dr. Mike had attended, as had Lacey, John, and Besa. Edward had stopped being a patient of Dr. Mike's six months earlier, and he'd been surprised by how happy he was to see the therapist. Mrs. Cox's graduation gift was a copy of her son's newly published book of poetry, and both Edward and Shay grinned widely when the wrapping paper was pulled off. "Harrison is very talented," Mrs. Cox said, holding up the book so everyone could see the cover. "He won the Walt Whitman Award, which is *quite* prestigious."

Afterward, when Principal Arundhi was finished with his official responsibilities, they had gone out to a fancy dinner with a lot of wine for all the adults except Mrs. Cox, who drank martinis. Dr. Mike and Principal Arundhi had a long conversation about a particular baseball series that had been important to both of them when they were kids. Mrs. Cox misheard them talking about the Mets and told everyone what she had seen at the Met that season. Edward and Shay were allowed a glass of wine each, due to the special occasion.

During dessert, Edward had surprised himself and everyone present by lurching up out of his chair, holding his glass. The collected faces had turned toward him, and just the sight of each familiar person had moved a piece of furniture inside him. He said, "I wanted to say thank you. To each of you. Thank you so much." There was a pause, and Shay raised her glass and then everyone else did too and it was possible that they were all crying a little. John looked at Lacey and said, "We did it." Lacey, her eyes shining with tears, laughed and said, "I guess we did." When Lacey leaned forward and kissed her husband, Edward sank into his chair, and everyone at the table applauded.

In Colorado, Shay and Edward drive to the hotel closest to the site and check in. The hotel receptionist gives them a look, like, *Aren't you a little young?* They have ID, but the receptionist shrugs, and they don't need to produce it. Edward and Shay had fought the grown-ups for weeks about taking this trip.

"Just wait a year or two," Besa had said. "Why does it have to be now? *Sólo tienes dieciocho.*"

Lacey said, "You think eighteen is old, but it's actually not. You need more experience driving, for a trip this ambitious."

Edward said, "I need to go before college, and I need to go alone with Shay." He didn't have a better reason to provide. He simply knew that this was something he had to do and this was when he had to do it. He and Shay will attend college together in the fall. As Shay predicted, Edward got into every school he applied to, but he'd applied to the same colleges as Shay, so he waited until she chose one that had accepted her, and then he enrolled there as well.

Besa had agreed to the trip only after Shay promised to respond to every single phone call and text from her mother. Besa also installed a tracking app on Shay's phone. "In case you get lost," she said. "So I can come find you."

They swim in the indoor pool. They have adjoining rooms and play gin rummy on Edward's queen-sized bed. They eat at the diner next to the hotel. The next morning, before the sun is fully over the horizon, they climb into the Acura and drive the twelve minutes to the site. Edward feels nauseous as they make their way there. This trip was his decision, and yet he feels like he had no choice. He wonders if returning to a place he had miraculously once escaped is a good idea. What if he doesn't get out the second time? He's had nightmares in which the ground takes a good look at him, shakes its shaggy head, and swallows him whole.

There's a small dirt parking lot next to the site. The sky is lined with pink and yellow; the sun is still working its way up. No one else is here. They'd planned their visit for a Tuesday, because Shay had found in her research that the fewest people visit the site on Tuesdays.

"We don't want anyone recognizing you," she said. They'd both read an article online about the memorial and how it had made the young sculptor famous, and the article had mentioned that any boy between the ages of fourteen and thirty who visited the site was approached and asked if he was Edward Adler.

A low wooden fence separates the parking area from the meadow. Edward climbs out of the car. The air tastes clean, and he gulps a few breaths. Ahead of him, in the center of the field, is the sculpture. A flock of 191 silver sparrows in the shape of a plane, taking to the air.

"It's beautiful," Shay whispers.

They walk together across the field. Tall grass swishes against their shins; they're wearing shorts and sweatshirts. When Edward reaches the tail of the bird-plane, he stops and looks up. The silver birds stretch away from him. The lowest ones are within his reach. The sculpture is smaller in person than it had looked in photos. It spans the length of a small Cessna, not a commercial airplane.

Edward turns in a circle. Other than the memorial, there is no sign of destruction.

Green grass spreads in every direction. He can see the road they drove on to get here, their car, and a wide expanse of pastel sky. There is so much sky, he feels like his proportions are off, as if most of the world is built into the horizon.

"Edward," Shay says. He sees that she is near the front of the sculpture, where the birds point upward into the air. There is a metal stake with a plaque. He stays where he is. He knows the facts: the date, the flight number, the accounting of lives lost.

The article they'd read had included a photograph taken the day the sculpture was unveiled. A group of perhaps fifty people encircled the birds. The families of the victims stood with their heads tipped back, watching, as the canvas covering the metal sculpture was tugged free. The people were all colors and ages. The only person not looking up was a curly-haired toddler, on her hands and knees, investigating the grass.

Edward spent a lot of time studying that photograph. He paid careful attention to the faces, looking for a woman who might be Benjamin Stillman's grandmother, looking for a man who might be in the midst of a search for Florida, in her new life and body. Edward looked for a poet who might be Harrison.

"Let's go sit on the hill," Edward says now.

Shay had checked the surrounding area on Google maps and found a slight hill about fifty yards past the memorial, which looked like a good place to rest. If other people do visit the site today, it's unlikely they will come anywhere near that spot.

When they get there Edward sits down, hard, because his legs have gone weak. He feels strange, but he expected to feel strange. After all, he'd half-expected this field to open up and swallow him in order to rectify an earlier error. Edward is aware, as if from a clock buried deep inside him, of a particular nanosecond that occurred six years earlier right above his head. The fleeting final moment when the plane was still a plane, and the people on it were still alive.

Only Edward had bridged that nanosecond, and here he is, again. Taller than his brother and father, able to bench-press his own body weight, with his mother's eyes. He's created a circle, created a whole, by coming here. When he leaves, he can carry this full circle — everything this moment and this place contains — in his arms.

Edward closes his eyes. He is the boy buckled into a plane seat, gripping his brother and father, and he is the young man sitting on the ground that plane crashed into. Eddie, and Edward.

When he opens his eyes, he realizes that the photograph he'd studied had been from this angle. Perhaps the photographer had stood on this hill, armed with a telephoto lens. Edward was unable, in the end, to identify a single person in the photograph. He knew what their loved one looked like, but he didn't know them. Did the red-haired doctor have red-haired parents? He didn't know. There were a handful of older women with brown skin — which one was related to the soldier? How many of the people in the scene had written him a letter?

The field waves with grass and shimmers with the people who died that day and their family members, who came to gaze at silver birds that reflect the light like perfectly polished spoons. Edward thinks, *Madame Victory was right: I'm not special. I'm not chosen.*

From beside him, propped up on her elbows, Shay says, "You were lucky."

He gives her a look, because she has finished his thought for him.

She says, her voice catching, "I mean, I was lucky too. I'm so lucky it was you."

Edward's instinct is to shrug this off, but he knows better now and stops himself.

Shay carries the presence of Edward, the same way Edward carries the loss of his brother. He knows the loss of Jordan will remain with him forever, even as Edward slowly leaves his parents behind. He was supposed to grow up and leave his mom and dad, after all, just like he will leave John and Lacey in the fall when he goes to college. That is part of the natural order. Edward wasn't supposed to leave Jordan, though. They were meant to age together. That loss continues to be spiked with pain; it will never be soothed. And he can see, objectively, that Shay's life without him would have been woven with different moments, friends or lack of friends, different fights with Besa, different books and different struggles.

As if she's heard his thoughts again, Shay says, "I might have kept planning to run away, without ever leaving. I never would have written to those children." She looks up at the sky. "I would have been so much less."

Shay is *this* Shay because of him. And he is alive — not just surviving, but *alive* — because of her. He wonders if the scientists who tend to the Large Hadron Collider are hoping to discover not only what happens in the air between two people but how that pressurized air changes those people inside their skin. He hears the science teacher say, *The air between us is not empty space.*

The air feels gentle against Edward's cheeks now; the tiny silver birds point at the sky. He and Shay regard the scene together. At a certain point, he looks at Shay and finds her already looking at him. The dimple is deep in her cheek.

"What is it?" he says.

She doesn't speak, but the undercurrent — the unspoken conversation that flows endlessly between them — is loud. Shay is the girl wearing pajamas with pink clouds on them the first time he entered her room, and she is the woman who will give birth to their daughter ten years from now, and she is *this* young woman, her face wide open, offering him everything.

Edward hears his brother's voice inside him. Jordan tells him not to waste any time. Not to waste any love. He watches Shay lean in his direction, and when she kisses him, she blots out the entire sky.

ACKNOWLEDGMENTS

One of the biggest surprises, and joys, of parenthood has been observing the profound, generous love between my sons. The two brothers in this novel are not similar to my boys, but the love between them is entirely inspired by the relationship between my children. Thank you, Malachy and Hendrix, for showing me more shades of love than I knew existed.

For legal advice on "who gets what" when a plane crashes, I thank the expert counsel of Alicia Butler. If I've made any errors in that department, they are my own. Many thanks to my friend Abbey Mather for connecting me with Alicia. I am grateful to Frank Fair for educating me about the military. Robert Zimmermann provided invaluable information on planes and piloting. He answered all my questions at the beginning of the writing process and helped correct my mistakes at the end. Any remaining pilot-related errors are definitely mine.

My agent, Julie Barer, is deeply wonderful, and I am grateful to have her in my life. I thank her and everyone at The Book Group for their help and support. Jenny Meyer, Caspian Dennis, Nicole Cunningham, and Heidi Gall deserve special thanks.

Whitney Frick loves this book as much as I do, and guided me through an editing process that turned out to be a joy. I am so glad to have her as my editor. Susan Kamil is brilliant, and I'm grateful to have had the chance to work with her. Thanks also to Clio Seraphim for her work on the novel. And I couldn't be happier that the book is in the hands of Venetia Butterfield at Viking Penguin in the UK.

Brettne Bloom and Courtney Sullivan believe in me and my work no matter what, which is a huge gift, and I love them. Stacey Bosworth and Libby Fearnley fall in this same camp, and have my equal gratitude. I am lucky to have many fierce, awesome women in my life.

My parents have always supported me, and I am fortunate to be their daughter. No one has done more for me than Cathy and Jim Napolitano. My niece, Annie, asked me to thank her in my book, so: thanks, Annie! And Katie too.

I love working at One Story (subscribe to One Story!) because of the people. I am thankful for Maribeth Batcha, Lena Valencia, and Patrick Ryan. I was one of the hundreds of people who loved Adina Talve-Goodman. She should have written many books, and beamed from many book jackets, so I wanted to put her name here. I miss you, Adina.

Helen Ellis, Hannah Tinti, and I are a three-legged stool. We've been reading one another's work since 1996, and it's their voices I hear in my head when I revise. Everything would be different, and less, without them in my life.

ABOUT THE AUTHOR

Ann Napolitano is the author of the novels *A Good Hard Look* and *Within Arm's Reach*. She is also the associate editor of *One Story* literary magazine. She received an MFA from New York University; she has taught fiction writing for Brooklyn College's MFA program, New York University's School of Continuing and Professional Studies, and Gotham Writers Workshop. She lives in Brooklyn with her husband and two children.